just Jack

Everything laid bare

K.L. Shandwick

Editor: Ellie Aspill

Cover Design: by Russell Cleary
Photograph: Andreas Vargas
Cover Model: Joseph Wareham

Disclaimer: This book has mature content and explicit reference to
sexual situations it is intended for adult readers aged 18+.

This book is a work of fiction, Names, places, characters, band names
and incidents are the product of the author's imagination or names are
used within the fictitious setting. Any resemblance to actual person's
living or dead. Band names or locales are entirely coincidental unless
quoted as artists.

OTHER TITLES BY K L SHANDWICK

Lily's story (The Everything Trilogy)

Book 1 Enough Isn't Everything

Book 2 Everything She Needs

Book 3 Everything I Want

The Last Score Series

Gibson's Legacy

Trusting Gibson

Foreword

I stared at the title 'foreword' and I'm struggling to know what to write because when I sat at down with my laptop to write a chapter of a book as a challenge, I had no idea that it would lead in to a world I never knew existed. The world of books. Twenty months after I published the first book I'm on the cusp of releasing book five from these characters. I can't put into words how this makes me feel. I'm so thankful to everyone who has read the 'Everything Trilogy' and 'Love With Every Beat' and loved the characters as much as I have loved writing about them. I am so honored to have the opportunity to entertain you through my 'overactive imagination'. Every morning I wake thinking that I must be dreaming, yet this little indie author is tirelessly promoted by a dedicated team of amazing people who do it for the love of my work. It is amazing how everyone I've met that have read the books, or have come to discuss them with me have got behind the story. I'm in awe of the support they have shown me. Thank you. I hope you like what I've done with Jack. KLx

Dedication

Many people love Jack Cunningham, the cheeky character in this book, but I hope none of you mind too much if I dedicate this book to Ashley Heather Appleby. Ashley is an avid reader who supports independent authors and promotes the work of the authors she reads, likes and reviews. Ashley has been with me since day one to promote my work and I wanted to write Jack's story especially for you. Ashley your comment, "Please, please, please, I need to know more about Jack," was one of the first comments I ever had in my inbox about the trilogy, and the very first one about Jack. Since the release day of the final trilogy book you have promoted my work relentlessly. I couldn't wish for a more fitting tribute than to share this book with you.

Thank you to my beta readers, Emma Louise Moorhead, Joanne Swinney and Elmarie Pieterse

I also need to mention KL's promo ladies. Without you, I doubt anyone would be reading this book because sharing the word is invaluable to someone who has no publishing house behind them. You are all amazing, thank you. Emma Moorhead, Jacqueline Dennison, Ashley Heather, Sarah Lintott, Debra Hiltz, Isa Jones, Joanne Swinney, Nicola Turner Anderson, Samantha Harrington, Janet Boyd, Angela Wallace Kawauchi, Isabel Adams, Leigh Black, Donna Tripi Salzano, Jennifer Pierson, Ann Meemken and Tammy Ann Dove for your tireless efforts to promote my work. #teamjack

Prologue

Lily Parnell and I have been friends since we were little. She was family that wasn't blood but was more than blood, if that makes any sense. Ever since she was a tiny, sassy playschool four year old, she has held a special place in my heart. If I close my eyes, I can still see her gorgeous smile lighting up her beautiful little face as she clapped with excitement at me back then.

The reason for this joyful outburst was because I had made a picture of a face out of pasta shapes glued onto a paper plate. I'd painted the hair around the face with bright acrylic paints in her favourite orange and yellow colours. Lily fell in love with it, and I fell in love with Lily, so I let her take it home with her.

On our first day of school our parents pushed us towards the gate, encouraging us to be independent. I can still remember the feel of her tiny hand squeezing mine tightly as we walked nervously into class together. Seeing the desolate look on her face when she was told we couldn't sit together destroyed me. Lily bawled her eyes out until Mrs. Moore, our exasperated class teacher quickly relented and sat us next to each other.

After that, it was pretty clear to everyone that we were two sides of the same coin and the grown-ups got a lot more out of us if we did things together. We were pretty popular kids and got invited to most things, but if one of us got invited to a single gender party, then that kid missed out on a gift because neither of us went.

We had a connection that was odd to most and some of my mates thought that I was in her knickers from the way we carried on. But Lily and I never crossed the friendship line because we already felt we had something higher and more spiritual than sex could offer us.

During my younger years there were times when I wondered what it would feel like to kiss her and there was one point where I had the horny teenage boy thing going on and wondered what it would be like to be with her. I wouldn't have been normal if I hadn't because my little Lily was absolutely stunning.

That was the one time when I had to distance myself from her because I knew that if I pursued that particular train of thought, our whole friendship would have been on the line.

Eventually we talked about it, and Lily admitted that there was a time where she'd had similar feelings to mine and had been struggling as well. But we both knew that if we went to that place and it didn't work out, our relationship, as we had always known it would never have been the same again.

Those months were some of the toughest of my life so far. How I dealt with them was how most sixteen year old boys would have; I screwed anyone who'd let me while I battled with my forbidden feelings for Lily.

My platonic love for her had bubbled over into lust. After five months of this, our relationship was pretty strained. We were both extremely miserable as we continued to fight against our surging hormones. Lily threw herself into music lessons to get by and even went as far as taking new classes, whilst I did a lot of extra-curricular activity as well—with Sally. Being six months

2

older than Lily, I acted like her older brother despite my more intimate feelings. Basically, I was confused about how I felt during a lot of that time. I used to growl like a bear at any guy that took notice of her.

Years eleven and twelve in secondary school were hell as I tried to keep Lily's suitors at bay. Instead of asking her out they would give her a wide berth, as I'd encouraged. Leaving her alone was far better than the alternative which would be me waiting for them after school if they didn't heed my warning.

Anyway, we got past that years ago and now... she's still the only girl in my heart. When she met Alfie Black I just knew she was slipping into another life, one where I wasn't number two anymore and was relegated to number three after her dad and him. Don't get me wrong, I knew I'd always be an important part of her life and I would always try to be there for her, but I could feel our relationship shifting to the point where we wouldn't necessarily be in each other's lives on a daily basis, much less spend any real time alone together.

When I saw how she was with Alfie and then I looked at my current girlfriend Rosie, it was obvious that there wasn't the same passion between us that you couldn't fail to see with them. When Alfie looked at Lily, it was as if she'd painted the moon in the sky. It was a shame that I didn't look at Rosie that way because she was a great girl, I just knew I couldn't commit to her. Maybe that was because I was sure there was someone out there who would look at her the way Alfie looked at Lily, but that someone wasn't me. With that revelation I suddenly felt that not everything in my life was cut and dried, especially after Lily left London.

Lily went to America to study music and became successful, very successful actually. And Alfie? Well, he was even more successful than she was. Being musicians, their lives were full on and their recent events had given

3

me food for thought with regards to my own life, and my relationship with Rosie. It dawned on me that Rosie just wasn't the one for me. Once I'd decided that, I plucked up the courage and went over to her house the same day. I told her how I felt and tried to let her down gently. I feel myself smirk wryly at the memory of Rosie's reaction. She didn't let me go without a fight calling me a fucked-up asshole and many more explicit adjectives as soon as her anger took hold.

However, at the end of the day, Rosie and me were never a forever kind of couple and as hard as it was, I walked away. I didn't consider myself a bad man, and I felt cruel about it at first because I could see she was upset and suffering. She rang me almost every day in a broken teary mess. I felt horrible but I had to be true to my own feelings and not stay with her out of pity. That would only have delayed the inevitable between us, so it was much better to let her go sooner rather than later.

Daily calls were one thing but when Rosie began to ring me late every night I felt she was checking up on me, eventually she asked me outright if there was someone else. There wasn't. That didn't stop the accusations though, and it got to the point that when I saw it was her, I almost didn't answer. But you know what? I'm not that guy and just because my feelings didn't run as deep as Rosie's did, it didn't mean I didn't still care about her. So I'd answer and reassure her.

Sometimes when she'd call and I was feeling lonely I'd almost cave and go over there, but I knew that she wasn't in my long term. There was no way I could've gone just to make us both feel better for a few hours and walk away again. That would only have made matters worse.

Being without Rosie put me in a weird place, mentally. It was only twenty seven days into the New Year and I had no personal direction. Thank God I had a great job and mates because I had no woman to keep me warm anymore.

I've always hated January with its horrible grey skies and rotten London weather, everything looked very drab without the sun in my hometown. If it wasn't for Dave and Sam, two of my best mates, I probably would have hibernated for the rest of the winter. At twenty five years old, I found myself in the position of starting again. It felt daunting and I was missing the one girl who was the closest to my heart, Lily. She was carving out a future for herself half way around the world and my life had stalled.

Like a lost soul, I woke daily with a hole in my world. I was accustomed to every one referring to me as part of the duo we used to be: Lily and Jack. We had always been inseparable, and although we hadn't been like that for the best part of three years, it still hurt. Lily was no longer a part of my day-to-day life and no one noticed that I still silently grieved for what I felt was missing—the other half of me. So I had to face the future without Lily and face the fact that we were never going to be referred to as Lily and Jack anymore.

I was…just Jack.

Chapter 1

Meetings

My Life was crazy at times. I made a mental note to get more organised in the mornings as I held a slice of toast between my teeth and hurriedly pulled hard on the brass knocker on my front door. The heavy wooden slab banged shut and I quickly skipped down the stairs of my apartment block two at a time. Living on the top floor of a Victorian building was great with the expanse of space and high ceilings, but there was no lift. It was solidly built and I had spacious living conditions, not to mention that my father gave it to me on my twenty-first birthday, so the fact there was no lift was a minor inconvenience.

Bus or Tube? I knew the underground would be quicker and I was running short on time. Taking off at speed, I was conscious of the loud slapping noise that echoed through the otherwise silent lane. The slippery leather soles of my Italian shoes pounded and slid against the wet cobble stones in a fast pit-pat rhythm as I took my regular short cut to the Tube station.

From past experience I knew it took me exactly four minutes to get to the underground. I'd inadvertently timed it one day, again when I was running late. I'm usually punctual, I just seemed to start out tardy and make a great recovery.

I knew it was my own fault. Every day started out with the potential to be the day I did things in a timely manner but other people then screwed me up. Daily, someone invariably invited me to one function or another for work, which generally meant late nights and not getting to bed the same day as I woke up. Sometimes when I got lucky, I didn't go to bed at all. On the whole I'm a very lucky guy, so I had to survive with very little actual sleep and keep myself buoyant with power naps and reenergising sessions at the gym. Some people are exhausted after a workout but I find it had the opposite effect on me.

I was running late for an interview I was scheduled to be at in The Dorchester Hotel, one of the plushest hotels in London, with a rock star from the band Cobham Street. Luckily, I knew Rick Fars pretty well through Lily and Alfie, and had interviewed him several times before. Questions formed in my mind and the order I would deliver them as I rushed to the Tube. I was feeling pretty relaxed about my morning but that didn't mean I could be late. Rick could be fucking awkward if he was kept waiting. Even with me.

In most other cities in the UK, I would have jumped in a cab to get me there on time, but in London it always felt like the world was trying to get to the same place at the same time. The quickest way to get anywhere was the underground. It was only a two stop ride to the hotel from my home in South Kensington to Hyde Park Corner and a five minute brisk walk up Park Lane. Checking my wristwatch, I had twenty minutes to get there, providing nothing went wrong I'd be there with minutes to spare.

When I hit the entrance of the underground station I went into auto-pilot, tapping my Oyster travel card on the reader and jostling my way for position with hundreds of other bodies trying to get onto the steep escalator. Once I'd reached it, I stayed to the left and ran past the stationary passengers down the metal moving stairway. Hearing the whine of a Tube grinding to a halt I felt the temperature of the suffocating stale air increase with the train's arrival.

I picked up my pace and swerved to the left, narrowly avoiding a plump girl with bright pink hair who was a walking multi-coloured spectacle. I took off down the short corridor between the tiled concourse and the concrete platform.

There was an open double door on the packed train directly opposite me and I launched myself into the crowded carriage. I pushed my way in and squeezed between some of the other commuters as the doors closed with a dull thud behind my back.

Looking ahead, my eyes scanned along the row of people seated and I began people watching. A grey haired guy in black rimmed glasses with pale pasty looking skin sat with a blank, worn look on his face to my right. He was wearing a white collar and dark tie, beige coloured raincoat and I automatically put him in the career category as a civil servant or an accountant.

In contrast, sitting next to him was a young student-type girl with dyed white hair and ruby red lips. She had her head in a book but was blowing bubbles with her gum and twirling her hair whilst reading a copy of 'Anarchy, State, and Utopia' by Robert Nozick. That made me smirk because just like books, you can never judge someone purely on appearances or I'd have expected her to be reading a topic less heavy.

In no time at all I'd travelled from South Kensington to Knightsbridge. Stepping off the carriage and onto the platform, I made way for tourists and commuters to disembark then stepped back on, this time facing the doors.

Just as the door was closing a petite sweet smelling brunette bundled her way on board and pushed up against me. Luckily the train was packed tight because she would have bowled me over if there had been the space. Adding to the initial squeeze, she was wearing a backpack so when the doors closed, her more than ample breasts were pushed hard against my chest. I automatically looked down and my eyes were drawn to the most perfect cleavage I'd ever seen. *Hot Damn.*

I swear my eyes, my hands, and my dick were wired oddly. I immediately wanted to know how her breasts would feel in my hands, and my dick was very interested in the visual I had as well.

Somehow, after a longer-than-was-comfortable glance, I dragged my eyes slowly up along a slender neck to the face of the breasts from heaven until I saw her face. The sweet, innocent face had the biggest, sexiest, come to bed eyes and the most incredible blowjob lips I'd ever encountered. All right—to most people she may have had an innocent face, but my mind was creative and I was a dirty bugger at times. To me she was a walking wet dream, especially with her being so up-close-and-personal. She smelled awesome as she stared up at me all doe-eyed through her long dark lashes. Towering above her I had about a nine inch advantage in height and a nine inch disadvantage in my trousers, but from where I was standing the view was damn near perfect.

When she cocked her eyebrow at me and smiled slowly, I bit my lip to contain a smirk that threatened to break out. I knew I'd been well and truly busted objectifying her. *Jesus, she's gorgeous.* The thing that initially struck me about her, besides her breasts, was that she had nerve. When our eyes met, she held my gaze looking completely unfazed. At least I had the grace to feel a bit awkward at the fact that her breasts were flat against my chest. And I was sporting a semi hard-on that I was desperately trying to talk down.

I was about to apologise because I felt that was expected when she winked at me and delivered a slyest looking smirk of her own. She knew the effect she was having on me. My smirk, no longer cooperating with my mind, morphed itself into a grin. So I did the only thing I could under the circumstances.

"Jack."

"Gini," she mirrored, still grinning up at me with a twinkle in her eye that hinted at her naughty side. Call me whatever you want, but I wanted to pull her off the train and show her what she was doing to me.

We didn't get any further than that, the whole encounter lasted less than two minutes but, I swear I experienced a greater connection with her than with any of the girls I'd previously dated. All too soon the Tube train began to brake at my stop and I had to get off. I did want to get off…but not to go to work. I was willing her to jump off the train at the same time as me, however I don't really believe in fate, and therefore knew that was never going to happen and it pissed me off.

The doors opened and I felt the pressure of her body against mine lessen as she stepped back to make room. As the warmth of her breasts left me, her palm brushed up my leg and across my groin. She eventually pushed herself clear and I had an instant ache to grab her and pull her against me again. Instead, I just smiled at her and began to leave the carriage. As one foot landed on the platform she grabbed my jacket, pulling me back momentarily to whisper sexily in my ear.

"Nice pack, Jack, I hope you know what to do with that."

Releasing her hold on my jacket, I fell back onto the platform and her hand came up to wave at me—her sly smile turning into a grin, probably at the stunned look on my face. In an instant the doors closed and the Tube with the incredible Gini on board was gone. All I could do was stand on the platform watching helplessly as my moment of pure joy disappeared into the blackness of the tunnel. As I stared after the Tube I wondered if she really had spoken or whether my fantasy gene was fucking with me because she'd inadvertently stroked my dick.

"Fuck!" *The one that got away.*

How was it that the best things seemed to present themselves at the worst times? I would definitely have liked a bit more time with her, and if it hadn't have been Rick Fars that I was interviewing that day I'd have blown off work and pulled a sick day. There was a wealth of untapped potential with Gini, but without time and a proper conversation I had been left with nothing.

A huge construction worker in a high visibility jacket shoulder-barged me out of my reverie, he knocked me in one direction as a middle aged man put out an arm to ensure I didn't stumble into him. Glancing at my wristwatch, I remembered why I'd been on the Tube in the first place. I turned on my heels and ran like Forrest Gump all the way up and out of the entrance, and up Park Lane to my appointment.

When I arrived at The Dorchester, Baxter the doorman, in his green uniform with yellow braiding, smiled and held it open for me. The guy never seemed to go home. No matter what day or time I rolled up, he was always on duty.

As Senior Music Correspondent for MuzikVibe, I was privileged to be invited to interview the crème of the music world. Sometimes those interviews involved travelling with the bands for a fly-on-the-wall kind of dossier and sometimes it was a one-off interview. These types of interviews were strategically scheduled to help plug the artists' new album or if an incident or event concerning the artist needed support—or a scandal to be sidestepped.

Walking through the marbled floor and opulent surroundings of the foyer I headed straight towards the highly polished dark wood reception desk.

"Jack!"

My steps faltered when a head bobbed up from behind the desk that I never expected to see in a million years. *Crap!*

Lynn was a girl I'd dated in secondary school in the last few weeks of my last year there. It was right before the summer holidays. She was a good lay but got pretty clingy very quickly. She began to stalk me. I used the summer holidays to create distance between us by picking up work experience with the local newspaper.

After that, I'd skipped out by changing university to one up north despite the fact I had everything I needed to learn about journalism right on my doorstep. Also, I wanted to experience living and working in another part of the country, so it kind of killed two birds with one stone in that respect.

"Well hello, Lynn! Fancy seeing you here. How are you doing, babe?"

"All the better for seeing you, Jack. Where have you been?" Immediately she flicked her hair back and smiled at me in a look-at-me-now kinda way. I was looking, but I wished I wasn't.

"Ah, you know how it is, studying, working, getting responsible. You?"

Lynn began to talk but suddenly I wasn't listening. I could hear my own blood swishing around in my ears and my heart pumped quickly as I stood quietly wondering if she could find me. I stared at the computer in front of her realising that my home address could be listed in their security system. I prayed that the magazine's address was the only one logged. There was no way I wanted to deal with her antics again.

"Jack?"

Spinning around, I was faced with the CEO of Sly Records, Keiron Hughes, the record label that Rick Fars and his band were signed to. I knew him quite well because Alfie's band, Crakt Soundzz, and Lily's XrAid were also signed to Sly. Keiron wouldn't normally be the one to meet me but he and Rick were close friends so sometimes he tagged along. It kind of screwed everything up when he turned up because things ran smoother when he wasn't around to meddle.

"Nice seeing you again, Lynn. Take care, honey."

Patting Keiron's back in an over-familiar way, I led him away from the reception area slightly more urgently than he was expecting.

"Keiron, I could kiss you."

Keiron smirked knowingly and raised his eyebrows whilst glancing back at Lynn, "I missed you too, Jack, but let's not get carried away, eh? Old flame?"

"Bonfire."

Keiron threw his head back with a loud hearty laugh that drew everyone's attention to us but I couldn't help chuckling at his reaction.

"Firecracker eh? She looks harmless enough."

"Looks can be deceiving, I moved county to get away from that, she was relentless in her pursuit, Keiron. I kid you not, it was almost at restraining order level."

"And does she get mental health help at all?"

I bunched my brow confused at what he meant then he smirked wickedly.

"Well her being attracted to you must qualify her for something, right?"

We both chuckled as he steered me towards the lifts and he nudged me in my side.

"Either she needs help or otherwise it means someone actually saw something in you the rest of us can't." he teased. "Anyway, I dug you out of that hole, so it looks like you owe me a beer, young Jack."

"Indeed, Keiron… for giving crazy-bird Lynn the slip so smoothly, I'll buy you a barrel."

Chapter 2

A little rash

After exiting the lift, Keiron stepped out in front of me with his arms stretched over his shoulder scratching his back before dropping back to walk beside me. As we made our way in the direction of the ornate doors that led to Rick's suite, he quickly briefed me on Lily, Alfie and their bands, their tours, and the pending release of both XrAid and Cobham Street's new albums. The latter being my reason for interviewing Rick.

When we reached the penthouse, I stood back to allow Keiron to lead the way along the short corridor to Rick's suite. Jed, Ricks's bodyguard, was sitting at a small desk by the door with another guy I'd never seen before. Looking up, Jed pushed his chair back and rose to his feet. The guy with his back to me instantly mirrored Jed's movements as his head swung in my direction. They were pretty intimidating looking guys, but I was fucked if I was going to let them know that.

"Well, well! If it isn't Jack Cunningham, the walking male Vogue model lookalike. Last time I saw you, buddy, the boss was telling you to get a room, if I remember correctly."

Smirking wickedly, I scratched the back of my head feeling a little sheepish at the memory of me being more than a little frisky in public with a couple of groupies at one of Rick's after parties.

"Hey, all I was doing was showing your boss how it's supposed to be done when you are a rock star. I felt he needed some pointers because I didn't see him getting much action while I was there."

"Time and place for that, Jack my boy, time and place. The boss prefers to keep his conquests away from prying eyes. Shots in the media from raggedy-assed bastards like you are as common as pissing in this game. Rick wouldn't want his pecker plastered all over the internet and besides, you were putting everyone off, dude. It was a regular one-man-sex-fest going on as I recall."

I couldn't argue with that. Four girls were vying for my attention after thinking that I must be famous because I had arrived with Alfie Black. I would have said something but I was enjoying myself a little too much at that point and it was all harmless fun. We were all adults and knew what we were doing. I had to agree, it was a little over the top though, even for me.

"True," I said, then I turned back to Keiron and continued to walk in after him.

On entering the suite, I somehow expected Rick to be sitting on a chair having breakfast, and I don't know why I even thought that, because I was dealing with a wayward rocker that was used to excess and late nights. Why they gave me a nine fifteen a.m. slot for the interview was beyond me because his PR team must have known he wouldn't even be out of bed by that time.

Keiron told me to make myself comfortable and then pushed the connecting door to his bedroom open just enough to ease his body through it. I felt awkward that he was dragging Rick out of bed for me to ask some pretty basic questions about his work. Seconds later I knew Rick was awake.

"Get the fuck out, pervert. I told you, I'll get up in a minute. It's only Jack for fuck's sake."

I could hear Keiron speaking in a low even tone until something banged against the door.

"Are you fucking deaf or just stupid? What the fuck are you even doing in here? I can manage an interview on my own."

There was more mumbling before Rick shouted angrily again.

"All right already! I'm fucking coming! Get the fuck out so that I can make myself decent."

I couldn't help but chuckle at the sound of hell-raising Rick Fars and the word decent in the same sentence. Since when did Rick Fars ever make himself decent for anyone? He was buck-naked on the last two occasions I'd seen him. Keiron slid back through the door and closed it. Turning to face me, he glanced nervously with a frustrated expression on his face before letting out an exacerbated sigh and throwing his hands out in an I-give-up gesture.

"Guess you heard that, huh? He's in a pissy mood this morning. Late night and a couple of exhausted looking chicks in there."

"Fuck...can you sign me, Keiron? All that pussy on tap and he's in a mood because he has to get up for work? Music lessons should have been mandatory in my school. If they had told me that I'd get hot women begging me to fuck them if I played the guitar in a rock band, I'd have learned those lame riffs in a heartbeat."

Rick cracked open the door and padded through it hacking a cough and reaching for the mini-bar.

"Mornin' Lothario," he croaked in my direction.

He had a sour look on his face and without making eye contact, he picked up the bottles and inspected the labels.

I chuckled loudly at his dry wit, there was just no way I was going to live down the notorious after party, but when I took in the sight of Rick I couldn't help but throw a come-back at him.

"Excuse me, Rick, did your mother send you that get up or are those pyjamas used as a signal for the woman in the room to leave?"

Rick looked down and checked himself out before smirking with embarrassment at the wine coloured paisley patterned silk pyjama bottoms he was wearing. They looked ridiculous on him.

Waving his hand at the chair in front of him for me to come over and sit closer to him, he picked up a glass and poured two miniatures of gin and a small bottle of tonic water into it. When he was finished he gave me a fleeting glance and threw the drink back before answering.

"Long story."

"Can't wait." My hurried comment was followed by a wide grin as I settled back in the chair with one leg crossed over the other, my ankle rested on my knee.

"Allergy. I got a rash from the starch on the hotel sheets the other night." When I saw the serious look on Rick's face, I almost lost it.

I knew he was going to regret his admission as soon as the words stumbled out of his mouth and judging from the startled look on his face, I'd caught him off guard and he didn't mean to be so open about it. Knowing he'd walked right into something that I could use against him, I literally saw him cringe with regret.

"A rash?" I couldn't keep the humour from my voice, and there was even the hint of a breakthrough chuckle as I spoke.

Rick stared pointedly at me as if to say, 'Laugh and I will tear you a new one', but my sense of humour overrode any potential fall-out or consequence he may plan in the future.

"That's a bit like saying I got pregnant from the sheets, Rick. Don't you think you're more likely to have caught something from one of the women in your bed than from the sheets? Or don't you want to believe that just in case you get pussy-fright?" Rick's reaction was quick. He threw the lid of one of the gin bottles at me and it bounced off my forehead, causing my chuckle to become a full on roar.

"Laugh all you want, but I'm allergic to starch. So they got me these pyjamas from the hotel store because I needed something to make sure I was protected in bed. It was fucking murder trying to play with the itch in my pants the night before last."

"Most guys wear condoms for protection, Rick not theatrical looking pyjamas."

I knew he was being completely serious but the more he defended himself, the more uncontrollable my laughter became until he stood up and pulled them down to show me the red welts on his legs while his dick bobbed at my eye level. Just as he did that, the door opened and the previous night's entertainment came through. Turning my head to look at the girls, I tried to stifle a grin.

Rick was true to form and had two classic groupies for a sleepover. They were skinny girls with big tits, no bras and dyed blonde hair with an inch of black root. Both were dressed in the usual rock-chick attire of leather mini-skirts, fishnet stockings and tight dark brown and cream t-shirts with the 'Cobham Street' motif on them.

"Sorry, ladies, I was just about to partake, would either of you like to join me?"

My quip was out before I'd even thought about it. *Hell, I'm probably going to be sacked after this.* I grinned widely and Rick smacked me around the head, making me cry out—partly in surprise and partly out of pain.

"You're such a smart ass, Jack Cunningham," he

growled as he twisted the top half of his body in the girls' direction.

Rick looked at them but gestured at me, standing with his pyjamas still at his ankles.

"I was just showing him my rash," he said with a serious tone to his voice.

Laughing raucously, I stared helplessly at Rick as I took in his pathetic form with the patterned material draped around his feet and his dick dangling out in front of him. As soon as I knew he felt the need to explain what was happening to them, all of my professionalism deserted me and I struggled to catch my breath, let alone stop laughing.

A second later the skinnier one of the girls gave a loud snort before her resolve disappeared and she joined in with my laughter. I think she was laughing because mine was so infectious more than anything else.

Rick continued to protest his innocence when the second girl who had been staring suddenly erupted in the oddest hee-haw laugh I've ever heard in my life. The look on Rick's face was a picture as he gawped in disbelief while the rest of us laughed hysterically at his expense. I was sure he was going to react badly, but even with that knowledge I just couldn't get it together, even when my sides hurt.

Rick bent down and pulled his pyjamas up. I found that even funnier. Striding over to open the door, Rick waved a finger in the direction of the two women, and without saying a word, Jed made short work of evacuating them from the scene. All I could do was watch helplessly because I couldn't get my laughing fit under control. I was sure he would throw me out next, but probably via the roof terrace.

Closing the door again, Rick bent forward with his hands on his knees then he suddenly cracked up with laughter too.

"Jack fucking Cunningham, I should bury my size eleven up your ass for what happened there, but for some reason I can't... I fucking love you, dude. You have no idea what a breath of fresh air you are in a world full of 'yes men'. How the fucking hell are you doing, buddy?"

I didn't know why these American's seemed to feel the need to say my full name all the time but just like that, Rick Fars switched gears and we were back on track with the interview, his rash forgotten. When we were done, he slipped me two backstage passes inviting me to his gig and another party the following Thursday.

"It's a sit down dinner, Jack, so no using your fingers," he commented when I raised my brow, and it was his turn to laugh.

In most circumstances I'd have been a social outcast after the stunt I pulled at his last UK event, but the most he did was chastise me because I got a little carried away and began a very public heavy petting session. When Rick called me out that night I pretended to act all innocent and said something like, 'doesn't everyone use their fingers at a buffet?' Or words to that effect.

Chapter 3

Dancing

Riding home on the Tube wasn't nearly as exciting as it was on the way over. Rick offered me a car but I wasn't in any rush. I had nothing planned for the first time in weeks and when I glanced at my phone I had two texts on there already from Rosie. I prayed at some point she would just move on. If I stayed home I knew I'd end up calling her out of guilt and then the never ending downward spiral of angst would begin. I didn't want to be involved with her intimately but although we weren't together anymore, I still missed her being around.

I struggled with my feelings sometimes and felt heartless about calling a halt to our relationship, but after almost a year I felt that our time had passed and I didn't feel the same about her anymore. She deserved better than that. If I'd stayed in the relationship, Rosie wouldn't have gotten the best of me when I clearly wasn't feeling the same as she did.

As I wandered out of the underground I pulled my phone from my jacket pocket and fired off a, 'rescue me' text to Dave and Sam because I really needed some down time with my mates. I'd been at events for the past two weeks and I just wanted to relax without having to socially 'perform'.

"Are you telepathic, man?" Dave answered his phone with a question and an incredulous tone.

"Might be. If there's a hot girl wearing just a string with three or four hours to spare in the thought." I quipped.

Dave chuckled down the line.

"Jack there's always a woman in a string where your thoughts are concerned. I was just talking to Sam..." he replied in an amused tone.

"True. You think that's a mental illness?" I interjected.

"Damn, Jack! Focus. Oh and talking about mental illness, I ran into Cat. You remember her, right? The mental health nurse you picked up on the Tube the day you had drinks at yours with Lily and Crakt Soundzz? You remember, Drew, Elle, and the body shot on the kitchen counter episode? That day?"

Humming into my phone, I thought for a minute before Cat's image flashed into my mind.

"Sure. Great legs, gave great head, great girl. Got on with everyone there, pretty kinky too from what I can recall. Why?"

"Well if you shut up long enough, I'll tell you. Jeez, Jack, focus."

"I am, shoot."

Dave cleared his throat before continuing.

"So Sam and I were talking, apparently he hooked up with her one night, and they've hit it off so he's dating her now."

"Well, fuck, that's going to be a bit awkward. Sam's the pretty jealous kind. Look at the way he got all possessive about sitting next to Lily in the restaurant when she came over from America that first Christmas she'd been away. What was that all about?"

There was a pregnant pause on the line and I thought my signal had dropped.

"Dave?"

"I'm here. Just don't want to answer the last question," he mumbled, sounding flat.

Initially I was confused both by what I'd asked and Dave's hesitancy to answer. Then the penny dropped. *Sam fucked Lily?*

"You had better be mind-fucking me, Dave. Lily would never get with Sam."

Dave sounded awkward and began to retract but I knew he was only doing that to make me feel better and to protect his position with Sam.

"Well, I could have picked up what he said wrong, or Sam might have been messing with me, Jack. We were both kinda wasted when he said it."

"Said what? Just tell me exactly how the conversation went and I'll make up my own mind," I demanded as I tried to keep the near hysteria out of my voice.

Dave was reluctant to go any further and tried to steer the conversation away from the subject of Sam and Lily but I continued to press the point.

"Just fucking tell me, Dave, you've gone this far. I'm not going to rest until I get it out of you."

Hearing him expel a loud breath was all the confirmation I needed. Sam had slept with Lily. I just couldn't get my head around that one.

"Sam slept with Lily, right before she left for the USA. From what I remember they were both pretty drunk that night. Sam said they did the deed the night Elle had the leaving party for her. After we'd all been clubbing, we headed back to Elle's and played spin-the-bottle. I don't remember much, but I do remember they disappeared at the same time."

Fuck! Suddenly I hated Sam. My emotions scattered in all directions. Firstly my anger at him, then I felt hurt that Lily had kept that from me, as well as Sam. I couldn't accept that he had gone there and that I had no fucking idea there had been anything between them. Lily confided in me about *everything*, or so I'd thought. And now there was this epic fucked-up secret between me and her that had been there for years. Of course it was her business. *But hell—with Sam?*

"You think he's making it up? You think if I ask Lily she'll tell me that the wires between Sam's fantasy and reality got crossed and he's imagined the whole thing? Being honest with you, Dave, Alfie, I totally get. The guy has it all, looks, rock star charisma, big dick..." I chucked sheepishly into the phone.

"Yeah, of course I checked him out in the loos, what guy isn't looking for a flaw in him? Like I said, Alfie I get. But Sam? I have a hard time seeing Lily having sex with a guy like Sam," I added.

Dave had remained completely silent during my rant.

"I'm sorry." Dave sounded remorseful that he'd been the one to tell me.

"No! Don't do that. Don't take responsibility for me being pissed off. I've got no right to feel anything. What Lily and Sam did of their own free will is none of my business. I'm the one that's being irrational here. Over the years I've developed this inbuilt protective mechanism that's at play here. I guess I'm just feeling annoyed because I was completely ignorant to the fact that she got with one of our close friends."

"Jeez, Jack, it was years ago now, and Lily has a whole other life. This isn't going to affect anything within our group is it? I mean, can you get past it?"

I wasn't sure about that, but I knew I had to try to get comfortable with my newfound knowledge. I had spoken to Dave all the way from the underground to home and by then part of me was wishing I hadn't called. Taking my keys out from my pocket, I stabbed the one to my front door into the lock, still trying to get a grip on my feelings. I closed the door quickly and decided there and then, I needed to burn off some steam.

"Right we're going out. What time do you finish?"

Dave reminded me he was on holiday for a few weeks and that he had actually called me to invite me to a club opening that evening. There was nothing I needed more than to get on the dance floor surrounded by hot women and forget myself for a while. Considering it was Friday, I had a whole weekend to recover from whatever trouble we got ourselves into. With that in mind I arranged to meet up with him at The Punch and Judy pub in Covent Garden a couple of hours later.

Normally I shower but I decided a soak in the hot tub was in order to soothe my suddenly weary body. When I thought about it, I hadn't stopped in weeks and I hadn't had a proper holiday since the previous summer. Travelling to Florida for Christmas didn't seem like a holiday. Lily was there, and our parents, so I'd felt like I was going home.

Once the bath was filled, I unzipped my pants and then heard my phone alert me to an incoming text. Taking it out of my pocket, I pushed my pants down my legs and stepped out of them as I swiped across the screen to see who it was.

Lily: Hiya handsome how is your day going? Miss you. Xx

Closing my eyes, I swallowed noisily. Her timing couldn't have been any better, it was as if she knew I was struggling with something. I brought up the onscreen keyboard to reply, but my usual witty response wasn't coming to mind. I guessed there was no time like the present for dealing with the Sam issue and getting it off my chest. My thumbs moved quickly over the screen.

Me: So-so. What's this smutty gossip I've been hearing about you?

As soon as I sent it I felt annoyed and disappointed with myself. I'd let Dave's comment get under my skin. More than that, I was frustrated because I hadn't been able to just let it go and was now going to get into it headlong with Lily. But I knew if I didn't talk to her about it now we'd have a wedge between us.

Placing the phone on the side of the bath, I stepped in and settled down before laying back and running both hands through my hair. My phone began to vibrate so I turned it over to see who was calling and my heart instantly started to race. It was Lily.

"Jack?" Hearing the hurt in her voice at the other end of the line made me feel sorry for mentioning it.

"Hi, beautiful. How is your day going?"

"No, you don't fire a text like that at me and when I call to find out what the deal is you act all innocent and sweet. I know you better than that Jack Cunningham. If you have something to say, man up and say it."

Boy, the temper in her voice made me glad there was a huge pond between us. Sighing heavily, my heart continued to pound as I plucked up the courage to talk to her. Even though it really had nothing to do with me, I felt it had because I needed her to be true to us by being honest.

"Well I was kind of sideswiped by Dave today. He rang me and somehow you getting fucked by Sam slipped into the conversation."

Lily remained silent at the other end and I thought we'd been cut off and I had been speaking to myself.

"Lily? Are you still there?"

Lily's voice sounded small and wounded when she answered.

"Yes, I'm here."

"So, is it true? You let Sam screw you? What the fuck

were you thinking, Lily?"

Clearing her throat, Lily spoke in a more self-assured manner.

"That's the whole point, Jack. I wasn't thinking, I was feeling. I've thought about it many times…"

"So he was that good? Damn, Lily…"

She was quick to cut across my impending rant.

"No. He was awful. It was awful. It was my first time, Jack, and it was really crap actually." Lily's voice broke and I instantly felt her pain.

"And, he didn't fuck me. He barely moved inside me before he came, but you know what? I'm glad it was him, Jack. Of all people, I'm glad it was Sam that night."

Listening to Lily tell me that was hard. Really hard. My heart ached that she was glad it was Sam that took her virginity. It took me a few seconds to recover from her admission before I could speak again.

"Sorry. This whole thing was shitty of me. I should never have sent that text. It's nothing to do with me and I don't know why it's affecting me so badly."

There was a silence between us as we struggled with what to say next, then I spoke more softly as I confessed the only thought coming to my mind.

"I'm not sure if that's because he shared something with you that I haven't, or because I was oblivious that it happened at all, or that he took advantage of your vulnerability."

"Stop!" Lily exhaled loudly from the other end of the line.

"Jack, I'm glad it was Sam and I'm glad you were away on an assignment. I'm glad you weren't there that night. If you had been, the way my emotions were, I know it would have been you. I was missing you and my feelings were all over the place. New life, new college, leaving everyone behind. Leaving *you* behind. I was struggling."

When I heard the pain in Lily's voice I realised how hard it had been for her to make the decision to study abroad and what it would mean for our friendship. It helped me to understand and in some weird way, accept that Sam had saved our friendship. If we said that out loud to anyone they'd think we were nuts. Maybe we are. Maybe I should have screwed Lily a long time ago and it would have been out of our systems. Hell, maybe we could have done that and still remained friends, then again, maybe not. Neither of us had been willing to take the chance. So now? It is what it is.

Chapter 4

Close calls

Talking to Lily really helped settle my mind, but I knew I still had to face Sam and swallow my thoughts about the two of them together. It also made it marginally better that Lily hadn't enjoyed being with him. Maybe I was just too sensitive and possessive because I had just come out of my own relationship with Rosie.

Seven hours after talking to Dave I walked into the crowded pub and immediately spotted Sam. It was as if he had a neon sign above him making him stand out from the crowd. It was like he was magnified or highlighted by my earlier thoughts of him and Lily.

By the time I reached him and Dave I actually wanted to thank Sam because Lily was right, I knew if the opportunity had presented itself when Lily was leaving, we probably would have had no fight in us. In all honesty it was the reason I took an assignment abroad right before she left. I was struggling with it; on the one hand it felt like she was dying and I had to say goodbye and on the other I was scared that I'd beg her not to go.

Glancing at Dave and then Sam, I knew instantly that

Dave had warned him that I knew his little secret and I immediately pushed it to one side. Sure I had to speak to him but it had to be at a time when we were relaxed and not right as I walked into the pub. What was I going to say anyway? *"So...I hear you fucked, Lily, how was that for you?"* What I actually did was our usual greeting of shaking hands and I pulled him in for a hug. When he stepped back he was struggling to meet my gaze so I just started to talk because I always try to make things okay for people.

"Am I buying or do I have one already?" Shifting my eyes between them, I planted myself onto the nearest chair.

Sam nodded his head in the direction of the glasses on the table. He'd bought me a pint. I hated beer. I used to drink Jack Daniels, not now. Call me a girl but I love tequila shots and my favourite drink is gin and tonic. 'Bombay Sapphire Gin' to be precise and it was even better that it used to be made in my hometown.

Shaking my head I raised my eyebrow incredulously at him. "You think? I'm not putting that in my stomach, I have a six-pack. I'd like to keep it when I'm middle aged. I'll stick with the G&T if you don't mind."

Staring at me with a deadpan expression, Sam inclined his head in the direction of the bar.

"Go on then, I'm not paying for another drink for you on my round. You want to play at being a snob, go finance it."

Smirking, I shoved the chair back and straightened to stand.

"Remember this moment when my body is still being used and abused by beautiful women, and you're lying on your sofa with a flabby paunch sticking out the bottom of your t-shirt, mate." I taunted.

Approaching the bar, a hand grabbed my arse. I was just about to turn when a stunning blonde crashed into me and sent the both of us flying forwards into a guy who was turning around with a tray heavily laden with drinks. Jumping back to dodge him and the drinks, I managed to get myself clear but my elbow caught the tray and the long stemmed glasses he was carrying toppled over. Every single one of the multi-coloured cocktails spattered all over the poor girl's expensive designer jumpsuit.

There was a freeze-frame moment where in a microsecond everyone fell silent before carrying on their conversations. The very attractive but irate looking girl tossed her hair over her shoulder and jabbed a long finger into my chest.

Damn. After staring down at her clothes she flipped her head up quickly to glare angrily at me in disbelief

"Oh. My. God. Look at what you've just done. You ruin me by soaking my pants. You make me very wet." She accused, gesturing towards the mess.

She was right, she was completely drenched. Her outfit was stained with the pink and yellow alcoholic beverages and there was one particular area that clung to her body just shy of her groin.   My eyes lingered there for a moment and having a healthy, filthy male mind and quick wit was sometimes a terrible affliction, that was one of those times. I couldn't help but take what she said in her sexy broken English accent with a certain amount of smutty humour. Before my brain had engaged I was grinning and I'd responded to her comment.

"I know, sweetheart, I seem to have a particular talent for doing that to women. Want to know what else I can do?" Out of the corner of my eye I saw the stocky guy's jaw drop as he stared wide eyed at me shocked that I would actually say something like that.

Turning my head slightly I raised my eyebrow and gave him a knowing smirk before I returned my attention to the distressed but very sexy, exotic sounding female in front of me.

"Now what you do to me? You make me wet you

must take care of me."

Glancing over at Dave who was quietly watching the whole exchange, I saw him almost choke on his beer, his eyes popped widely as he spluttered and chuckled at the same time. He tapped Sam's arm and pointed over at me, unable to speak. Sam turned and immediately smirked wickedly shaking his head at me. Undeterred I continued flirting.

"Sure, babe, I can do that. Your place or mine?"

The puzzled look she gave me made me think I was in the clear until she spoke.

"Why would you take me to your home? You have woman's dress there for me? You put me in the shower? You dirty me then you wash me?"

In my mind a mini movie began to play out her verbal storyboard, but I bet what I was thinking and what she meant were anything but the same thing.

I told myself I wasn't one for stereotyping blonde women because some of the smartest females I knew were blonde, but this one wasn't doing much for the argument.

"Of course I would. It would be my pleasure. If you get dirty with me then of course I'd clean you, I'm a gentleman after all. And if you play your cards right, you might get to wear this one hundred percent Egyptian cotton shirt in the morning."

As she mulled over my proposition a ginormous rough-looking guy came alongside her and rested his huge fat hand on her shoulder. He spoke to her in what I think may have been Russian and his abrupt tone alone was enough to frighten the crap out of me. Blondie replied in a hurried tone, gesticulating with her hands to me then to the guy with the tray, and then back to me again.

Another quick glance to the stocky guy, and he looked exactly how I was feeling—petrified. He was trying to look innocent and kind of pathetic, and I noted him swallowing roughly a few times as we both held our breaths waiting to see what our fate was going to be at the hands of man mountain.

I was sure he was going to lay me out on the floor and was trying desperately to work out my exit strategy but instead, he leaned in and clapped his large hand on my shoulder. The weight of his touch almost made my legs buckle.

"Excuse me. My wife she is very… how you say?… clumsy? I apologise for the wrongness she do to you."

My heart never missed a beat as I pulled out the performance of my life.

"No problem. I'm used to women throwing themselves at me, it's a curse. I hope she gets the drink stains out." I said, glancing again at the wrecked material of her clothing.

As quick as the words were out of my mouth I smirked wickedly and created some distance by swerving around her and heading over to the guys.

"Out. Now. Hurry. I'm not staying here in case he suddenly changes his mind."

Without waiting for them I spun on my heels and made for the door. Once out on the street, Sam chuckled and shook his head while shoving his arm into the sleeve of his coat.

"Tell me your secret, Jack. How come, when that guy should have been whipping your arse, you get an apology? I was sitting there thinking, Shit! Jack's really got himself in trouble this time. I even started sizing up your opponent and wondering if I was going to try to help if he started beating on you."

Dave was slower to join us outside and looked pissed off about leaving as he closed the door behind him. Standing still, he shoved his hands deep into his jacket pockets and examined his shoes before giving me a burning stare with a scowl on his face.

"Now what? It's still two hours before the club even

opens. I'm not up for us being the first there, that makes us look sad," he moaned.

Chuckling at their lack of adventure, I shrugged and bumped Dave's shoulder before pushing my own hands into the pockets of my open suit jacket.

"We can get something to eat. I hate drinking on an empty stomach anyway it makes me tired by ten o'clock. Besides, the drinks will be cheaper in the restaurant than in the club."

Dave was a bit of a snob, and like me he came from a family with money, but he couldn't quite 'get' why I made life so hard for myself by not accepting family handouts all the time. He was happy to take whatever was given to him by his parents and couldn't get that, although I was a man of means, I refused to use money I hadn't earned myself. Not that he was a shirker when it came to work. He had a great work ethic and put in long hours as a sound engineer in a recording studio.

Expelling air heavily, his breath misted into the January coldness and he nodded before walking in the direction of the restaurants.

"Fine by me, but I'm not going Japanese. All that writing on paper place settings and sharing a table with strangers isn't for me. Especially when you start talking about how your sex life has been in the last week, Jack. It's a tad embarrassing, especially when you start going into graphic detail and we get sat next to women."

I raised my brow not sure what he was talking about and looked at Sam who nodded in agreement with Dave. At that point I thought, maybe I needed to be a little more aware of who was around me.

After some negotiation we settled on Chinese. I had no idea why we'd even started a discussion about where to eat. We always ended up in a Chinese restaurant when Dave was with us. Our dinner was delicious and relatively uneventful. We'd had a fair few drinks by the time we finally set off for the club. It was still only ten thirty however it was a more respectable time than if we had turned up at nine when the doors opened.

There was already a queue forming outside Konnect, the newest addition to the club scene in London, but Dave walked to the front with a confident air and stuck a purple and gold coloured ticket into the bouncer's hand. Checking it quickly, he nodded at another guy who was holding the door handle and let us in.

Plush purple carpet with a lilac border ran along the wide reception area. To the left there was a sign for the cloak room and another for toilets in gold and purple writing strategically placed above an archway.

"Jack Cunningham. Where have you been hiding yourself? I haven't seen you in years." Spinning around in the direction of the distinctive sexy voice that I knew belonged to Sally Whittington, another a girl I had an on and off relationship with while at secondary school.

Sally was an extremely attractive girl of about five feet eight inches, mousey brown hair cut in a layered style framing her face and was immaculately groomed. Time had changed her for the better. Slender and tall, my eyes scanned her frame from top to bottom. At the end of her long slender legs were the tallest red patent heels I'd seen in a long time. She was as beautiful as I remembered.

Both Sam and Dave stood with their jaws gaping and I saw Dave's eyes raking up and down her body as well, he looked like he was mentally devouring her. Smiling seductively, Sally leaned in towards me like a hawk stalking her prey. She placed a splayed hand on my chest as she closed the space between us. Luckily I turned my head slightly to the side at the last moment and she planted a kiss with her ruby red lips at the side of my mouth. Although I had to admit Sally was stunning to look at and she smelled fucking awesome, I knew already what I'd be getting; an athletic bang with plenty of exchange in body fluids. Unfortunately, I also knew that she was a dead certainty and I preferred a chase these days.

"Come on, Sal, we need to get to the bar before it's five deep, I'm drying out over here."

Looking over my shoulder I saw a much shorter blonde girl wearing a skirt that made me wonder why she'd bothered with clothes at all. It was like a thin belt below her low cut chiffon light blue blouse, her navy bra showed through it like a beacon. How she was dressed left nothing to the imagination. Sally smiled seductively at me.

"I'll see you later, hon. Don't worry, I'll find you."

Dave shuffled his feet and twisted his lips at me, looking more than a little weary of my women.

"And she'd be?" he commented, gesturing his thumb in her direction with a note of sarcasm his voice.

"Sally. Great shag but I'm moving forward tonight, if I was moving backwards it would be Rosie's door I'd be knocking on, not hers. She's a great girl, but not a great girl for me." I explained as I watched her walk away. Dave was struggling to tear his eyes away from her as she sashayed her way towards the bar,

"Feel free to press on my friend, she's all yours. You'll have fun, I guarantee it."

Chapter 5

Hands full

Sweaty, clammy bodies were already in abundance by the time I had a few tequila shots and a couple of double gins inside me. Pushing my way through the various groups of people, I was perusing the faces of some of the girls on the dance floor until one grabbed my hand. She squeezed it tightly and yanked me towards her beaming face. Familiar eyes caught mine as I smiled in recognition when I made a connection between the face and the name.

"Hey, Jack." She hollered, straining to be heard above the music.

An instantaneous flashback of a wild night I'd spent at my apartment with the girl in front of me sprang to mind. My next thought was that she was also one of Sam's conquests. *Great another one of my girls that Sam has fucked.* Not that Lily was 'my girl' in that way, but for the second time in a day I had to mind myself around Sam, the women in my life spilled over into his. Reacting less naturally than I normally would have, I remembered that Dave had told me Sam was seeing her. I smiled warmly and gently squeezed her delicate hand back.

"Hello, Cat, how are you doing, babe?"

"All the better for seeing you here, Jack. Where have you been? You never called me."

Fuck I hadn't. "Oh, you know my crazy life... and then I met this girl..."

"Rosie, yeah, Sam told me about her." Despite the music Cat's voice sounded a bit flat.

Well, damn. They'd been talking about me.

"So, you and Sam?"

Cat looked slightly embarrassed probably because the night we had shared together was pretty debauched and she hadn't held a single thing back. I'd fucked her senseless and she had loved it. Her eyes dropped to look at the floor then flicked back at me with an air of defiance. We started to dance to the beat that was vibrating through our feet when she pinched my shirt with her thumb and forefinger and drew me back into her chest again. Her mouth brushed my ear and she raised her voice to be heard again.

"You never called back. When I ran into Sam a few months ago in a club we hit it off. I hadn't recognised him at all from that night at your place. It wasn't until he mentioned Elle and Drew that I realised he was even there."

I smirked because she was literally telling me that if I had called she wouldn't be with Sam. That somehow, made me feel better, which was stupid because I didn't want her in that way anymore.

"It's not a problem, Cat. Don't feel awkward about it, I don't. Sam obviously doesn't care that we've been together, so why should you? Besides, that was years before you guys got together."

Cat's gaze rose above my shoulder and I felt Sam's presence behind me before he moved past and slipped a possessive arm around Cat's waist. Leaning forward he dipped his mouth and planted a slow sensual kiss on her neck. Cat shivered and I suddenly felt like the third wheel dancing lamely in front of them.

Taking her hand, Sam gestured with his head in the direction of the table like I wasn't even there. They began weaving their way through the crowded dance floor and Cat tottered in her high-heeled shoes. Her arse swayed from side to side hugged by her sexy satin pencil skirt with a slit up the back and I hung back just enough to watch as I followed them to our table.

It was marginally quieter back in the seating area and Sam sat down pulling Cat onto his lap. He glanced at me as if to ask if I had any comment for him. I didn't, he was more than welcome to her. Cat's arms snaked around his neck and they instantly looked like they were trying to eat one another's faces the way they were devouring each other.

Dave was at the bar in deep conversation with Sally and my night was taking a nose dive as my wing men disappeared. Slipping out of my seat, I headed for another area of the bar because I'd seen enough of Cat and Sam, and I didn't want to scupper Dave's chances with Sally.

Seeing a gap in the four-bodies-deep crowd at the bar, I managed to squeeze in and lean on the counter with one elbow. A couple stepped closer to me and I was trapped against it. A pretty barmaid smiled warmly from the other side of the counter and her eye contact silently communicated to me I was next to be served.

As I began to give her my order a hand brushed over my dick. I immediately straightened and turned my head to the side. Gini, the hot girl from the Tube, was staring at me with a wicked smile on her face. I grinned at her forwardness and began to chuckle before my eyes widened as she proceeded to pull my zipper down ever so slowly. My dick was stirring in my pants at the possibility of what she was up to, but above the counter top I was trying to act very normal.

"Where I come from, people usually greet each other with a hand shake." I mumbled.

"I'm not from where you're from," Gini replied. She stuck her tongue out in concentration as she tried to fit her hand through the zipper to fiddle around in my boxer briefs.

"I'm beginning to believe that."

I'd never met anyone as blatantly forward before and I couldn't help but grin widely. I found it increasingly hard to stand still and keep the conversation going while she fished around inside my trousers. Her hand suddenly found the fly-hole in my boxers and without hesitation she slipped it inside. When I felt her gentle soft fingers wrap around my solid shaft her eyes widened, as if she'd found treasure down there.

"Where are you from, anyway?" Gini asked casually, and I marvelled at how innocent she appeared whilst she felt me up in a public place with hundreds of people packed tightly around us.

"South Kensington," I answered honestly. My voice was slightly affected as her fingers tried to tug my dick while it was still inside my boxers. The sensation of what she was doing sent sparks of electricity charging through my body and my length strained for release from its confined space and movements of her hand.

Gini grinned and licked her luscious glossy lips as she got frustrated. She then began to free my dick from my trousers and held it in both hands under the bar. I could feel the fresh air on my exposed dick even though it was baking hot in the club.

My head spun as I checked out the crowd to ensure that no one could see what she was doing. Gini raised an eyebrow and smirked as I stood staring at the blue burning gaze in her eyes with wonder. From her appearance she didn't seem like the type of girl that would have the nerve to do something as outrageous as that in a room full of people with a virtual stranger.

"Oh, well that explains it. This is how we do it south of the river. We're much more 'hands on' since our ancestors were mainly manual workers."

I chuckled as I stood trying to look nonchalant to the barmaid and continue to hold a conversation with Gini. Our discussion wasn't one of the most fluent ones I'd achieved, and when Gini started running her thumb over the crown of my dick, I thought I was going to burst.

"Well can't say I've mixed with anyone south of the river before, because I've never had someone feel me up in public with a dick shake until today. Twice," I added, remembering her fondling me on the Tube train.

"Poor Jack. The women in my neck of the woods are obviously much handier than the socialites in yours."

She stated piling on a thicker South London accent to highlight the differences between her own accent and my refined North London one.

With a dry mouth and a longing to be somewhere else entirely with her, I fought desperately to appear calm and not at all fazed by her breaching my personal body space and tackling what was now not in my trousers without a care. I was trying to think of a smart comeback but when I spoke back, my voice was an octave lower and there was a newfound urgency in it.

"It would seem so." I swallowed with some difficulty.

I gazied hungrily into her glittering eyes, and I watched her mouth curl up at the sides with pleasure. She lifted one of her hands to her mouth and licked her fingertips. Smirking mischievously, her hand disappeared back below the counter and I felt the wetness skim the length of my dick from root to tip. Gini leaned in, her perfume smelled alluring and I breathed in deeply, inhaling her seductive aroma.

"Vodka Cranberry please."

Hearing Gini's request dragged my mind back to the

barmaid who had been standing watching me the whole time and I realised she was waiting to be paid. Nodding slowly, the girl behind the bar started making the drink and Gini suddenly tucked my dick back in my trousers and pulled my zipper back up. By the time the barmaid was finished and I'd paid, she had me respectable and good to go.

Picking up the beverage, she raised the glass to her lips and tipped her head back, downing the rosy coloured drink in one go. She placed the empty glass back on the bar and licked her lips again. Her fingertips rose to her mouth and traced her wet lips in a sexy move that had my erect neglected dick twitching in my trousers once more.

"Dancing?"

My lips curved in a half smile and I was tempted to say an old clichéd phrase, "No, it's just the way I'm standing," but my boner was aching and straining against my zipper. If I had tried to walk I was sure I'd have a limp.

Gini was just incredible. Sassy mouthed, a great body and gorgeous features, and to me she was a very pretty little package. Definitely the type of girl I was attracted to. Dressed in a short red dress with two patched pockets at the front, she looked classically beautiful. The material wasn't too clingy, but it suited her perfectly. The innocence of the dress made her more provocative with a hint of her amazing creamy cleavage just visible from the square cut neckline. Overall, she alluded that she'd be explosive if I ever got inside her.

I felt her hand slip into mine, her fingers closed around it. She tugged me through the crush until we ran out of carpet and skidded onto the polished floor beside hundreds of other dancing clubbers.

Still holding my hand, Gini twirled around and managed to wrap herself in my arms with my front to her back and my hand tightly around her waist. Vertical spooning, my second favourite position after horizontal spooning, and the way Gini expertly manoeuvred herself left very little in the way of air between our bodies.

Wiggling her arse against my erection, Gini leaned her head back to look up at me. The sexy-as-fuck smile she gave me made me want to bend down and kiss her. Gazing at her luscious lips I almost gave into the urge until she broke the moment.

"Comfortable?" she asked waggling her eyebrows.

She smiled before her lips stretched to a devilish grin as she watched me intently, her eyes twinkled in the dim club lighting.

"You can feel how comfortable I am," I commented as she arched her back and stuck out her arse.

Then she began to twerk it up and down the front of my groin, all over my dick. A low growl tore from my throat as I put my free hand on her belly and pressed her further against me, enjoying the feel of her there.

I dipped my head forwards and my mouth found her slender neck, I licked down to her shoulder and back up towards her ear. I felt her body shiver in my hands and I lifted my head to see her face turned in my direction and her mouth slightly open. When I saw her tongue dart out and lick her lips there was no hesitation on my part, my mouth immediately covered hers in a kiss.

Shockwaves of electrical pleasure rode through my alert body as I hungrily explored her mouth. Gini wriggled her slender body free of my grip and turned to face me properly. Smiling seductively with lust-filled eyes, her hands slid up my sides over my pecs and up my neck. Clutching my hair with her fingers she pulled my head back down and reignited the kiss with even more passion.

My hands were initially resting innocently at her mid-back but after that they found their own way to her arse without any help from me. Cupping her cheeks, I pressed her closer against me again. Breaking the kiss, Gini leaned back to meet my heated gaze and smirked smugly but a little breathless.

"Well one thing's for sure, I affect you in all the right places. It would seem you're very pleased to meet me. You ladies south of The Thames may be handy, but we're a little more... holistic in our greetings. All I need to know is whether we're going to extend the acquaintance status we currently hold onto a more firm footing. If so, we may need to find somewhere a little more private, with some clean sheets, a few drinks and a thick springy mattress maybe?" I asked innocently.

Gini's eyes popped widely, surprised by my suggestion and she bit back a grin as she ran her forefinger over her lip in thought.

"Interesting proposition and you would know where to find a suitable location with those items listed?"

"Hmm...I thought you'd be the one with the clean sheets. I'm the bloke remember? We guys wait for our mothers to visit for that to happen. Or we take a girlfriend and keep her just long enough for her to notice and do it."

Gini placed her hands firmly on my chest and pushed me away as she started to dance again. My initial thought was that I'd overstepped the line between humour and sexism and I'd blown my chances. I was confused as I watched her moving to the music with a sudden disinterest in me. Strobe lighting disrupted me from reading her reaction fully as she swayed to the beat with her head down. When the lighting changed at the beginning of a new song, Gini turned her head slowly to the side. After a few minutes she glanced up through the parting in her hair and met my concerned gaze with a naughty grin.

Honestly, it felt like she had cast a net and I was becoming trapped in it. I'd never met a girl as playful as Lily before, but Gini was definitely beginning to fill that void. Amazed that my comment hadn't put her off, I began dancing beside her. I followed her lead and within a couple of minutes it was her that re-established physical contact with me. She was edgy and different, and I could feel myself becoming more tangled up in her by the minute.

Chapter 6

Different strokes

Every time Gini touched me, my flesh reacted. Goose bumps broke out when she ran her hands down my spine. My dick ached to breaking point when she turned her back to me and pushed her body against mine. I wanted to rip her knickers off and ride her within an inch of her life.

I'd used the phrase 'a sure thing' many times during nights out and I'm not ashamed to say I've had my share of one night stands—after all it was almost a given when you're a half decent looking guy at university like I was. But with Gini I'd never been more certain of how the evening was going to end.

"Do you want to get something else to drink? Or do you want to get out of here?" I looked at her seriously, willing her to choose the second option.

Being in a crowded place was suddenly incredibly annoying and although I had been enjoying my time at the club with her, I really wanted us to be alone. When she opted for another drink my heart sunk a little, all I wanted was somewhere quiet to get to know her better.

As we ordered drinks at the bar, we started talking

about how we earned our living. I shared my work in vague terms, before asking her about her career choice and she started to say she worked in the media field as well when she came to an abrupt halt mid-sentence. Suddenly, she dipped her knees digging her hand into one of her dress pockets and taking out her phone, she held up an index finger and signalled to me to wait as she took the call. Tucking some strands of hair behind her ear, she moved the phone from one ear to the other. Her brow furrowed as she placed a finger in her other ear to block out the background noise. I silently watched her, taking in her beauty while she listened intensely to the caller. Shaking her head, Gini bit her lip then raised her voice further in an effort to be heard.

"Hang on I can't hear you."

Mouthing a, 'Sorry,' to me, she briskly turned and hurried toward the foyer pushing through a couple of girls who looked in her direction then angrily back at each other because she hadn't been careful where she was going. I looked over to Dave and saw him smile and raise an eyebrow making light of what she'd just done.

"Is that her backup call?" he asked, nodding in the direction of Gini.

"Huh?"

Chuckling, he continued to try to get a rise out of me and inclined his head in the direction of the lobby where I could still see Gini on the phone.

"Oh, you really like this one, Jack? You looked like a kid that dropped their ice-cream when she pulled that phone out of her pocket," he taunted.

"Dunno, Dave, there's something different about her but really familiar. Do you understand what I mean?"

Sniggering at me, Dave tilted his head and stared intensely at me before raising his eyebrow.

"Jack, I thought you'd have caught on by now with the number of women you've had. They're all different."

When I didn't respond Dave commented further.

"Hmm, if I didn't know better, I'd say Jack was smitten with the little cutie over there. How do you know her anyway? From the way you were instantly all over each other there's definitely chemistry, but you both looked like you already knew each other."

"Her name's Gini and I met her on the Tube this morning."

"Damn, Jack. Do you stalk the underground looking for women? You seem to have the luck of the Irish. No one speaks on the Tube so how come you're able to pull these beautiful looking women down there? I mean, there were a few before Cat and now this one."

"Gini... her name is Gini." I interrupted, repeating her name again and feeling annoyed that he had referred to her as 'this one'.

I glanced again in the direction of the purple lights of the foyer, and saw that Gini was no longer leaning against the wall where I'd last seen her. My eyes quickly scanned the bodies and faces but she wasn't anywhere.

After a couple of minutes it dawned on me that she may not be coming back, so I excused myself and went off in search of her. Initially, I hung around the foyer with a drink in my hand and at that point, to most people, it probably looked like I was just having a breather from the noise and crush of the bar. After a few minutes I just knew she wasn't coming back. During that time I felt conscious of women passing me on their way to the restrooms and then again on the way back. Some smiled or winked suggestively in my direction. I was used to that, it happened a lot. Lily used to get pretty mad when we were talking in public because my eyes roamed. It was usually because girls would look at me and catch my eye. I wasn't consciously trying to piss her off; it was just that some girls were more adept at getting my attention than others. Gini was very adept.

Slowly, I began to make my way towards the loos and asked a tall skinny girl that came out if a girl fitting Gini's description was in there. Shaking her head she told me there was no one else in there at all. Turning on my heels again, I craned my neck to see if she was anywhere in the crowd. She wasn't.

Shoving my way through the crowds of merry clubbers I made it back to the bar thinking that Gini may have gone back to look for me, and we'd somehow missed each other. It would have been understandable in a dark room packed with people who were mulling around.

Glancing towards the foyer again, I noticed it was empty; Gini had obviously left.. I'd been watching the entrance to the bar when she was outside, and I was pretty sure she hadn't returned.

Disappointed, I figured she must have got a better offer I so went back to the bar. Cat and Sam were just talking and seemed the best bet for me because Dave and Sally were getting on like a house on fire if Dave's hand resting on her arse was anything to go by.

Sliding into the seat next to Sam I did a double take when I realised they were sitting next to two girls. They looked so similar that they could have been twins, and were even dressed the same. I'd had a few to drink so that may have confused the matter further. Cat introduced me to her friends, Lizzie and Yvonne, and explained that she'd actually met us by chance that evening; she'd originally been on a girl's night out.

My interest was immediately piqued by the girls because their jobs said a lot about them. Lizzie was a party planner for a sex toy company and Yvonne was a strip-o-gram. Glancing at Sam, I saw him give me a small smirk around his beer bottle before he tossed his head back taking a huge swig when they'd told me what they did for a living. I'd thought they were messing with me, but as we talked more I'd realised they weren't joking. I kept trying to focus on their names because I just knew I was going to get them mixed up.

It seemed funny that I should find two single girls with those particular careers and skills at one table. They seemed to be so attuned to each other as well. When one spoke the other nodded as if she was thinking exactly the same thing. Their voices were sexy with the hint of an Australian accent, and they were great fun to be around.

When I asked how they had met Cat, Yvonne explained she was at an event where Cat was a guest. Some guy had overstepped his boundaries with Yvonne and tried to sexually assault her, Cat supported her and told her to go to the police and report him. She explained they had been friends ever since.

During the conversation a song came on that I loved but asking one to dance would have meant giving one preferential treatment and because they looked so similar, I couldn't have chosen between them. To be perfectly frank, in the absence of Gini I fancied the both of them. My dilemma was resolved when Lizzie grabbed my arm and pulled me towards the dance floor.

"Come on, Sexy Jack, show us your moves."

Yvonne reached out and grabbed my other hand.

"Whoop! Me, too, I really fancy a Jack sandwich."

Lizzie dropped my hand, leaned closer and slid it down and over the waistband of my jeans, tucking it in my back pocket. I glanced down at her and saw that she was biting the side of her lip by way of a sexy challenge to me. Turning to look over my shoulder in the direction of the bar, Dave's eyes met mine and he stared back at me with a sickened look on his face. I raised my eyebrow and gave him a smug smirk before throwing my arms around both girls as I led them to the polished wooden dance floor.

Yvonne wasn't joking about her sandwich comment either, within seconds of us starting to dance she turned her back to me. Her ass slowly grazed back and forth over my groin as she swayed to the music and Lizzie was snug up behind me. By the time the first song had ended I was as stiff as a board with my dick struggling for attention. It ached after having been teased so many times in one night and denied a release.

Two more songs passed before Lizzie swapped places with Yvonne and faced me that time, her fingers instantly sneaked up my firm pecs and tangled in my hair. Her touch made me break out in a rash of goose bumps and to be frank, I'd have shagged anything that moved at that point I was so horny.

Glancing down, Lizzie met my gaze; her eyes glittered with want as she gave me a seductive smile. A second later I felt her pushing the back of my head forwards. She paused when her mouth was an inch away and suddenly she fluttered her tongue across her bottom lip. I was still processing that when she pushed my head closer and began kissing me hungrily.

I had no time to react before Yvonne, who was still behind me and not wanting to be left out, slipped her hands around to my groin. She started to drag my ass away from Lizzie and closer to her hot little body. *Hmm, wonder if they are up for a threesome?* With that thought my heart started to pound in my chest causing me to almost give up on all sense of decency on the dance floor.

I couldn't fully lose myself when kissing Lizzie because I couldn't tell if Yvonne actually knew what Lizzie was doing in front of me. Lizzie's hands were still in my hair, so I thought that Yvonne might have had no idea what her friend was doing and that they were both hitting on me without the other being aware.

Just as that thought entered my head and without a word, Yvonne let go and came around to stand next to her friend. Lizzie broke the kiss and stepped away. Yvonne took Lizzie's position and picked up where her friend had left off, exploring my mouth deeply with her tongue. With my fantasy confirmed, I almost burst out of my zipper with excitement of the possibilities the rest of my night held.

When Yvonne kissed me I could really tell the difference, she was an amazing kisser and by the time she broke away, I was breathless. My heart was beating rapidly and my boxers were sticky with the excitement of both, what they could offer and what they were doing to me.

"So, Jack. You seem like a fun guy but this place is getting old, want to come back to our place to continue the party?"

Fuck. Erm...yeah! I stared incredulously at Yvonne, shocked that she should even have to ask me that, hell would have had to freeze over before I'd have been able to ignore that comment. Gini was a distant memory as the girls successfully lifted my mood and the little guy in my underwear. I just grinned salaciously, nodded and allowed myself to be led back to the table.

Cat was sitting on Sam's lap with her arms draped around his neck looking a little worse for wear. His eyes flicked up to look at both girls and then back to me. Biting back a grin, he nodded at them, but spoke to me.

"You've cheered up, Jack. Dirty dancing always seems to perk you up. Want another drink?"

"Oh, Sam, there are parts of me that are definitely perky enough and I'm so thirsty but, it isn't a drink I need. Besides, looking at these two ladies I think the only drink that would come close to fitting the bill right now is a Slow Comfortable Screw and they don't sell those in doubles."

Lizzie chuckled, grinning wickedly as she elbowed me playfully in my side.

"Jack, slow and comfortable isn't our style, we're more wet and wild."

"That's a wet ride honey, not a drink," I sniggered with a grin on my face.

Yvonne cut me off by saying, "Exactly."

Chapter 7

Taxi

Twelve minutes after Yvonne's comment we were in the back of a taxi with me sandwiched between them again and enjoying the attention I was receiving. Believe me, the girls were *very* attentive. As Yvonne's gorgeous pouty mouth fused with mine, Lizzie was fiddling with the fly of my jeans.

Thirty five minutes after my night seemed to be going in one direction with Gini, it had shot off at a tangent and there I was riding off to a whole different fantasy.

We'd all got carried away during the journey back to their place, but I drew the line when Lizzie bent her head and started to pull my dick free from my underwear in the cab. Those things had CCTV in them. Pulling up in front of the plush St. John's Wood London apartment block, I was getting pretty lost in my horny feelings when somewhere in the distance, the sound of a male clearing his throat broke through my lusty haze. When I opened my eyes and glanced up, the taxi driver was glaring at us with his mouth pursed closed through the glass partition of his cab. When my eyes met his, he spoke in a gruff cockney accent.

"You might want to take that upstairs, you lucky bugger."

Staring at his expressionless face I felt a little sheepish at getting so carried away with the heavy petting in his place of work, until I saw the humour in his eyes as he fought to keep a straight face.

"Yeah, sorry. I couldn't tell the difference between these two, they look so similar. I'm still trying to find something that will help me to identify who's who.

Chuckling heartily at me, he nodded his head as if in agreement.

"And don't tell me, even when you've had your hands in their knickers, you can't tell, right?"

I sniggered at his audacity but I couldn't help but like him.

"Ah! That's where you're wrong. I know who's who now, and I'll have no problem about mixing them up."

Shifting in his seat for a better view, he looked long and hard at Lizzie then at Yvonne and sighed heavily because they really were that similar. Finally he turned back to look at me with a defeated expression on his wrinkled face.

"Okay, you're going to have to tell me. I have no idea what you're seeing. They're like peas in a pod."

Smirking knowingly, I shrugged my shoulders. "Well it wasn't so hard really. I just had to think logically. I'm a multi-sensory kind of guy, so although I found it difficult on sight, I just had to use my body to tell me who was who. They kiss differently and now I've been around them for a while, I know they wear different perfume, and I know one other difference between the two."

Both girls looked surprised and chimed in at the same time.

"Really, what's that?"

Grinning wickedly, I knew I risked the chance of

offending them but I figured if they were into threesomes, they'd be fine with my discoveries and sharing with a random stranger they probably would never meet again.

"One of these ladies is clean shaven while the other has a landing strip if you know what I mean."

The driver started to laugh and cough at the same time and both girls' mouths dropped open in shock at my disclosure.

Yvonne turned to Lizzie and gasped before asking in a high pitched voice, "Did he just tell him about our..."

"Yep." Lizzie cut her off, sounding flat.

Glancing sheepishly again at the taxi driver, I briefly wondered if he'd be taking me home alone, but Lizzie began giggling and blurted out, "See! I told you that random bit of hair was stupid and now everyone knows about it."

Both the cabbie and I began laughing openly at Lizzie chiding her friend for her personal grooming preferences while Yvonne looked completely unfazed by the reprimand.

"At least my pussy doesn't look like a Sphynx cat."

A roar of laughter escaped from my belly and the cab driver frowned at me, looking puzzled.

"It's a weird breed of cat that's wrinkly and hairless, mate." I said, educating him like I was suddenly some feline expert or something.

We finally made to get out of the cab as the cabbie closed the dividing window, but not quickly enough to stop us from hearing his muffled laughter as he lost control at my comment.

Leaving the cab, Yvonne turned and curled into herself as she laughed raucously and told her friend off.

"I don't believe you, Lizzie. You have no filter!"

"Yeah, and she doesn't have any pubes either," I stated still grinning.

Both of them giggled simultaneously and I breathed a

sigh of relief. I had barely stopped laughing by the time we reached the lifts before taking control to ask which floor they were on.

"Sixth," they both commented together.

I didn't let on that I'd been in their building more than a few times already. The girls apartment block was where Sly Records and a few other record labels had a couple of apartments for their new signings to shack up, during the first few months in the city. Most new artists were from outside of London so needed a base, and I guessed this way the labels could keep a close eye on their new prodigies.

If I wasn't mistaken, Alfie Black had stayed on the tenth floor for a couple of months with Crakt Soundzz before they were moved to a secure house in the countryside as they became famous. I had previously been sent to the apartments to conduct interviews a couple of times, especially for the teenage bands.

Stepping into the lift, Lizzie patted my arse and for a moment I felt more like one of her sex toys than a person. There was no need for any pretence; it was a one night stand pure and simple. No real thoughts or feelings for any of us. For me it was all about the fantasy and experience.

I was just crossing the threshold and began to shrug out of my navy suit jacket when Lizzie pinned me to the wall and pressed her hot little body against mine.

"Yvonne's just getting us something to drink," she said, linking her hand in mine as she led me to their sitting room.

It was expensively decorated and the only furniture in the room was an oversized cream leather sofa and two wide brown leather chairs. It was apparent that the girls were very successful from the quality of their stuff, and their address. I wondered how much money was involved in their line of work.

Lizzie turned me around as she sat down on one of

the chairs, her mouth level with my groin. Leaning in she placed it against my jeans and pressed hard against my now semi-hard dick, blowing hot air into the material. At that point I would have sold my grandma to have her blow me.

"Mmm, I've been dying to do this since we'd been on the dance floor," she cooed, and I silently wished she had.

The continuous hum that passed her lips vibrated like an electrical charge and sent shivers of expectation right through me. I couldn't help myself and tilted my hips towards her mouth, needing more contact and more than enjoying what she was doing.

"Oh, you like that, huh? Let's see about this then."

Without a moment's hesitation she unbuttoned my jeans, unzipped me and frantically begun tugging the jeans down my legs, exposing my boxer briefs.

"Hey, slow down where's the fire?" I remarked. She was rough in her desperation to have me naked.

"Wet and wild, Jack. We promised you, remember?" I did.

Lizzie smiled up at me, her eyes glittered with lust as her fingertips tickled my skin on their journey along the edge of my waistband. Suddenly she yanked back the elastic and my dick sprang up, freeing itself from the confines of the cotton.

"Wow. Yvonne, he's as big as I suspected. Pretty too," Lizzie commented.

She tilted her head from side to side holding me in her hands like my dick was some expensive trinket she was thinking of purchasing. Southeby's auctioneers would have been proud of the scrutiny she gave me as she lifted me forwards and up, checking the underside to get an 'all round view'. When she was satisfied she stopped and just stared with a look of wonder on her face.

A few women had commented that I had a nice dick in the past but I'd never had anyone check me out to that extent before. I mean, a dick's a dick, right? When she finally took me in her warm palm, she immediately began stroking me and continued to stare at it, eventually she glanced up at me. My head was about to roll back on my shoulders but then she spoke and ruined the moment a little for me.

"Feel good?"

Is the pope Roman Catholic? Is there ice in the Antarctic? She's stroking my ridged boner and she asks if it feels good?

"Mmm." I hadn't been there five minutes and I was already standing in front of her with my jeans and boxers around my knees. A few yards away her friend was mulling around in their open plan kitchen which was less than sexually inspiring. Being able to relax was harder than usual and I just hoped they weren't going to keep up with the questions. I didn't want my double ride to feel like an exam. I just wanted to fuck them both and go. Any probing would come from me alone.

Yvonne seemed pretty busy in the kitchen and once again I was distracted when I heard a series of beeps. I imagined her pushing buttons on what sounded like the microwave. I wondered what the fuck was so important that she had to cook at that particular moment.

Meanwhile, Lizzie continued to play with me. I stood quietly waiting for them to make their next move because they were obviously the kind of girls that liked to take charge. I didn't mind that now and again, and with them being a double act and me being a threesome virgin, I was more than happy for them to lead the way.

A few seconds later the microwave dinged and gave three beeps indicating that whatever was in there was ready. Yvonne took out a small red bowl and glanced over at Lizzie who grinned widely and raised her eyebrows at her as she walked towards us.

Yvonne came alongside me, turned and ran her hands

up under my shirt. She raked her nails a little sharply back down towards my dick before leaning in to kiss me. My hands automatically found her hip and her arse as she sucked hungrily on my bottom lip then sunk her tongue deep in exploration. A low groan fell from my mouth into hers. Suddenly breaking the kiss, Yvonne began unbuttoning my shirt while Lizzie tugged my jeans and boxers down to my ankles.

As soon as I pulled both legs free from the rough material, Lizzie pushed herself to a stand and pressed her hands against my shoulders. She shoved me backwards until I landed on one of the soft leather chairs. The leather felt notably cold under my warm body.

Lizzie placed her palms on my inner thighs and spread my legs wide, kneeling between them. I had to admit that I was a tad nervous at what they had planned for me. She smiled seductively as Yvonne smirked and scooped some white foamy looking substance from the bowl onto her fingertips. It looked like shaving foam but didn't smell of anything.

Passing the bowl to Lizzie to hold, Yvonne then reached out and wrapped her fingers around my shaft applying the foam to my length. The texture was silky smooth and creamy and felt exquisite against my skin. My eyes rolled involuntarily at the sensation it evoked in me.

"Nice? Yvonne asked quite genuinely.

"Stop doing that and I will bite you, hard," I groaned and let a low growl pass my lips.

I'd never felt anything like it and immediately I reminded myself to find out it's name when I was in a less horny state.

"Hmm…tempting offer," Lizzie purred as Yvonne continued to stroke me her gaze transfixed on what she was doing.

Yvonne's thumb grazed over my head and I sucked in a deep breath because it felt incredible, but I still cracked an eye open at Lizzie's comment.

"I wasn't addressing you, love. I don't see you doing anything." I said provocatively, teasing her.

Lizzie smirked knowingly at Yvonne and nodded before turning back to meet my gaze, her eyes heavy with lust.

"Well I guess I'd better get to it then." I don't know why but that statement made me swallow hard.

Yvonne drew her hands away and exactly one breath later, Lizzie took me in her mouth shoving my dick all the way to the back of her throat before giving an exaggerated hum.The sudden vibrations sent a shockwave through me and I felt myself leak into her mouth. I was starting to get lost in the full attention of two females when Yvonne crouched down beside her friend.

"Slide down a bit Jack, I want to get your balls."

No sooner were the words out of her mouth than a ripping noise sounded from the chair as my skin peeled away from the leather and I quickly scooted down to allow both girls access to me. My skin erupted in a fresh batch of goose bumps as her words took hold of my hormones. My arousal was just about off the scale with them and right then I'd have done anything they asked of me.

Yvonne's eyes captured mine just as her mouth inched towards my scrotum. They sparkled with a mixture of mischief and lust as she smiled salaciously before she touched me. The anticipation of what she was about to do was almost enough to make me come on its own. Taking my right ball in her mouth, she rolled it around with her tongue and had me growling loudly in ecstasy. The sensation felt like my dick was going to burst at being teased when the both of them stimulated me at the same time.

The scene was downright scandalous from where I was sitting. Two amazing looking women giving me an oral sex experience I'd never forget. Cupping the back of

Lizzie's head to hold her in place I began fucking her mouth as gently as I could, mindful that Yvonne had one of my jewels between her lips. I was no longer holding back and fully invested. Just the thought of what they were going to do to me was off-the-charts hot and I knew we were going to have fun.

Chapter 8

Lift-off

Sometimes it can take a while for me to get fully hard even when I receive good head. It has something to do with the size and blood flow I'm told, and I can handle being sucked off. I'm not normally a one orgasm guy either, but I am a gentleman. I always take care of any lady I'm with before I finish. However, the way both girls were playing my body, I seriously thought they could give classes to the masses on exactly what would get a guy off. They were like the ultimate oral experts.

Ever felt dizzy with desire? I swear that was exactly what happened to me with those girls. If a woman had two mouths and I had one wish, that's exactly what I'd have her do to me all day long. Suck my balls and blow me at the same time.

Mentally, one minute I was like, *Oh, jeez that's incredible I wonder where they learned to do that. Fuck!* The next, *I'm going to come* and then, *do fishermen use worms or something bigger for bait to catch a shark?* I kept asking myself stupid questions and thinking of anything that might take my attention away from what their mouths were doing to me. I wanted it to last for as long as possible.

Before long I was feeling close to the edge again, I gently pushed Yvonne's head away and pulled my dick out of Lizzie's mouth with a pop. There was no way I was going to be satisfied with just oral with their skill set. I wanted to see what other talents they had to offer. Glancing at me over my dick, Lizzie's eyes were tinted pink and filled to the brim with lust as she gave me a naughty smirk before wiping her mouth with the back of her hand. It was a scene I'd witnessed in many porn movies when I was away on assignment and bored in some hotel room or another.

Yvonne was already on her feet. She peeled the figure hugging lime green dress she was wearing over her head. Her hair crackled with electricity as it rubbed against the material, and I wondered if she stripped that fast in her day job.

My eyes scanned her from head to toe, appraising every inch of her fine body with her even light brown skin's shiny appearance. She was either olive skinned or she'd been on holiday, but I didn't see any tan lines. Wearing a small black lacy thong and suspenders, with a matching lacy see-through bra, I was in awe at her perfect female form.

Lizzie slicked her hands down over the outline of her small breasts and stood fully clothed in an identical dress to Yvonne's, I was mesmerised. I couldn't say which view I liked the best, the hint of hidden pleasures she had to offer underneath her dress, or the image of Yvonne stripped down to her underwear before me.

Reaching down, Lizzie ran her fingers along the edge of the dress toying with the hem, lifting it slightly in a teasing manner, she stroked between her thighs before allowing it to drop again. For a moment she had me thinking that she'd make a better stripper than Yvonne.

My thoughts were disrupted when Yvonne reached out and took my hand as she leaned in. She planted another kiss on my dry lips as she shoved my hand between her thighs onto the wet, lacy gusset of her thong. Instantly my dick twitched, bouncing on my belly as I enjoyed the foreplay.

Pushing her away, my mind was ready to explode with the fantasies that were forming in my head. I tried to hurry things along by moving my arse forward in the chair and sitting up. As I was about to stand, Lizzie lifted one foot and placed her green stiletto shoe between my legs, only a hair's breadth from my balls, then placing her hands on my shoulders, she pushed me back into the chair.

Gulping noisily, I silently thanked God that she'd missed my wedding tackle with her killer heel. My eyes flicked nervously to Yvonne for her reaction. I was relieved when she began laughing softly whilst Lizzie shook her head at me with a stern look on her face.

"I think you should have figured out how this works by now, Jack. You do the fucking, we do the preparation and warm-up."

When she put it like that I knew exactly what I needed to do, nothing, until I was called upon to perform. I just hoped I was half as desirable to them as they were to me.

Smiling, I stared wide eyed at the both of them and nodded in approval.

"Indeed, ladies. I know my place. I think I know how this works now. I'm happy to take your lead. Just tag me by slapping my arse and I'll fire up."

Both girls chuckled at my comment; my response obviously pleased them as everything began to make sense to me. There were two of them and one of me, so I wasn't losing face by allowing them to master me.

Swallowing a small chuckle, Lizzie pursed her lips and lifted my hand. She placed it back on Yvonne's lacy underwear then inclined her head in the direction of her friend's pussy. Lizzie's eyes bored into mine with one eyebrow raised quizzically at me.

"Pay attention, Jack, we won't tolerate any more interruptions, understand?"

I could feel my lips curl up at the edges because I liked stern Lizzie; the edge in her voice was more of a turn on than what she was saying. No doubt about it, the girls were very different in their approach to sex, but both were smoking hot. I became increasingly aroused and excited at the prospect of them telling me what to do, and when to do it, than I thought I'd ever be.

It was the first time I'd allowed someone else to take complete control. The anticipation of what was coming began to make me feel desperate for them to do whatever they needed to so that I could have my turn. As soon as I received my instruction, my focus was immediately back on Yvonne.

Slipping my fingers inside the elastic of her thong I cupped her mound and began to stroke the silky smooth outer lips of her pussy. My dick twitched at the stimulus of the slick texture of her soaking wet lips. Gliding my finger across her seam, Yvonne moaned softly and her head rolled back stretching her neck upwards so that her long hair cascaded down her back. And that my friends, was an amazingly sexy pose.

Under my touch she instinctively spread her knees wider, inviting my fingers to slip between her outer and inner lips. My touch instantly made her moan again, but that time much louder as her pelvis tilted in the direction of my wandering hand. At that point I was in no doubt Yvonne was the more submissive of the two girls.

I stroked the length of her pussy while her head rolled forward onto her chest, her eyes were brimming with lust and her face displayed pure pleasure. Yvonne made me want to hurry things along, but Lizzie interrupted the flow by climbing up and straddling the arms of the chair.

Suddenly my view was even more appealing.

I was delighted when I glanced up and saw her teasing me more than I thought possible by displaying her bare pussy under her dress.

My hands wrapped around the smooth skin of her ankles. I glanced up to meet her gaze a little unsure that I could take the initiative without her direct say so. Lizzie smirked knowingly and chuckled.

"You have my permission, Jack, you may touch me."

Applying firm pressure, I gripped her ankles and squeezed gently before relaxing and began to glide my palms up the outside contours of her legs. Staring intently, her eyes locked on mine but there was no outward reaction from her to what I was doing. I stopped short of her hips because my hands couldn't reach that far. I repeated my sweeping movements on the inside of her legs, which again stopped short of her pussy. We groaned slightly as it affected the both of us.

Lizzie jumped up from the seat and Yvonne pulled away. Both girls took my hands and yanked me out of the chair. I was sweating from my heightened arousal so as I got up from the leather chair it felt like a giant Band Aid had been torn away from my back. It stung so badly that I wondered if I'd left some skin behind, but the pain just added something else to what was happening in some sadistic way.

Dragging me through to the bedroom I noticed they had a huge king sized bed with only a single pure white fitted sheet. I briefly wondered if they'd be filming this to post online as a porn movie. Frankly, I couldn't have cared less by that point.

Lizzie walked over to a walk-in closet and I heard what I thought was briefcase locks snap open against leather. Yvonne threw me on the bed and climbed on top me, pressing her full body the length of me. All I wanted to do at that point was push her back, roll over her and sink my dick inside her. I'd been a patient man considering what they'd done to me so far but, I was getting to the point where my rock hard dick was communicating with my brain and it was screaming for some overdue action.

Kissing me hard, I could feel that Yvonne was wired and ready to go, her pussy rocked back and forth across my thick erection. Grabbing her arse cheeks I pulled her even harder against me and growled with a primal need to take the party up a level.

Lizzie came out of the closet with two black items in her hands and an excited look on her face. My thinking at that point was that she had gone to get a vibrator of some kind and thought she'd obviously never had a guy who fulfilled her sexually if she needed to use a battery operated boyfriend. Previously, I'd had some kinky shit in my love life, spanking, soft biting, rough sex, and the like, but never had the need to use sex toys. I wasn't sure what she needed from me, but I was happy to experiment with her.

Lizzie slapped my hands away then slapped her friend's arse.

"All in good time, Yvonne, I want a little fun first."

My heart sunk at those words when it was my dick that should have been doing any sinking. And there was I thinking we were already having fun, not enough for Lizzie it seemed. Yvonne rolled off me and Lizzie's hand immediately grabbed my dick. She must have seen the startled look on my face when I saw the toys and chuckled at me.

"Don't tell me you've never used one of these before. This is tame but very effective. I figured you were a straight fucking guy, so we'll go easy on you," she said shaking the Perspex box at me.

Why did that particular comment worry me? Because I was already getting to the point of no return.

Any more teasing and I felt I'd blow like an

uncontrollable garden hose. Lizzie cracked open the little clear plastic box and took out a black ring of stretchy latex with what looked like a three inch massage bar across the top. Very adeptly, she fed my dick through the hole, quickly pushing the ring with the course bar on the underside all the way to my root.

Twisting her body she reached into the case again and brought out a little black box and my excitement went to another level. I raised my eyebrow at her in question when I saw her flick a switch. As soon as I heard the click, I felt a slow vibration at the base of my dick. A second click later it intensified and gripped me harder. Lizzie used the remote control again and within seconds she'd taken it from zero to what I guessed was the maximum judging from the speed of the vibrations and buzzing. My dick felt like it was resting on a highly charged engine waiting for the clutch to be released.

Adding to the heightened pleasure, Lizzie was on the bed and took my dick in her mouth while Yvonne straddled my face. Suddenly I was lapping and sucking at her clit to the vocal responses of, "Oh hell, yeah, right there. Lizzie this guy is amazing with his tongue."

Chuckling, I pulled away and murmured, "Of course I am, I'm a journalist, we're known for our excellent oral skills."

Lizzie hummed again and the sensation was fucking wicked. All of a sudden I was done with the foreplay. Pulling my mouth away from Yvonne I shouted, "Jeez, stop that, you're going to make me come."

Lizzie sucked harder while Yvonne demanded, "Do it. Come. Now!"

Being commanded just as I felt my release pending was too much. Lizzie took me in her mouth again and sucked, making me come hard and fast. Her tongue circled the head of my shaft as she drank every drop of my seed. I felt dizzy with the force of my release and I seriously thought the top of my head was going to burst open. She continued to suck me dry and was still slurping long after I'd stopped pulsating. I became aware of the vibrating cock ring again once I had stopped jerking. Lizzie pulled it off of me, but continued massaging my balls.

"My turn." She grinned and straddled my face sitting back and giving me no choice but to perform oral sex on her, she tasted sweeter than Yvonne.

Although I'd felt drained from coming, I soon felt myself stiffening again. The sounds Lizzie made while I pleasured her were a constant source of stimulation to me.

"Holy fuck, Jack. You weren't kidding, Yvonne. He has a pretty talented tongue here, honey."

Grinning against her pussy that I'd passed her test, I gave her some of her own medicine when I hummed deeply in agreement.

Suddenly Yvonne grasped my dick in her hand again and stroked it a few times.

"All right, we have lift-off down here, Lizzie. I think our gorgeous Jack is ready to take the reins."

Lizzie lifted her herself away from my mouth and cocked her leg over my head to position herself to one side of me. She then knelt beside me with her arse in the air.

"Well, what are you waiting for, Jack? Think you're up to handling the both of us?"

"Fuck! Ladies if I can't, I'll die a happy man trying!"

Chapter 9

Toys

Knowing how controlling Lizzie had been during the foreplay gave me an overwhelming urge to put her in her place. I rolled over slowly on to my belly and dragged myself to my hands and knees. My slow movements lulled her into a false sense of security. I quickly grabbed her around the waist, holding her in place and spanked her arse hard. She yelped like an injured puppy and my eyes flicked quickly to Yvonne for her reaction.

Biting back a grin, Yvonne's eyes sparkled with humour and she glanced at Lizzie as both of us held our breath waiting to see how Lizzie would react. Lizzie growled and turned quickly knocking me on my side, she overpowered me and eventually managed to roll me on to my back. She was on me in an instant, cocking her leg over my body to straddle me. She grabbed my wrists roughly and placed them above my head. I'd underestimated her strength, she had made me look like a weakling.

"Sorry, I should have told you, we're both 3rd Dan black belts in judo."

Well fuck! I was overpowered by a self-defence expert so that at least made me feel a little better about her gaining the upper hand.

"Well to be honest, Lizzie I was kind of hoping this was how it would go. I'm tired out. It's been a long day so fucking you on my back definitely works for me." I teased playfully trying to save face.

Lizzie glanced at Yvonne who came over and stood behind her with her knees against the side of the bed. She reached over and placed her hand on Lizzie's right shoulder. Lizzie; who was still in her dress, stretched her arms up as her friend peeled it from her body. Her breasts were slightly smaller than Yvonne's, but they were still a handful.

Leaning up, I took Lizzie's nipple in my mouth and sucked hard earning me a gasp. She ground her pussy against my hard dick coating me in her wet nectar. Yvonne chuckled and poured what looked like maple syrup on Lizzie. I was in awe, firstly at the sight of Lizzie's breasts covered in maple syrup while sitting in my lap, and secondly that Yvonne even had maple syrup. I never saw her leave the room.

After dribbling the sticky liquid down her friend's chest, Yvonne suddenly climbed onto the bed next to me and found my mouth with her hot wet tongue. Once again I was vibrating with excitement at the prospect of what they were doing to me, and when Yvonne's hands snaked their way to my hair and began tugging, my arousal grew tenfold.

We both moaned and I felt Lizzie position the crown of my dick at her entrance, sliding it back and forth for lubrication.

"Wait. Condoms," I groaned, tearing my mouth from Yvonne's.

Lizzie nodded and Yvonne reached into a small jar with a Chinese pattern on the bedside table. She ripped open the gold coloured foil pack with her teeth and handed it to Lizzie, watching as Lizzie applied it to my stiff, aching dick.

"Thanks, almost got carried away," Lizzie confessed, more than a little anxious to resume where we left off.

Her hand was once again wrapped around my length as she guided me back to her entrance. Randomly, I was conscious of an email alert on my phone and it momentarily distracted me, but as Lizzie mounted me and lowered her body slowly, the alert was quickly forgotten. I felt every inch of me sink deeper as her walls spread to receive me. I felt her tighten as she held me still inside her.

Lizzie gasped and rolled her head back in pleasure. As soon as she started to move up and down my shaft she moaned.

"Fuck, you're dick is so thick. I've never got off without clit-play before but the way you're going, you'll make me come."

She started to roll her hips back on me and it felt amazing. I'd been teased almost to breaking point but as she was riding me, all the foreplay had been worth it.

Suddenly I grabbed her tightly pinning her arms by her sides, and pulled her down onto my chest, holding her firmly in place. BI brought my knees up for more leverage and fucked her hard. She was completely immobile and at my mercy by then.

Less than a minute later she was shaking uncontrollably and coming so hard she almost broke my dick when she bore down.

Screaming loudly she shouted, "Oh Fuck! Stop. Oh my God, stop. Stop it's too much."

"So that you can overpower me again, Lizzie? I'm not falling for that one," I sniggered.

She peered up grinning at me and I knew I my intuition was right, so I continued to fuck her hard as she rode out the last of her orgasm. When I released my grip on her she fell exhausted to the side of me. Yvonne cocked an eyebrow at me, questioning what I was going to do with her.

I pulled her against me and kissed her hard. Her body immediately sagged as she dropped down beside me. Instantly I pulled the condom off and got onto my knees. I placed Yvonne's legs over my shoulders. I buried my head between her thighs poking my tongue out gently and licked her clit. When I made contact, Yvonne drew in a deep breath and exhaled in a long groan as my tongue glided the length of her warm, wet pussy. She tasted amazing and was more than ready for me.

Clasping my hands around her thighs I began to stand at the edge of the bed and dragged her arse towards my dick with her legs still draped over my shoulders.

"Condom?" I enquired. That time Yvonne reached up for the pillow.

"Right here," she smirked, pulling another golden foil wrapped condom from underneath it.

I rolled it on quickly and placed myself at her entrance. I leaned forwards to kiss her while I entered. I swallowed her sexy moan as she felt me pushing my way inside. She was tighter than Lizzie so I had to be a little more forceful. Yet another difference between them. *Oh my God. I can't believe what's happening.*

Yvonne's style was much more leisurely than Lizzie's and she never made me feel like I had to perform the way her friend did. Her lips curved into a sweet smile as she stared up at me.

"Damn, Jack, you have a great body, you know that?"

I'd been told that by many women but I thought I was on the skinny side. I wasn't bulky and built from hours at the gym. I was a swimmer from an early age so my abs had developed long before the rest of me but I was glad that Yvonne liked it.

We continued to enjoy each other's bodies until I

recognised the signs that Yvonne was about to come, and the main difference between her and Lizzie was Yvonne voiced it.

"I'm coming, Jack, fuck that feels *sooo* good."

A sexy moan tore from her throat and she made a mewling noise that aroused me even more as she became less in control of her body.

"Yeah, you like that, huh?" I asked as I continued to fuck her in a more attentive way than the competitive way I had done with Lizzie.

It didn't feel that bad from my perspective either I had to admit. Lizzie and Yvonne may have been very similar to begin with, but I definitely had my favourite now. Yvonne was much more sensual than Lizzie and, I hated to say it, but I felt that Lizzie regarded sex in much the same way as a bloke getting his rocks off did.

I began to ignore Lizzie by that point, but she was trying to get back in the game by stroking my arse. When she raked her nails down my back as I fucked her friend, shivers ran up my spine, but it was Yvonne that was causing me to break out in a sweat. Her pussy felt so good.

I could feel that Yvonne was beginning to come again and the sensation of her tightening made me fuck her hard. In no time she was screaming my name.

"God, Jack, your dick is incredible."

Smirking, I bent down and lifted her up, falling out of her at the same time. Placing her in the centre of the bed, I climbed on and turned her over on to her hands and knees then pulled her arse in the air to re-enter her from behind. That time I was more primal in my thoughts so I fucked her more for me than for her, but she seemed delighted with what I was doing. She just felt so good.

"Harder, Jack, harder, oh yeah, right there, right there."

I knew I was hitting her G-spot and her legs began to shake uncontrollably. Spreading them wider I moved even closer, bending over her back to bite her gently on the neck. At that point I was aware of Lizzie moving alongside us when the thought entered my head that she'd been quiet for a few minutes.

As soon as I realised that, the thought was quickly dispelled when she suddenly began lubricating my arsehole and massaging it with her finger. Now, I couldn't say I hadn't had a finger in my arse a time or two in the heat of the moment, and I wasn't adverse to a little kinky play, but I wasn't sure I trusted someone like Lizzie with my most sensitive spot. Unfortunately, I had that thought a tad too late as Lizzie was pushing something into my arse. I tried to straighten up in protest, but Lizzie put all of her weight on my back pushing me further into Yvonne. I felt her begin to gently push something that felt like it had small baubles on it in and out of my arse.

"Has anyone used one of these on you before, Jack?"

I shook my head, too afraid to speak because she was definitely in charge while that thing was in my arsehole.

"This is a prostate stimulator. You may think you've had some good orgasms before, but I'm going to teach you what a really great one feels like. Fuck him hard, Yvonne."

Yvonne then started rocking back onto me while I hardly moved, I was scared to do anything with that thing sticking out of my arse. I was even more scared of the person holding on to it. Yvonne was keeping me hard with her peachy little pussy sliding up and down and after a few petrifying minutes I could feel myself getting near the edge.

Yvonne put her hand between her legs and began to play with my balls. They weren't playing fair, because with the stimulation from Lizzie, Yvonne riding me, and the extra fondling, I could feel my orgasm coming to a crescendo. Lizzie pushed the toy deeper and began to massage my prostate as promised and the sensation of that little rubber toy was mind blowing.

Without any warning I was coming harder than I ever had in my life, I was spurting hot cum into the condom like I was being milked. I quickly pulled out of Yvonne and whipped the condom off, spurting small strands of my seed all over her arse and back. I'd never emptied myself to that extent, ever. I was wobbly on my knees and collapsed over Yvonne's back feeling completely wrung out.

I felt the rubber toy leave me as Lizzie pushed me off of Yvonne and on to my back.

"So, you want more or have you had enough?"

I put my hands up in protest. My arse stung and I felt raw. Call me a wimp but I was already thinking I'd had enough of Lizzie's toys for one night.

"I'd be up for more, but I figure I'd better be heading home, ladies. I have a date tomorrow and I want to save some energy for her if that's all right with you both?" I said, delivering my barefaced lie with what I hoped was a warm smile.

"Sure. I'm more of a dick sucker than a fucker anyway, Jack. If you ever want another lesson just call us," Lizzie responded, completely at ease by the fact that I wasn't going to stay longer.

Just like that, we were done. Who would have thought I'd shy away from the opportunity they were offering me? I think maybe if Lizzie hadn't been the way she was, I'd have been more experimental. However, in my fantasies about threesomes the women were doing things to each other. They weren't, and, in hindsight, I was actually relieved about that for some reason. So I cleaned up, thanked my hostesses for their service, and called a cab to take me home.

Chapter 10

Ham

Arriving home, I threw my keys on the table and headed straight for the fridge. It was almost five in the morning and I hadn't eaten anything for about eight hours. Rummaging through the various open, half eaten packets of stuff I spied my favourite snack, Wiltshire ham straight from the packet. The taste was one of the best after Lily's mum's lasagne.

If there was one job in the world I'd like more than the one I had it would be as a taster in the Wiltshire Ham production and packaging plant. Well, maybe not exactly, but I was addicted to the stuff and I knew it sounded stupid, but if there was only one packet left in my fridge, it played on my mind until I bought more.

Taking out the Bombay Sapphire gin bottle from the shelf next to the fridge, I poured myself a two finger measure and then added some slim-line tonic. Screwing the caps on, I placed both bottles on the shelf. Thrusting the Edinburgh crystal glass under the ice dispenser, two cubes dropped neatly into the oversized glass. Some of the drink splashed onto my fingers, which I licked off as I headed over to my sofa.

Despite what I told the girls about having to save my energy, I was wide-awake. I just wanted to be out of there as soon as I was done, and because I felt there was something seriously off about Lizzie. As I travelled back in the taxi at the end of the night, it entered my head that she could probably be a sadomasochist given half the chance.

Glancing at my phone, I saw that it had been Lily that messaged me earlier, and I realised she would be finishing her day in Los Angeles. I walked across my open plan sitting room to switch on my desktop computer. The touch screen monitor was three feet in diameter and a poor substitute for Lily, but it made me feel like she was at least a little closer when we Skyped.

Swiping my screen I selected the Skype icon to call her. When I touched her name the machine instantly connected to her line. I made several attempts before I accepted that she wasn't available. Each time it disconnected I felt a pang of annoyance that I couldn't just see her when I wanted to. Staring down at my hand, I realised I'd eaten the whole pack of ham when I had been absent-mindedly fishing around inside and found it empty. I had been comfort eating while trying to call her and that only irritated me further.

I placed my hands on the table and dragged myself to my feet feeling disappointed and suddenly tired. I wandered down through my bedroom and into the bathroom to clean myself before bed. I loved my power shower, it was a luxury I afforded myself because I spent a lot of time travelling and some of the hotel showers I'd stayed in were less than desirable.

My shower was a natural stone tiled wet room cubicle with seven jets. Six to the side and a massive shower head at the top. Multi-force settings gave me everything from a fine mist spray to pulsating and regular flows, and also a more forceful massage water pressure. My varying moods and time dictated which setting I used. Flicking the lever from left to right, the shower instantly sprang to life. The water from the side jets caused the mirrors over the countertop to fog up and the room filled with steam.

Peeling myself out of my jeans, I threw them in the laundry basket and pulled my shirt over my head. I couldn't ignore the fact that I reeked of sex. Stepping into the steamy space and feeling the warmth and the force of the jets was an exceptional experience. I didn't know why, but Rosie popped into my head. I couldn't help feeling a tad guilty about being with the girls. I did miss her a lot, we'd been together for a while, but she had become more of a habit than a permanent feature. Once I had made my hard decision about her, I knew I would not go back on it.

Running my hands through my wet hair, I closed my eyes and let the warm water cascade down my body before eventually reaching for the shower gel. Squirting a load onto my hand I began to rub the soothing bubbles over my abs and belly then down to my groin. My dick twitched and I wrapped my hand around it pulling the skin back and forth gently as I cleaned myself. My hand lingered there for a few seconds while I let my mind go blank, then I swung the shower lever one hundred and eighty degrees and the water stopped immediately.

I walked over to the shelves in the corner and pulled a green towel off of one, wrapping it loosely around my hips. I also grabbed a hand towel from the pile and walked over to the mirror. Wiping the steam from the glass, I stared at myself while I briskly rubbed my hair to stop it dripping. I then used the other side to dry my face. I noted that I looked less tired and much fresher than I had before my shower.

From the bathroom, I heard the distinctive sound of an incoming call on Skype and quickly walked back to the sitting room. Lily's face filled the screen as I moved the cursor onto the green phone icon. Clicking on it, the call instantly connected and I leant back in my chair with a wide smile on my face.

"Hey sweetheart, how are you? Don't tell me you're tired of that big pierced dick over there and want to try some British beef for a change?"

Lily giggled and threw her head back while I automatically leaned forward stretching my arms out on my desk to be nearer her. Watching her happy face, I realised how much I missed that smile.

"Stop being so jealous, Jack. Alfie isn't a dick." Lily was as quick as ever.

"I was talking about his penis, Lily, if I wanted to insult him I'd have called him an arsehole."

Lily chuckled again, tucking her hair behind her ear, then she looked at the screen and reached out as if she were trying to touch me.

"God, I miss you, Jack." I could hear the hint of sadness in her voice as she stared wistfully at me, she then took a deep breath and sat back sighing.

My heart sunk to my stomach, my arms suddenly ached to hug her because she looked so sad.

"To be honest, Jack, I could do with a little spooning right now, I'm kind of lonely. Alfie is in Las Vegas this weekend keeping Drew company because Elle insisted Drew went with her. A couple of her dance students are auditioning for a show there. XrAid have been recording and although Alfie came and hung around the studio, I could see he was going stir crazy, so I suggested he go with them."

"So, how are things with you apart from not getting any?" I asked not wanting to talk about Alfie and focus on how she was.

Lily blushed and squirmed in her seat at my comment then rolled her eyes, she dipped her head before glancing back at me through her eyelashes, "Good. You?"

"Oh, I'm getting plenty, in fact I just got home."

I knew I'd make her uncomfortable but I loved the look on her face when I did that. Lily's mouth gaped and she covered it with her hand chuckling and a little embarrassed by my disclosure.

"Yeah? Was she nice?" Lily's tone sounded intrigued.

"They, Lily, *they* were nice."

"Huh? What do you mean?" Lily sat forward and clasped her hands on her lap shaking her head like she'd thought she misheard me.

"Well there was someone at the start of the evening that I definitely wanted to pursue but that didn't pan out so I went to talk to Sam and these girls were sitting with him and Cat. You remember Cat from that time at my place when I was volunteered by you to host a drinks party?"

"You hooked up with Cat again?"

"No, Sam's with Cat."

"God, you boys are like dogs sometimes."

"Cat is Sam's girlfriend now."

"Since...?"

"Whenever they got together. I don't know, I was just mentioning her because the girls were with her."

Lily's eyes popped wide. "The girls? You were with two girls? You and Sam? What happened with Cat."

"Fuck. Stop, Lily. No."

Taking a deep breath I sat forward and started jabbing my hand on the desk to punctuate my explanation.

"Sam and Cat *are* an item. Cat brought her friends clubbing. Sam and I met her in the club by accident when we were with Dave. Dave hooked up with Sally, you remember, Sally from high-school? And I hooked up with Cat's friends."

Lily's jaw dropped again, her head bobbed about in a half-nod-half-shake in disbelief before she recovered and started giggling again.

"For a moment I thought you said you hooked up

with her friends. You mean one of them right?"

Twisting my mouth, I felt a little embarrassed about my admission but I'd always been open about my sex life with her.

"Nope, Lily, you heard me correctly." I held my fingers up in a V sign indicating the two of them.

"Jack Cunningham! You didn't." Lily pursed her lips swallowing a giggle.

Nodding with a wry grin I reaffirmed my statement. "Uh huh, I did."

Lily's eyes were like saucers by that time, "Two? You had sex with two women at the same time? Did they have sex with each…"

"Nuh huh, one at a time," I admitted, my head wagging from side to side as I struggled with the best way of explaining what we did without going into detail.

Lily was quiet for a moment then stared seriously at the camera. I meant, really stared at me, and I saw a fleeting look of distress pass over her face.

"You think Alfie…?"

I knew what she was thinking and I wasn't going to lie to her. Alfie was a man whore in his day, but I was kicking myself for putting the thought in her head.

"Probably… definitely. He's a rock star for Christ's sake, Lily, but that just shows you that your pussy was better than a double ride, you should be proud of that, sweetheart," I countered, going for crude to distract her in the hope of relieving the pain of that revelation.

Lily looked more than a bit perturbed and pursed her lips again looking like she might cry.

"Hey. You both had pasts." I said softly with a resignation in my voice.

"Shit happens or threesomes in mine and Alfie's case, but when the right woman comes along we sure as hell don't want someone that's willing to do that. We want our women as pure as snow but capable of being sluts in the bedroom, or elsewhere we choose to take them when the mood strikes us, but sluts only for us, if you know what I mean."

Watching her tussle with the thought, I knew I'd given her something else to worry about. *Shut the fuck up, Jack, you aren't selling this explanation very well.*

Lily's head was bowed down, looking at her lap and she smoothed her skirt down in a gesture I knew too well. She always did that when she was upset, and I tried again to make her feel better.

"Lily, sweetheart, who is Alfie with? You. Why is he with you? Because you are all he wants. You're the end of the rainbow as far as women go for him. You think he'd throw away everything he'd had before to be with you, if the guy didn't think you weren't the real deal? You're 'it' for him. And sure, I'll continue to screw around, but only because I haven't found my 'it' yet, that's all. When I do I'd, never want to hurt her like that."

My comment seemed to settle Lily's mind and we talked a little longer about her and her band before she told me she'd be coming to London soon. My heart sped up with excitement at the thought that she was coming for four whole days to see her parents. It would be towards the end of my holiday and I was delighted that I'd be able to devote some rare time to just the two of us.

The only thing that was difficult was being able to take her out somewhere. Now that Lily was famous; it was nigh on impossible to get any private time outside of her parent's place or mine. And even then she had a massive bodyguard in tow with her.

"So, you and Rosie are definitely done, Jack? You won't change your mind?"

"I told you, Lily, I wish I felt differently about her. I do love her and I miss her sometimes, but I really don't think I was ever *in* love with her."

Lily nodded like she understood and leant back in her

chair crossing her legs and her eyes rolled slowly to the top of her head in thought. I knew she'd started to warm to Rosie and Rosie to her.

"I think I felt like that about Zack, but I didn't keep letting him think I was serious for over a year, Jack." Lily chided, reminding me about a guy she went out with briefly when she and Alfie were on a break.

"Just a sec," I ran to the fridge to get myself a coke.

I was parched after all the alcohol I'd consumed. I quickly opened the can and began slugging it down on the way back to the screen. Lily took her small denim jacket off and threw it over the back of the chair then flicked her hair behind her ears.

"Okay, beautiful, where were we?"

"You were avoiding talking about Rosie."

Running my fingers through my hair I sunk down in the chair and sighed deeply at how Lily's opinion about me dumping Rosie grated on me. Especially after all the support I'd givden her with the car-crash-of-a-relationship her and Alfie had.

"Listen, Lily, I'm going to tell you something and then maybe you'll understand where I'm at. When I was going to interview Rick yesterday morning, I had a chance meeting with a girl on the Tube. Her name was Gini. I'd never seen her before but the connection I had with her left me dumbfounded on the underground platform. We met for all of a minute and I was speechless at the effect she had on me. Rosie never had anything close to that effect on me."

Grinning, Lily leaned forward seeming really interested.

"Mmm, Jack sounds love struck. You got her number, right? When am I meeting her? And if you're chasing her, what the hell are you doing with other women? You know how I feel about that."

"That's just it, Lily. I have no clue where to find her.

I bumped into her twice. *Twice*, and then she disappeared just when I was getting to know her. I have no idea where she went, but I guess that was our chance. I wasn't quick enough, one moment she was there the next she'd gone."

Lily, in her own little hippie style, tried to throw me a lifeline.

"If you're meant to be together you'll find each other again. I mean, sometimes I think about 'ifs', if I hadn't gone to Florida to study I'd never have met Alfie, if I hadn't gone to that open mic…"

Cutting across her speech I interjected, "If we'd given in to our hormones when we were teenagers, if I hadn't been so fucking laid back I'd have followed Gini out to the lobby when her phone rang."

"So her phone rang and she went to take the call?" Lily said either ignoring my first comment or because all of that was years ago, and those feelings for her were insignificant now.

"Yeah, and that was the last I saw of her," I answered, letting everything else I was feeling slide. I wondered if I was just feeling that way because of the finality of our situation.

"Well she may have had an emergency and had to leave. Try going back there at the same time next week. You never know she may be feeling the same."

Armed with a glimmer of hope, I decided it was a long shot but I had nothing to lose. I dropped the subject and we talked about our friends for a few minutes before I told Lily to go, she'd yawned and it was ten in the evening in LA. When the call finished I headed to bed feeling slightly better about my encounter with Gini after talking to Lily about it. I was going to try her suggestion and go back to the club at the same time the following week.

Chapter 11

Chances

A shrill repetitive noise interrupted my weirdly erotic dream and I glanced bleary eyed at my bedside alarm clock but then remembered I was on holiday. I focused on my mobile which was ringing on the bedside table.

The time read two in the afternoon. I tried to get my bearings then shoved myself up and scrubbed my hand over my face. The acidic feeling in my stomach was a dull nauseating ache and my mouth felt like I'd been licking a floor clean. Grabbing my phone I answered, even though my brain still felt foggy. I cleared my throat in an effort to sound even halfway decent.

"Hello?" I said, gruffly.

"So?"

Clearing my throat again, I started to answer but suddenly felt the full effects of my late night drinking.

"Who's this?" I asked, sounding hoarse.

Dave's voice came back at me sounding way too chirpy for someone who'd been out late clubbing.

"Dave, who else? Damn, Jack, you weren't kidding about Sally! The girl rode me until I thought my cock was going to break. She only left about fifteen minutes ago.

Jesus man, I thought I had struck gold until I saw who you were leaving with. How come I suddenly I felt as if you'd handed me a consolation prize?"

"Dave, Sally isn't a consolation prize, and if you ever see her again you'd better not let her hear you talking about her like that. She's a nice girl. Very easy I'll admit, but you wouldn't find a better natured girl anywhere, apart from Lily."

"Whatever. You are one jammy bastard, Jack. I've yet to find one woman on this planet that doesn't want to fuck you!"

"Well you aren't looking very far. What about, Lily?"

"She doesn't count, that would be like you fucking family."

"Well, that's why I never pursued her in that way."

"Oh my God, sounds to me like you've considered it, Jack. Revelation here, the guy is human like the rest of us after all."

"Nope never considered it for the reason I just said, Dave, that's not to say that I didn't."

"You didn't what?"

"Want to. Of course I wanted to fuck Lily. Who didn't? For a while the lines got a little crossed when we were teenagers."

Confessing felt good. It was the first time I'd ever openly told anyone about my thoughts in regard to feeling horny about Lily back in the day.

Dave seemed to jump on my comment. "Oh I wanted to as well, and thought about it *many times*. Mainly in the shower."

"Shut the fuck up, Dave. A hand date would be as far as you'd have gotten with Lily. She's way out of your league mate!"

"How would I know that? You never let any of us even speak to her in high-school."

Smiling at his honest assessment of me, I wandered

through to my kitchen and pulled a bottle of water from the fridge. Swigging it down, I winced when the coldness hit the back of my throat; it was almost painful to swallow.

I considered what he was saying. I knew that even though Dave was a good looking guy he would have been completely wrong for Lily. It wasn't that I was against anyone dating her. Well I was, but it was more that I felt she was meant for better things. If one of those spotty school boys had stolen her heart she wouldn't have pursued all the dreams she had when she was sixteen.

I guessed what I really thought was that I didn't think Lily was mature enough to see the bigger picture at that age, and even though I acted immaturely at times, I just knew that Lily was going to be extra special to the world at some point. She just needed to find her inner confidence to realise she could be.

"Can we change the subject? You're making my hangover a whole lot worse with this conversation, Dave. Besides, as far as Lily is concerned, no one can compete with Alfie. Anyway, did you only call to get a run down on my performance last night, or was there another reason?"

Dave chuckled down the line at me then made a long humming sound like he was deliberating about my question.

"I don't even know if I want to share with you now, you grumpy shithead. I called you out of the goodness of my heart and all I've had with this conversation so far is verbal abuse."

I heard him snigger down the phone. *Fucker.*

"You mean there was an *actual* reason for calling me besides wanting to hear about my night of drunken debauchery?"

"Gini?"

Hearing her name made me stop in my tracks. Suddenly Dave had my full and undivided attention.

"Gini?"

"Yeah, that smoking hot little thing from the nightclub. She came back just after you left last night."

"Fuck! She did?"

Just the mention of her name had my heart racing in my chest, the shock of hearing that I'd missed her when I'd skipped out with Cat's friends suddenly made me feel sick. I really was a man-whore. Not that me hooking up with those girls was the right thing to do immediately afterwards, but at that point she was gone and I never thought she'd come back. Also, I was a bit drunk and horny after everything she'd done to me.

"Yup, and she was looking for you. God only knows why, I tried to set her straight about you and your three-inch cock. I told her she'd be far better off letting me take care of her needs, but she insisted that I pass her number on to you."

Dave started chuckling at his own joke and my body was suddenly filled with excitement and a longing to see her again. I was amazed that she'd gone back to find me and asked him to pass her number to make sure that we got the chance to get together.

"Oh, by the way, Sam told her that you'd already left with someone."

As soon as he finished speaking I wanted to find Sam and punch him in the throat. The more I found out about him lately, the more I was going off of him. He'd already given me a couple of awkward moments with Lily and Cat, and if he'd fucked with my chances of seeing Gini again, we'd be having words there was no doubt about it.

"Let me get a pen."

"You didn't see it? I sent it straight to your email last night when she gave it to me."

I was no longer listening to Dave and made my way over to my desktop. I fired it up and opened my emails. There it was, in the eleventh email down.

Dave. '***While you were getting your rocks off with the hot blondes***' was the subject heading. In the email, he went on to describe Gini as a hot bird with a cute ass before listing her number. There were a few drunken expletives from him about my sexual prowess before the email ended.

"Dave, I fucking love you."

"Bet you made the exact same declaration to those females in the heat of the moment last night as well, Jack. I know what you're like when you've had a few."

"All right, I promise I'll fill you in about them later. I have a call to make."

We arranged to meet for a late pub lunch an hour later before hanging up. I quickly dialled the number he'd sent me, praying he hadn't taken it down wrong. When it started ringing I realised I was calling before I'd even thought about what I was going to say to her. My heart pounded wildly in my chest and my body was buzzing, and all I was doing was talking to her on the phone.

"Yes?"

"Gini?"

"Jack?"

"Hello, Gini, I believe you wanted me to call you? Dave sent me your number." I said nonchalantly.

"You left the club before I got back."

"I wasn't aware you were coming back."

"Did you leave with those twins I saw you with?"

Fuck! She had actually come back while I was still there. I had no idea how to answer her question except honestly.

"Um, yeah I did, sweetheart, but they weren't twins, they just happened to look similar."

"Okay. So, are you seeing one of them?"

What was I supposed to say? So again I decided to be blunt and honest.

"Oh no, they're nothing to me. I just hooked up with

them for a night of domination and a double ride, then I came home."

The moment the words were out of my mouth I convinced myself I had Tourette's Syndrome because I was sure I'd just blown my chances after my outburst.

"You're funny. I love a man who can make me laugh."

She giggled infectiously. So I laughed as well.

I had been honest and she thought I was joking, relief flooded me.

"Then you're going to fall hard for me, sweetheart."

Desperate to change the subject I put the focus back on to her.

"Was there any particular reason you wanted me to call or did you just want to reacquaint me with another south-of-the-Thames 'hand shake'?"

Gini chuckled and it was incredibly sexy.

"Umm, sorry I was a bit drunk," she replied, sounding a little embarrassed about her forwardness in the club.

"Hmm, so you were drunk when you brushed your hand over my dick on the Tube as well? What do you drink? I'll make sure I have some in if you ever come over."

"I like you already," she laughed.

"I kind of got that feeling when you grabbed my dick under the bar. That was not fair play by the way."

"No, you're right, it was foreplay."

"Hmm, that suggests there should have been a 'play and an after play'."

"Well that would have depended on how well the foreplay went but we never got to finish that."

It was my turn to laugh. She wasn't at all shy with what she said or how she said it. and instantly my dick was hard. All that just from talking to her.

"So, do you want to get another drink sometime?"

Gini laughed again and I quickly added, "In public

with your hands tied behind your back this time."

"Just adding exhibitionism and bondage to the list of things I'm finding out about you, Jack."

I was grinning widely, "You're a funny girl."

"Jack, I'm a lot of things, love. Funny, sexy, intense, horny, playful, sensual and amorous..."

"You forgot modest, and aren't horny and amorous the same thing?"

"I have a high sex drive so it's fitting that both words are there."

My dick twitched at her confession and I was even more intrigued by her.

"So, Gini. Do you? Want to meet for a drink, I mean. Dinner too, if you want." Jeez, I had never sounded so inept at asking someone on a date before.

She hummed into the phone like she was thinking about it and I felt less cock-sure about her wanting to spend time with me.

"I don't know, do you think you can handle me?"

"I'm sure I can give you all the handling you need, Gini."

"I want a man that I can call when I want a night out. No strings, no questions, just fun. If you don't have a significant other, I'd be interested in getting to know you a little better."

Alarm bells sounded. I knew I definitely wanted to see her again, but the first thought that sprang to mind was Lily and a no-strings-thing she had been a part of previously. I quickly dismissed the thought because Gini's proposal was way different. We were just two people who had met and wanted to spend some more time with each other. Wasn't that how all friendships and relationships started?

"Sure. Sounds good to me. I've just got out of a serious relationship so having some fun would be perfect for me right now. When did you have in mind?"

Gini was hesitant at the other end of the line, then she sighed heavily. "All right, I can do Thursday evening, but I need to be home by ten. Can you make that?"

My week was completely free but I didn't want to wait until Thursday. "Um, Thursday's a bit tight for me, anything earlier in the week?"

"Nothing in the evening, but I have a few hours on Tuesday from eleven thirty. We could go for a coffee or something."

My plan wasn't working so I knew I had to take what I could get. "Okay Tuesday, eleven thirty, sounds good and I'll see if I can move some things around for Thursday," I lied.

"Do you want to take my number in case something comes up?" I asked.

"You rang me, so I have it. Do you know 'Bar 45' in Mayfair?"

I did know the bar. It wasn't a three-shots-for-ten quid kind of bar. It was an upmarket, classy and intimate establishment, and one of my favourite places to take a girl if I wanted to actually talk to them. It was also where I'd taken Rosie for drinks on our first proper date.

"Umm, that's like a local bar for me, ever been to the China Tang restaurant at the Dorchester? Fancy trying that instead? Cocktails and Asian food?"

"Cocktails in the morning? Not sure about those but I'll see you there on Tuesday, Jack."

Click. The line went dead and I immediately had an unpleasant feeling in the pit of my stomach at the loss. No goodbye, no finalising the arrangements, she'd just ended the call. The briskness of it all made me feel a little controlled again. It was something I wasn't used to and something I was learning I didn't care for very much. I began to wonder if I was giving off some kind of vibe lately because women were behaving differently towards me, or maybe I was just out of practice.

Chapter 12

Regrets

Meeting Dave on his own turned out to be a great idea. We talked music, bands, cars and women. Sally had made quite an impact on him and even though he was trying to play it down, he didn't fool me. He never usually spoke about any of his sexual conquests, and when I thought about it, apart from a short time with Maddie, I'd never known him to have a girlfriend.

When I had to answer all Dave's questions about the two girls I felt, surprisingly, a little embarrassed reliving it all.

"Thanks." Dave smirked, then a wide smile spread over his smug looking face.

"For what?"

"Test driving them, Yvonne it is then."

"Excuse me?"

"Well from what you told me, if I ever get the urge to ask one of them on a date, I'd go for Yvonne. I don't do bossy females."

"Ah, but from how you were talking about Sally, I'd say that Yvonne's going to have to wait a while."

"What about Gini? Did you call her? Damn, that girl has the perfect arse." Dave said, changing the subject quickly.

Even though my immediate reaction was to tense at the mention of Gini's name, I felt defensive that he was talking about her in that way.

"Jeez, is that all women are to you, tits and an arse?"

"Of course not, that would make me shallow. I love everything about women. I love women in general, I just happen to talk about their tits and arses more than any other part of their anatomy. I mean, come on, Jack, if I said wow she has great knees or something you'd think I was a freak!"

Smirking wryly at him, Dave had a point. I probably would have thought that was a fetish. After a few more rounds at the bar we both went back to my place and drank shots until we ran out of lemons, limes, and then the tequila. By the end of it we couldn't really stand any more. Dave was plastered drunk and I wasn't that far behind.

"So best lay?" Dave asked as he was lying flat out on the floor staring at the ceiling with a glazed look in his eyes and a bottle of beer resting on his chest.

He turned his head to squint up at me with one arm extended in my direction. I was lying on the sofa flat out with my head faced in his direction and one leg stretched over the back of the couch. I had a packet of ham on my chest. Waving the pack in Dave's direction, he wrinkled his nose in disgust and shook his head so I shrugged and took it back.

"Simone. A hot airline stewardess. Twenty minutes of pure ecstasy in the disabled restroom at Gate 21 in Charlotte Airport, Atlanta. I was on my way home from an assignment." I chuckled at the memory and even though I was drunk my dick twitched at the mental image the memory called forward.

"You?"

He looked almost comatosed with his eyes open and for a moment I thought he'd passed out until he drew a deep breath and spoke.

"Not sure, I'm torn. I want to say Isabella from Italy, who I spent a long but very quiet night with. Something about her complete silence just did it for me, or perhaps it was that her parents were three feet away in the next tent on our annual camping trip to Tuscany. But, there's also Sally, she held nothing back and the noises that came out of her mouth made me feel like a fucking stud. There is one other but I'd prefer to hang on to that thought."

Chuckling at that I asked, "Regrets? Who do you regret having sex with and who you didn't?"

"Emily." Dave answered a little wistfully.

Emily was one of our close friends and I was surprised if they had ever had sex because she was very particular about her type of man. She loved bald, well-built guys. Dave had a full head of hair and was a little on the slim side. I had to admit that Emily was a sexy, voluptuous girl who oozed femininity. She was also the type of woman that Dave avoided like the plague.

"Oh come on, I can't wait to hear this one." My interest was piqued and I was suddenly more alert.

Dave glanced at me with a drunken sheepish grin on his face and I knew instantly I'd got my assessment totally wrong. *Damn they hid that one well. I must have been walking around with my head up my arse not knowing everyone was screwing each other in our group.*

"We did. Then she ignored me for three weeks, it was painful."

"The sex was painful?" Lifting myself up onto my elbow and turned on my side to face him, I rested my head on the palm of my hand as I tried to focus on him.

"No the sex was... incredible. It was the way she ignored me afterwards that was painful. So much for hanging on to that thought, looks like I'm not able to do that anymore."

I could see by the look on his face that he was still affected from his encounter with her.

"You still like her don't you? Is that why things are tense around the two of you? I mean I've felt it a lot since..."

Thinking back, their relationship changed not long after Lily left for the USA. I thought that everyone was in a funk at that time because we'd all lost a big part of our group when she went. Lily was infectious and she held a special place in the hearts of all of us.

"This was a few years ago, after Lily left?" I asked for clarification.

"Right after. Emily called me feeling a bit low. Sam and Elle had gone on holiday with their parents, you were away on assignment, Maddie was loved up, and Emily and I were at a loose end."

"Yeah very loose by the sounds of it," I commented, waggling my eyebrows at him.

I chuckled at his confession, but when I saw the look on his face I felt bad for making light of it.

"It just happened. One minute I was cooking dinner the next I was pinned to the kitchen counter and she was kissing me like I was going off to war. Man, the passion in that kiss."

Dave drifted off for a second then sighed heavily.

"By the time she broke it off I was dizzy. The next thing I knew we were ripping one another's clothes off and I was staring at the most beautiful body I'd ever seen. We didn't just have sex, Jack. It was much more than that. It was animalistic, raw passion and we didn't stop until we physically couldn't keep going anymore."

"Hmm. Emily. She doesn't look..."

"Well, all I can say is, looks can be deceiving, mate." Dave looked sad and then turned his head to face the ceiling, sighing deeply again.

"So if it was that good, why didn't you both get together?"

"I tried to talk about it with her afterwards but her rejection hurt. She said it was just a moment and we were to leave it at that."

I dropped down onto my back again and now it was my turn to stare at the ceiling.

"So you regret having something because it was awesome and you know you can never have it again, right?"

"Got it in one. It's been difficult being around her ever since. I've tried to get over it for the sake of the group, but the feelings I have are still there after all this time."

"Love?"

"Yeah…no…an ache…I don't know. All I know is she's not interested and she left me confused by her come on and then shunning me afterwards. Well, I felt like my performance wasn't good enough."

"Did you tell her that?"

"God no. Why would I do that?"

"Maybe she has no idea that's how she's made you feel. Maybe she's embarrassed that she started it. Maybe she liked it too much as well and thinks she's not your usual type and you're not attracted to her. Maybe, just maybe she feels the same way about you as you do about her, but she can't bring herself to talk about it because she doesn't want you to excuse what happened."

"Fuck, Jack. That's a lot of 'maybe's' right there, this is that fucking philosophy class coming out in you, right?"

"Well, when was the last time you tried to talk to her about it?"

"A couple of months after we hooked up."

"All this time and those feelings are still there? You two need to be locked in a room until you work it out."

Dave sighed and rolled onto his side to look at me,

pushing himself up onto his elbow, he supported his head on his hand.

"So your regret?"

Inhaling deeply in my drunken state, I allowed myself to be completely honest.

"Lily."

"Lily? But you said…"

"Oh we never…"

"But you said you wanted to?"

"Fuck, it was more than want with her. She's still everything I measure every other woman by. I don't want to feel the way I do for her at times, it feels wrong on so many levels. Sometimes I'd imagine that if I'd gone for it and it worked out… Then I'd get stronger again and we'd keep moving our lives in different directions. I'm an ordinary guy. I'd have held her back, Dave. And like you said before, I wouldn't be a red blooded man if I hadn't lusted after her at some point."

Dave swallowed and looked at the wooden floor, placed his bottle down and began tracing the grain in the wood with his forefinger before staring me square in the eye again.

"And now? Is it too late to wonder? An opportunity missed you feel you should have pursued?"

"I think about it now and again. And in the past couple of years, hell yeah, especially during some of the darker moments she was having with Alfie. I just wanted to take her away somewhere and make her realise everything we meant to each other. Then I'd get rational again and know that we were always meant to be friends and nothing more, and want to punch Alfie for being such a dick."

Dave lay silent, his gaze burned into me as I dug deep and dragged up all the confused feelings I've had about Lily that had been buried since I was as a spotty teenager.

"I mean she admitted once she had struggled with her

feelings about us as well."

Dave sat up and exhaled heavily. He reached out and placed his hand on my shoulder trying to look supportive as he stared at me bleary eyed.

"What you're telling me is that, if Lily had made the first move you'd have grabbed the opportunity with both hands."

I drew in a deep, shuddery breath and shook my head confused by my drunken thoughts. My mind was foggy and I fought to resist the feeling that I'd wallow in if I allowed those thoughts to consume me the way they had when I was sixteen.

"Jeez, I'm drunk. No. It is what it is, Dave. We are what we are. Friends forever."

Dave struggled to his feet, swaying a little above me and for a moment he almost tipped the balance and crashed into me but he managed to pull himself back.

"I've got to take a leak, but, Jack, if you had those feelings for Lily and didn't go there. Shit, I admire your stance to preserve your friendship. You have the reserve of an ox mate. Me? I'd have fucked her brains out and worried about where we went from there afterwards."

Staggering towards the bathroom, Dave swayed again as he reached the door, I smirked wryly at his comment because he probably would have as well. I resigned myself to the fact that I'd done the right thing by Lily and not complicated her life. By making sexual demands of her we may have both lived to regret it later and ended up with nothing. So my decision had at least left me with something. I knew I was important to her and Lily meant the world to me, so I could live with that.

Hearing the toilet flush I swung my leg around and sat up on the sofa, my stomach caught up with the motion and I became slightly light-headed and nauseous. Dave wandered back into the room, his hands out in front to steady himself, while I pushed myself to stand up.

"Fuck, Jack. I'm sorry. What you just told me sucks. That was a crass remark I just made. You, Jack, are one hell of a gentleman to care for Lily the way you have and not to have taken advantage of your privileged position with her. I fucking commend you, mate," he said, slurring his words.

Sniggering, he leaned over and hugged me. We both swayed unsteadily on our feet until I pushed him away and he lost his balance. His arms flailed in an effort to steady himself until he landed heavily on the sofa and I changed tact a little.

"I regret having sex with Rosie because unfortunately I think I'm the love of her life and I don't feel the same. I worry about her as well. I guess I've made her feel the same ache I have in my heart and the insight to know how that feels. I'm just praying there is a way past that for the both of us.

By the time I made it to the bathroom, my mood was low and all I wanted to do was sleep. Once I had relieved myself I made my way to bed. Dave was adult enough to take care of himself and I didn't want to wallow in the sadness I felt in my heart right then.

Chapter 13

Making plans

Waking up to the sound of someone passing wind wasn't a great start to the day. Dave was wandering back and forth just outside my bedroom door making various animalistic grunting sounds before proceeding to pee like a horse into the toilet bowl. Through the hazy fog of my hangover, I managed to pull myself up and leant back against my headboard, mentally struggling to remember what day it was.

Sunday. I threw back the covers at the exact same moment Dave cracked open my door. I chuckled as I watched him avert his eyes briefly before quickly glancing back at my groin.

"Don't worry, Dave, I have that effect on women as well. They can't believe what they're looking at. They, like you, look away only to stare straight back in amazement at the gorgeous wood I have first thing in the morning."

Dave snorted and chuckled again, then flung the cover back over me.

"Dear God in Heaven, grant this guy a lame cock

before he blinds himself in the shower."

"Thanks for that, but I'd rather save it for my date with Gini on Tuesday, if you don't mind."

"Oh, the confidence."

"Nope, the promise. It's a dead cert. She just about said as much."

"Okay, we all know how you can get carried away with your imagination, Jack. What did she say exactly that has you jumping to that conclusion?"

"I believe it was, 'Nice pack, Jack, I hope you know how to use it', or words to that effect. Oh, and she was rubbing my dick through my jeans when she said it. Is that enough for you?"

"Man, she really did that? Or was that some fantasy you envisaged?"

"Nope, it really happened, on the Tube, that was the first time I rubbed up against her."

"You rubbed...never mind I don't need that image stuck in my head. I'm due at my parents at quarter to ten, that's trauma enough for one day. I'll call you on Wednesday to find out how your 'promise' goes."

Glancing at the Omega wristwatch Lily gave me for my eighteenth birthday, I could see that he only had twenty minutes to get there. Dave tapped the bedroom door with the palm of his hand and left the room, a few seconds later I heard the latch click on my front door. Once he'd gone I took a shower and tidied up my bathroom. The guy really was a disgusting slob. He had used my toothbrush and left toothpaste spittle all over the sink.

When I went to transfer my phone from my old jeans into the fresh pair I'd worn, I noticed that I had received three text messages.

The first phone number wasn't one I recognised.

Unknown: I just found out I have three hours free tomorrow night do you want to grab a bite to eat?

Flicking back through my phone, I compared the number from the last call with Gini and smiled slowly. It appeared as if she couldn't wait either. I added her name and saved it to my phone before texting back.

Me: Sorry just found this. Sure I'd love to meet. I have no plans tomorrow night, where and when?

Less than two minutes later, Gini replied.

Gini: This is Gini's husband. Who the fuck is this? Gini won't be going anywhere and if I get my hands on you, you'll be dead meat, got it?

I stood frozen in the middle of my bedroom staring at the phone screen feeling shocked. It was as if a sudden jolt of electricity ran through my body when I read the message. I felt infuriated. The one girl I'd had an instant connection with was married. There was no way I was getting mixed up in anything like that. *What the fuck?*

My mind flitted through all our conversations and how forward she was and yet she had a husband at home. At first I was numb, then I was so angry with her. Coming to terms with the fact that I wouldn't get to see Gini again was a real body blow. Even though my loins were already in love with her, my head rationalised that I'd had a narrow escape and was partly glad. At least I found out she was married before I'd gotten in too deep. It didn't feel like much of a consolation though.

Besides, if Gini could cheat on someone she loved enough to marry, who's to say she wouldn't do the same to me? Frustrated, I threw my phone on the bed and with mixed feelings bubbling away inside, and a heavy heart, I raided the fridge for some breakfast before crawling back into bed to watch MTV for a while.

As usual when I watched any of the music channels it wasn't long before XrAid came on the screen. It still felt a bit weird watching Lily and her band on television or when her songs came over the sound systems in shops. Lily was born to play music, but it didn't stop the ache in my heart that she wasn't here with me. The separation and loss of her in my daily life made it almost painful to watch her out there, all grown up and living life without me. Especially when I recalled my sweet memories of the innocent little girl I knew when we were growing up.

Lying around gave me plenty of time to think and I came to the conclusion that I just needed to be on my own for a while until I got over Rosie. There was no use figuring out what I wanted from life until I was completely over that relationship, and I decided there and then that I wouldn't be going out with another girl until I had done some healing. I wasn't heartbroken like she was; my feelings for her didn't go as deeply as hers.

That evening Sam called. From the conversation I got the impression that he thought I was a man-whore for life. He was damn near in hysterics when I tried to talk to him seriously about how I felt and what I thought.

"Jack Cunningham giving up women? Jack, that's like a barman saying he won't serve any beer. Both scenarios are ridiculous and it's never going to happen. What do you think will happen when you go clubbing? I've never known you to go home alone in all the time we've been going out. Or maybe you're planning on getting into trouble and being locked away for a while to help stop you getting any action?"

When I didn't laugh or come back with a quick remark, Sam became quiet. After telling him what had happened with Cat's man-eater friends and then the incident with Gini and the text message, he was more sympathetic towards my situation.

"Okay, are there a set number of days you are aiming for, or is it a minute by minute goal you're setting for yourself? I mean, how long can you go before your dick shrivels up and you have to take stimulators like Viagra?"

What Sam asked was a fair question. I had a high sex drive and Rosie had been an incredible match in bed. I hadn't met anyone like her, which is why she made it onto the girlfriend list in the first place. I didn't mean to sound shallow but at twenty-three I wasn't looking for anything more when I'd met Rosie. I was relatively happy with her until I saw Alfie with Lily and couldn't help comparing.

"Well, Sam, maybe a stint of celibacy will do me good. It may balance my hormones because I've been feeling a bit like a teenage boy one minute and a girl the next. On the one hand being without Rosie has me in the mind-set that I should fuck anything that moves, and on the other I'm looking for 'the one'. You know? That significant other that your sister, Elle, and Lily seem to have found without even trying."

Hearing myself say it out loud was even more painful than thinking it, and it suddenly dawned on me that I was having some kind of midlife crisis but in my twenties. Thinking like that may have made me sound crazy, but I had no better way of putting it. I was missing Lily, and Rosie in a weird way. I wondered if I had allowed myself to become too dependent on the women in my life instead of just being me.

"You know what, Sam? I think I'm going to take a sabbatical from work. I think I'll go somewhere and do something, anything. Six months of doing something worthwhile instead of sitting with my finger up my arse thinking about women and the drudgery of waiting for the next exciting project to come along."

"Jack, you don't know *how* to do anything else. You don't know you're living mate. You get to sit and have personal time with the likes of Kylie Minogue and Beyoncé for God's sake. Most men would give their right nut to do what you do, and most music lovers would think you've gone insane to even think about having time off.

What on earth would you do with six months, Jack?"

"Hell, anything I want. Think about it. I could go to Colorado or Montana and get work as a ski-instructor in Keystone or one of those small towns up there. I hear their season runs to about June and I could travel the rest of the time. I don't know...I could learn a new skill like surfing or ballroom dancing or something."

Sam laughed uncontrollably at my last suggestion then between chuckles choked out, "Jack Cunningham in tight dance trousers with a blue sequenced shirt and baggy sleeves, or a male tailored onesie with a V down to your belly button? I'd pay to see that!"

Suddenly I was laughing with him. His description of ballroom dancing apparel brought a genuine grin to my face. It was just like Sam to be so uncultured that he'd bring urban dress like 'onesies' into something as refined as ballroom dancing.

I wasn't one for indulging in my feelings normally, but I felt that I'd reached a junction in my life where it felt almost like I was suffocating, and that there was a gaping hole in my heart.

Normally, my personality was extrovert and I was definitely one of the 'glass half full' types who lived life to the maximum. However, since the New Year I'd recognised that I'd had been struggling. And it wasn't getting any better. I had no idea why I felt like that, but it could possibly be something to do with splitting with Rosie.

Sam continued to talk, but my mind whirled with ideas of how I could shake myself out of that depressive state and start to view life more positively again.

My research began immediately when I hung up the phone. *Creative writing? Learn to surf? Trek to Kilimanjaro base camp? Work in an orphanage? Teach English to rich kids from another country?* If I was being brutally honest with myself, I knew I couldn't have done a couple of those things. I had a soft heart so I'd have either tried to adopt all the kids and bring them home with me, or in the scenario of English teacher, I may have given the rich kids pushy parents a piece of my mind.

Scrolling down the Google list of suggestions, I knew instantly what I wanted to try and do. There were several options that hit my soft spots. Detox. 'Four weeks of yoga, meditation and detoxifying from all of life's indulgences', that sounded perfect. Without a doubt four weeks without anything to distract me, I believed would put me right. I'd lived in the fast lane ever since university and with Lily being half way around the world, any holidays I had seemed to include long haul flights.

A thought had popped into my head. *Wouldn't it be really cool to surprise all those rock stars I interview if I knew enough to ask questions that were really fresh?* I knew about bands and genres of music. I had extensive knowledge of each accolade every band had ever achieved, but what if I started talking about their instruments, or the actual music styles they were playing with a level of expertise?

I'd convinced myself that would take my skill set to a new level and perhaps open doors for me in my future career. It would also give me an edge over some of the other reporters that seemed to have tapped into a vein of artists that were well acquainted with each other. It was like there were cliques of performers who had their favourite or trusted journalists, and it was so difficult to break into those circles.

There was no hesitation after that. I went straight to the site organiser and fifteen minutes later my place was confirmed and reservations made to fly into Granada in just over a week. With each minute that passed, I formed my ideas for what I wanted to achieve. Twenty minutes after confirming my place at the health retreat, I'd booked my place on a multi instrument taster course in the south of Spain, followed by whatever instrument or instruments the instructor decided I had an aptitude for. I was going to do what I should have done a long time ago—learn to play an instrument properly.

Learning to play a few tunes on the guitar, and six months of weekly drum lessons when I was a teenager, had been a chore. I knew that if it hadn't been rammed down my throat to practice, I would probably have enjoyed playing those more.

I wasn't the best guitar student because my fingers were all thumbs, but during my training as a journalist my typing speed had improved and was on par with speaking speed. I figured that my fingers were more agile than what they were when I was just a lad.

Hopefully my plans would give me back some of the 'Jack spark' that was missing. Once motivated, I'd also made my mind up not to tell anyone what I was up to. If what I planned worked? It would be worth it to see their shocked reactions.

Chapter 14

Visitors

During the following few days, I scoured YouTube for tutorials about making and playing music. Surprised at the amount of guidance there was out there, I purchased a new guitar; a Fender CD-60. It wasn't the best guitar available but was a really good budget acoustic one. I could tell that it had a great tone even with my rusty attempts at playing it. The projection was amazing for a guitar at that price.

By the Thursday everything was in order and after finalising some last minute maintenance on my place while I was gone, I'd sat back feeling antsy about the challenge I had set myself. Dave had been really supportive when I'd told him. He encouraged me, even when he had no idea what I was going to do, and I hadn't felt such drive since I'd studied for my interview for my current job.

My doorbell rang while I was in the middle of yet more research. I closed my laptop immediately then quickly took my new guitar and placed it on the bed in my spare room before opening the door in case it was one of my friends. With only five days until I left, I didn't want to let anyone know what I was going to attempt.

When I'd opened the door my jaw dropped open, my eyes popped open wide and my heart began to race. Lily stood in front of me looking sensational. She wasn't due for another week but I was pleased because I would have left by the time she'd arrived. Squealing loudly she bundled through the doorway and reached out for me excitedly. Her slender toned arms wrapped around my neck and she peppered my surprised face in little kisses. Instantly my arms were wrapped around her and it was she who pressed her warm, familiar little body flush against mine.

Lily's reaction was reassuring. The way she clung tightly to me showed that she'd missed me a lot. She squeezed me even tighter and that said she was as desperate to hold me as I was to hold her. My heart was thudding hard with excitement because she had managed to surprise me. I'd expected a phone call when she arrived in London, not for her to come to my apartment.

Suddenly I felt at peace. The feel of her in my arms, the smell of her long, silky hair, and the way she pressed the palms of her hands against my back trying to get even closer to me made me feel at home.

"Hello, Jack. I have missed you *so* much."

That refined but sexy rock-chick voice laced with her posh London accent was so distinctive, but it had changed slightly and there was a slight hint of 'Americanisms' in her language. Normally I would have had a quick witted answer for her but I was just so happy that she was in front of me that I'd remained speechless. I'd felt a little choked with emotion at how demonstrative her greeting was.

We stood there hugging in the hallway for what seemed like ages, rocking back and forth, but then Lily pulled her head back enough to look at my face with a huge grin. For the last few years it had usually been me

113

going to see her, and although she was always the one to rush at me, this felt very different, she'd turned the tables by arriving at my door.

"Damn, Jack. You look incredible. I was worried about you after the last time we skyped, but seeing you in the flesh has put my mind at ease. Maybe the fact you had been up all night being a dirty boy had made you look a little tired."

Smiling widely with pleasure, I responded, "What can I say? Two for one, you know me ,Lily, I've always been a sucker for a bargain. Anyway, it's your fault. You know I sleep better when your sweet smelling little body is tucked up in my arms."

I gave her a squeeze and dropped my mouth to her neck in mock seduction. Lily's neck disappeared into her shoulder as goose bumps instantly spread over her arms in reaction to my lips on her skin. Pulling away from me she shook her head and swatted my arm.

"Behave, Jack Cunningham. Alfie has a sixth sense when it comes to you. Henry will be knocking on the door in a few minutes to deal with your inappropriate handling of his girl."

Henry was Alfie's security detail; he didn't trust anyone else with Lily when she came to London.

Lily threatening me with Alfie's bodyguard was a new thing. Normally she wouldn't have let anything come between us. The now familiar pang of loss of what we were was back in an instant with her chiding remark.

"Tell me you're kidding. I'm sure I can persuade you to stay the night with me. We never get to spend time together anymore, Lily."

"Jack, I promised Alfie that habit was one that we wouldn't be repeating anymore. Please, don't make this any harder for the both of us than it already is."

Swallowing hard, my anger and hurt were getting the better of me. It might even have been jealousy at that moment. I'd felt I'd lost a huge part of my life, yet that time she was the one that was redefining the boundaries. Lily's eyes lost their sparkle and were instantly glistening with tears. I saw that it was hurting her.

We both felt the same ache for what we had and I knew Lily was as badly affected by it as I was. So, in a more rational frame of mind, I knew that it was up to me to make it all okay between us, just like I did when I stepped away years ago so that I wouldn't cross the line with her.

"Come here. It's okay. Whatever it is, it's okay. Everything is always okay with you. I adore you, Lily. That will never change. I'll always love you no matter what. It's right that Alfie should be pissed off about how I behave around you. If you were my girl and he behaved the way I do, I'd have decked him long ago. You deserve to be happy. You love him with most of your heart and you've saved a little piece of it just for me. It's a huge privilege to still be in there at all, sweetheart, so I'll take whatever time I can get with you, whenever I can get it, as long as you're happy."

Lily stared up at me through her tear stained eye lashes, her huge pretty blue eyes that always melted my heart had begun to get red and puffy. She gave me a weak smile of resignation. I kissed over each eye and pulled her close for another hug, and then rubbed her back. When I had, I felt Lily's fingers curl tightly around my shirt as she clung to me for reassurance.

The following two days felt idyllic having Lily home, we even spent one rare evening with our whole group because Elle was in town as well. Apart from one occasion, we hadn't all been together in over three years. We had takeaway delivered and spent hours and hours talking about Lily, her band, XrAid, and hearing funny things that had happened during their tours. While she spoke I watched her with awe, she had become an incredibly confident woman. Lily was *everything* I knew she could be when we were growing up.

Everyone else shared their news and afterwards we just reminisced about all the funny stuff that had happened between us in the past. I had sworn Dave and Sam to secrecy about my sabbatical because I didn't want to answer any questions, and because I hadn't told Lily.

When Alfie rang I did my usual stunt of winding him up about spending time alone with Lily and I could hear the aggravation in his voice. I imagined him standing with a grim look on his face, his jaw clenched tight with anger, and that made me laugh even more. Eventually he threatened me outright which made both Lily and me chuckle, just like we had when people got the wrong idea about us when we were younger.

My heart felt full when I'd woken in the morning to find Lily's head in my lap. At one point during the previous evening as we'd talked, Lily had lay her head there and I'd ran my fingers through her hair, just like I always had when we talked into the night. When I'd looked down and watched her sleeping peacefully, I couldn't resist reaching out to gently stroke her face. Lily's eyes fluttered open and she'd looked up slightly alarmed before her face relaxed. She turned over onto her back, stretched her arms above her head and smiled sleepily at me.

"Morning," she murmured in her sweet husky morning voice.

Wagging my finger between us I smirked mischievously.

"Just wait until I spin this one to Alfie. He's definitely going to burst a blood vessel."

Lily giggled, grabbed my wagging finger, opened my hand and placed it against her cheek before closing her eyes again. I could tell she was savouring our little private guilt-free moment just as much as I was.

As with all good things, Lily's days in London came to an end too quickly and on her last day she met up with Rosie for lunch. I kind of wished I could have gone as well, but I wasn't sure if that was to spend more time with Lily, or to see Rosie. I'd realised it had been over a week since I'd last spoken to her. Once that had dawned on me, I felt a bit weird, it meant that she must be coming to terms with our spilt as she hadn't felt the need to call me again. I didn't quite know what to think about that. Gini never called me back either, so I assumed her husband must have been for real. All of those things left me feeling lost again.

Lily was cagey after lunch and I'd thought I should respect what they had talked about, even if it was probably about me, and not broach the subject. Plus we would inevitably have different views on the matter and I was too busy insisting on travelling back to the airport with her. She was too famous for me to drive her on my own and I didn't want Henry sitting in my car with us, so she ordered a limo with a privacy screen and had Henry ride up front. During the journey she asked me when the last time I had spoken to Rosie was, I calculated it had been ten days by then.

"You two really need to sit down and talk, Jack. Promise me that you'll go and see her."

Since Lily had told me she was going to lunch with Rosie, I had wanted to see her. I really did.

"How did she look?"

"Tired. She looked tired, and sad, she's devastated actually. I really think you need to talk to her, Jack."

Hearing the concern in Lily's voice was enough for me to know I had to see Rosie for myself. Whatever had happened between us, I still cared about her and I knew I shouldn't go away without speaking to her.

"All right, I'll call her later, promise." Lily gave me a tight smile and nodded, content that she'd got her point across.

Funny how the things you don't want to happen seem to come a lot faster than those you do want. In what felt like the shortest car journey I'd ever had, we arrived at the airport. Lily and I sat hugging in the back of the limo in the car park of a fast food restaurant that lay just outside the tunnel that led to the terminals, because once she arrived, it would be a media circus. Even I thought that, and I *was* the media. I wasn't going all the way with her. I hated saying goodbye in that frenzy.

Saying goodbye to her was always painfully hard for me, but that time I knew I definitely wouldn't see her for at least six months. I'd only told her I was going at the last minute and it was horrible for the both of us, especially since I still didn't tell her where I was going or why. Bizarrely, she tried to discourage me from going by saying that six months was hell of a long time, and anything could happen in that time. That pissed me off considering she was the one that lived half way around the world for most of the year and out of a suitcase for the rest of it.

Lily looked alarmed and pretty anxious about my news and yet the most urgent thing on her mind was to remind me again to talk to Rosie before I went. Once I reassured her that I would, Lily and Henry slipped out of the limo and transferred into the back of her security detail's car that had been following us. I sat in the limousine watching her disappear into the tunnel that would take her to the departure terminal.

At that moment, I was glad I was leaving as well. Convincing myself to do it was the easy part, making a go of it would be something else entirely different, but I was determined to make it work. Learning to play an instrument adeptly would be hard to pull off, especially when my friends were some of the most famous rock stars in the world. It was them I'd have to impress and not some visiting family member that I wanted to show off to.

With just over a day to go until I left, I made good on

my promise and called Rosie. I didn't know what I had expected when I'd offered to go and see her, but it wasn't to be brushed off because she had friends coming. I'd almost asked her who, because apart from her friend, Kay, there wasn't anyone she normally socialised with that wasn't in my group of friends. Then I remembered, *it isn't any of my business*, but it kind of struck a chord with me that I wasn't invited. I wondered if it meant that she had finally moved on.

After speaking to Rosie, and after Lily's visit, I was even more certain that I was doing the right thing. Once I had time away from everyone and everything, I'd find perspective and get an idea of what I should do with the next chapter of my life.

Going to bed that night, I felt excited. It wasn't a case of me running away, I had nothing to run away from. But over the past few weeks, I'd been feeling lost so it was actually more about running to find myself.

Chapter 15

Detox

Apprehension flooded through my body and nerves had gripped my stomach by the time I reached London City Airport to catch my flight to Granada. It was weird considering I flew on interview assignments regularly. Perhaps it was because the significance of it was that it was my own journey of self-discovery. Then again, everything felt weirdly perfect about it as I was the only person that knew precisely where I was going.

My parents were as supportive as they always were but my mother still wept buckets when I was leaving their house that morning to head to the airport. It was hard for me to deal with and I had to swallow the lump in my throat when I hugged her goodbye.

Flying to Spain was uneventful and darkness had already descended on Granada by the time we touched down. It felt late even though it was only twenty five to seven. Surprisingly there were five of us being met at the airport and I was the last one to be collected. Two had arrived the evening before and had stayed in a local hotel. They shared their experience of their last minute indulgences from the previous night. I was instantly jealous that I hadn't had the foresight to do that as well.

The journey in the minibus was quite a good icebreaker and everyone was friendly but stilted in their conversations. As with all groups of new people who are thrown together, everyone discussed their work, the weather, and what they hoped to get from the retreat. I was the only one taking a sabbatical, the rest were all there to de-stress from their careers.

Travelling with me was a lawyer, a social worker, a banker and a heart surgeon; the mix of people accompanying me tickled my sense of humour. If I had a heart attack due to junk food withdrawal, I had expert medical on hand to save me. If he fucked up I had someone to help me sue him, if I was still alive, a banker to tell me where to put the money I won and a social worker to counsel me from the trauma of it all.

The snow-covered mountainside that led to the retreat seemed to add an element of drama to what I was about to do, and the reality of six months away from home began to sink in.

I had no idea what to expect from the experience, but in my mind there were massage beds with sheer curtain drapes and sweet looking beautician types helping me to feel relaxed and in control.

After the short journey it was clear that what was in my imagination about the living conditions of the retreat and the reality were very different. It was sparsely furnished accommodation. A single bed, two blankets, a small bedside table, and what looked like a dining room chair were the only items in the room.

Three square meals a day consisting of mainly superfoods, such as whole grains, berry fruits, vegetables and water by the gallon was my new diet. My one luxury was an incredible view to enhance my contemplation.

Apart from meal times and the yoga class, I never saw another soul. Every electronic device I had brought with me was locked away and I was totally reliant on my memories for entertainment.

Reflecting on my past would never have entered my head before, however being high up on the mountain was very cathartic from a 'finding oneself' perspective. Every day more and more issues came to the surface about how I had behaved with women and how I figured they regarded me. It also occurred to me that I probably deserved the attention I got because of the aura I emitted.

Apart from unpicking the inner workings of my mind, I found myself missing people. Basically, my thoughts led me to have the biggest reality check and I concluded that I was one majorly selfish bastard, apart from where Lily was concerned.

My reflections became vividly clear on day four and I had a major revelation. When I processed my time with Rosie I accepted that I hadn't really tried much with her. Everyone tells me you only get out what you put into a relationship and I hadn't put much in. Once I realised that, I began to see all the positive things in Rosie that I had taken for granted. Sometimes I wondered if what I was feeling then was because she shunned me before I left, and that was really what was eating me up. But it didn't stop me from dreaming steamy scenes of having sex with her.

Four intimately vivid dreams in nine days about my ex-girlfriend was either my conscience trying to tell me something or I was so deprived of sex that Rosie was suddenly back in favour. But it couldn't be the latter because my heart was missing her as well. Either way she was great material for my wet dreams.

In one erotic interlude Rosie crawled across to sit astride me, her favourite position. My hands instantly fondled her amazingly firm and heavy breasts, my thumbs stroked across her small pebbled nipples. She leaned in to kiss me, positioning my dick at her entrance then sat up straight. Her wet swollen pussy engulfed my dick as it sunk deep inside her, inch by delicious inch. Watching her eyes close in reaction like it was all too much for her was the one thing that always got to me. That and the soft sigh she always expelled at the same time. The dreams were so vivid that I could even smell her and usually woke with a start, automatically reaching out to find that she wasn't there.

My time on the mountain gave me a greater understanding of how I wanted to conduct myself in the future. Thanks to all of the yoga, I weighed ten pounds less and I was as supple as a female gymnast. My muscles were toned, I was fitter, and I felt completely reenergised. I was buzzing about moving on to the next part of my journey and felt I was already changing for the better. The only thing that was playing on my mind was Rosie. She was still drilling away at my conscience.

Leaving the retreat, I travelled to Seville and to the home of a couple who had been teachers to some of the most popular music artists and songwriters of the twentieth century.

Beverly Saunders was in her seventies but looked like she was in her fifties and had an amazing, infectious personality. Her fair British skin had seen too many sun rays and I resisted my urge to tell her if she wasn't careful she'd start to resemble an expensive tanned leather handbag in the near future. Beverly was an incredible creative writer and lyricist. Graham Pope, her toy-boy partner was in his sixties and had been song writing with her as a career for all of his adult life. Judging by the place they owned they were incredibly successful, but they still only provided their students with very basic accommodation.

Somehow I expected to find everyone arriving at the same time like the detox retreat. But what was waiting for me was music and song writing workshops with four other people, all at various stages of their time there.

The workshops catered to suit all genres of music. Jazz, blues, country, indie rock, hard rock and power ballad style, had specialist songwriters available to work with. According to my research, every month a celebrity guest came to talk, give a master class and each person received feedback regarding progress. My only worry was I hoped there was no one I knew.

Graham was a genius, a music graduate and a multi-instrumentalist. He played piano, guitar, cello, violin and percussions. After a consultation with him, I felt embarrassed when he gave me a short piece to play and had written a tab score for me to follow. Suddenly I was at school again and felt extremely nervous showing him my attempt on the guitar. His feedback was much better than I expected, and he was incredibly patient, reassuring me that I was there to learn, not to be a master on day one.

Six days of experimenting with different genres and musical instruments later, I was stunned by how much I'd achieved given my very limited musical ability. Graham suggested I either focus on the drums or the guitar as both were my strengths. I chose the guitar because I couldn't really carry a set of drums around to practise with when I left there.

By the time I'd resided there for a couple of weeks I totally got what spurred Lily, Alfie, Rick Fars, and all other musicians, on. Once I knew how, playing music was incredibly addictive. As soon as my eyes opened in the morning, I'd lean over pulling my guitar onto the bed beside me to play.

I practised my scales first thing every morning, giving me a sense of routine, then I picked out all the riffs I had learned so far. After that I would play some songs, singing quietly. The sense of peace the music gave me was phenomenal.

I found myself grinning from ear to ear when I managed to play a song all the way through that actually sounded like music and not like a six year old that had been given a toy guitar for Christmas. I suddenly had a sense of pride in how far I had come.

Song writing was another particular strength of mine, maybe because of my journalism studies, although my lyrics never seemed to be romantic. I was more of a situational lyricist and tended to focus on world events and my feelings around them. Penning a score of music to match the words was easier than I imagined, but finding a melody that worked to lay over the words was a little harder for me.

Two months in and my skills had grown considerably. In fact, Graham had invited a couple of guys to listen to two of the songs I had written. I was too embarrassed to sing them, so another student that I had been partnered with sang them for me. Listening to Diane left me speechless. Her delivery of my little tunes to musicians who sang for a living was perfect and I couldn't get past how smoothly the words and music blended together.

Finally, twenty weeks after I first met Graham and Beverly, the day came for me to leave my safe haven and step back into reality. After six months away, I had no idea what to expect upon my return to London, but I had gained a wealth of experience and was more in tune with my own identity.

Before I'd left I had given my parents the name and address of the retreat post office box, but as promised they hadn't sent any mail. The reason I had told them was for emergencies only. They were as good as their promise and never contacted me so at least I knew nothing too urgent would be waiting for me.

If I was being honest, I felt apprehensive as I turned the key in my apartment lock and slowly pushed the door open. Everything looked the same; bare and spacious. My home hadn't changed but I had. How had I changed? Well, for one thing I wasn't starving all the time. I knew now that it was boredom that made me eat to fill the void. I hadn't flirted or gotten laid in six months. Apart from Diane, who was an amazing girl but finalising a messy marriage, there was no one to flirt with, and lastly, I was now an unaccomplished musician/songwriter.

Staring in the hall mirror, I knew I looked better than I had in a long while. My appearance was a little rougher because my hair had grown and I hadn't shaved for a couple of days, but personally, I felt the unshaven, casual look suited me better. I was stress free and had boundless energy. Fifteen pounds lighter in weight, I could concede that I looked and felt super fit. With that and my couldn't-care-less attitude, I felt like I was on top of the world.

Wandering over to my desk I saw my answerphone was full. I hesitated before pressing the play button; I didn't want to spoil my new found centred life. Eventually I did and sat down on the sofa to listen. Familiar voices flooded the room and my heart reacted to each and every one of them. I felt the strings of my heart being pulled in all different directions. The effect of hearing them again for the first time in a long time caused a lump to form in my throat.

Dave: Hello! It's Saturday, are you back yet? I hope so, I fucking missed you, mate.

Emily: Hi, Jack, we're having tapas on Sunday evening if you want to join us. Give me a call. Missed you.

Sam: Jack? You there? Fuck, when do you come home again? Tell me and I'll pick you up from the airport.

Laughing I shook my head in disbelief at Sam's message, doubting that I could even begin to explain the flaws in Sam's logic.

Mum: Oh, goodness. You aren't home yet. Ring me when you get home. Your dad and I missed you so much.

The anguish in my mother's voice made me feel terrible that I had gone and left her in the first place. I wasn't left to my thoughts for long as the next message started.

Lily: Call me when you get home. I'm worried. Why didn't you go and see Rosie, Jack?

Joe Crawley: All right now that you've got all that hippie shit out of your system perhaps you're ready do some work now. Call Linda, you're seat has to be booked for the Rock Fest event next weekend. Schedule some time for a catch up, a lot has happened in six months.

Joe was my editor and I almost called him back right away, but for once I did the right thing. Normally Lily would have been my first call, but during my time away from her, I'd gained a more objective view of how our behaviour might affect other people, namely Rosie and Alfie.

As much as I loved Lily, continuing our relationship as it stood when I'd left seemed very wrong. Behaving risqué with each other when we were young and single was one thing, doing it to the extent we still were, when we had both had partners was just wrong and disrespectful.

Punching the numbers into my phone, I placed the phone to my ear and heard the connection click before the sound of the call ringing.

"Jack! Thank goodness."

My mum was suddenly crying hysterically and I felt a huge pang of guilt again for leaving her without any real way of communicating with me. Choked with emotion, my dad took over but I could hear him struggle to maintain the conversation as well. I found myself tearing up at the sound of their voices and I'd thought about how I'd needed to do better by them, they weren't getting any younger.

With my new outlook on living and being in tune with my feelings, it was clear to me how selfish a person I had been. Even though I had gone to 'find myself' I hadn't really considered the effect it would have on others, especially my parents.

Dave was my next call and he sounded genuinely happy that I was home. He wanted to come over there and then, but I needed a day to get myself together. I worked my way through the people who had called, making sure I spent enough time talking to them, they were, after all, the ones who seemed to miss me the most.

Lily was the only one I never called. Her message was odd and the subject of her call, Rosie, was very much on my mind. After spending months writing songs concerned with political statements than with prose, towards the end of my time, my lyrics about missing Rosie began to flow from my pen. It was through the lyrics that I came to realise how much I truly missed her.

Needing some comfort, I slid between the sheets of my own bed feeling both incredibly tired and lonely. During my time on the retreat I had begun thinking more and more about Rosie and less about Lily. Glancing at the clock, I noted that it was only ten to nine; it wasn't too late to call her. Just the thought of speaking to her made me nervous, I'd never felt like that with her before. Six months was a hell of a long time not to speak to an ex-girlfriend, let alone call her out of the blue to see how she was doing. I could only hope that I wasn't ripping open the scars that had started to heal.

Rosie loved me, I knew that without a doubt and I also knew from the way my mind seemed to wander to her, that not only did I miss her, but I actually loved her as well. Pity it took trekking to the top of a mountain to make me realise that. Being away from home, I had felt with each passing day that my heart ached more and more for her. Hesitating, I tapped my phone against my chin, contemplating whether I should risk opening old wounds and also wondering if this was a selfish act. I was sure that I had made a huge mistake in letting her go and it was only right she knew this, even if she didn't feel the same.

A huge part of me was worried about how she would feel hearing from me after all that time, but if there was a chance she'd take me back I had to try. Finding my courage, I scrolled through my contacts and pressed on her name. Taking in a deep breath, I readied myself and pressed the call button. I held that breath and waited nervously for the call to connect.

Chapter 16

Gutted

When Rosie's line started to ring my heart jumped into my mouth. Its wild beat matching my excitement at the thought of hearing her voice and telling her how I felt after all that time. The longer I waited for her to answer, the more wired and excited I became.

"Yes?"

I was taken aback by Rosie's abrupt greeting as if she had no idea who was calling. She had to have known it was me, she knew my number off by heart. I couldn't help but snigger at her dismissive reaction because I deserved that and more after everything I'd put her through.

"Hi Rosie, I just wanted to tell you I'm home, sweetheart."

An unexpected silence hung between us until eventually Rosie responded with a slight brush off. Her voice sounded a little too high pitched in surprise to be genuine.

"Oh right. Thanks for letting me know."

Huh? I didn't exactly expect a welcome mat but I wasn't prepared for that either. Feeling awkward, I tried to reach out to her again and tell her how I felt.

"Um, I missed you when I was away. How are you doing?"

The low timbre of a slightly irritated male voice interrupted our conversation.

"Where did you go? What's taking you so long out here?"

My heart sunk like a stone to the pit of my stomach and almost stopped in shock, before a deep seated rage began to build up inside of me. Rosie was with another man. Flattened at hearing someone else in my shoes, I had no idea what to say next.

My beautiful Rosie had moved on, that was my reward for the shoddy way I had treated her. All the time I had wasted thinking the grass was greener elsewhere had cost me what I then thought was probably the only girl I had ever loved in a non-platonic way.

"Sorry, Jack. I have to go, I have company right now, I can't talk. Can we do this another time?"

Awkward wasn't the word for how I was feeling by then. It was out of character for Rosie to dismiss anyone, but there was little doubt in my mind that was exactly what was happening to me. *And for the second time. Serves me right, I've been the biggest arse to her.*

"Sure, of course, sorry, Rosie. I'll leave it with you then. Give me a call if you want to go for a drink or something."

Rosie abruptly ended the call but not before I recognised the barely disguised tension in her voice. I hung up feeling totally deflated. *How could we get back together now?*

But what did I really expect? I had been away for six months. Did I think that she'd be sitting by the fire with a book waiting for me? Maybe. Had I been so presumptuous as to think she'd still love me and would take me back again? I started to question whether I'd actually learned anything about myself in my time away. Everything I am as a person got switched up while I was away, she didn't know that yet. I wondered how I could make her listen with the cold vibe I got from the tone of her voice? A feeling of panic took me over. Six months without contact and I was too late. She was over me and would never see the changes I had made.

I was deep in thought, distracted by the effect the call had on me that I hadn't realised the doorbell had rung, it was only when it rang again that the first buzz sunk in. I made my way to the door but I wasn't in the mood for company and prayed to God it wasn't Sam. Out of everyone I knew, he was the last person I felt I could have coped with at that moment.

Dave grinned, holding up a brown paper carrier bag full of Chinese food.

"Dinner is served," he announced loudly.

I wasn't hungry at all. The old Jack would have inhaled the bag of food within seconds; the new Jack couldn't stomach the thought of eating at that moment. Pushing his way past me he wandered into the kitchen and laid the takeaway on the counter before turning around and grabbing me in a bear hug.

"Come the fuck here, Jack. I missed your ugly face. You look like shit, as usual."

Dave squeezed me firmly and I knew his greeting was entirely genuine. Stepping back he smirked and shook his head as he appraised me from head to toe. He grinned wickedly but was obviously happy at having me back. It felt good to know that he'd missed me.

"Well, well, well, Jack my man, the women of London won't know what the fuck to do with you now. You're better looking than when you left. You've just made 'longer hair and scruff in an English gentleman', a new trend, Jack. Best be careful, I might give you *my* number as well."

I chuckled and slapped Dave's back. We walked into

the kitchen and I slid the takeaway bag across the counter. Even though I had put him off coming, I was pleased to see him.

"After six months of celibacy, Dave, you might just find you get lucky if you do. I believe I have the strength in my right arm now to match Roger Federer's."

Cracking up with laughter at my tennis player analogy, Dave shook his head at me again.

"Fuck. See, I missed that Jack, the funny, insulting arse who has a quick line on the tip of his tongue for anything that's thrown at him. I take it you didn't find a little hottie on your travels and shag yourself senseless then? Oh wait, that statement would imply you had some sense in the first place."

Laughing at his own joke, Dave shrugged his jacket off, hung it over one of my kitchen chairs and leaned his elbows on the counter with his hands clasped in front of him.

"Not even a blow job?"

"Nope, not one. No women in the last six months. My right hand and I have been totally monogamous."

What I didn't say was it damn near killed me, and I was sure I had tennis elbow. I lifted my hand and talked to it as if it were going to reply.

"Isn't that right, darling?"

I stared back at Dave's gaping mouth and leaned over the counter, clamping it shut with my finger. I started to unpack the takeaway containers from the bag before I continued.

"Mindless fucking won't do it for me anymore, Dave. I've got it all figured out in my head now. I don't want to be 'Jack the lad' any more. Jack the man has finally arrived and he knows exactly what he wants."

Dave looked intrigued and straightened up with his hands on the counter, obviously surprised by my statement.

"Seriously? And that 'want' would be what, exactly?"

Dishing the noodles onto two plates, I threw the empty carton back in the bag and licked the stray sauce on my fingers before meeting his scrutinising gaze.

"Rosie."

For the second time in as many minutes I was staring at the inside of Dave's mouth. His jaw looked like it was dislocated as he stared at me in disbelief. He started pacing back and forth behind the counter, raking his hands through his hair before he stopped and looked me square in the eye.

"Jesus H. What the fuck is it with you? Between you and Lily's love lives I'm at a loss at times. Talk about drama and angst? I hate to tell you this, Jack, but I think you've missed the boat with Rosie. I saw her a few months ago with a guy ten times better looking than you, and she was actually smiling again."

"Who is he? What's his name? How did she meet him?"

Dave put his hands up in defence of my rapid questions.

"Whoa! I don't know. I just saw them coming up Kings Street near the hospital when I was at Accident and Emergency. I'd taken a colleague there who had fractured his ankle on the stairs at work."

"You haven't talked to her since I left? She hasn't been over to see Emily or Sam?"

"Nope, apart from that sighting, I've not seen or heard from Rosie since the day you dumped her."

Dave's assessment of how I'd treated Rosie at the end smarted and I could feel frustration building up inside, I was going to lose my temper with him really soon.

"I didn't dump her, Dave. It wasn't like that. I let her go because I didn't think she was the love of my life. I couldn't let her waste any more time with me. Now I know how wrong I was about that, but I didn't dump her."

"Yup, you did, Jack. Don't try to sugar coat it. You came back from that assignment and after Lily's…whatever, you walked away from her and none of us have seen her since. I stood by your decision because you're my friend. It's your life and you have the right to decide what you want, but don't try to make it sound less than it was. You cut all ties with her and she lost all of us because we were your friends first."

"Damn. I never meant for her not to have anyone. I miss her being around too. Why are relationships so fucking complicated?" I groaned angrily.

All Rosie had done was love me and I hadn't been fair to her. Acting the way I did with Lily must have been humiliating for her, and then for me to cast her aside because I thought I was the most important person in all of that was downright shameful.

"And after all that, you want to go to Rosie and say what? Hey, maybe I was a little hasty about us? Let's give it another go and see if I feel differently about you this time? She's moved on, she's happy from what I saw, leave well enough alone, Jack. Rosie's a lovely girl; she doesn't need to be messed with any further. You had your shot and you fucked it up."

Dave thankfully changed the subject when he tucked into the food like he hadn't seen any in a while and commented that my appetite had changed. He excused my poor eating due to not getting laid and consoled me that my love of food would return once I started 'riding' again. Dave definitely had a way with words when it came to having sex.

When he'd started to fill me in on all our friends news I felt annoyed that Lily had been over three times and I'd missed her. He'd said she was coming over again in August for an extended stay but he only had half the story because he'd forgotten to ask what the occasion was.

Being the great friend he was, it wasn't long before

Dave found a bottle three quarters full of gin in my kitchen cupboard and was soon helping me drown my sorrows. Another thing I'd learned was that I was a very cheap drunk due to my self-imposed abstinence from alcohol.

Dave squinted at me and with a slightly inebriated voice said, "So I guess you got over your little Lily crush while you were away."

Thinking back to how I felt six months prior, I never protested that I didn't have feelings for her. My feelings were all over the place when I'd split from Rosie, so I could very well have been looking for a safe place to give my heart and Lily was the safest person I knew I could trust to handle it.

"Yeah, I suppose if that's what was happening, but I think I was more fucked-up than I realised. I guess my emotional state is more settled because I haven't even tried to ring her yet."

Once the bottle of gin was finished, I sent Dave to the spare room as I headed to bed. I stared up at the ceiling and my mind replayed my call with Rosie and how familiar that guy's voice was with her. All I knew was since hearing her voice and how she'd responded to me, I had to accept that she was over us. I'd lost out big time and had no one to blame but myself. I had to make it easier for her by staying away so that she could get on with her life.

Sleep just wouldn't come no matter how exhausted stepping back into my real life had made me. No matter which way I looked at things, I'd made a proper arse of what may possibly have been the most important relationship in my life. I'd heard people say that, 'sometimes one has to lose something before the significance of it is fully understood', and that couldn't be truer right then. I was too immature to understand the significance of what I had at the time and I was paying for it then.

Chapter 17

Bump

Stretching out like a star on my king size mattress felt incredible after my single bed at the retreat. Graham and Beverley had been amazing and accommodating hosts, but their lumpy mattresses definitely needed replacing. I bet the one I slept on had been there since they first opened twenty five years before. I shuddered as I thought about who and how many had slept on it before me. I spent a lot of time napping on their rope hammock during my breaks because of my lack of sleep in that bed.

Dave had left by the time I had gotten out of bed the following morning but had left a note.

Time to get back in the saddle. Tonight, Ministry of Sound, just you and me. I'll even be your wingman. Your need is greater than mine.

Chuckling softly at Dave's note I wandered over to my desk. It felt strange pressing the button on my laptop after all that time and seeing the familiar wallpaper of my desktop. It was a picture of the whole group, including Lily, her band, her friend,s Holly, Brett, Mandy and Neil, as well as Alfie and his band. It was taken during a night out when we were all together in Florida shortly after Lily's graduation.

Bloody hell time flies, it had been just over a year ago and a huge amount of drama had happened for the group of people staring back at me from the screen. When I opened Skype I saw that there were eight missed calls from Lily that had ranged in time from the afternoon before until three that morning. I had deleted the Skype app on my phone to stop me from getting side-tracked when I was working. Glancing at my wristwatch I noted that it was only eleven in the morning so would be six in Florida where she currently was according to her messages.

Figuring she would still be asleep I typed a reply to say that I'd missed her tremendously and that I'd catch up with her later. As soon as I pressed send the round icon featuring her face came up with the familiar Skype ringtone.

I scrubbed my face with my hand suddenly unsure of what we were going to say to each other. We had been through so much together but six months apart was a long time. A part of me was apprehensive about getting too close to her again because of the feelings I had right before I went away whilst the other just wanted to talk to my best friend.

Plucking up courage I answered the call and Lily's gorgeous but perplexed face filled my screen.

"Well? Put your bloody camera on Jack. I've missed you and I can't see your handsome face."

I clicked on the camera icon and heard her breath catch before her face broke into the most beautiful smile. Her eyes searched the screen, she had obviously noticed the differences in my appearance.

"Jack! You look incredible. You are even more handsome than you were before you left. I love the longer hair and the scruff! It's almost criminal how hot you look. No guy should look that stunning that's not on my arm. I may have to abandon Alfie and get the first flight home."

I was unsure of how to reply, I didn't want to fall into the same pattern of behaviour as before, but this was Lily and I didn't want to upset her either so I flirted back in a subtle and appropriate way.

"Hmm, I think Mr. Black would be sending his 'Men in Black' to deal with me if you did, but it's a great thought thank you, Lily, you look stunning as usual. It's great to see you again."

Lily asked me what I'd been doing and I told the bit about my detox retreat. I didn't lie to her but she'd assumed that's what I'd been doing all of this time and I never once corrected her. We spoke for a few minutes about her band and what was going on with Alfie before her face took on an intense stare.

"Jack, does Rosie know you are back? You really should call her."

And there it was—the one thing that would put a dampener on my mood during our first conversation in half a year.

"I already did, Lily."

"You have?"

"I just said so didn't I? Don't you believe me?"

I'd sounded irritated and Lily tucked her hair behind her ears looking a little embarrassed that she'd questioned me. She began to chew the side of her mouth like she did when she was worried about something, so I sighed and softened my face.

"Lily, I called her before I left on your suggestion and I called her yesterday afternoon when I got back. Both times she brushed me off. Besides, yesterday she had her new guy with her and according to Dave it's been going on for a few months, if it's the same guy. Why are you so hung up on this?"

139

Lily nodded slowly, confusing the shit out of me. If she knew all of that why was she pushing me to speak to Rosie in the first place? Lily leaned back in her chair and tried to press the point again.

"Jack, I just think you two still need to talk. It doesn't matter who else is in the frame, you really need to make the effort to make peace with her. I'm talking as your friend here."

By that point Lily was annoying me, but that was her all over, she was always the peacemaker. Growing up, she wanted everything in her world to be rainbows, unicorns and fluffy clouds. She always saw the best in everyone when the reality was quite often the complete opposite, as was the case for Rosie and me. She had a guy in tow, there was no way I was going to fuck it up for her after skipping out and messing her about the way I had, Lily would just have to like it or lump it.

"Leave it, Lily. I offered her an opportunity to meet for a drink, so the ball is in her court. I'm not going to force the issue. Anyway, I'm back to work tomorrow and I'm off on assignment on Thursday so my week, apart from tonight, is fully booked. I'll have research to do and there is a stack of other stuff to catch up on before I can even think about relationships and having a social life again."

Changing the subject, I spoke to her about Rick Fars' band, Cobham Street, because we were going to be meeting up at the festival at the end of the week. Lily was quite tight with Rick and she allowed me to steer her away from the subject of Rosie.

I had another interview scheduled with Rick as his band had just released yet another album. The guy was a machine, but his constant success meant I got to go and spend time with him and his bandmates quite regularly. I'd interviewed him a couple of times before Lily met him, but since her friendship with him had blossomed, and because of my relationship with her, he treated me more as the friend I'd become, rather than Jack Cunningham, music reporter.

When my phone rang, I had to finish my call with Lily, Joe, my editor at the magazine was calling and I knew it wouldn't be a two minute conversation. Even then Lily had to have the last word about Rosie.

"Do yourself a favour Jack, call Rosie."

It was like she had this sixth sense about my feelings and I hadn't even discussed my thoughts over the last few months about Rosie with her.

"Talk to you later, Lily."

"Tomorrow. Ring me tomorrow, Jack, promise."

Lifting the phone towards my face, I hit the green icon to accept Joe's call.

"Just a sec Joe. I'll speak to you then, Lily."

Turning the Skype call off I opened my organiser in readiness to receive Joe's instructions.

"Lily? Lily Parnell?"

"Yeah, my Lily."

"Fuck, she's the cutest woman I've ever laid eyes on."

"There will be no use of the word laid in the same sentence as Lily while I am around."

Joe chuckled heartily.

"Lily and laid in the same sentence equals fantasy in my book."

I made a growling noise down the phone to which he laughed out loud before coughing. He did this thing where his laugh made a kind of deflated-coming-down-sound into normal conversation speech.

"So, festival on Thursday, you all set?"

"Not really apart from knowing I'm going. How many days is it? Do I have onsite accommodation or do I take a tent? What's the deal?"

"Two days, no tent, no onsite accommodation. Rick

Fars has you covered. You're staying at the Hilton with the band."

"No shit? Really?"

"Yes, Rick wants to talk to you about chronicling their tour or something."

In the past Rick had made plenty of references to me going on tour with them but I always thought that was an alcohol induced idea. The kind of thing someone says when they're drunk and it can conveniently be forgotten in the sober light of day.

I was more than excited at the thought of touring with Cobham Street. It would be just the pick me up I needed to try to get over Rosie. Not that I wanted to forget her, just that I had to. She had moved on and was happy, according to Dave.

For the next forty five minutes Joe fed me information about the festival I would be attending, from bands to research, personal information I needed, and who to avoid being in the same room as. Eventually Joe had given me all the details necessary that made it look like I knew what I was doing. I was glad he was so thorough.

Following my calls, I did some necessary but very mundane stuff, like going food shopping and stopping by my favourite tailor's. I took three suits to be altered because the trousers fell off me when I'd tried them on. I'd gone down two sizes and my jackets looked like they had belonged to my dad. Zachery, my tailor, told me they would be ready in forty-eight hours. I doubted many people get that kind of service in London from an old school tailor.

Leaving the Saville Row shop in Mayfair, I made my way up to Bar 45 for a bite to eat and to find out the latest on bands. A lot of the reporters hung out there and I had a few contacts who worked at the bar, they would overhear gossip so I usually got the information before it hit the wire.

Walking into the bar, the last person I expected to see sitting there was Rosie. It had been our favourite place to eat, but I never expected that she'd be here on her own. Shocked was the only word I could use to describe the look on her face when she saw me walk through the door. I highly doubted mine looked any different to hers.

We were in the same place, she had no option *but* to speak to me. When I wandered over to her table she stayed seated, looking radiant in a loose fitting purple dress and black patent flats. She'd put on some weight but it suited her. She was simply stunning. I couldn't take my eyes off her but she looked uncomfortable, it was then I realised that she was probably meeting her guy at the bar and I wasn't sure how I felt about that.

Placing all my feelings for her to one side, I couldn't let her feel awkward about my untimely arrival which was obviously going to scupper her lunch plans.

"Hey, Rosie. How are you doing, sweetheart?" I asked crouching down beside her.

I'd kissed her lightly on the cheek and when I'd pulled back to look at her, I saw that her eyes were brimming with tears. My heart squeezed at how my presence had upset her and I placed a hand on her arm in reassurance.

"Oh, hey. No, Rosie."

Pulling a chair close from another table I'd sat next to her. My arm instantly wrapped around her shoulder and I pulled her into me to comfort her. Kissing her temple, I'd tried to soothe her but it only upset her more and a strangled sounding sob escaped from her lips. Seeing her like that made me feel even shittier than I had when we'd broke up.

"Please don't cry, Rosie. I hate seeing you cry. It's all right. Everything's going to be all right." I cooed in a soft tone, desperately wanting to make her feel better.

A dark shadow cast over us at the table and when I'd

looked up, a huge guy with mousy brown hair in a smart tailored suit spoke to me.

"Rosie knows everything is going to be all right. We've talked about it often enough. You're Jack, I presume? Don't you think you've done enough to Rosie? Now if you don't mind, I think you need to back off, Rosie's happy now and that's down to me, so we'd be grateful if you left us both to get on with our life together."

Shit, on the one hand I was glad Rosie had someone who wanted to protect her, but on the other I was pissed off that he thought she needed protecting from me.

Rosie glanced up at her guy with a small smile and he reached out to wipe a tear from her cheek. Taking her hand, he began to help her out of the chair.

"Come on, darling, let's go somewhere else."

Rosie began to stand and her guy put a protective arm around her waist. She pulled her jacket around her belly, if she hadn't done that it probably wouldn't have taken my attention away from his hand. My eyes were drawn to the front of her dress and that's when I saw it—a neat little bump. Rosie was pregnant and by the looks of things was about four or five months. No wonder she didn't want to talk to me. She was having someone else's baby.

"Rosie and I are leaving now," he barked and turned towards the door.

I slid out of the leather seat and stood face to face with Rosie, I could feel her breath on my cheek.

"You know where I am if you want to talk. Call me." What else could I say? *Have a nice life?*

Rosie remained silent as her boyfriend ushered her from the restaurant, his hand resting on the small of her back in a protective gesture. All I could do was watch with a gaping hole in my heart, willing her to turn around so I could see her one last time. Just as they were about through the door, Rosie's head turned in my direction. I kicked myself for watching her because the look she gave me will haunt me forever.

Chapter 18

Back in the saddle

I was devastated. Everything Rose and I had had was gone. I was so shocked when I'd seen that she was having a baby, it was the last thing I expected. My thoughts of convincing her to take me back suddenly became impossible. We were irretrievable. No second chance and no discussion. Anything we were together, had to be left in the past. There was no opportunity to rake over the coals and find any passion from the embers that had been burning inside me during my months of solitude.

Rosie was building another life that I had no place in. She'd given me her heart and I hadn't realized how precious it was. In fact, I'd trampled on it and it was my turn to feel the full impact of my decisions.

I wanted to apologise but I knew at that stage apologies would mean nothing and would sound hollow given that she was carrying another man's child. No wonder I'd become an inconvenience on the phone. Maybe she'd even begun to see me as a nuisance. All I seemed to be doing was disrupting the harmony she had with her new boyfriend. Suddenly my emotions caught up and cut through the shock, I couldn't breathe. I had to get out of the bar as it taunted me with memories of happier times.

When I was safely in a cab, I asked the cabbie to take me to Dave's place. Given the mood I was in, if I went home I felt I'd do something rash, like call Lily and give her a telling-off for making me see Rosie in the first place.

Texting ahead to Dave, I'd asked him to be ready to help me drown my sorrows, maybe not in so many words but I gave him the heads up there was some heavy drinking to be done that evening.

Me: On my way. Need to get pissed in a hurry, be prepared for the worst kind of drinking session. I'm on my way.

Two minutes later Dave replied.

Dave: Rosie said no?

As I replied my thumbs moved quickly across the keyboard and my temper rose as I replied.

Me: Rosie said never. New guy and pregnant.

Less than thirty seconds Dave replied.

Dave: Holy fuck I'm sorry, Jack. Damn, pregnant? No wonder she's not been around. See you in a mo.

Dave was already at the kerb when we'd pulled up and he climbed into the back of the cab.

"Soho," he called out to the driver as he sat back heavily in the seat beside me.

The taxi driver did a U-turn throwing us both off balance for a moment and begun to retrace his journey back into the centre of town.

147

"Jack, I'm in charge. No arguments. Leave it to me to arrange your wake. Soho has the best Chinese food, tits and arse are aplenty and we're two single, hot guys. I know it's the last thing you'll want to do but you're going have the time of your life and you'll be worshiping at my feet with gratitude by the end of the night. I won't hear any lovesick shit or I'll punch you unconscious and put you out of your misery, got it?"

He was right. The last thing I'd wanted was another meaningless one night stand, but... I didn't even feel like I could've fought for her. I had no choice. There *was* no going back for Rosie and me. Dave was right and that was my wake, it was as if Rosie had died as far as I was concerned. I wasn't sure how the night was going to end but one thing I was sure of, I had to push through the pain even though all I'd wanted to do was lay down and die. I was miserable but Dave was in charge and I had no energy to argue with him.

With wine, brandy, liquors and a couple of gins behind me, my pain was still there, it just wasn't killing me at that point. We had just finished eating and were thinking of moving on with the evening when a couple of great looking girls came in and sat in the booth opposite us. Dave grinned wickedly at me and I rolled my eyes. Dave signalled the waiter and asked him to offer the girls drinks on us.

Both girls giggled and accepted vodka and something drinks, the waiter made his way behind the bar to get their order. Meanwhile, Dave leaned over and introduced himself.

"Hi, I'm Dave, and this ugly bugger here is Jack. I'm the eye candy of this duo, ladies." Dave winked at me and grinned back at the girls.

Chuckling, one of the girls placed her elbow on the table, her chin rested on her hand as she stared straight at me.

"Hey, ugly Jack. I'm Billie the charity case lover of our duo, so I guess your mine for the night?"

Dave shook his head and laughed heartily.

"Jeez, you have no idea what you've just let yourself in for, Billie. Jack's out of practise so you may need to help him with that as well."

I'd given Dave a what-the-fuck stare; I couldn't believe he'd just said that. I turned and addressed both girls, giving them my sexiest smile and placed my hand over Dave's mouth to silence him.

"Forgive my friend, ladies, he has no filter. What Dave means is that I have been away for a while, so he thinks I may have forgotten how to treat a lady."

Billie grinned knowingly, the banter obviously appealing to her sense of humour and I couldn't help but notice her beautiful green eyes were rimmed with a black halo. She flicked her long dark brown hair back and straightened up in her seat. My eyes were drawn to her legs as she crossed them under the table.

"Hmm, so let me see? Ugly, out of practise, and been away for a while. What can I say? I'm into ugly guys like Jack, Dave. The more out of practise the better because I love a challenge. I'm studying to be an occupational therapist so Jack here could very well be an interesting case study, I'm also a great teacher."

I was instantly drawn to the way the light danced in her eyes when she tried to look as if she were being completely serious.

Dave suddenly spat out the mouthful of beer he was drinking, he coughed and sputtered, choking from the burning alcohol that was going down the wrong pipe. He inhaled deeply trying to catch his breath. Billie's friend was out of her seat in a flash, reacting instinctively as she began slapping Dave's back between his shoulder blades with a concerned look on her face.

"Jeez, are you okay? Try to remain calm. You'll only

antagonise your bronchus if you carry on."

Dave tried to smile, embarrassed that he'd almost choked himself while trying to impress her and I lost my composure. I began to laugh uncontrollably as I invariably do when something tips me over the edge and Billie joined in, laughing with me, or because of me, I wasn't sure which.

"Sorry," I said, but when I looked at Dave's face, I was off again.

"I might be the ugly one, Dave, but at least I can swallow."

Chuckling again, I was breathless and realised that I hadn't laughed that hard in a long time. Billie turned to look at her friend with a gorgeous smile, winked, and nodded her head at Dave.

"Well that's that sorted, Michelle, he's definitely yours."

Turning to me, she smirked knowingly before informing me, "Michelle's a geriatric nurse."

All three of us erupted into a howl of laughter that brought the waiter scurrying over shushing us and gesturing at the other patrons of the restaurant. Even Dave saw the funny side but he didn't let me off with that remark.

"Fuck you, you're definitely paying for dinner after that remark."

Billie asked where we were going and Dave told her that we were on the hunt for strippers and that I was drowning my sorrows due to my ex-girlfriend being pregnant. To which I quickly added, "Not by me."

I'm not sure what happened after that but all four of us somehow ended up in the street, the girls having foregone their food to stick around with us. Even when Dave said we were heading to a strip club, neither girl was fazed by our choice of venue and were quite excited to tag along.

At first a little déjà vu hit me and I wondered if they'd had threesomes or even foursomes, if so, I'd be bowing out of that. Although, if it was a little one on one with Billie I was definitely up for breaking my duck, as they say in cricket terms, and jumping back into the game with her.

Dave grabbed Michelle's hand and dragged her behind him as he weaved his way through the tourists. His enthusiasm and sense of purpose made me smirk at Billie and I felt a little embarrassed at Dave's over-keen attitude to see women peel their clothes off in a dingy bar.

"Just for the record this isn't our usual kind of night out. I think he's trying to make me feel better by indulging in what he thinks would make him feel better if he was in my situation." I commented, trying to look suitably mortified.

Grinning back, she looked at me as if she was checking me out before giving me a sexy giggle and rolled her eyes.

"Yeah, you're way too hot to hang around strip clubs. I'd have had you pegged more for an upmarket sex club if you were into voyeurism."

"Oh I'm definitely into voyeurism. I just prefer it to be one on one if you know what I mean. I'm not exactly an exhibitionist, but not prudish about being naked either you understand." *Fuck. I'm babbling now.*

Billie stopped dead in the street, raised her eyebrow and licked her lips slowly, staring me out for a second.

"Hmm, nice thought, Jack. You naked, I mean. You certainly look like you take care of yourself. Do you work out?"

"Yoga."

"Damn! Me too. Are you into tantric sex?"

Jeez. I'd read about it, but didn't know that much apart from Sting and his wife were splashed all over the gossip mags a few years ago with stories pertaining to it.

151

"Actually never had a partner that was into yoga so it's not something I've been able to try."

"Well, Jack. Like I said, I'm a good teacher. Play your cards right, I might blow your mind tonight."

At that point I was relaxed and all the talk of sex was making me horny so, as far as I was concerned, she could blow any part of me she wanted.

By the time we reached Dave he was standing outside what looked like the trashiest, tackiest establishment in all of Soho.

Blue lights and multi-coloured plastic fringes outlined a door that led the way inside with a guy, I swear looked close to seven feet tall and the same wide, standing guard.

"Well, Jack. Here we are. This is where the fun begins. I hope you have plenty of fivers on you. Are you sure you girls are up for this?"

Billie smiled at me before turning to Dave. She smirked knowingly at him and placed her hand on his arm.

"Oh, we're definitely coming, Dave. If I have to sit through a little tit jiggling in order to teach Jack a few tricks then I'm in. You never know, I may pick up a tip or two for my own repertoire."

Winking at me, Billie pulled the plastic fringes apart and stepped into the blue lit foyer, Dave shook his head at me again.

"Like I said, I've yet to meet a woman that doesn't want to shag you, Jack. It looks like your luck is in. Pity I had to nearly choke myself to help you to get laid."

Patting Dave's back I'd grinned and followed him into the foyer thinking how lucky I was, not for getting laid, possibly, but for having Dave as my mate.

Chapter 19

Enjoying yourself

Staggering behind one another as we followed the cocktail waitress in the dimly lit strip club was funny in itself but Dave kept turning to look at me, grinned then gestured at the cocktail waitresses arse with his head. I couldn't see anything except for his purplish, white teeth and shirt collar because the light was florescent strip lighting that ran around the stage. The actual seating area was so dark. Possibly to hide how shabby and run down the place was.

Our table was next to the stage and I wasn't sure how to behave with the girls in tow. I figured I'd just be myself and if they didn't like it they were free to leave. I liked the look of Billie she seemed like a fun girl but my heart had been scorched to fuck by Rosie earlier that day so I wasn't looking for anyone to try and lay claims to it. If anything happened it would be just for fun.

We'd come in during an interval, so ordering drinks was difficult; everyone wanted the waitresses' attention. Dave ordered a bottle of tequila and the girls ordered vodka and cokes before Dave then added three double gins to the order to 'loosen me up'. I was already pretty much hammered and if I got much 'looser' I was sure I was going to be the one swinging around the pole. Funny I should have thought that because that's exactly what happened an hour later.

One of the girls on stage took a shine to me and came down to give me a lap dance. She was a skinny little blonde-haired thing, with pretty big tits and a fit body. She was wearing the one thing that screamed of sin—those horrible cheap glass stripper shoes. Anyway, she crawled towards me on her hands and knees, looking all seductive and wanton and the next thing I knew she was all over me and I was being pushed up onto the stage by Dave and Michelle.

I protested profusely because being in that place with a couple of girls was one thing, getting on stage was something else. Yet, less than two minutes later I was down to my boxers dementedly gyrating against her in an impromptu dry humping session. Completely brazen in my behaviour I got carried away in the moment. Actually it was like I didn't care about anyone or anything. I'll admit that on previous nights out with the lads I had some unruly behaviour but I'd never stooped to that before. But then again, I'd never been celibate for six months before, either.

Dave was clapping his hands thinking it was all hysterical and that's when I looked at Billie to gauge just how ridiculous I appeared to others. Billie was sitting back staring intently at me and she looked completely mesmerised. When I'd made eye contact with her I could see she was totally turned on, aroused by my simulated sex with the little stripper next to me.

Loud cheers egged us on and only got louder as soon as we'd finished. Goading remarks rang around the room and guys were pushing money in my boxers with more than one copping a feel of my dick as I fended them off with my hands. Dave stepped in eventually and told one guy in particular to, "Get the fuck off", and I blew Dave a kiss telling him not to be jealous because I was saving myself for him. Billie laughed loudly and winked sexily at me. I didn't care about anything; I was completely rat-assed drunk.

When I'd managed to focus on my wristwatch and saw it was three in the morning, I'd had enough. Dave had abandoned the strip show for the 'feel show' and was busy running his hands up and down Michelle's legs, as she perched on his lap with her tongue well and truly down his throat. I was exhausted, pretty drunk and in need of a horizontal position, but at least I felt much more in control of my heart; I was pretty numb.

Billie offered for us to go back to their place. Dave opted that we went to his because there was no way anyone was coming to mine. I wasn't ready to have another girl in my bed. The only girls that had ever been there were Lily, Cat and Rosie.

Finding a taxi wasn't easy. No cab driver in his right mind wants to take rowdy inebriated people home, but with the girls it was easier to be picked up as two couples than as two stray drunk guys.

Arriving home, Dave pulled a coin out from his pocket and placed it on his thumb ready to toss it in the air. "Heads big bed, tails little bed."

Staring at Billie to see how she reacted to Dave's question, I could see she wasn't at all put off by that or by the fact that I was stinking drunk and could barely stand. She hadn't stopped looking at me all evening and despite everything, she seemed to accept my terrible behaviour in the club with the stripper without comment.

"Take whatever bed you want, Dave. Jack and I won't be sleeping and I'll either be on top or under him so I'm not expecting to be comfortable."

I was staring at my feet and trying to remember how

to work my legs and when I heard that, I smiled slowly and glanced up at my friend. Dave tugged at Michelle's hand, almost yanking her off her feet as he half-jogged to his room.

"My bed it is then."

Sniggering, Billie turned towards me and wandered over to sit next to me on the sofa. When she'd flicked her hair back, it drew my eyes to the olive silky skin on her slender neck that was waiting to be savoured. She was incredibly hot and her directness to Dave had my dick solid, even though I'd been drinking all night. Her amazing body hadn't escaped my notice either. She was stunning and that had nothing to do with how drunk I was.

Dave's living room had great lighting and I'd thought she was a good-looking girl in the restaurant, but when I'd checked her out properly, I realised just how beautiful she was. She sat down next to me and her left leg pressed against mine. The warmth from it radiated towards mine.

My favourite feature of a woman was usually her breasts, but Billie's legs were the longest I'd ever seen, and I had a compulsion to touch them. But a part of me was worried about starting something and then not being able to satisfy her. After a six-month dry spell, I was like a pressure cooker, but her pull was so strong. I'd felt so randy and drunk and I was thinking that, if we had sex I might not last longer than a few minutes. I'd never had an issue getting it up no matter how drunk I was if the conditions were right. And the conditions were definitely right.

Reaching out, I stroked her leg with my middle finger drawing it slowly to the top of her stocking. My finger traced her soft, silky skin just under the hem of her skirt. I glanced at her face quickly to gauge the effect of my action and when her lips curved upwards in a wicked, seductive smile I was hooked.

"And?" I mirrored her smile and raised my eyebrow

156

in question to her.

Billie's brow furrowed and she shook her head slightly yet maintaining her intense stare into my eyes.

"And what?"

"And do you like a challenge?"

"I do." Staring silently for a moment she allowed her words to sink in to my drunken brain.

"And is a guy who's been celibate for the last six months and drunk as a skunk enough of a challenge to you or too much?"

Billie hummed as she pretended to ponder my question which drew my attention to her beautiful, full lips. I couldn't tear my eyes away from them. I'd wanted to kiss her so badly at that moment then realised I hadn't even kissed her. *Why hadn't I done that?* But before I could, she spoke again.

"Of course it is." She hesitated then shrugged her shoulders. "So you may need some tuning up. I get it, but I'm in no doubt you're a great screw, Jack," she added.

"And you'd know that how?"

"Watching you with that stripper had me so fucking hot for you. I almost straddled you in that flee ridden hole. How I sat there and didn't climb on stage to bitch slap that little whore up there with you is beyond me. If you work me half as well as you simulated with that little display on stage, I know I'll be leaving here with a smile on my face."

Raising my eyebrow I gave her a drunken smile as I thought back to my stage performance and how she had been watching me intensely. Maybe that was one of the reasons I'd gotten carried away. Billie turned to face me and I reached up, placing one hand on the side of her head, and pulled her head closer to me. I placed a chaste kiss on her lips before pulling back slightly, I grinned when our eyes met and she immediately kissed me back. Her tongue penetrated my mouth with an urgency that has only ever

157

been matched by Rosie as she began pulling my shirt out of my trouser waistband in an effort to slide her hand under it.

Billie was undressing me and I was pretty compliant with it. I lifted my arms and legs to free the garments when she told me to, and I dropped them again when ordered. Before I knew it, I was butt-naked whilst she was still fully dressed. I had gotten so caught up in what she was doing to me that I hadn't thought of undressing her. She didn't seem that bothered about that, because she stood up after pulling my pants off and dragged the top she was wearing over her head. I watched in awe as her braless breasts sprang free and saw electricity sparks crackling in the air from the synthetic material reacting with her hair.

She popped the button on her waistband and pulled the zipper down sliding the small skirt over her hips to expose a pair of beautiful lacy boy short panties. They were intricately designed with lacy strips in black and pink and when she turned, her arse was covered in delicate lace criss-cross bands of material that made me want to rip them off with my teeth. They fitted her perfectly as the strings of material strained gently against the paleness of her skin beneath them.

Dropping to her knees in front of me, Billie slid her hands from my knees to my groin and then glanced up at me, smiling very seductively.

"So you weren't lying, you do like to watch."

"Always."

My inaction was actually due to my inebriated state but I was more than happy for her to think that I had that much self-restraint.

Billie licked her lips as she wrapped her fingers around my dick and held me firmly in the palm of her hand. Bending forward she inspected my length closely before licking from my root to the tip. Concentrating on the glands, she swirled her tongue around and over it in superbly slow wet strokes.

As much as I'd wanted to watch, my eyes rolled back into my head and I fell against the back of the sofa. I'd let a small growl fall from my mouth as I basked in the delicious sensation of a woman's tongue on the most intimate and sensitive area of my body for the first time in six months.

Needless to say, I was a two-minute wonder but Billie was relaxed about it and had told me afterwards that she'd expected it from someone in my position. I was embarrassed to say that I fell asleep within seconds of shooting my load all over her face as well. I didn't know how long I was out but when I woke up she was lying on the floor masturbating without any trace of shame on her face at being caught.

I smiled because I was enjoying the view and when her eyes met mine, I couldn't hold back from commenting.

"Ah, are you enjoying yourself down there?"

Billie grabbed her breast and squeezed it tightly still trying to get herself off.

"So are you still watching or are you going to get down and dirty with me."

My dick was semi interested again and I really wanted to taste her so I crawled to the floor and in between her legs.

"Sorry I'm a gentleman, just a little out of practice," I said.

I grabbed her legs and opened them further so I could stare at her swollen pussy, mesmerised by the way her finger was still moving back and forth on her clitoris.

"You're forgiven," she said.

I dipped my head and nudged her hand out of the way with my nose. A gasp of pleasure escaped her chest when my tongue stroked her wet seam.

"Oh, God, yeah, do that," she commanded.

I'd lifted my head to look at her and she had a sexy

frustrated look on her face that registered in my brain, then my dick a millisecond later. I teased her slowly and enjoyed how her arse bucked and squirmed in my hands until I was fucking her with my tongue. What started out as, "Oh yeah…do that," quickly became, "Oh fuck, that is sooooo good. Damn! You're so fucking good at this." Eventually the vocals became one continuous scream and I knew there and then, despite all my time away, I hadn't lost my touch.

Billie rolled over and reached for her little black handbag. She began rifling through it until she produced a red and silver foil packet.

"Here," she said, throwing it at me in a hurried gesture.

Without another word, I ripped the pack with my teeth, took out the condom and quickly rolled it down my dick. Having a barrier down there felt very weird after all that time and for the first time that night, I hesitated about being with another girl when Rosie was the one I wanted. I had to make myself remember that she didn't want me anymore so I had nothing to lose. Billie looked at me and grinned when I grabbed her by her legs and yanked her closer up my thighs so that my dick was at her entrance.

"All right Jack let's find out what you have in the sack."

Chapter 20

Early shift

I was conscious someone was watching me, my eyes darted open and I stretched out on the floor to see Michelle leaning over me trying to reach Billie. She grabbed her shoulder and began shaking her awake.

"Billie, come on, you're going to be late for your shift," she called in an urgent tone.

Billie groaned, rolled over and pulled the single duvet up around her chin. I'd huddled closer glad I'd grabbed the cover from the spare room for us at some point in the night.

"Fuck off, Michelle, I'm not moving. I can't move. Jack here had a steep learning curve that jolted his memory and broke his vow of celibacy last night. Once he got going there was no stopping him. I'm sore, call me in sick and it's still dark so it must be stupid o'clock."

Michelle gave out an evil chuckle and towered over the top of us, she then tried to pull the duvet away but I grabbed it. I clutched it tightly just before she exposed my dick. Giving her an angry glare in the dark room because she was disrupting my recovery time, I mumbled to Billie that she should go home with her friend because I was exhausted.

Billie and I had given each other quite a work out and I was tempted to say I'd fucked myself sober, but that would be a lie because I still felt dizzy when I eventually lay down. Both of us demonstrated our stamina thanks to our yoga lessons but it was a fun sloppy session and without going into the details, I think it was safe to say that we both really enjoyed ourselves.

"Billie what did you say to me before we went out last night? 'Don't let me stay out. Don't let me get hung up on some guy to the point where I miss my shift. I really can't miss this, no matter what I say drag me the fuck home because I really need to go to work tomorrow'."

Wandering around me to get to Billie she crouched down and suddenly flung the duvet away from her body, smacking her arse hard. Billie jumped to her feet and shoved Michelle backwards on to the couch.

"Fuck! All right, all right, give me a minute. I'm coming."

Standing naked in the dark with her hand on her head, I could see that Billie was still half asleep and confused, trying to pull herself together.

I chuckled at her annoyance and frustration, it was the same frustrated tone I'd heard when I'd found her masturbating. I rolled over on the floor and stretched out again before I turned my head in Michelle's direction.

"You may have to hang around a while she said she was coming a lot to me last night as well."

Billie's posture relaxed and she laughed then swiped her skirt off the floor and waved it in front of her before stepping into it, pulling it over her hips and fastening it. Straightening up she flicked her hair behind her shoulders and picked up her top, turning it the right way out.

"Yeah at least I could say give me a minute Jack," she chided back.

Smiling sheepishly I knew Billie was referring to the two minute blow she gave me. Although I'd have to give myself some credit, six months without sex and being drunk, one night was still all it took to get my mojo back.

Three minutes later Billie knelt down beside me and gave me what I can only describe as a tongue flossing. Her tongue swept my teeth from top to bottom before she tried to wedge it at the back of my throat. When she eventually pulled away I was breathless. She stood grinning above me while under the duvet my morning wood could probably have withstood a category five hurricane.

"Thanks for an epic night, Jack. It was awesome. Take care."

With that, Michelle turned and left the room followed by Billie. Neither of them looked back. Dave came into the living room when he heard the door to his apartment close and climbed onto the sofa pulling the duvet off of me as he went passed. I sat up in the semi-darkness with only the light from the hallway and shivered when the cold air hit me.

"Nice girls, eh? Did you get Billie's number?"

Sitting naked, I rubbed my arms to get warm.

"Not looking to get into anything, Dave, that was just a bit of fun last night, she felt the same, I think. My head's not on straight, it's Rosie that's in here." I said tapping my temple.

"Fuck it's freezing. Give me that back," I said trying to grab the duvet, but Dave held on tightly yawned and snuggled himself further into the duvet.

"Nope you need to go home and get some work done before you leave for the festival in a couple of days. I have to get up for work in ten minutes. You can have the shower first."

He was right. I should have been doing research and I still had to speak with Lily about Rick Fars and her own band, not to mention Alfie's band, Crakt Soundzz. I wasn't sure I had the energy for any of it and even though I'd been home only a day or two, I was already worn out. Lily was in California the previous night so I knew that if I got home then, she'd be just finishing her day and I could probably catch her before she went to bed. I did as Dave suggested and went home.

As soon as I pushed my apartment door closed I headed over to my desk, fired up my laptop, and then walked to the fridge. I grabbed some bagels and cream cheese before heading back and began my Skype call to Lily. When the call connected it was Alfie's face that lit up the screen.

"Ouch! That's assault seeing that ugly face this time in the morning. I don't know how Lily does it every day. The girl deserves a medal for waking up to you all the time."

Alfie smirked and gave me a lopsided grin before lying back on the bed looking relaxed and naked from the waist up. I wasn't that keen on tattoos, except maybe Lily's, but his looked right on his body.

"Tell me you've got boxers on at least, I'm not having a naked conversation with you. I'd have to write about it. Lily's a saint I tell you, having to look at your ugly face and body," I added.

Alfie was probably one of the best looking guys in the world. Not my opinion but those of the polls done regularly worldwide by the gossip magazines, but it did him good to get some shit at times.

"Anyone ever tell you that jealously is a curse, Jack? You'd love to be me. Pity you can't play the guitar and sing, 'cause you're almost hot enough to be in my band. I seem to remember that you did have some groupie skills though." Alfie sniggered at the memory of my antics during Rick's after party. *I was never going to live that down.*

"Where is my little hottie? Put her on, I'm fed up

looking at your ugly mug I want to speak to my girl."

"*My* woman is in the shower in *my* favourite state, naked, wet and all *mine!* You need to start getting your head around that, Jack," Alfie goaded, bringing his face closer to the screen as he grinned devilishly at me.

Lily's voice interrupted our conversation.

"What did I tell you two about playing nicely when I'm not in the room?"

Lily perched herself on the bed beside Alfie dressed in a bathrobe, her hair was hidden by a towel turban. Smiling widely, she pulled the laptop away from Alfie and wandered over to the chair leaving Alfie sitting naked on the bed behind her.

"She's mine now, Alfie." I called out to annoy him and Lily smirked at the screen.

"Stop it, Jack."

Alfie threw two fingers up at me in the distance and I couldn't help but reply again.

"Oh, very grown up, Alfie. Put those fingers away and get some boxers on, I don't want to see your todger while I'm talking to my lovely friend here."

Lily was giggling and turned to look at Alfie then back at the screen with wide eyes.

"Oh god, can you see him behind me?"

"Indeed and he's fucking traumatising me here."

Lily giggled again and Alfie got off the bed and wandered right up to the screen still naked.

"Good. Have a good look at what a man looks like, Jack. Best get down to the doctors' office to see what they can do for you. I hear they have all sorts of solutions for guys like you these days."

I couldn't help but chuckle at him at that point. It was just banter between us now, but at one time I'd really wound him up about Lily and I was determined not to do that anymore. Especially now that I understood how it must have felt for him to have me constantly making suggestive comments to her. A little remark here or there was okay but I knew where to stop.

Alfie wandered out of the shot and I could hear him laughing while Lily shook her head looking mortified that Alfie had shaken his dick at me like that.

"Boys. Stop it!"

Alfie wandered back with some jeans on that time and was in the process of pulling a t-shirt over his head.

"I'm off along the corridor to talk with Andy for a while. When you two get together you forget I'm in the room anyway."

Lily shrugged her shoulders but nodded in agreement. I didn't say anything, not wanting to encourage her, so I waited in silence for Alfie to leave the room. When the door closed Lily turned back to the screen.

"So…did you take my advice about Rosie?"

Lily had a bee in her bonnet and it was all she wanted to talk about since I had come back.

"No, but I saw her anyway."

Lily looked worried, "And?"

"I bumped into her at Bar45 and oh yeah, talking about bumps, she's pregnant."

"You talked about that? What did she say?"

"You knew?" I stared wide-eyed at the screen that she hadn't thought to mention it to me.

Lily looked shocked by her slip and I'd instantly became annoyed that she knew and hadn't said anything to me, but there was no point in getting in a state about it. The situation wasn't Lily's fault either.

"We're done. Rosie's with someone else and she's having a baby."

Lily seemed to struggle for a minute then pulled the towel off of her head and leaned in.

"Rosie told you she's with someone else?"

"She didn't have to, I went into Bar45 and she was sitting waiting for him. She seemed to accept everything he said to me and they pretty much told me to back off. What is there to talk about anyway? I think it's pretty final that she's moved on, Lily. Stop trying to play matchmaker. It sucks. I had my chance and I blew it. Pity it took going to a mountain in Spain to realise I'd already had what I wanted and it was too late. I keep thinking maybe I should have come back after a couple of weeks and spoken to her. Maybe she wouldn't have met him at that point. Maybe I could have salvaged our relationship."

"Oh my God, Jack. You really love her don't you?"

Lily's exclamation reminded me that she didn't know and that I hadn't discussed some of the thoughts and feelings I'd had during my time away.

She sighed wearily and spoke in a concerned tone, "I'm coming over to see you. I have Wednesday, Thursday and Friday off this week. Where will you be?"

Excitement flooded my veins, but it was quickly replaced by disappointment when I'd remembered I was working and I wouldn't be around to spend time with her.

"I'm covering the festival, Lily. I'll be working all weekend and apart from that it's ridiculous to fly for ten hours to arrive sometime on Wednesday then spend one whole day here on Thursday and fly back on Friday."

"What's ridiculous is my friend is hurting and I can't be there. I'm coming. When do you have to leave for the festival?"

"Don't. I'm going on Thursday and I'm staying at the Hilton in Leeds with Rick and the rest of the guys. I have a job to do, sweetheart, and the boss expects results. I've been off gallivanting in Spain for so long I need to re-establish myself there."

"I'll call Rick. He told me last week that he's flying into London on Wednesday night. I'll catch a ride over with him."

No matter what I'd said Lily wasn't going to be put off and it had been a long time since we'd seen each other.

Six months and four days to be precise, but I didn't want to see her at all if she was only coming over to talk about Rosie. There was no point in talking about her anymore. No matter how I'd felt, it was too late and I had nothing else to say on the subject. Our call lasted another hour while Lily filled me in on all the music deals and plans she knew about.

Alfie came back and told me he needed some time alone with 'his woman' making a point of emphasising that she was his. To be honest, I was grateful that he let me speak to her at all given that their time together was pretty precious. I thanked him for being a mate and letting us catch up properly before hanging up.

Chapter 21

Detour

Productive and informative would be the best way to describe the rest of my day after talking to Lily. She'd given me a head start on everything that was current and I did some research to fill in the blanks. By about four that afternoon I was ready for my assignment, so I switched off my computer and slid my office chair back. I was starving and in need of some comfort food. I grabbed my jacket and keys and headed down to the basement car park.

Slipping behind the wheel of my car, I headed out to my parent's place on the outskirts of London. By the time I'd got there I was ready to see them. The sound of my parent's gravel driveway was one of the main things I remembered as a child, and as soon as it crunched under my tires my mum threw the front door open and came rushing out to meet me.

"Jack! Oh, Jack. It's great to see you. You look wonderful, darling." She exclaimed as she flung her arms around me and pulled me in for a hug. The familiar smell and touch brought me instant comfort.

Five hours and two meals later my parents and I were

relaxing in their drawing room and I filled them in on almost every part of my journey of self-discovery. My mum asked me if I had heard from Rosie and I told them that she had found someone else. I didn't discuss my own feelings about that because I knew my parents missed her too; they'd loved Rosie.

Sometimes I used to feel like they were too involved in my business, but as I matured I've realised their worries were born out of love and not the need to control me. I had long since accepted their need for information about me.

It was getting late and they were pressing me to stay the night, but I had to get home. I had put a call into Rick Fars' PA and was waiting for him to get back to me at five the following morning.

As I was driving home I found myself taking a detour past Rosie's place and saw that her light was still on. Rosie's first floor apartment had floor to ceiling picture windows and she never bothered to close the curtains. I could see her clearly as she sat in a chair near her open window, her legs curled underneath her as she read a book. I cut the car engine and sat across the street to watch her.

Sitting motionless, she looked deep in concentration and my heart ached for her. I really wanted to tell her how I felt, but it would be wrong of me to do that now she was finally happy. A sudden wave of emotion caused a huge lump to form in my throat that almost choked me and I swallowed it back down. I was once the man in her life but I wasn't anymore.

Angry feelings began to bubble up from the depths of my stomach and I found myself incredibly jealous of the guy who got to hold my Rosie in his arms. She should have been mine. After a while I turned the engine back on, wallowing wasn't going to change anything. I glanced up at her one last time then headed home.

I'd like to say I slept that night but I didn't. When my grandfather died, I had the same kind of feeling in my heart as I did about Rosie. It was like my heart had constricted but my brain hadn't told it to expand again and I needed something to release the pressure. I was mourning my loss and although I had accepted she was no longer mine, I knew I would never be the same without her. I'd just have to figure out a different kind of normal in my life.

In the morning, Rick Fars' Personal Assistant called me right on time and asked me to meet him at the hotel at five the following evening. There were a few things Rick wanted to talk to me about before the festival, as an exclusive for me, and he also wanted to catch up with me and Lily. She'd spoken to him about tagging along and he was apparently excited to see her. Not as excited as me, I'd bet.

During my final preparations for my work assignment that evening, the image of Rosie's face looking back at me as she left the bar tugged at my heart. A part of me wondered if I only wanted her because we weren't together any more, but considering the way that my heart felt, I doubted that.

Finally, I gave up working. I was as ready as I'd ever be. I was only trying to keep myself busy. Closing my laptop down, I rubbed my eyes with my thumb and forefinger and headed to the bathroom to prepare for bed. When I'd slid between the sheets, I hoped sleep would take over quickly, but once again, that didn't happen.

Rick called me during the night and I was barely coherent so he kept what he wanted to say brief and I went back to bed. I woke again and thought I'd dreamed it. I lay wondering if the call had taken place. Eventually I fell asleep again.

I was awakened by my phone ringing and it was daylight. I squinted at the screen and saw Lily's face. Swiping it to answer, her excited voice made me instantly alert.

"Well am I going to stand out here all morning, Jack? I've been ringing your door bell for ages!"

Throwing back the duvet, I was half way down the hall before I realised that I was still naked. I grabbed a towel from the bathroom and wrapped it around me before opening the door.

Lily flung her arms around me and squeezed me so tight I struggled to breathe.

"Oh, God this feels incredible. I missed you so much, Jack. Don't ever do that to me again. Don't leave me without being able to reach you."

Her hug was fierce but she felt perfectly familiar to me. Being at my parents the day before had been great, but I had still felt tense. I could feel the last of the stress and tension leave my body in that hug.

I let Lily in and then went to my room to get ready. Once I was dressed I walked into the kitchen where she was making coffee. She'd found some fruit and croissants and had laid out jam, butter and my favourite, chocolate spread.

"Wow, Lily. Since when did you become so domesticated?"

"Since my neglected friend needed some TLC," she replied looking pleased with herself and sitting down at the table.

Wandering around to her, I kissed the top of her head and slipped into the seat beside her still grinning at her beautiful face.

"I need to talk to you, Jack."

Lily's face became very serious and took on an ashen appearance. I could tell immediately that whatever she needed to get off her chest was huge. Reaching out, I took her hand in both of mine and brought them to my lips kissing her fingers in reassurance. Lily's beautiful blue almond shaped eyes filled with tears. I hated seeing her sad face. My gut twisted as she visibly struggled to tell me what was wrong.

"Whatever it is, it's okay, Lily. Take your time." I held my breath while she gathered her thoughts.

Lily swallowed audibly, her eyes searched my face for a little longer than was comfortable before she sighed heavily.

"You're going to hate me, Jack."

My response was immediate. "I could never hate you. What's happened? Did you have an affair or something?"

Lily's eyes went wide as a look of horror registered on her face.

"Of course not," she exclaimed hurriedly and I sighed with relief.

"It's Rosie."

My heart sped at the mention of Rosie as did my temper, and I wondered what was wrong and why Lily was so fixated about her that she had to mention her all the time?

Anything I said would open wounds and now that Lily was in front of me I was sure to break down. So I just stared blankly at her and said nothing while I waited for her to speak. It was different talking to her on skype and then sucking it up and dealing with it in front of everyone else. But Lily knew me better than anyone and she knew that giving my heart to someone wasn't something that was going to happen a lot in my life.

"I've been a terrible friend. I *am* a terrible friend."

"Fuck, Lily. Spit it out, you're killing me here."

Pushing my chair back I'd stood and paced back and forth in front of her, raking my hands through my hair.

"The baby's yours, Jack. Rosie's baby is your baby."

Shocked wasn't the word I'd use to describe my reaction as I froze on the spot. All I could do was search Lily's worried face as she stared back at me. I was speechless. My mind raced around in circles. How could it be at all possible that it was mine? Based on her appearance she wasn't far enough along. Then another thought overrode the first one. If there was a remote possibility the baby she was carrying *was* mine, both Rosie and Lily had betrayed me by not telling me.

In a startled, jerky movement, I shook my head and began to pace my kitchen floor again, raking both hands through my hair once again and then shoving them deeply into my pockets. Hurriedly, I started doing the maths and concluded I hadn't had sex with Rosie for six months and twenty three days. I knew that because the last time we had sex was Drew's birthday.

"Lily, you've got this wrong. I was gone at least a month before she got pregnant, she can't be any more than five months gone, I wasn't even here then."

"Jack, remember when I went to lunch with her that day? She told me then. I wanted to tell you but she swore me to secrecy."

"You knew? You fucking knew? You never thought that your best friend might like to know that his ex-girlfriend was pregnant and he was skipping town? What the fuck, Lily? What the hell am I to you? Are you fucking serious, you did that to me?"

Rage coursed through my body and I swiped the plate of croissants off the table, sending it crashing to the tiled floor, shattering it into tiny pieces. Lily jumped in her seat, her back straightening as tears began to roll down her face. That made me even angrier.

"No use fucking crying this time, Lily. I'm not fucking comforting you. How could *you* do that to *me*? You are supposed to be *my* friend. *My* fucking friend. If there is any possibility that I am that baby's father I'd do everything and anything to support it but you have no idea how fucking crazy I feel right now. Who are you both to deny that child its true father? I can't fucking believe you let me go away knowing this and you kept it from me. Why the fuck did you do that, Lily?"

"Jack, she wasn't even going to tell me. When I met her for lunch she was acting weirdly. I couldn't put my finger on it but something was off. Every time I spoke about you she almost burst into tears, but I thought that was just…"

I interrupted her, my tone was clipped as I bit back the seething feeling that was threatening to tear out of my throat. I was incensed that she'd taken a decision not to share information about me that was so massively important.

"Save it. I'm not fucking interested in your excuses. This is a child's life, Lily. Maybe *my* child's life and you kept it from me. That's fucking monumental in my book. Who the fuck are you? I mean where did the girl go who had principles, morals? Your lifestyle has fucked with your sense of reason and decency, Lily."

Lily stood with tears streaming down her face and for the first time in all the time I'd known her, I couldn't stand the sight of her.

"You need to leave."

"Jack. Stop."

"No, you stop. You fucking stop. Out. I want you out of here. I have no fucking idea how you justified in your head that it was okay not to tell me. Even if that baby isn't mine, I had the right to know of its existence."

Lily was sobbing but I was already heading for the front door. Opening it, I turned to see her still standing in the doorway of the kitchen.

"Get the fuck out, Lily. If you don't go then I'm going."

Lily walked slowly down the hall hugging herself. She looked pathetic.

"Jack I know you're upset…"

"Upset? Up-fucking-set? Oh I'm more than upset, Lily. I'm fucking livid. You need to get out of here before I say something the both of us can't recover from. What a shitty thing to do to me, Lily Parnell. We're done. I want nothing more to do with you."

A strangled sob tore from her chest and for the first time, I felt nothing. I was drowning, my lungs weren't expanding and the pressure in my head felt like it was preventing me from seeing anything other than red mist.

Lily stepped over the threshold and turned to give me a pleading look. I vaguely saw her draw in a deep breath but I swung the door and it banged shut in her face. *With friends like her who needs enemies?* How I felt about Lily was immaterial. I had reasonable cause to speak to Rosie and I was definitely not leaving until I'd had my say and got some answers. Passing the mirror I noticed my cheeks were flame red with anger. All the prompting Lily had done about speaking to Rosie made sense now, but Lily had definitely done the wrong thing in my opinion.

Chapter 22

Futile

My rage built inside the more I'd thought about it and I began gathering my keys and wallet. I had to know what the deal was. I was furious that I had been excluded from knowing there was the potential I could be the father of Rosie's baby, and Lily and Rosie had kept that from me. I drove like a bat out of hell and knew I was going too fast but I had to confront Rosie straight away. I'd seen Rosie for myself and she didn't look far enough along for the baby to be mine, but if she'd said that to Lily then she had to have thought it in the first place.

It was still only quarter to nine, but I didn't care when the most appropriate time for waking a pregnant woman was. Taking her steps three at a time, I rang her apartment bell, holding my finger on it until I saw her shadow walk towards the door.

Cracking the door open slightly, Rosie's face peered round it, her eyes going wide with shock when she saw it was me. She made to close the door but my foot was in the way.

"Wait. We need to talk," I said, a little breathlessly as

the oxygen deficit caught up with me. Rosie pushed the door hard in her effort to shut me out.

"Jack, I have nothing to say to you. Go home."

I pushed back harder but was careful considering her condition.

"Rosie, I'm not going away until we've talked. You may have nothing to say but please let me come in. Give me ten minutes and if you want me to leave then, I'm gone. No arguments."

Rosie relaxed her weight from the door, turned and began walking down the hallway and then into her kitchen. From behind, she was the same sexy Rosie and didn't look pregnant at all. Maybe it was wrong to think like that at that moment but I wasn't really in control of my thoughts. I followed behind her cautiously peering in each room as I passed for signs that her boyfriend was around. I was relieved when I found nothing to suggest he was there.

Rosie walked over to the sink and leaned her arse against it before folding her arms. Her lips were pursed in anger, but the fire in her eyes made her look even more beautiful.

"Say what you want to say, Jack, then leave me alone," she spat, throwing one arm in my direction.

The pressure I'd felt to get what I wanted to say right was insurmountable. I was scared to open my mouth in case I fucked up the moment where we were actually in the same space and I had my one chance to say everything I wanted to tell her. More importantly, she should have heard from me six months ago.

"How far along are you? I mean when is your due date? I mean..." *Fuck.*

I didn't know what I meant. I sighed and sat down at her kitchen table.

"Listen, Rosie, we need to talk. Not like this..." I gestured between us because she was still standing in a hostile pose and I thought she was going to erupt any second.

"It's not yours. If that's what you're asking."

Is she lying? Rosie couldn't look me in the eye and her head dropped to look at her chest, her teeth biting the side of her cheek. *Is she biting back a lie?*

"I never asked if it was. So why would you feel the need to say that? Unless you think that it may be mine?"

I was trying desperately to keep calm and control my temper because I knew I'd get nothing if I acted volatile.

"I guess you did the maths, Rosie. When Lily told me, I did it myself and there's a small chance it *is* mine. But that's not why I'm here. Well it is." *Damn, I'm ruining this.*

Gone was the quick-witted music reporter who could talk his way into and out of anything, in his place sat an inept arsehole of an ex who was waiting to see if his past was going to catch up with him. Well that's how it may have looked from Rosie's perspective.

"Rosie, I don't care about the baby. No…I do. That's not what I mean. Let me start again. If it isn't min;, whose baby is it? Is it a boy or a girl? God, if it's mine I want to help you."

Rosie glared angrily at me and I could see how hard she was fighting to stay in control of her emotions. It was clear that she was upset, her knee bobbed nervously on her bent leg as her arms unfolded to reach back on either side of the sink for support. Blood had begun to drain from her hands with the pressure she was exerting on them and her stance screamed tension. Clasping my hands in a praying gesture I tried again.

"Please, Rosie. I didn't plan what I was going to say this morning. I'm going to talk, please just listen and I'll leave. If you don't want to hear from me again, I'll respect your decision. Just let me talk."

Shrugging her shoulders, Rosie waved a hand out in front of her for me to continue. She pushed off of the sink and walked over to sit in the chair furthest away from me before chewing the side of her mouth again as she stared nervously at me.

"Rosie, I was wrong. I was so wrong about giving you up. I had no idea what a dickhead I had been to you when we were together. This here..." I waved my finger between us, "This is our one opportunity to take stock of everything we were to each other. I love you, Rosie. I'm not saying that because you're pregnant and there's a chance that baby is mine. I'm saying it because you deserve to hear it. It's the truth."

For the second time that morning I made a woman cry. The difference that time was that I felt every tear she shed. It was as if each tear was shredding my heart. My voice cracked with emotion and Rosie's eyes flicked to my mouth before returning to my eyes. I watched her swallow and then continued.

"Sweetheart, I love you. I am *in* love with you. I don't know what else to say other than I'm so sorry I walked away. I had to step away to realise what I had. What *we* had. I'm so sorry that I hurt you so badly. It took being away from everything for me to understand just what was important to me; who was important to me. All the time I was with you I was looking for something. Being away from you made me realise that all that time I was looking, I was looking for *you* even though you were right in front of me. I didn't realise it was that we were meant to be together."

Rosie pushed herself to stand and stared down at me as she dried her tears on her sleeve, her face was blotchy. When she spoke she was so calm it was scary.

"Apology accepted, Jack, but I don't want you back."

"So that's it, Rosie, nothing else to say?" I shrugged thinking Rosie would never be this callous.

Rosie nodded. "Yes, actually, when we were together all I wanted was for us to mean everything to each other.

But I found myself searching too, Jack. Searching for the moment when you would notice *me*, I mean *really* notice me like your world had suddenly turned upside down, like mine did the first time you kissed me."

Rosie stared straight through me and drew a long shuddery breath, "You were the one man I thought would treat me right, Jack. Looking back, I don't believe you did, but I stayed with you because I thought, or hoped, that in time you would find in me what I believed I had found in you. For over a year that didn't happen. I gave my heart to you. You just didn't know what to do with it. So in the time you were away, guess what? I took it back."

Hearing Rosie put our relationship and how I had treated her into words was excruciatingly painful. My heart was crushed and I was disgusted at myself. Rosie had been feeling exactly what I'd been feeling and I never knew. The difference was she knew it was because of me. I was the one that wouldn't take us to the next level, the one holding us back and I didn't do anything to help matters. I was questioning the meaning of us when the explanation was right there, I should have understood what she was to me. Rosie was right. She wasn't allowed to be happy because of me.

"Sorry. Jesus, I'm sorry." I whispered huskily.

My hands reached out automatically as I pulled her into a hug before I'd even thought about what I was doing. Rosie was stiff in my arms and I recognised I was taking a hug rather than her volunteering one so I stepped away to a safe distance.

"Rosie, I know my timing sucks but I need to tell you this. Not to be selfish, but just so that you know. It's *you*. You were right. My heart *is* yours whether you take it or not. I'm sorry I'm doing this now, but I need you to understand that my heart burns for you. It's a horrible feeling but I know why now. It's you I'm supposed to be with."

Rosie started to walk past me without acknowledging anything I had said and made for the door. Pulling it open she stood and swept her hand towards the corridor outside.

"Too little, too late, Jack. Obviously things have moved forwards for me. While you were working out who the lucky girl was, she moved on."

Rubbing her bump she commented, "Stewart thinks I'm supposed to be with him too. Funny thing is, it only took him a month to figure that out and this baby? He doesn't care who the father is because he loves *me*. He's excited for her to come and I know without a shadow of a doubt that he's going to be an amazing father. I love him, Jack, really love him."

Shifting on her feet impatiently, Rosie tried to get me to leave again.

"Thanks for coming, Jack, the baby isn't yours. She was conceived two weeks after the last time we shared a bed. Ultrasound scans can date conception to the day. She's the result of a one night stand I had with a colleague from work when he was consoling me about losing you."

I was completely gutted. Somewhere in my subconscious, I had accepted I was going to be a father and Rosie had just dispelled all of that.

"Why did you tell Lily it was mine?"

Rosie nodded slowly in thought and shrugged confirming that she had indeed told Lily.

"I thought it was yours until they did an early scan to date her, but you're not. Personally I'm glad she's not yours, Jack. You're not ready to be a father. I love Stewart and I'm not going to hurt him because you've come back on a whim. I love you, Jack. I'll always love you but I'm not *in* love with you anymore. Stewart and this baby are my life now, I'm happy." Rosie rubbed her bump again as she shifted her weight from one leg to the other.

Clearly expressing her own wishes, Rosie blew me off. No matter how much I loved her, she'd explicitly told me that she no longer felt the same about me. I could have thrown myself on the floor and begged her for a second chance, but she was carrying another man's baby and was in love with someone else. What else could I say?

I stepped out of her doorway without another word as she quietly closed it behind me. I could hear her crying softly in her hallway and my initial reaction was that I wanted to break down the door, but I sucked it up and headed back to my car. In just one day I'd been betrayed by my best friend, struggled with the possibility of being a father, and had the girl I'd finally given my heart to, reject me. Sliding behind the wheel I sat staring at it for a few minutes, feeling numb before realising that was probably the last time I'd ever see Rosie.

Turning the key in the ignition, I looked over my shoulder then aggressively pushed the stick into reverse, driving back sharply to make room for me to get out of the space. Selecting drive on the automatic gear sticks I drove out into the flow of the morning traffic, my screeching tyres echoed in the street and I saw Rosie watching from the window in my rear view mirror. *Fuck, time to move on Jack.*

I parked the car and went upstairs to pack a bag before starting my journey to Leeds and the festival. When I'd got to the hotel, I asked for a room under a pseudonym because I didn't want Lily finding out where I was. If I saw her, I was likely to destroy our friendship with the way I was feeling.

As far as Rick was concerned, I was checked into the room his team had arranged for me but I had no intention of sleeping in there. Lily would be gone in a day, so all I had to do was do what I got paid for and spend time with Rick in a professional capacity. After that I'd have to be clever with avoiding her until she flew back to California. I had nothing to say to her that was of any value.

Chapter 23

Avoidance

Clearing security on Rick's floor, I'd had to endure the same banter yet again about my after party behaviour from the band. I was tempted to do something else that time, if there was an after party, just so that they would change their tune about me. That particular joke was getting old or maybe I was just in the mood to punch someone into next week after my conversations with Lily and Rosie.

Entering the suite Rick provided for me at the hotel, I threw my leather weekend bag on the sofa and headed straight to the mini-bar. I quickly snapped the lid on two miniature bottles of gin and a bottle of tonic water. I made myself a long drink and plugged in my laptop to make sure it was fully charged. Kicking off my shoes, I sat on the bed with my back to the headboard and began to read the other reporter's coverage from the lead up to the festival event.

It was amazing how much leg work the internet saved me. All I had to do was collate all the other reporters' bits and pieces and verify a few of their comments and I was up to speed. Twenty minutes after I'd arrived, Cobham

Street's PA, Paul called.

"Jack? Are you all set? Rick wants to talk in ten minutes. Please come to the suite, he's expecting you."

"Is Lily with him?" I wasn't really in a position to place demands on anybody but I had to ask because I didn't want to see her.

"No she's at her parent's right now. She's arriving at seven forty five for dinner."

Immediately my jaw went tight at the thought of her and I began seething all over again that she had chosen to be loyal to Rosie over me. I was determined not to see her that weekend, I really didn't care if she'd flown over especially; it was, afterall, only to tell me something she should have six months ago.

Ten minutes later I had freshened up and was walking into Rick's suite, he was sitting on the sofa with a glass of whiskey and a smug smirk on his face as I walked passed his security.

"Holy fuck, Jack. What have you done to yourself?" Rick commented with a surprised look on his face as he walked around me studying my new look.

"You're not half as ugly as the last time I saw you, love the longer hair. In fact, I'd say you have a hot rock star look about you. It's good to see you, dude. I thought you had died when they sent that pimply teenager in your place a couple of months back, but then I never got an invite to the Jack Cunningham Memorial Service so I figured you were still alive. The next assumption I made was that you'd been sacked for your promiscuous behaviour during some after party event or other."

"Nah, I had post-traumatic stress from interviewing these fucked-up rock stars who were catching all sorts from bed-hopping and trying to pass it off as a starch rash. They kept waving their dicks in my face whenever they got the opportunity, Rick."

Rick threw his head back, arching his back as he

laughed loudly before he gestured at the sofa offering me a seat.

"See, Jack, I fucking missed you. Do you know how tiring it gets hearing everyone telling you how wonderful you are all the time?

"All the time." I said like it happened to me as well.

Chuckling again, he leaned over and clamped his hand on my knee, squeezing it and making me jump.

"Jack Cunningham, seriously dude, I fucking missed you."

When Rick said it for the second time I started to feel good about myself for the first time that day. He was one of the world's biggest rock stars and yet he had always remembered me even though we'd first met at the start of his career. I had no idea how he did that. He was very personable to the people he liked and I was grateful that, although we were becoming friends and I loved the banter between us, we were able to keep our 'professional hats' on when I interviewed him.

Rick quickly changed tact and suddenly we were discussing his work and the band's new direction. I guessed I had begun to ask questions that were more in depth and technical than what he was used to because suddenly his expression changed.

"Damn, Jack! This is fucking refreshing. I've never been asked these questions before. You've been doing your homework or I'd swear you were an accomplished musician with the stuff your testing me with here."

I smirked knowingly because that was exactly the kind of reaction I'd dreamed about from someone like him. Even a reaction from someone like Lily who knew me well would have been amazing after everything I'd worked for during those months of study. The five months of sixteen hour days playing music was pretty intense and considering Rick's response, it had obviously paid off.

"Let's just say I know more than you'd ever give me

credit for." I responded, smiling wickedly.

"Fuck, do you play an instrument? I've never really thought about it, Jack. You growing up with Lily n'all, I've never thought to ask before," Rick drawled in his thick American accent, still staring incredulously at me.

At first I wasn't sure what to tell him but then I decided I wanted to keep the mystery going a little longer.

"We're not all glory hounds, Rick. I've just never felt the need to share my talent with the world like you. Anyway, you're older than me and I'd hate to deprive you of a living when you're so near pension age."

Laughing hysterically at my reply he turned and patted my back.

"So, Jack. Do you want to come on a short tour with us? Document us for posterity? It'll be late September until mid-November, what do you say? You want in?"

Of course I did. Who wouldn't give anything to go on tour with a band like Cobham Street? Dave was going to bust a gut when I told him because he worshipped the ground Cobham Street walked on.

"Depends. Do I have to listen to the after party episode from your crew again? Because I am so fucking sick of hearing about it. It was one night. One night, Rick and it's been on repeat for about two years now."

Rick chuckled and shook his head, glancing sideways at me.

"Fuck, Jack. It was classic, dude. There was just no regard for anyone around you. We've all done some stupid things, but Jesus, we're the ones known for doing wild things and there you were supposed to be reporting on us, but were giving us a sexual exhibition instead."

I glanced sheepishly, still a little embarrassed about my drunken frolic.

"What can I say? I got carried away. Are you sure one of your guys didn't slip the reporter something in his drink so you could have a hold over me?"

Rick scratched his chin in jest pretending he was thinking about that.

"Hmm, now there's a thought. Anyway, you've survived with your career intact and that's what I love about you, Jack. Fall into a barrel of thumbs you come out sucking a tit."

We both started laughing, that may have been true to some extent before but it wasn't how it was anymore. My conversation with Rosie earlier taught me that. After a few more questions we concluded our interview and as soon as we did, Rick mentioned Lily.

"I hear you and Lily have had a disagreement. Did hell freeze over and no one informed me?" Rick eyed me suspiciously, telling me he knew more than he was giving away.

"Well, Rick, I figure if you know that much then you'll know exactly why I'm pissed off. You'd be the same if the circumstances were like mine."

"Jack, if I fell out with everyone around me that kept the possibility of me being a father to themselves, I'd have no one in my crew. Lily had been subject to one conversation with Rosie. She didn't feel you should hear it from her."

"Don't defend her, Rick. Lily and I go back too far to hide anything from each other. She fucked up royally and I can't see past it right now. If you are meeting her for dinner, have fun but count me out, I really have nothing I want to say to the girl. If I went I would just make the situation worse."

"She flew all the way from California to be here for you, Jack." Rick's tone was one of frustration but as far as I was concerned, Lily still should have told me before I went away.

"If she'd told me before, at least I'd have been able to speak to Rosie about it before there was another guy in her life and Lily wouldn't have felt the need to fly here in the first place."

"All right, have it your way, but I reckon Lily thought she was protecting you. I've got to meet her in twenty minutes so I guess you'll be ordering room service on your own tonight. I'll see you at the festival tomorrow, Jack." Rick stood up and began to wander towards his bedroom and never looked back. With that action, I was dismissed and left his suite.

My plan for solace away from Lily had worked but it was a difficult night knowing that she was there and was with Rick. But I wasn't remotely ready to forgive her and the way I felt at the time, I wasn't sure if I would ever be able forgive her. Even though Rosie's baby wasn't mine, I should still have known there was a possibility it could have been. If Lily had told me at the time maybe it would have got me thinking and I would have realised what Rosie meant to me sooner as well.

I left the suite Rick's team had booked me into and went to my own room in the hotel to ensure that Lily wouldn't barge into my room on her way to or from meeting Rick. I couldn't have her disrespect my feelings any further by trying to push me into an uncomfortable friendship just because of our past. If I forgave her for what she'd done, it would be on my terms, not Lily's as had always been the case in the past.

Switching my phone to silent I went and sat in the tub. I was feeling exhausted again, maybe being away from all the stresses for so long meant that I was struggling to pick up the pace of my life back in the fast lane.

Reaching for my phone, I went to set the alarm for the following day when I noticed that Lily had tried to call me five times. I immediately deleted the five voicemails she'd left because I wasn't going to cave to her emotional blackmail this time.

When I'd climbed into bed I expected my mind to go around and around in circles like it had been all day but I was physically and mentally exhausted, and ended up passing out instead.

When I awoke, the sun was streaming through the window. I hadn't bothered to close the curtains when I had climbed into bed. I'd gotten used to waking up like that in Spain. Everyone thought I was weird for not using the blackout blinds to keep my room cool, but I actually preferred the heat to being in a dark, cool place. I wondered if that had something to do with me being part Spanish.

Room service brought up the breakfast I'd ordered and after I ate, I headed for the shower. It was still early and I wasn't sure where Lily was staying but since I'd avoided her so far, I was sure I could do it for another couple of hours. Once she was gone I'd be able to think about things better because I wouldn't be worrying about another run-in with her.

It was a beautiful day and sunshine usually made me feel light hearted but not whilst I had all that shit floating around in my head. I hit the shower and stayed there for ages before dragging myself out from under the warm jets and breathing the soothing steam into my lungs. I wrapped a towel around my waist. Walking out of the bathroom, I picked up my phone and saw yet more texts from Lily. I deleted them without reading again and then moved on to my voicemails. Three from Lily crying, I deleted them as well, then I heard Alfie's voice.

"What the fuck is going on over there, dude? Lily's been skyping and getting all hysterical because apparently you won't talk to her. If I was over there I'd kick your ass, you little shit. All this time I've tolerated your fucked up behaviour because of my girl and now I find you're fucking upsetting her when she's flown halfway around the fucking world to be with you during our measly time off. I'm warning you, Jack, if she comes back with this unresolved it's the last time I'll listen to her where you're concerned."

I ignored his rant and pressed to delete before moving on to the last message. I was relieved to hear it was Rick's PA saying that he'd knocked on my door that morning and got no reply. He also informed me that he'd left the passes to the after party for me and my 'plus one' with reception. I didn't hear him knock because I wasn't in my allocated room. Then I wondered if Lily had tried to find me there as well. My last thought was that I was definitely a minus one.

All day after that, my mind was solely focused on my work. Studying the new bands performing on the minor stages, I'd found a couple of good ones that I felt would go far and then worked my way up to the headliners. Four stages, each with five bands playing, gave me plenty of research to catch up on. I Googled everything I needed to know to give some background for my article, and tried to imagine how different my job must have been for those reporters that had gone before me. They never had that kind of technology at their fingertips, and yet I used to hang on their every word in those magazines.

By the time Cobham Street came on stage it was dark. It was the end of the first day. The claustrophobic atmosphere felt awesome and we actually had a balmy evening in the North for a change. Huge waves of bodies were swaying in time to the music, all fully engaged and hanging on every word Rick sang. I'd missed this.

Cobham Street's set was staged with an expensive technical extravaganza of laser technology, it was phenomenal and their ability to hold the tens of thousands of people watching in the palm of their hands was awe inspiring.

Rick Fars was more than just an international rock superstar, he was a genius. His delivery and interaction with the audience was completely effortless. Apart from Alfie Black, I'd never seen anyone with such talent, stamina and natural ability, who could deliver time after time, no matter how many gigs they had done. Rick was known for always giving a fresh performance and his fans were incredibly grateful. Cobham Street was a worldwide phenomenon with a following of tens of millions. Every time I'd covered one of their gigs I always forgot my job and got carried away by their musical showmanship.

All through the encore my thumbs were going ten to the dozen taking notes as I made observations, and by the time I was done I had everything I needed to write an article. All I had to do was reconfigure it to look polished for the editor by the time their final notes were still ringing in my ears. I could report that stuff with my eyes shut, and with all the experience I'd had over the past few years, it took no time at all to get it to proof readers for the first read.

I had sent myself notes on fourteen bands so I knew that there was more than enough material for the next edition, the problem was which new band to cover because there were three that stood out for me. I'd been in contact with three photographers that were freelanced for the magazine and they'd already sent me some 'money shots' they'd captured during the performances. I felt sure that we'd definitely exceeded my boss's expectations for the festival by the time we were done.

Normally, I'd have been desperate to go to one of Cobham Street's after parties, but I just wasn't feeling it that night. All was not right in my world; Lily was on her way back to the USA, Rosie had rejected me and I'd had another meaningless one night stand even though I hadn't wanted to fall back to my old habits.

I knew that if I hung out with the guys there was every chance that I'd get drunk and repeat my mistakes. Not going was risky and Rick could have taken exception, but I sent a text to Paul saying that I wasn't feeling good and regretfully I had to bow out. Obviously I made it sound like I was gutted to be missing out, and luckily it was clearly so out of character, because the text that came back offered for them to send Rick's medic to me. I managed to persuade them that I'd be fine.

Something inside told me that I had to take care of myself because unless I got my head straight, it was going to drag me down again.

Chapter 24

Disloyalty

Careful diplomacy got me through the following day. Rick and the rest of Cobham Street were flying out directly after their last gig to make an appearance somewhere in Australia at an awards ceremony, so I was let off the hook without too much interrogation regarding my absence the previous night. I felt relieved when I was finally leaving.

Rick had said that he'd send someone from their PR department to brief me on the tour in a couple of weeks, but gave me the dates to mark off on my calendar. My boss was freaking out at the fact that I had a seven week exclusive with one of the world's most popular bands and he was already carving out ideas for a special edition. Joe told me that it would be a compilation of the best bits of all the interviews and photographs that I'd take during our time on the road.

During the following seven weeks I was prepped for the tour learning as much about all of the guys in the band, not just Rick. I knew all the guys but I had no real understanding of their families or what they were about because everything with Cobham Street seemed to be centred around Rick.

Lily had tried to break the ice between us but I just couldn't get past her disloyalty. Dave said he thought it was because I was hurting from Rosie and that I was taking my frustration out on Lily. He then started to spout some bullshit theory about me transferring my anger to Lily because I couldn't deal with Rosie's rejection. Maybe some of that was valid, I'd never had a girl dump me before, but then again, I'd never really had a girlfriend before Rosie.

Each passing week helped me feel a bit less hurt and a bit more resigned to moving on from Rosie. I had started to miss Lily because she would have been my go-to person in all of that, but she was the one who had let me down. She had stopped calling me and used Emily and Dave to fight her case instead.

Emily kept telling me time healed but I guessed that not enough time had passed because Lily's betrayal still festered inside me. So I spent the time leading up to the tour doing nothing except work, going to bed and nothing much in between. But I was in a better place by the time I was leaving for the tour.

Two weeks after I visited her, I'd heard, via Dave, Rosie had become a mother to a little girl. I was alarmed because by my calculations she shouldn't have been due for another two months, I then wondered if I had upset her to the extent she'd gone into labour early. Dave had been to see her and they told him that although the baby was small she was going to be fine. However, as painful as it was to hear, Rosie being a mum helped me to overcome my final hurdle and finally accept that I had lost her. I left the conversation there with Dave because there was nothing left to say. By then I was ready to step back and become myself again instead of the lonely pitiful guy that was having an affair with his sofa.

Gillian, another PR person from Sly Records brought me a media packet just as Rick had instructed. The pack contained everything I could possibly need to know about the band and the tour before travelling. At first I saw that a lot of it was promotional stuff for the fans, but there were a few gems in it like Rick's favourite cologne and the fact that his favourite animals were all cats. *Who asks those kinds of questions?* Then there were the disclaimers and confidentiality clauses which told me what I could and couldn't talk about, For example, I couldn't write or discuss anything in relation to the band's behaviour. Personally I thought that was a bit rich coming from a group of guys that gave me shit at every turn about my behaviour.

Even though I knew all the guys pretty well, I was wary because I was going to be living with them for seven weeks. It made me a bit nervous because they were pretty much my idols and I didn't want the myth tainted if I found out that they weren't as awesome as I regarded them to be.

Twelve hours later I was in a mini bus on the way to the airport with a photographer called Phil, who I'd come across a few times at one event or another, and a blogger called Rachel. She was really friendly and gave me a few pointers about how the guys liked things done. I was about to ask how she knew that when she explained that she'd been blogging for the band for several years and always worked on some part of their tours with them.

For the first couple of days after arriving in Paris the band and crew seemed pretty tense due to a new set they were in the process of working with. Everything from where the guys needed to be on stage and where and how they were going to project the sound to the audience was mapped out.

There were plenty of rehearsals for me to watch and I had to admit that although the band was extremely talented and effortless, the time they put into their practise was ridiculously long. They didn't just go on stage and assume they were going to be great, they spent hours perfecting their performance.

By day three they were starting to get into their stride and more and more women started to hang around backstage. I spent a great deal of time wondering how they could have possibly got in because I arrived with the actual band yet my ID was checked at every turn, whereas those girls seemed to just meander around without anyone batting an eyelid. If Dave was there he would have said it was their tits and arse that opened doors for them.

Being a fly-on-the-wall journalist, I was able to wander under the stage and into the pit to see where it all happened, and where the sound engineers, lighting guys, riggers and the rest of the crew diligently worked their magic to make the set work for the band. I was impressed at their level of professionalism and skill. One thing that did surprise me was the band's guitar technician: she was a young woman, something that I was not used to seeing.

There were two sets of metal stairs leading up to the stage, one directly off the stage and one to the side but further back to allow technical assistance for the band once they were on stage. I sat down on the ones furthest away to watch the girl who had caught my eye while she worked.

A long look passed between us as she pulled a guitar from the stand and began to tune it. She had balls. I don't think I could ever pick up Rick Fars' guitar and just play it like she was. Her fingers worked quickly over the fret and damn she could play. I was captivated by her. She was a very petite and sweet looking girl with her dark hair swept back in a messy bun. She obviously didn't care too much about her appearance, but her shabby jeans and tight crew t-shirt made her all the more feminine and appealing somehow. Her femininity in that environment was very refreshing and I just couldn't stop staring at her.

197

I don't know how long I'd been watching her but she suddenly glanced back over at me, smiled widely and continued with what she was doing. When she'd finished, she placed the guitar on a stand and picked up a second one repeating the same process. After tuning a third, she picked up all three guitars and took them on stage, placing them strategically where the band members could easily access them.

My mouth was dry from watching her, she looked divine and I couldn't look at anything else because I was too busy noticing her. When she came down from the stage, she began to restring a guitar and spoke to me without looking up.

"Enjoying the view?"

Smirking wryly because I was busted checking her out which seems to be common for me, I answered truthfully.

"Sure, very much."

Glancing up with her head to the side she grinned, her eyes glittered with humour.

"Forward as well, huh?" she said, sounding playful.

"Always, it's a curse," I commented, winking cheekily at her.

The girl chuckled and shook her head.

"Honest if nothing else. So, what would your girlfriend say about you checking me out?"

"I'm sure I'd get a slap at the very least, if I had one. What would your guy say if he caught me?"

"Oh he'd come after you with his shotgun screaming that I belonged to him and shoot you in the ass for even looking in the first place," she said humorously with a soft American accent.

Smiling sheepishly I apologised to her.

"I'm sorry but that," I said pointing at the stage, "was definitely a testosterone booster. I mean you, a smoking hot woman handling awesome guitars that belong to legends and playing them expertly... The whole visual was a pretty intoxicating combination. He's a very lucky guy your boyfriend."

My tone was a little wistful and bordering on lust. I stood and walked closer, leaning my shoulder against the wall, my legs crossed at the ankle. She placed the guitar down then sat on the stage steps with her elbows on her knees supporting her head.

"What's your name?"

"Jack, yours?"

"Mya. I'm just about finished here, want to get a coffee?" *Fuck, yeah!*

"Hmm, that depends if your boyfriend is lurking with that shotgun or not."

"Oh he's not here at the moment so I guarantee you're pretty safe."

For about twenty-five minutes Mya and I swapped intros and she told me she had been playing guitar for about fifteen years and was five when she'd started. A quick calculation later and I'd gathered that she was only twenty, but she had a maturity about her that gave me a feeling of calm. I'd only met her minutes before but she was really easy to talk to and we were talking like old friends. I quickly found myself watching her mannerisms as she spoke and I could feel myself being drawn to her.

Ten minutes later I knew I wanted to know a lot more about her. The small hospitality area wasn't very private and people were constantly coming and going, it wasn't really conducive to forming friendships. We were going to be spending seven weeks in each other's company at pretty close quarters so it was only natural to want to get to know someone I felt I could gel with.

"So what do you do when the gig is finished and you've packed up?" I was thinking of asking her to dinner or something.

"I usually go fuck one of the guys in the band for

something to eat."

The coffee cup at my mouth almost scalded me when my hand jerked the hot liquid at her comment. I almost choked because her reply was so unexpected and I wasn't sure if she was being serious or not. Her expression was deadpan and I was still figuring out my reply when Rick walked into view.

"Well if it isn't beauty and the beast. Jack Cunningham you leave that girl alone. She's taken."

Rick stalked across to the couch we were sitting on and lifted her off the seat, sat in her place and plonked her onto his lap.

"Hey, darlin', don't waste your time on this cheap specimen. Come here and feel a real man." He flirted shamelessly in front of me.

Mya giggled and snuggled into his chest and I felt instantly pissed off that he could just do that. I then felt even more pissed off when she responded like a weak, giggling teenager around him just because he was a rock star until Rick spoke.

"Jack, I see you've met my niece, Mya."

Rick raised his eyebrow in question with a knowing smirk.

"Her daddy and me are brothers, so don't go getting any ideas about her."

My head was all over the place thinking, *thank god she isn't interested in him* then thinking, *shit, she's related to Rick* and then finally, *Rick has a brother?*

Turning to Mya, he nodded in my direction whilst looking at her.

"This is Lily's best friend, although you'd never know it right now because he's being an ass and not talking to her."

Mya's eyes widened in surprise; her eyes darting all over, taking me in from head to toe.

"Oh My God, you're *that* Jack?" she said her voice

rising in exclamation.

"I mean she said you were hot but…"

Mya blushed when she realised her spontaneous outburst. What she meant by that I had no idea but I was intrigued to hear that she'd heard about me and I wondered what she'd been told. I just hoped the after party incident hadn't come up.

"You know Lily?" The conversation was becoming weirder by the minute.

"I sure do, we've met several times, once during a weekend we all spent together when she came to Uncle Rick's place. She's very cool and an extremely talented musician. We jammed a lot the weekend she stayed over." Glancing at Rick with affection, she took his hand and smiled and then looked back at me.

"Uncle Rick taught me to play guitar and I'm really grateful to him for this job. I'm studying music myself but I wanted to have a year out. Cobham Street's usual technician has just had surgery so it seemed logical for me to step in and take his place. I get to travel, spend time with my favourite uncle, help him out technically and meet tons of cool people."

"Like me, you mean?" I grinned cheekily, quickly glancing at Rick who was staring at me with humour in his eyes.

"Jack, I'm supposed to be a fuckin' deterrent you moron, you're not supposed to be flirting with my niece you asshole."

Mya chuckled enjoying the show and nudged Rick's shoulder.

"I love it when you get all protective of me, Uncle Rick. Wait until I tell Dad you really can do the whole parenting thing, he'll never believe me. I'm looking forward to that conversation because as far as he's concerned he's the sensible one and you're the crazy irresponsible one. But then again he did make the decision to let me tour with a group of horny rock star men for a year. Jack is as near to a normal guy I'm going to find hanging around you lot."

Rick pushed himself to stand shaking his head and began tucking his t-shirt in the back of his waistband as he wandered over to the door.

"All right, Mya, have it your way honey, you know what a soft touch I am with you so I'm not going to tell you what you can and can't do with Jack."

Mya glanced at me and her face flushed pink as Rick turned to me.

"However, Jack's on my payroll and if he fucks you, I'll fuck him big time. She's twenty years old, Jack. Remember that. Have fun kids."

Rick gave me a forced smile and began to laugh as he walked out of the room, leaving us alone. I felt as awkward as hell sitting in front of her after his exit.

I knew my smile was frozen on my face because although I was confident Rick was messing with me, I wasn't going to do anything that would cause a problem either. Plus he was right, at twenty Mya was a bit too young for me. At twenty five I had lived a big life so far. *Yeah, okay it's only five years but still...*

Mya chuckled again and I noticed how beautiful she was, but I wasn't looking to get into trouble and I wasn't looking for a casual type of relationship with someone who had a partner either.

"Well, he made it sound like I was going to come on to you. Can't two people of the opposite sex chat without it coming down to sex?" I said quickly trying to make her feel at ease again.

"Not in Uncle Rick's world but, aww, I'm disappointed now, and there was me thinking it was my amazing rack and awesome looks that were keeping your attention when really you were babysitting me."

"No! Don't get me wrong you're stunningly

attractive, Mya. I'm just not looking to get into anything right now, besides being fucked by Rick would terrify me, you know how many women he's had?"

Although I'd made a joke of it, I smiled sincerely thinking that if I was looking for a woman and she was just a little older, I'd be all over her. But I wasn't quite ready for anyone else to fill the hole Rosie had left. Spending time with Mya for the following seven weeks was an attractive proposition I was enjoying her company already.

Luckily, she chuckled and shook her head, grinning widely.

"You forgot the boyfriend with the shotgun and the short temper."

Sniggering, I nodded in agreement.

"Damn, and there's that too."

Mya put her hand on my arm and her familiarity wasn't contrite, there was genuine affection in her touch. It made my heart race a little and the hairs on my arms stand on end as my flesh reacted in a rash of goose bumps.

"There is no boyfriend, Jack. I was teasing. I'm not looking for anyone either, so we can hang out without any hang-ups about charming the pants off each other."

I was delighted by what she said, but then wasn't sure if I was delighted about the no boyfriend thing or the not looking for anyone comment.

"Sounds good to me, Mya, we can never have enough friends, right?"

A guy with a grey beard and a pot belly wearing a crew t-shirt called out to her and Mya stood slowly.

"A few of us are getting pizza at this late night place when the gig's finished, you want to come with us?" *Yes I bloody do.*

"Sure."

Mya arranged where to meet me and turned, waving her arm over her head without looking back as she left the room. *At least I'll have someone to hang out with sometimes during the next seven weeks.*

Chapter 25

A word

In my imagination touring with Cobham Street led me to make the assumption there would be excess alcohol and partying, but in my experience most of their time consisted of quiet time, full on performances and constant rehearsals. The guys hardly ever took a break but Rick power napped *a lot*. That was as much of a revelation to me as his allergy to starch. I knew from Lily that the life these guys led was one of privilege and they had access to things the rest of us only imagined was commonplace, but the level of commitment to their work was beyond most people's capability. In a nutshell, they earned every minute of privilege they got. Freedom was non-existent and their days off were mainly spent sleeping.

Mya and I grew closer and I'm not sure when it happened, but I began to watch how she moved, ate, came back at me when I flirted with her, and I loved the way that she laughed. She was the cutest girl I'd ever seen, in fact I'd even go as far as to say she'd give Lily a run for her money with how attractive she was. I just couldn't stop looking at her. I loved her mannerisms and the way she carried herself and without realising it, I'd become enthralled by her. More and more I found myself seeking reasons to sit next to her or asking for help with things just to spend time with her.

Once, in passing, our arms brushed together and the delicious current that was sent through my body gave me a fierce erection. I'd never had such a physical connection from such an innocent accidental contact before. I thought I was being subtle about being close to her but when Rick cornered me one day I realised that I was kidding myself.

"A word." Rick's tone was brisk and I was immediately on my guard, wondering what I'd done as I walked behind him. I felt like a naughty school boy about to face the headmaster's wrath. Pushing the door open to his dressing room, Rick emptied his pockets throwing a pack of cards and some chewing gum on the table before turning around and perching his arse on the end of it.

Twisting his mouth he then took a deep breath and stared me square in the eye.

"Mya."

I knew straight away he'd caught me checking her out. I figured I had to play it how I normally would or he'd be even more scathing towards me.

"Yup. Very good that's a word. It's also a pronoun. Good job, Rick." I smirked cheekily, raising one eyebrow to try and look cock-sure of myself even though I was feeling anything but.

"You can stop with the shit, Jack. I've seen how you look at her, you've been eye-fucking her for the last week. Let's get something straight. I'm not keen. Not because I don't like you. I do. And I don't think that you aren't good enough for her because you are. My issue is that she's young and quite innocent, so if you fuck with her heart and let her down I'll have to break your balls. It would be a problem for me because I've grown fond of you, but as much as I like you, we'd no longer be friends. So make sure your intentions are of the best kind, I'd hate for you to piss me off. Your life could suddenly get pretty uncomfortable."

Sweat beads had formed on my back during our conversation. I had been expecting him to warn me off instead he'd kind of given me his blessing, as long as I didn't fuck it up. All of that was supposition though because I'd never given Mya any hint that my feelings were shifting, and as far as I knew hers hadn't.

"If I'm honest, I do like Mya, Rick, however, we've never been anything but friends and although I feel ready to take a risk, I'm not sure Mya sees me that way. And like you said, she's very young."

Rick snorted and shook his head in disbelief.

"For fuck's sake, Jack, *all* women see you *that* way. You are a walking, talking cock as far as they're concerned. Funny as fuck and not bad to look at, that's a lethal combination to them. Even when you're with me, they notice you." Rick sniggered and ran his hand through his hair looking slightly embarrassed.

"Shit that sounded big headed, what I mean is, I'm supposed to be the main attraction, right? But not when you're in the room as well. You have a kind of draw, like your cock is magnetic and I can't think of one person that doesn't like you. Anyway, ask her out if you want because she's boring the fuck out of me with her, 'Jack this and Jack that' shit. I'm tired of her talking about you all the fucking time so you better put her, and me, out of our misery."

"It's only been a month since Rosie blew me out, Rick, I'm not sure."

Rick cut across. "Why are you even talking about that girl? She wasn't right for you, Jack. You need someone that's going to be able to deal with your smart mouth and from what I saw of her, she had no idea how to handle you. Mya's mature for her age, but the kid inside bursts out of her every now and again. She'd give as good as she gets from you, you're a match made in heaven on that score. I've watched the two of you and it's hilarious. I can't think of another word for it."

"Let's just see where it goes, I'm not going to force anything." I replied, feeling happier about liking her.

After my talk with Rick I was more self-aware when Mya was near me. I felt a bit awkward around her and wondered if Rick had mentioned anything to her because there was an air of expectation between us. Something had shifted and I wasn't sure if it was because I knew that Rick knew or because of what he'd said about Mya, or maybe it was because I was behaving differently without being aware.

Our feelings bubbled over in a completely natural way one night soon after. Cobham Street had just given a particularly awesome performance and had taken to the stage to perform their encore. The song they had chosen wasn't their usual closing song but an older one that was especially popular during their early days.

Mya and I were standing under the stage talking between numbers when she instantly went nuts when she heard the intro. Watching her bobbing around with her eyes closed as she sang along and got lost in the music was amazing. She was an incredibly beautiful girl and loved by all the crew and at times like that I could see why. Mya had no inhibitions as far as music was concerned and couldn't have cared less whether anyone saw her enjoying the song.

Singing loudly, she opened her eyes and saw me staring, totally captivated by her. I knew I was grinning like a fool because I loved it when she did stuff like this. Suddenly she grabbed my hand and began to dance with me and I let myself go and joined in.

We were both laughing and Mya was striking some silly poses so I threw in a few of my own until we were helplessly chuckling. Somehow we started to compete against each other as to who could pull the most outrageous moves. I didn't feel stupid at all around her being that playful.

When the song had finished, she collapsed into me and my arms automatically curled around her little body. As she stared up at me, it just felt right to dip my head and plant a chaste kiss on her lips. I was just about to release my hold on her when Mya reached up, placing her hand at the back of my head and pushed my mouth back towards hers.

Instantly, desire rushed through my body with the heady effect of Mya's sensual kiss. My hormones ignited passion in all the right places. The sensation of her tongue when it met mine felt incredible and our kiss was slow and unhurried as we enjoyed the taste of each other.

She groaned into my mouth and I walked slowly backwards, still holding her tightly against me and continued our kiss. When my heels hit the wall I spun her around sharply, pinning her back firmly against it with my body.

Instinctively, my hands slid from her waist down her hips and over the globes of her arse pulling her closer to me, but it still wasn't close enough. Mya whimpered and sagged against me, her hand sliding under my shirt to sweep up over my skin. Goosebumps erupted over me and I growled, breathlessly breaking the kiss as I pushed her away from me gently and stared at her for a moment.

"Wow. Um...wow."

Mya stared back at me wide-eyed and panted slightly. Her eyes became heavy with lust and her face flushed from the aftermath of our kiss. Her chest rose and fell rapidly as she visibly fought to get her feelings in check and I imagined that I looked pretty similar to her. After a moment Mya hugged herself then started to fidget awkwardly with her clothing.

"Um…I don't know why I did that." Her eyes searched mine for some reassurance and she tucked a lock of stray hair behind her ear.

Mya had definitely lit a spark in me that I hadn't felt in a while and although I wanted to reassure her, I was too busy enjoying the moment so I kept it going by flirting with her.

"Oh, sweetheart, don't worry, I always have that effect on women, I think it's this aftershave I'm wearing. Women have been known to throw their underwear at me. You've shown amazing restraint, I was beginning to think you were a guy or I was the wrong gender."

Mya grinned her eyes widening at what I said and replied, "Actually, I was thinking you were a bit dense and that I was going to have to resort to that if this didn't work."

Rick was right. Mya knew exactly how to deal with my stupid banter. She was a lot like Lily in that way. My comparison made me think about Lily for a moment. I missed her. About two weeks ago she stopped texting and I noticed the day she did.

Mya dragged me out of my reverie when she coughed to get my attention.

"Hey where did you go? Did I say something wrong?" Glancing back at her, I realised I had been daydreaming and quickly recovered my train of thought.

"Actually, I was just reminding myself about all that lingerie. I have them in a drawer in my office desk at work in London, if you come back with me I'll show them to you. You never know, you may pick up some fashion tips for under those ripped jeans of yours."

Suddenly my stomach rumbled with hunger and I began to lead her up towards the seating at the side of the stage that's reserved for band members' wives and guests. Turning to her, I asked if she'd like to go out to dinner, just the two of us. I knew instantly that she was delighted at my suggestion to spend time alone together, her face lit up as she smiled warmly at me. Her eyes glittered as the stage lighting reflected in them when she looked happily back at me. I was expecting her to agree but her next comment blew me away.

"Dinner's good but I'd rather go home and have sex with you. We've been doing dinners and a lot of safe-touching foreplay for weeks and I'm about ready for the play. And anyway, I've seen how you eat, I'd like to see what other skills you have."

Mya's words had a direct hit on my dick and my hard erection willed me to grab a hold of her. I was choked by her bluntness for a second before I regained my composure and swept my hand around her waist to pull her tightly against me. Her eyes flicked to my mouth then back to my eyes again as she licked her lips. Her chest heaved in response to my sudden move on her. Smiling slowly at how my actions had caught her off guard just like her words had me; I dipped my head and placed a quick soft kiss on her closed mouth.

"Hmm…not sure, that depends on those all-important knickers you're wearing. I'm very particular in my tastes."

Mya's smile was as sexy as sin and she patted her own arse.

"Aww well sorry, Jack. I think you are definitely going to be disappointed there. I don't wear any."

"Well non-existent lingerie is my favourite type of underwear, how did you know? In that case, Mya, I'd *love* to have sex with you." I replied, playfully wagging my eyebrows.

If I was being honest I wasn't sure if she was serious or not but I wasn't taking any chances. I excused myself to go to the toilet and went in search of a condom machine. My dick felt like it was going to break in my trousers after her suggestion, and I honestly thought the casual way she delivered it was off-the-charts hot. I knew I'd definitely go along with her request but after my nearly-a-father moment with Rosie, I wasn't going anywhere without protection.

Mya was sitting alone when I got back to the hospitality area and I wasn't sure what to say so I offered her dinner again. She opted for takeout and we set off back to the hotel, collecting it on the way. I'll admit I was nervous, it was probably the first time I had ever really felt nervous about being one-on-one with a girl. I had a feeling it was because she had the potential to mean a lot to me, but at the same time, I kept thinking about how young she was, where she lived and a whole list of other things that told me to proceed with caution.

With Rosie it was a physical attraction that turned into more for us, with Mya, we had an amazing emotional connection, our hidden desires for each other have only just surfaced.

A couple of things worried me; I was still getting over my feelings for Rosie and I didn't want Mya playing with my fragile emotions, and I certainly didn't want to play with hers. However, when she kissed me, the moment her lips touched mine, I had to admit that I'd been falling for her from the moment I set eyes on her.

Chapter 26

Different

As we stood waiting for the lift in the hotel foyer, I began to think about how the last two girls I had been with had treated me. It was like I was more of an object than a person, a means to an end. I couldn't pretend to be surprised, that's exactly what they were to me. We'd used each other—it's the definition of a one-night stand.

In normal circumstances everyone saw me as some kind of playboy. For a long time I thought the girls I had been with was by mutual consent and everything between us was on equal terms. However, in hindsight it was actually more like they'd hit on me that we'd ended up together, rather than me actively seeking them out.

Glancing down at Mya I saw the way she was staring up at me and if I wasn't mistaken it looked like adoration. We stepped into the lift and there was an awkward silence between us as we stood side by side. Since our kiss, I'd caught her watching me intensely but it wasn't like some lust-crazed drunken female who wanted a quick fuck. No, Mya's observations of me were measured and her smile was open when we had made eye contact during those times. She didn't give me the usual predatory appraisal I had become accustomed to from the women I usually slept with.

From spending time with Mya, I had learned a lot about her. We'd shared some intense and intimate conversations during the previous few weeks and often sat together late into the night when everyone else had disappeared off to bed. She was incredibly easy to talk to and I opened up to her about my thoughts and feelings for Rosie and why I wasn't talking to Lily. She empathised with me about that, but was careful not to take a side. It showed her honest character and I noted she was actually quite a dignified and refined girl despite her playful flirting.

Touring with Cobham Street was disconcerting at times, and yet Mya absorbed all of the crude banter and coarse behaviour whilst still managing to stay grounded and feminine. I loved that about her.

Above everything else, Mya was the only girl who had taken the time to know me before deciding she wanted more. That put her in a class all by herself. But it made me nervous. I'd never thought about how I performed sexually with women before, sex came naturally and I knew exactly what I needed to do to please them, but I somehow felt a pressure to get it right for her.

Suddenly my experience with women was something I was pretty ashamed of when I looked at Mya. Maybe it was because she looked young and quite innocent, but sometimes it takes that experience to know when someone special comes along, and I had a feeling that Mya was definitely something special.

When she leaned over to press the lift button, I noted that she had pressed the button for her floor instead of mine and I wondered if she was backing out. *Was she just joking around earlier and isn't serious about taking us further?* Suddenly my head was full of doubts when all I

214

wanted was for this to be real between us. Quickly thinking back to the journey back to the hotel, I realised that we hadn't touched since that one simple kiss.

I was still musing about the plan when the lift door opened on Mya's floor and immediately her hand reached out, slipping into mine. My fingers clasped around it instantly and I felt the warmth emanated with the comfort of her touch.

"We're going to my room is that okay with you?" A faint quiver in her smile gave away her nervousness, so I tried to put her at her ease.

"Sure, whatever makes you most comfortable, love."

Mya smiled up at me again but that time it was more one of relief anything else. Swiping the key card in the lock, the green light flashed and we heard the soft click of the latch. Mya leaned her weight on the door and pulled down on the handle to open the door. She flicked the light switch on with me tagging along behind her because I was still holding her hand.

Placing the key on the dressing table, Mya turned and sat against it. She stared nervously at me and her appearance gave me an immediate understanding. Mya wasn't used to inviting men back to her room. My heart squeezed at the thought that she'd had the balls to do it in the first place, and I knew that I had to take charge of the situation to put her at her ease.

Slowly I let go of her hand and stepped into her space, placing my hands either side of the dressing table but making sure not to touch her.

"What are we doing, Mya? Are you sure this is what you want?"

Her eyes were piercing as she stared back into mine, they quickly flicked to my mouth and then back before she answered.

"As sure as a girl can be in a strange hotel room, miles from home, but this won't be a one night stand, Jack.

I don't screw around. If that's what you're after then I am not the girl for you."

"Good, because I'm so bored of those girls. I know you're different, Mya. I can feel it in here."

I took one hand off the dresser to tap my chest before placing it back next to hers. Mya's eyes nervously searched mine as she swallowed audibly, took a deep breath and exhaled a shaky sigh.

"Actually, I'm scared, Jack." She bit her lip in thought and inhaled sharply before shaking her head.

"I don't know what I'm doing. I like you a lot. No, that's wrong, I'm kind of infatuated with you, but I don't want to start something and lose our friendship. I really connect with you and I've had that with a guy before but only once. Girls, yes, but another guy..."

My gut reaction was to offer her reassurance and I surprised myself at my openness.

"I understand, love. I get where you are, I imagine you're feeling exactly how I felt when I had a crush on Lily years ago."

Mya looked alarmed by my confession, but I pushed through it and continued to explain myself.

"But being with Lily would have been wrong. She's like family and that would have ruined what we had and fucked the both of us up for relationships with other people because the lines would have been blurred. This thing that you're feeling, correct me if I'm wrong, but we're two people who have no sexual or personal history, who have connected on an emotional level and it doesn't seem enough for either of us anymore. You want to get closer physically, right?"

Slowly, her lips curved upwards until she had a wide beaming smile on her face.

"Jack Cunningham you really get it, don't you? You feel that as well? Do you know how many days I've wanted to just climb over your knees and straddle you, then kiss your face off?"

I laughed at her comment and waggled my eyebrows at her in an attempt to cover my own nervousness. I understood her completely, and I was definitely on the same page.

"Oh, I'd say do it, Mya. When you have an urge like that, I don't think it's the kind of thing that should be ignored."

She lifted her hands and placed them on my chest, pushed herself off the dressing table and propelled me backwards. I barely managed one step back before I collapsed onto her bed. My heart raced as my body became flooded with arousal. Mya climbed over me and took my head in her hands, hesitated and stared intensely down at me, her eyes searching for the connection she found in mine.

Although Mya acted like she was dominating me, I could feel her body tremble above me. She was trying to be brave and I wasn't going to leave her to struggle so I quickly wrapped my arms around her and flipped her onto her back, hovering above her.

"Hmm, not quite fast enough, Mya. I think I'm going to take it from here if you don't mind."

From her breathless reaction I could see that she hadn't expected my response and the element of surprise had taken her off guard. Her huge blue eyes widened before her coy smile made an appearance and helped me feel more confident about touching her intimately. In fact, the draw to do so was becoming increasingly overwhelming. That was when, for the second time in my life, I felt what I had felt with Lily, that urge for more, but that time it was with Mya and I knew that I'd never pass up the opportunity of seeing where this could lead us.

"You're so beautiful, Mya."

I found myself staring in silence into her sparkling, bright blue eyes after my statement. It felt like the sky would fall if I looked away. Mya licked her lips slowly and drew her hands up both sides of my body and under my shirt. I shivered at her touch and my dick twitched uncomfortably in my trousers. I had to get closer.

Dropping my arms, I allowed the weight of my hips to sag and I lay on top of her causing us to sink deeper into the mattress. Her small soft hands slowly traced over my skin, her gentle touch and tender attention was a very new experience for me. I couldn't hold back much longer and dropped my head until my forehead was resting against hers.

Once again, we shared a quiet moment where we just absorbed each other. We both swallowed at the same time, our mouths dry in anticipation of what was going to happen next. Mya smelled incredible, her soft sweet perfume overwhelmed my senses.

Cutting into our silence, Mya's hands moved to my head and she began to run her fingers through my hair.

"I love your hair, Jack. I've wondered what it would feel like to run my fingers through it for weeks. It's so not fair for a guy to have hair like this and you aren't even in a rock band."

Chuckling softly, she gently slid the strands of hair pass through her fingers. A few times her fingertips touched my scalp and it sent an electrical pulse through me, which was both delicious and teasing.

Reaching up I brushed a wisp of her hair from her face and placed my lips on hers in a hesitant kiss and then began to move down her neck. I peppered kisses from her ear to the collar of her little white t-shirt. I began to push her leather jacket over her shoulders and she sat up briefly as I pulled the sleeves down her arms. One at a time she lifted her arms so that I could pull the sleeves off and when her jacket was free of her body, I threw it behind me onto the floor.

Glancing back at Mya, I saw that she had lain back

onto the mattress with her hands placed casually above her head. As my eyes began to rake down her body, I saw her erect nipples through her t-shirt, holy hell when I saw she was braless my restraint cracked.

Cupping her firm breast in my hand, I took it into my mouth and sucked on her nipple though the material. Mya gasped loudly before a soft moan of pleasure followed and she wriggled under me arching her back, pushing her breasts closer. What I was doing wasn't enough for either of us so I pulled the material down and took her sweet flesh in my hand before placing my mouth over it again. I sucked and flicked my tongue around her nipple before biting it gently and I felt her body gently vibrate.

"Jeez, Jack. You're wreaking havoc with me, I almost came then." When I looked up at her I expected her to be joking but the expression on her face said she was deadly serious.

"Is that so? Well best we get the first one out of the way then because I have a night planned for us."

I knew I sounded big headed, but I wanted to show her that I wasn't a one-and-done kind of guy in any sense of the words and that I was a considerate and passionate man. Besides, there was nothing sexier than seeing a woman in a perpetual state of orgasm.

Too many people in my life had an idea of what I was without knowing the man inside, even Lily. I wasn't just a guy that wanted to sleep around. I was a guy that wasn't given much of an option. Other than Rosie, no one had truly wanted to know the real me and all the while I found girls attractive and I was having fun, I knew it wasn't really who I was inside. It was more a case of living up to my image.

But Mya was different. That felt different—all the others paled in comparison and I was desperately hoping that she was feeling the same about me.

Chapter 27

Infatuation

Both hands trailed down the sides of her body until I reached the hem of her t-shirt. My breath was ragged as I pushed the cotton material above her breasts and saw her tight little abs for the first time. Mya's beautiful skin had a string tan line where her bikini interrupted her bronzed skin. She had a small metal ring in her belly button and I wanted nothing more than to take it between my teeth. I dipped my head near her neck and traced slow, delicate, light kisses down her body.

Watching Mya's skin respond to my touch as it erupted in goose bumps was more than erotic. Her rapid, excited heartbeat caused a ripple of vibration on her belly and seeing her visibly excited like that turned me on even more.

Arching her back again, Mya's head rolled to the side as she suppressed a low moan and her hips squirmed into the mattress. I dipped my tongue into her belly button and caught the ring between my teeth, tugging gently on it. Everything I was doing was calm and deliberate, but inside I was anything but. My heart was hammering inside my chest and I was fighting to stay in control. I just wanted to eat her, she smelled and tasted so damn good. I had never felt as weak willed around a woman before.

Pulling back to look up at her, I took in her appearance. Her eyes were full of want, her face slightly flushed and it struck me how young and vulnerable she looked. My willpower not to devour her was definitely waning and I had to give her one last chance to back out, because after that there would be no turning back.

"Mya are you sure you really want to do this with me? I need to know because I'm going to lose myself in you any minute now, love."

"Of course I am. I wouldn't be here if I wasn't. Are you?"

Still staring back at her, I dropped my arms and sat back on my legs to place several light kisses on her belly again. I crawled up to her and took her in my arms. I placed my mouth at her ear and whispered, "I don't think I could start something physical with you and walk away. The way I feel, I just want to do *everything* to you, so I have to be sure this is what you want."

Mya leaned back to look at me and seemed pleased with my reply, her hands cradled my head as she pulled me close for a kiss. That time there was nothing gentle about it, we were hungry and our kiss felt desperate. Maybe we were both on the edge of our friendship ledge and were nervously jumping off, becoming lovers was a game changer but Mya wasn't hesitant like I was.

Quickly, she sat up, lifted my shirt and pulled it over my head. That was all the reassurance I needed. Within seconds I reacted, flipping the button of her jeans open and I hurriedly unzipped them, tugging them down her slender, toned legs in a frantic attempt to get her naked as quickly as possible. She was telling the truth, there was no underwear in my way.

The time it had taken to pull her jeans off, kneel at the

foot of the bed, separate her legs and place my mouth on her inner thighs was impressive, even if I do say so myself. She giggled when my mouth connected with her leg and in an act of modesty she covered her little clean-shaven pussy with her hand. I wrapped her hand in mine and lifted it away. Placing it firmly at her side, I applied a slight pressure to it to keep it there while I studied her. She smirked wryly at the intimacy of what I was doing and turned her head away, blushing slightly.

"What are you embarrassed about?" I asked, turning my head to look up at her before chastely kissing her mound. "This is beautiful, it's an amazing part of the gorgeous girl you are, love. Don't be shy around me."

She cringed and covered her face with her other hand, so I went back to licking my way up her thigh to stop myself from staring. I became aware of a slight tremor of anticipation that gripped her as she waited to see what was going to happen next. Her body was literally buzzing under my touch.

Breathing in deeply, I enjoyed her sexy intimate fragrance and suddenly had to hold back my pressing need to be buried inside her. My dick twitched in protest at not having her immediate attention.

Slipping my hands under her arse, I tipped her pelvis up to make her most sensitive spot more open to me. Leaning forward, I glanced briefly at her serious face as it watched me intensely and drew my tongue along the length of her seam. She shuddered, her back arched as she tried to clamp my head between her thighs, her body instantly tensed in reaction to my expert oral attention.

"Oh fuck. Mmm." I exclaimed.

Mya's hands were trying to push me away like what I was doing was too much for her to tolerate even though I had only touched her once. Writhing and twisting her body, I could see her tolerance for teasing wasn't very high. Warm slick syrupy juices flowed freely down towards her arse and I caught them on the end of my tongue.

We made eye contact and I reached up to tease her entrance with my middle finger. Mya's mouth fell open and she gasped. "Ahhh."

When I touched her clit with my forefinger, she moaned loudly and spread her legs wider for me. Then when I started lapping at her clitoris with my tongue, her arse began to buck in my hands and I had to squeeze her arse cheek to keep her where I wanted her.

Inserting a single finger into her wet and swollen pussy as I flicked her clit with my tongue earned me another soft moan followed by a deep breath as she writhed wantonly on the bed. Less than a minute later she fell apart screaming, fisting the sheets tightly in her hands.

I stopped briefly to look up at Mya again and couldn't help but smile at her rolling eyes as she squirmed. She exhaled shakily and I saw her relax before she murmured, sated. It took less than a minute and I knew she couldn't take much more of my teasing but I was enjoying her. Mya's post-come face looked incredible and I grinned wickedly at the effect my touch had on her. She was so responsive.

"I think I just found my new favourite pastime." I commented playfully.

Teasing her with my tongue and fingers was one thing but I didn't think I'd be able to be so playful once I was inside her. My dick was aching and harder than it had been for months. She just felt perfect in my arms.

One thing struck me about Mya. She was happy to be led by me, she wasn't aggressive or pushy at all and for the most part all she had done, apart from kiss me and trace her fingers tentatively over my abs, was to stroke my hair and lie almost completely passively while I explored her. Tugging my clothing was one thing, pushing me sexually apparently wasn't her style. I briefly wondered whether she had much experience with men.

"Are you okay? You sure you want to do this, Mya?" Her eyes searched mine for a moment and she drew her tongue over her bottom lip and drew in a deep breath.

"Jack, that's the second time you've asked me that, I wouldn't have brought you here if I didn't. It's making me wonder whether it's what you want. Are you getting cold feet?"

"Fuck no. I guess I'm just a little scared of taking this further and ruining what we have. What if it's awkward between us, we've got three weeks left on tour."

Mya giggled and shifted her way out from under me to kneel beside me at the bottom of the bed.

"Jack, the thought of you inside me is all I've thought about for weeks. If you don't, I probably won't talk to you again. I have wanted you since the moment I saw you. Does that help you decide what's next?" Smiling warmly, she placed her hands on the sides of my head and kissed me in reassurance.

The kiss was tender and unhurried like she had kissed me before. Slowly I stood up; my hands mirrored hers and guarded her head whilst keeping her lips in place on mine. Easing her back on the bed, I crawled over her and lay on top of her, keeping my weight on my elbows.

"It does. Fuck, Mya, of course I want you. You're so beautiful. I can't stop staring at you now that I know I can." Smirking, I dipped and lightly licked her neck from her collarbone to her ear.

My dick twitched when she let out a sexy giggle while scrunching her neck away from my touch. Her skin had reacted in instant goose bumps and once again I knew the chemistry between us was hot.

"Jack, I don't want to wait any longer. Make love to me."

Begging was something I was used to from women but no girl had ever asked me to make love to them. Not even Rosie. They all wanted me to ride them hard and for most of them, the wilder the ride the better. What did that mean? We've only known each other for a few weeks and wanted to take it further but was this infatuation I was feeling or a friendship that had bubbled over into lust? *Aren't I feeling like I did with Lily when we were teenagers? Is that it? Am I replicating the thing with Lily here?*

Rolling over I managed to reach the floor and pull the box of condoms as I fought against that last thought. *This isn't Lily and this is different.* Trying to open the cellophane was like trying to enter Fort Knox and when I surrendered and handed the condoms to Mya we were both chuckling heartily. I was definitely out of practice. In the end Mya ripped it with her teeth, then peeled the little gold opener strip and produced a foil wrapper. Without hesitating she tore it open and pulled the latex sheath from it.

"Are you doing the honours or am I?" she smirked, holding the condom between her thumb and forefinger.

"Hmm, I don't think you have anything to fill that, but it might be fun watching you try to wear it."

"Jack, I was rather hoping you could help me with that. You may have something that can pack it out."

Smirking wickedly at how sassy she was, I grinned and took the condom from her and began rolling it down my dick.

"Always happy to help a damsel in distress or in this case, undressed."

As soon as it was on I didn't want to wait a moment longer. Mya smiled wickedly up at me and bit her bottom lip. Her eyes were seductively heavy and her skin tinted pink with arousal. Her shyness forgotten, Mya reached out and wrapped her little hand around my length.

"Anyone ever told you, your penis is very big?"

"All the time. I've never found a vagina it didn't fit

though, but that doesn't sound like much of a compliment to give a woman, does it?"

Dropping her jaw at me, Mya smacked me on the side of my arse.

"Well you've obviously had a lot of loose women, Jack."

"Are you implying it won't fit inside you?"

"I don't know, Jack, do you think we should find out?"

"Is that your pathetic attempt at begging me to fuck you?"

"I'm not going to beg and you're not going to fuck me, Jack. Look at me, I'm not the kind of girl you fuck. I'm the kind of girl you make love to."

Smiling sweetly at me, Mya was goading me into taking the next step. She was trying to sound confident and slightly arrogant with her statement, but I saw the nervous look was back in her eyes. I was feeling pretty desperate to have her, but recognised her warning was about taking care of her. So I tried to tread carefully because I was determined to give myself the best chance with her and get it right.

This girl wasn't the type you did a one-and-done with. Mya was in a class of her own. Apart from being funny, smart and beautiful, she was very talented and independent as well as being ball-crushingly innocent looking and sweet as sin. She was like bright sunlight suddenly flooding a darkened room and had exactly what I needed to help me feel like myself again. She was definitely girlfriend material but I still felt that five years difference between us could create some problems and I had a bit of a hang up about that for some reason.

Chapter 28

You don't play fair

The strange thing about us lying on that bed was that, if I'd been with anyone else I'd probably have been twenty minutes into a nice sexual workout. Even though I was feeling extremely horny, I didn't want my first time with Mya to be a frantic groping session. The fact that I was thinking of it being the first time made me think I was more invested in this thing with her than I'd been willing to accept until we were both naked and all the bullshit had been stripped away.

Mya chewed the side of her mouth and I placed my fingers against her lips to stop her. She was driving me nuts with her sexy little innocent ways so I drew my fingers across them and poked one of my fingers into her mouth. She took my breath away with the power she put behind sucking it. My dick bounced heavily against her leg as the feeling radiated through me.

Mya rubbed her knee against my groin and a low gravelly sound tore from my throat. I took my wet finger out and began trailing it down her chin then between her breasts and down the length of her body to her pussy.

Goose bumps appeared on her skin again, her nipples hardened and her breath caught in her throat.

"Oh, god, you taste delicious." I murmured, moving my head back to her nipple before my mouth engulfed it and sucked hard.

She writhed and drew her palm up my arm and shoulder to grab a handful of my hair at the nape of my neck. My scalp tingled under her touch stimulating my own erogenous reaction.

My fingers were moving across Mya's clitoris and I slid them down the wet channel to her entrance, she felt open and ready for me.

"Open your legs wider for me."

She spread her legs and I pulled her knees up as I crawled over her to place the head of my dick at her entrance. She looked nervously at me and then smiled, letting me know that she was happy with what we were doing. So I cradled her head between my arms and held her face to mine with my forehead resting against hers. She held my gaze for a couple of seconds before lowering her eyes.

"Look at me, Mya. I want to see how you feel when I'm entering your body for the first time. I want you to see me and what you do to me too."

Heavy eyelids and serious, lust filled eyes stared back at me. I bent my head to whisper in her ear.

"Tell me you want me inside you." I needed that final consent before I went any further.

"Do it." Mya's voice sounded strained.

"What Mya? What do you want me to do? Say the words." I whispered seductively again.

Mya stared intently and looked a little pissed that I wasn't already balls deep inside her.

"Put it in." She said gruffly. I smiled against her ear at her attempt to consent and whispered playfully again.

"Tell me what you want, you have to say it or I can't

228

do it."

"Jack don't you dare mess with me. Come on I'm waiting." Mya's school ma'am tone was urgent.

"For what? What are you waiting for, Mya? A bus?"

"Jack, this isn't funny. Please…"

Nudging forward I began to enter her slowly and Mya's eyes widened before half closing as she began to absorb the sensation of me filling her warm, tight pussy. She was hugging me from within and her head extended back as her back arched when she reacted to our union. I began to kiss her in that first couple of seconds and I swallowed the gasp that escaped from her.

"Thank you for begging, Mya, I knew you could do it." I whispered into her ear and smiled as I started to move in and out of her slowly. Mya's brow bunched as she thought over what she'd said.

"You don't play fair do you?"

"Oh, I do. When I'm not burying myself deep inside the beautiful woman I'm trying to impress." My dick was enjoying the feel of her and the rest of me was screaming to ride her hard because she felt so good.

"Any beautiful woman or just me?" Mya's tone was playful but I knew she wanted some kind of reassurance that I wasn't just using her.

"I can't see anyone else here with us, can you?"

Bending to kiss her again, I decided enough was enough. It was time to satisfy my beautiful bed mate and make sure I left her feeling like she'd made the right decision to press me for more.

I pulled my dick out and slapped it gently against her as I moved myself onto my knees in front of her. I pulled her up my legs so she was sitting in my lap. Sliding back inside her, Mya's soft moan and little growl as she ground herself against me was all the encouragement I needed. I began to fuck her gently and pick up the pace when I saw her brow begin to furrow in frustration, so I paid special attention to her clit to increase her pleasure.

Within a few minutes I could feel her legs begin to tremble and I knew I had her right where I wanted her. My speed picked up and less than a minute later her mouth formed a silent scream before she made this sexy high pitched noise with every wave of her climax as it tore through her. Mya's pussy clenched so tightly I thought my dick was going to break.

"Ohhh, fuck. Mmm. Damn that feels so good."

Watching her recover, she licked her lips and her eyes stared up at me with pure unadulterated lust. I felt ecstatic that I'd help put that look on her face. Turning her on her side, I spooned her from behind and pulled her knees up to her stomach. Sliding back inside her felt like perfection. This was one of my favourite positions and she was taking all of me now. I held her in my arms, pulling her close to me and turned her head to kiss her while I rocked in and out of her at a steady pace.

All the while I was doing that, my hands were stroking her body and squeezing her breasts. Mya groaned and moaned softly, enjoying everything I could give her. She tried to turn and I was instantly aware of her need to change position so I released my grasp, letting her pull away from me. She rose onto her knees, pushed me back on the bed and straddled me, her hands tracing down my shoulders to rest on my hips. She then reached behind her with one hand and positioned me back at her entrance before sinking slowly down onto me.

I glanced up at her, she looked perfect in that position as she begun to rise and fall slowly at first and then much quicker. Her breasts bounced up and down gently and her hair flopped to one side. When she began to rock back and forth on me she looked a little frustrated, in fact she was a hot mess and I don't think I'd ever seen anything sexier than how she looked at that point.

Mya was a little hard to work out because she seemed

shy in one sense and completely unabashed in another. I liked the intricacy of her; she was complex and yet appeared to live a simple life at the same time. She was deep and brooding when she was concentrating and quick witted and playful when she was relaxed. And, right at the point where she was about to come, open and shameless.

The night was all about pleasing her. I don't know how I did it, but I kept myself in check as I pleasured her until she said she was dizzy and I pulled out. I pulled the condom off and stroked myself until I came on her belly while she watched. Afterwards, I cleaned her with a wash cloth from the bathroom and pulled her tight to me, holding her in place in front of my body.

It had been a long time since I cradled someone the way I was holding Mya. Rosie hated to be cuddled in bed she liked to sprawl out and hog most of the bed. Actually, the only other person I slept this way with was Lily.

Hearing her breathing change from breathlessness to deep and her heartbeat slowed to a soft rhythm, I noticed she had fallen into a deep sleep. I was exhausted but my mind wandered to Lily and the differences between her and Mya. They were a lot alike but completely different. Mya was much more astute than Lily was at her age, and Lily was less independent.

Sleep escaped me as my mind went around and around about Lily and how difficult life had been for her during the past couple of years and I wondered if I had been enough of a friend to her during those times. Had we grown apart that much that she felt she couldn't share something so life altering with me? I knew I'd have to put the past behind me at some point and I promised myself I'd deal with Lily once I was back home after the tour.

After that, my mind flitted to Rosie. Life in the past year was one that I'd never forget. We had gone from almost living together to never speaking again. How does a relationship like that go downhill so fast? We'd gone from being together all of the time, to acting like strangers and we lived like an estranged married couple with one cutting the other out of their life altogether as if they'd died. Except Rosie hadn't died, she had built a new life where I had no place, and I was beginning to build mine. Maybe I had developed an infatuation with her during my time away that would have burned out again if we'd gotten back together.

Once I had reconciled myself about the other women who were a big part of my life, I turned my focus back to the wonderful girl sleeping peacefully in my arms and felt fortunate for the chance to see how things would develop between us. After that, sleep began to close on me and I snuggled in tightly. Mya sighed in my arms and I kissed her neck; that was the last thing I remembered before sleep took over.

I woke to the feeling of someone watching me and opened my eyes. Mya was sitting cross legged on the bed in my shirt and she was a vision first thing in the morning. The bun had gone and her hair cascaded down her back and over her shoulders, stopping just over her breasts.

"I expected you to leave in the night, Jack. You're full of surprises. I never figured you for the kind of guy that stayed."

I wanted to call her on that but I couldn't because apart from Rosie and Lily, I had been exactly that kind of guy. Admitting it wouldn't have been a wise move when I was trying to impress her though.

"I wanted to stay to prove to myself that last night really did happen and that it wasn't a dream. If I'd gone back to my own room things could have been awkward this morning between us. I didn't want that to happen."

"Me neither. I was surprised you'd stayed to be honest."

"Why?"

"I'm not the type of girl who sleeps around, Jack. I've

had two partners in two years and never a one night stand. I prayed you weren't my first, but I took that chance anyway to be with you." She blushed and picked at the bed sheet before she looked up nervously, unsure whether her admission had freaked me out or maybe she thought I was going to let her down.

Pulling myself up the bed, I leaned back against the headboard and pulled the sheet across my morning wood that I was trying to ignore during our serious conversation. Covering it up just made it all the more obvious and when I looked back at her she had a smirk on her face that was threatening to become a full on grin at any moment. I wanted to hug her and reassure her that this wasn't a casual thing for me.

"Come here, Mya. I want to talk to you."

"No, Jack. Don't. It's okay. We're okay. I know we live very different lives and there's an ocean between us. I don't regret last night, but we're going to go our separate ways in a few weeks, I get that and I'm cool with it." Her comment left me stunned.

Hearing Mya's thoughts made me bottle up my own and my heart sunk to my stomach. How was I supposed to reassure her that I'd make time for her despite the distance between us and her life already mapped out in front of her at music school? I knew her plans and she was only twenty years old. Of course she didn't want the complication of a guy like me who wasn't even able to live in the same country unless I jumped through a million hoops to be there, and that wasn't an option for me at this moment in time.

All I could do was nod. It wasn't how I was feeling but I had to accept what she was telling me. She'd had second thoughts. Trying to have a long distance romance at twenty wasn't going to get either of us far, so I just reached forward and kissed her softly.

"Thank you for last night, Mya. It was beautiful.

You're an incredibly beautiful girl. I had a wonderful time."

As soon as I said it I knew it sounded shitty and I wished I'd never met her. She was a friend that I'd crossed the line with and now she wanted to walk away.

We spent another awkward ten minutes in each other's company before she went into the bathroom and came out a short time later wearing her jeans and a clean t-shirt. Throwing my shirt onto the bed, she turned and picked up a few sachets of coffee. Sensing I'd outstayed my welcome I stood and began to excuse myself by saying that I had some articles to catch up on. Mya didn't respond as she wandered over to the coffee machine in her room and began to organise her morning drink. She could barely stand to look at me. As I picked up my shirt and pulled it over my head I then shook my jeans out, stepped in and shrugged them up over my arse.

Once I'd dressed I wandered over to her placing my hands on her upper arms and forced her to turn and face me. Bending down I kissed her lightly on the mouth and hugged her tightly against my chest. As her body pressed into mine, I inhaled her scent and kissed the top of her head. My heart squeezed as I struggled with the huge lump that had formed in my throat and I really wanted to challenge her about her decision, but I felt she'd made herself crystal clear. I sighed deeply, released my hold and pulled back slightly to meet her awkward fleeting eye contact.

"See you later? What time will you be at the hall?" It was all I could think of to say that was completely platonic, giving her the opportunity to stay friends.

Mya looked up and I stared at her face intently, trying to figure out what she was thinking because her expression was blank. I couldn't decipher anything from our interaction that clued me in one way or another about her feelings.

"Sure. Around two." She said chirpily, and then went back to making her coffee.

I could sense she just wanted me to leave so I walked over to the chair, picked my jacket up then looked back over my shoulder at her one last time. When she didn't turn back I opened her hotel room door and left.

Chapter 29

Throat punch

I felt sick as I walked back to my room, her rejection had stung and I had started to think that there was something wrong with me. I must give out a vibe to these girls that makes them all want to fuck me, but not get involved. I thought Mya was different, or maybe I wanted to think that and it wasn't really there at all.

The mixed messages I'd received from Rick and Mya led me to believe that there would be more than just casual sex or I wouldn't have ventured there in the first place. So much for Mya's comment about her not being a 'one night stand', kind of girl.

The more I thought about it, the more I felt used. At least with the other girls I knew exactly what I was getting myself into. With Mya, I took it slowly, did everything at what I thought was her pace and yet in the end, she just climbed on and rode me; just like all the rest.

Complicated thought processes ran through my mind about myself. After the retreat I thought I had everything figured out and where had all that thinking got me? Rosie hated me and I had let two more women use me. Feeling angry with myself, I headed for the shower wondering if

I'd ever learn. Inside I was hurting because I had begun to fall for someone I thought actually cared about me.

Several days of awkward conversations and minimal contact followed and I began to avoid being where I thought she might be. My feelings towards her were still strong. When a heart wants something bad enough it cuts deeper when it is deprived, but I wasn't going to force something between us.

Mya had made it clear what she wanted and I hadn't been written into her plans. Instead of joining the others for dinner or hanging out, I became a little reclusive during the final days of the tour. Even though I thought I'd been clever it didn't escape Rick's attention.

"Jack, come to my suite after rehearsals. I want to talk to you."

And there it was. Rick was probably going to fire my arse for screwing his niece. By that time I knew the whole episode had affected me, but it was interfering with my work as well. I didn't really care what he did to me. I'd been moping around and avoiding everyone like they were a plague of lepers. I also knew from Phil, the photographer, that Mya wasn't hanging out with anyone either.

For the first time I really understood Dave's feelings about Emily. He hadn't talked to her about how he felt about it and years later was still feeling like shit because there was stuff that should have been said at the time, but it was too late to talk.

The bigger lesson for me in all of that was that I'd been right not to get involved with Lily all those years ago. Getting close to Mya and then having sex with her taught me how easily people's relationships transformed from a close emotional connection to complete avoidance.

My social life may have been in the toilet but my work ethic had always been exceptional and I couldn't afford to upset Rick that late in the day. Until then I knew

Joe, my editor was impressed. Every morning there were emails from him sounding pumped about every article he received. With my exclusives and Phil's amazing shots, we were able to put together some really wicked media packets on the band.

As I walked through the hotel on the way to face Rick, I still couldn't fail to be impressed with how immaculately kept it seemed. Even the cream velvet chairs seemed pristine with no evidence that anyone had ever sat in them. Then it struck me that it all seemed kind of clinical. When I stepped into the lift my stomach churned in anticipation of what may be facing me when I reached the penthouse. After Jed, Rick's bodyguard, had given me the nod I knocked on suite door. It was our last day in Munich and we only had four days left of the tour. I heard Rick call out from inside.

"Yep, come on in," he shouted, in his distinctive southern drawl.

Pushing the heavy oak door open I saw Rick sitting in a chair with large glass of brandy. Holding the stem between his second and third fingers and the glass cradled in his palm and thumb.

"Sit down, Jack, we need to talk," he said in a serious tone. His expression was solemn.

Rick's eyes narrowed as he scrutinized me carefully then sighed heavily and gestured for me to sit on the other sofa with a wave of his glass as he tipped his chin up toward it. Stepping forward I turned and sat as he'd directed me to.

"All right, spare me the graphic details or I might have to throat punch you, but what's going on between you and my niece?"

Rick flicked some imaginary lint off of his trousers then leaned back and placed his arm the length of his sofa waiting for my reply.

I was trying to appear innocent. And I was really. I

hadn't done anything wrong, to my mind it was Mya that had called the halt between us.

"Nothing."

Rick snorted incredulously and looked slightly peeved at my response.

"Well fuck, Jack, I wouldn't have to be Einstein to see that she chokes every time you're in the room or your name is mentioned, and today she was staring at the wall while we were all sharing a laugh. What's the deal?"

I shrugged trying to look nonchalant but inside I felt sad because she was upset but I reminded myself once again, that it was her decision.

"What can I say, Rick? She was the one that told me not to push it and I haven't. She's twenty years old with a future that doesn't include me. I get it we never should have strained the friendship we had."

"Jesus, Jack, I never had you marked down as a fucking martyr. I've noticed you've had the same sour pathetic look about you that she has. You want her, you'll have to fight for her, Jack. I never pegged you as a quitter. Don't make me have to reassess my judgement. Distance, time, fucking career prospects—they're all bullshit. Didn't watching Lily teach you anything about relationships?"

"I'll talk to her at least. See where she's at now that the dust has settled on our date night. I know she's young, Rick, I'd never toy with her feelings."

Rick looked satisfied with my answer and slapped his hands on his knees pushing himself to stand.

"All right see that you do, Jack. Now get the fuck out of my space, I need to get laid and catch a nap before the gig later."

Turning away from me he headed into his bedroom and I had to smile at his blunt list of chores for the afternoon. He'd said it like it was the most natural thing in the world to say. But then again both of those things *were* probably the most natural things in the world.

Avoiding people wasn't really my style so I left Rick's suite and headed straight for Mya's. I had no idea what I was going to say and walking down the corridor transported me back in time to when I went to see Rosie. I knocked on her door and Mya opened it with red rimmed eyes making my breath catch in the back of my throat.

"Jeez, Mya, what's the matter love?"

Covering her face with her hands, Mya bent her head towards the floor in her effort to hide it from me.

"Sorry, I was watching a weepy chick-flick on the TV."

I called bull on that particular excuse because I couldn't hear the television and Mya looked like she'd been bawling her eyes out.

"From your appearance, I'd say you were watching the same movie that's playing out in my mind and fucking with my head. I miss talking to you, love. Where did we go wrong? I'm really sorry we slept together if this is the outcome."

Glancing up at me through her tearstained eyes, Mya gave me a weak smile and I immediately wrapped my arms around her, pulling her into my chest. She felt like she belonged there. I didn't care how old she was or that she was leaving to go to California in four days. I wanted her so badly.

Mya broke down and started crying again. Her body was racked by her shaky breathless sobs and my heart bled for the pain she was in.

"Hey, nothing's this bad, love. Tell me what's upsetting you and we'll work it out."

Suddenly Mya pushed me away and walked into the bathroom closing the door behind her. That irritated me because Lily had done that to me once and instead of talking to me she just shut me out, but then I heard the toilet flush and the water running in the sink, so I relaxed and sat on her bed waiting for her to return. When she did

I saw that she had washed her face but her eyes were still tear-stained and puffy.

"Sorry." Wiping her nose on a tissue she placed a knee on the bed and folded it underneath her as she sat facing me. "I didn't mean to do that, it just...overwhelmed me."

"What did, Mya?"

"The sadness of our whole situation. I really like you and the thought that in a few days..."

Mya's voice trailed off and in my mind all I wanted to do was tell her how I felt, but the chances of us surviving a relationship so far apart was a major barrier. Plus she had everything ahead of her. Maybe if I hadn't studied music at the retreat and grew up knowing how important music was to Lily it would have felt simpler. But I had and I knew how time consuming and emotionally absorbing it was. It would be unfair to try to make her share her time between that and me, never mind try to maintain it with the distance between us.

"I know, I feel the same but I'm not going to come between you and your studies."

Mya glanced at me and took another deep shuddery breath.

"Uncle Rick said that I can study music anywhere but it's too early, we're too early to know... I mean, I don't want to move to London to find that you don't want me a month later."

Fuck. The dilemma facing me was tricky. Did I care enough for Mya to commit to a relationship of that kind that early on? Was it sustainable enough for her to give up her college place and relocate to my city to be near me?

I knew I really liked her to the point where I thought about her a lot, loved being with her, loved the closeness of minds we shared and we had a lot of chemistry, but it was very early days. Was what we were both feeling that early infatuation one feels for someone when it's all very new or could this be the beginning of something special?

"Mya, if it makes you feel any better this isn't easy for me either. I like you a lot as well. I have since day one, and I've loved the time we've shared during the tour, but think about it sweetheart, being in this environment we've kind of been thrown together. We've been travelling, sleeping, and eating in the same places, and us both working with the band, none of that provides normality does it?"

Mya looked like she was going to cry again at any second and I could see tears welling in her beautiful big blue eyes as they searched my face, waiting for me to say something that would make everything okay for her. From my own perspective, since I had her in my arms again I knew that I couldn't just let her go.

"You're not throwing away everything you've got planned because you met me. I won't allow it. I think we both feel enough that we want to see each other again after the tour, right?"

Nodding slowly, Mya wiped a stray tear away with her sleeve and looked at me intensely. A sob tore from her throat and I pulled her to me for another hug. Rubbing her back, I lowered my head to kiss the top of hers and stroked her hair before speaking.

"All right, love, we'll work something out, but the plans for your college stand. I agree that we both need some time to see how we work in a normal setting. How does that sound?"

Mya leaned back to look at me with a weak smile, her eyes slowly brightening with hope.

"Sounds like a great plan. I'd like that Jack."

Leaning forward, I pressed my lips against her wet cheek and tasted her salty tears before pressing them to her lips.

"No more tears. If we're supposed to be together we'll find a way."

Chapter 30

Honesty

The following three days were incredible. Mya and I spent as much time with each other as possible and I had definitely put the smile back on her face again. Slipping away from the others, we stole intimate moments together and although my head kept telling me she'd be leaving soon, my heart was behaving as if I was a love struck teenager. I was elated with every moment we were together and yearned for her when we had to spend time apart.

Obviously, neither of us was looking forward to that final goodbye when the tour ended and we had to go back to our regular lives. The mere thought of it gave me a horrible ache in the pit of my stomach. Life was unfair because I'd finally found someone that could mean everything to me and we were being torn apart by circumstance.

During the last night of the tour, I stood watching Rick on stage performing with boundless energy rocking out in all his glory and wondered how the hell he did that year in, year out. Playing to millions, filling their heads and their hearts with joy from his ability to make music and write songs that struck a chord with his fans, as well as spreading himself so thinly that his own life seemed owned by everyone else. I no longer envied him his position.

I understood why he had sex with so many women. I believed it was Rick's way of having no time to commit to one person. He was transient, constantly leaving people behind or there was the expectation for anyone that became involved to basically give up their own dreams to allow him to follow his. My opinion used to be that Rick had become a selfish man-whore because of his fame and that his lifestyle was incredibly self-centred. But actually, the fact that he hadn't attached himself to a woman that could give him what his life was lacking was pretty selfless, because he already knew his ability to return their devotion was extremely limited.

When the concert finally finished and the last song rang out, the crowd went berserk, cheering and screaming. The band made their exit into the blacked-out people carrier I knew was waiting for them. As they disappeared into the night the hall was still full of people, who were only just coming down from the enthralling performance they'd just witnessed.

As the lighting was turned on in the auditorium, my eyes were drawn to the small familiar figure that had appeared on the stage and a sharp pang hit me square in the chest. Reality dawned that would be the last time I'd see Mya tending to the band's guitars. Tomorrow we'd both be going home, alone.

Depression was no excuse for not getting my final article written so I sat in the family and friends seating area and punched my article out on my tablet, my feet resting on the seat in front of me. I was fulfilling the last of my work obligations while I waited for Mya to finish doing what she had to do as well. My heart wasn't really in the final assignment but I knew once it was done we could go back to the hotel and I could devote the rest of the night to spending time with her.

I'd called ahead and ordered room service and bought some things that would make it feel more romantic and less like we were in a work-related hotel room. I wanted that night to be intimate and special so that I could show her that this wasn't the end of us. I'd bought fifty-one candles, a cheap guitar and an iPad.

During the journey back from the concert venue Mya was quiet and deep in thought and I knew she had to be feeling the same ache about this as I was. When someone was grieving the loss of something it's so easy to say, 'Everything's going to be okay'. And at that early stage of our relationship, I didn't know that for sure, so I kept quiet and hoped that one day I would be able to.

Entering the lift, she went to push the button for her floor. We'd spent the past three nights in her room, but that night I pushed her hand gently to the side and pressed the button for my floor.

"Tonight I want you in my bed if that's okay with you? Tonight is going to be a good night for us. I won't have it any other way, understand? This is the beginning not the end, right?"

Staring up at me I could see my three questions being digested and their effect on her. She pursed her lips in an effort to bite back her emotions that were just below the surface. Mya nodded quickly then dipped her head because her eyes had started to fill with tears. She wasn't quick enough though and I saw her trying to blink them back rapidly before her hair fell in front of her face.

Bending my knees, I crooked my finger under her chin and lifted her face to make eye contact with me. When her gaze met mine I swallowed hard when I saw the vulnerability of her youth in the way she looked at me. I know it sounded like there was twenty years between us but with her going to college on the other side of the world, there may as well have been. There and then I vowed silently I'd never intentionally hurt her. The lift arrived on my floor and I smiled warmly, kissed her forehead, wrapped my arm around her shoulder and led her to my door.

When we'd entered the hotel, I'd nodded at the receptionist and they had lit the candles I had arranged along the dresser in front of the mirror as we made our way up. The small table by the window was set with two places for dinner and also lit by a single candle. The hot food trolley was already in place. When Mya saw my small efforts her breath caught in her throat and her hand gripped mine tightly as she walked ahead of me into the room.

Turning to face me, her face was in the shadows but I could see her expression was very different to when we'd left the lift. A wide smile had spread across her face and when she leaned into me and extended her neck, the flickers from the candles reflected in her eyes.

"You did all of this just for me, Jack?"

"Not at all, you have the first hour. There are three more girls after you. Candles aren't cheap these days, you know."

Mya giggled and smacked her hand against my chest and I instantly caught her wrist turning her quickly to press her against the wall by the side of the bed. Lifting her arm above her head I kissed her neck while she squirmed against me before meeting her lips with mine. She reached around my back and started to pull my shirt from the waistband of my pants but I grabbed a hold of her hand and lifted it. I held them both together above her head while my lips wandered down to her neck again.

Groaning loudly, she shivered at the sensation and sagged against my body, her head rolling to the side while her back arched her groin closer to my raging hard-on.

Responding to my every touch, kiss, lick and soft nibble, Mya continued to express the pleasure she was feeling through a series of soft moans and sighs. Each erotic sound she made turned me on more than the last, but I was determined not to treat her like all the others by throwing her on the bed and simply having my wicked way with her. I didn't want our last evening to be purely about sex. If we were trying to go forwards I wanted her to know things about me, the Jack that no one else knew.

Kissing her again, I brought her hands down by her side and stepped away, stretching her arms out in front of her as I continued to hold them.

"Come here and sit with me, Mya. I want to feed you first. You're going to need as much energy as you can muster for later."

I was being humorous but distracting her at the same time as I led her to the table. Mya rolled her eyes because, I thought, based on the last few days in bed she had me pegged as a sensual lover rather than a passionate one. So far my willpower had held out. Mya had to survive dinner to find out about the other side of me.

If I had allowed myself to get fully lost in her before it would have made it more difficult for both of us and I was being careful in case I was experiencing rebound feelings after Rosie, but the last few days taught me that I was becoming more and more drawn in by her. That was the saddest part. The follow day, I imagined, we would both be emotionally drained by the separation and that would be our ground zero for whatever happened next for us.

Mya glanced over at the candles and smiled affectionately at me.

"So, candles, Jack? I never had you down as a romantic guy."

My eyes flicked to the melting array of wax shapes and their flames dancing gently with the low air condition, and then looked back at their reflection in her eyes.

"I didn't think I was either, until now."

"Lots of candles. They made a good job of the display, don't you think?"

"Thank you. I picked them out, bought them myself then arranged them here like that especially for you."

Mya leaned forward then turned to look at me again then began to chuckle as her gaze changed to one of disbelief.

"You almost had me there, Jack. You should consider acting as a career."

Her words stung because I had really thought that out and for a second I wondered whether I should just let it go, but I decided honesty was a necessity in this relationship. I'd seen too many people play with each other and ruin their relationships.

"Actually, Mya, I'm serious. What you see was all me. Fifty-one candles. Forty-nine marking one for each day since the first time I saw you tuning those guitars in the pit."

Inclining my head in the direction of them I added, "Look closely at them love, each candle is different just like every day has been on this tour."

I could see Mya wondering about the remaining two. Her brow was furrowed in question and I thought my spur of the moment romantic gesture sounded cheesy, I hesitated about saying it out loud, but the sentiment was genuine.

"That leaves two candles I haven't mentioned. Those two are the same and are standing side by side. They represent us. Similar people with a burning desire to be together. If you look at the dresser they are at the centre surrounded by the flames and melting wax of all the others. That makes them fragile. If we choose to do this it won't be easy, Mya, and it's going to mean constant separations and trusting each other. I'll do my best as long as it's what we both want. If it isn't, we have to be honest with each other. You're young and just beginning to live your life and I know I'm only five years older, but I have done so much in the last five years that have shaped the person I am today. I don't want to hurt you, and I don't want you to regret your decision."

Mya looking into my eyes like she was searching my soul then she sighed and the sound was like her heart was heavy. She stood up and walked over to my side of the table, wrapped her arms around my neck and sat on my lap.

"Jack, I know you're worried about my age and I don't understand that it's only five years. I'm a woman and I'm as sure about this as I have been about anything in my life. This isn't an adolescent crush I'm experiencing it is much deeper and more life changing than anything I ever expected to feel about another person. My heart feels hollow and my focus is patchy when you're not in the room."

Looking at me in desperation she took a deep breath and tried again.

"Look, I know now isn't the time and that you probably don't want to hear it but, I've fallen in love with you. The best way I can describe it is that, being with you is like watching a new born baby grow day by day. Each day when I look at you, or when I hold you, I love you a little more."

All I could do was stare back at her. She'd just told me she loved me, but I wasn't sure it was love for me yet. I was still in the honeymoon stage of our relationship. If I was being truthful, I was crazy about her but being crazy about her didn't mean it was going to last a lifetime. So I hugged her and mumbled something about loving someone being a wonderful gift or something just as shitty.

I had to be honest with Mya, it had only been a few weeks since we moved the relationship on and she had bolted the morning after. With everything I'd been through with Rosie, I couldn't tell her the same back. I needed to protect myself as much as I needed to protect her.

Chapter 31

Bathroom

Declaring she loved me was a brave move on her part and I wanted to respect her feelings, but Mya's admission was almost a conversation killer. I quickly recovered the moment by asking her to tell me something about herself that I didn't know which caught her off guard and she rolled her eyes upward in thought.

"I have a Vintage Volkswagen Beetle called Stanley who's the same age as me. My father bought him for me when I was sixteen. Your turn."

Not wanting to focus on material things I tried to share something personal about me.

"I'm an only child, the last male heir in my family, actually. My father has three brothers who all had girls so the pressure is on me to produce a male Cunningham to keep my family linage going." *Jesus Christ, Jack, what in the hell did you say that for? How pompous did that sound? She's telling you she loves you and you're sending a message that she has to give you a son?*

Gesturing for her to take her seat, I began to dish up the food between us and tried to change the subject yet again because I was making a real arse of things as they were.

"Tell me another thing that no one else knows about you," I quickly added.

"I used to hate playing the guitar because it caused so many fights between my dad and Uncle Rick. My father is a corporate money-man and Uncle Rick...? well my father thought he was just a wayward layabout."

Chuckling at her comment, I wondered if her dad had changed his mind when Rick became a world famous rock star earning shed-loads of money and a very big and loyal fan-base. I bet he felt pissed off about that.

As the evening wore on, we continued to share a few very basic things about each other, although there was nothing earth shattering in our revelations. Mya wanted to know about Lily, but that would have lowered my mood so I excused the topic as being too long to go into and she let the subject drop. By the time we'd finished eating we'd drunk an entire bottle of white wine between us and I was feeling more relaxed again so decided to surprise her with the second thing I had purchased that day. The iPad.

"I know you have a tablet already but I've put a few things on this one to keep you company when we're apart." Glancing between me and the parcel she had just finished unwrapping, she took out the iPad and sat it on her lap.

"Check out the camera gallery," I told her.

Mya scrolled to the apps and opened the camera gallery, there were about a hundred pictures waiting for her. I had chosen them from several hundred and uploaded them earlier. As well as the band photographs, Phil had taken tons of candid shots of us together, ones of her doing her job or conversing with various members of the band and crew. I found one of the pictures incredibly inspiring and I wrote a song about it, recorded it using some voice software on my computer and uploaded it to the iPad as well. It wasn't exactly about her but more about life on the road and it was fitting for that night because it referenced a couple going their separate ways for a while.

"Oh, Jack, this is awesome. I love it. Aww, look at this one of us, we look amazing together." She was right, we did and the look shared between us was so passionate it could have been a book cover for a hot romance novel.

Tilting her head to the side she looked at me out of the corner of her eye.

"You did all this for me?"

I had, and I'd wanted to do a lot more for her, especially with the sexy way she was smiling at the pictures. Leaning over I placed my hand on her cheek.

"I wish I could do a hell of a lot more, but we'll work it out."

I sounded more confident than I felt. America seemed a long way away and I was a spontaneous sort of guy, how I was going to achieve that spontaneity I had no idea.

Mya excused herself and went to the bathroom, leaving me worried the night was going to go downhill and we'd end up all tears and tantrums before bed. I decided to surprise her again, that time by playing a tune on my guitar. I had planned on sharing my secret talent with her during the night at some point but there was no time like the present.

It was either going to work or it was game over and we'd leave feeling like shit about not making the most of our time left together. Finding some courage, I pulled off my shirt and sat cross legged on the bed feeling nervous because it would be the first time I had performed to anyone other than Graham and the others at the retreat. Plus Mya was pretty much an expert on the guitar so I wasn't that confident about impressing her.

The first song I thought of was one that got me through some bad memories while I was on retreat.

'Living In The Moment' by Jason Mraz. I began to quietly play the intro, and took a deep breath. I'd never really played and sang at the same time in front of anyone and I hadn't realised how nerve-wracking it would be until now.

I'd sung Karaoke hundreds of times, but not to impress anyone other than myself. Then there was the fact that Mya's uncle was one of the best singer-performers in the world. *No pressure there then.*

It's strange how music lightens the heart with just a few beats of the right song and before I knew it, I was singing loudly and lost myself in the spirit of the song. Forgetting my inhibitions was very liberating and I figured that if I was going to play for her, I had to commit completely or I would have sounded half-arsed and made mistakes as soon as my confidence waivered.

When I'd finished, I opened my eyes to find Mya standing in the bathroom doorway wearing sexy matching lingerie with suspenders, black fishnet stockings and stiletto shoes. Initially I was having difficulty figuring out how all of that had gone into the little bag she was carrying earlier. I quickly dismissed the thought as my dick woke up and hardened painfully.

"So...Clark Kent has a phone box and you have a bathroom? Are you figuring on saving me in that outfit? Because it's giving me heart palpitations and if I look at you without touching for much longer I think I'm going to need mouth to mouth resuscitation, love."

Mya stood still as she blinked a couple more times before shaking her head as if she had been day dreaming. She then brought her hands in front of her chest with her palms facing me in a 'stop right there' gesture.

"Hold it right there, Jack. You never told me you played the guitar and could sing like that. Were you in a band? Are you in a band, back home in London I mean? You're incredible, amazing, fucking hot. No one ever mentioned you playing. Fuck, Jack, I didn't think it was

possible to be any more attracted to you but after that..."
Mya's eyes were wide with lust as she wandered over to
me, her legs looking ultra-sexy in her stockings.

What is it with me and legs all of a sudden, I used to
be an arse man.

When she reached me, she took the guitar from my
hands and placed it on the floor before pushing me
backwards onto the bed. She climbed on, straddled me and
lowering herself. She sat directly on my dick and began to
rock back and forth. The friction her dry humping created
made me desperate for more, so I rolled her over face first
on the bed. Mya protested weakly, but I pulled her up onto
her knees and pushed her shoulders into the mattress so
that her arse was up in the air.

"Fuck, Mya. You can't do that kind of thing to me
and expect me to carry a rational conversation. You're
attire foreplay outshines my guitar playing foreplay any
day of the week."

Mya started giggling and tried to protest again.

"It's only underwear, Jack."

"Only underwear? Fuck it's lacy, matching, black
see-through underwear with nipples and a hint of clit
showing and silky skin next to lacy fish net stockings and
fuck me heels..."

Mya interrupted my distracted lust-filled babble, "All
right take a breath, Jack, I get the message. Note to self,
order fresh supplies of kinky lingerie for Jack's visits."

"Yay! And they don't have to be fresh as long as they
were worn recently..."

Mya tried to turn and look up at me with her mouth
gaping in shock at my smutty comment. To pull her out of
it, I pulled the straps on the back of the suspenders and let
go, snapping them against her skin. They made a sharp
slapping noise against her thighs and I was so turned on by
the sound that I wanted to do everything to her.

"Ohh. Jack, Let me get up," she cried out, pretending

to struggle underneath me. The smile she was wearing told me she was coping just fine.

"Nope. You think you can tease me in that lot, get me all hot and horny and I'm going to say sure, Mya, let me assist you baby?" Chuckling at her weak attempts to move, I knelt on the bed with one knee and placed the other foot on the floor.

"Let me show you how it feels to be on the other end of that sexy get-up you're wearing."

Yanking her small knickers down as far as I could with the suspenders still in place, I gave her a short, sharp smack on her arse cheek. Mya cried out and I bent over to lick her stinging flesh before spanking it again. That time I had struck it hard enough to sting my hand and I'd branded her with a red handprint. I immediately kissed it better and rubbed my hand over it. Mya wriggled her arse in my face until my mouth was between her legs and my tongue sought her wet pussy. Instantly her attention turned to making those erotic sounds I loved hearing.

"Oh, Jack, ah, ooo."

I straightened up and my dick was almost bursting out of its skin never mind my trousers. It was getting harder by the minute and was screaming to be inside her.

"Hmm, you like a little kinky play do you, Mya? That's my girl."

My dick felt uncomfortably restricted by the seam of my trousers so I quickly unfastened the buttons and yanked them down my legs before pulling my boxers low enough to let it spring free. From that point on I lost all control. I stepped off of the bed and quickly dropped my trousers, I fumbled for the condoms that were in my back pocket and eagerly sheathed myself as quickly as I could.

I'd been trying to be gentle with Mya since I'd met her, given her age and experience, and because I'd never been around a girl as innocent as her apart from Lily. However, if we were going to try and have a relationship then it was only fair she knew how I liked to have sex. I felt I had to be more how I wanted to take her that time. We had no more time to take things slowly and to my mind it was a now or never moment.

With her shoulders still on the bed, I knelt beside the bed and pulled her arse up to meet my face, instantly tongue-fucking her without warning. Mya gasped loudly as her body sagged in my arms while my dick leaked into the condom with the thrill of tasting her. I kept swirling my tongue and poking into her entrance until her flimsy knickers became too restrictive. I stopped momentarily to push my thumb into the lace, making a hole before quickly ripping them clean off of her.

Mya's breath caught in her throat as I climbed on the bed and knelt behind her. I held her shoulders down with one hand on her neck then licked my other hand and stroked it down my sheath before pushing my dick inside her in one long steady thrust. The long even-toned moan she emitted was all I needed to hear. My eyes closed momentarily at the exquisite feeling as her tight pussy engulfed me. The combination of the two things temporarily rendered me silent. I gathered her hair and leaned over to kiss the back of her neck.

Seeing Mya completely submitting to me without any trust issues drove me on to ride her harder. I straightened back up on my knees and as soon as I grabbed her hips, she turned to look up at me. I could see she loved what I was doing. Her eyes were heavy with lust and her open mouth was making occasional breathy sounds alongside soft moans and little growls before she pushed herself up onto her hands.

I gathered her hair again at both sides of her shoulders and pulled it into a pony tail tugging it back to extend her neck all the way until I could see her face properly. She looked fucking sensational in that position, her plump little arse cheeks were accentuated by the way her spine curved in at her tiny waist then rose again up towards her shoulders.

Mya made more erotic noises and swallowed audibly before licking her lips. I licked mine then ran my tongue the length of hers and kissed her hard. All of me was working hard to please her. My dick was rocking in and out of her steadily, my tongue was tantalising her, I scraped nails the length of her back while my other hand held her firmly by the hair. There was no doubt who was the boss.

Trembling from her legs to her shoulders Mya began to come, her core tightened and almost incapacitated me inside her. Her pussy walls temporarily crushed me with the force of her pending orgasm. I let go of her hair and grabbed her shoulders to increase my traction and speed to take her over the edge in a screaming, shaking experience that she had been overdue for.

As soon as I stopped she collapsed onto the bed with beads of sweat on her back, her neck red and her legs trembling. .

"Jesus, Jack. Where did that come from? That was the best sex I've ever had in my life." Mya croaked in her weakened state and I smirked, satisfied she could handle me in the bedroom.

Chapter 32

Expressions

Mya turned over to stare up at me, her eyes clear and sparkling in her post-come glow and suddenly my heart was fucking with my head again. I didn't want her to leave but I couldn't ask her to stay. I almost choked with emotion at the thought that this was all we could have for the moment.

With that thought I didn't want to waste another minute so I crawled on top of her and held her head in place, kissing her deeply. I absorbed the moan she breathed out and I pressed my hips against hers. Mya's hand slid in between us to hold my length and she positioned it at her entrance again. I pushed myself inside with one long glide and began to fuck her hard again, taking her by surprise. A groan of pleasure tore from her chest and she wrapped her legs around me, digging her heels into my back in her effort to get even closer to me.

Placing my forehead on hers, I rode her at a punishing pace while we stared intensely into each other's eyes. I struggled again with how I was going home without her. A couple of times I caught sight of what I was feeling reflected in Mya's expression so I kissed her, and told her how beautiful she was, and how much I liked her. But I couldn't allow myself to say what I really felt because that would only have made it more difficult for us to be apart.

Entertaining the thought I loved Rosie had taken a lot out of me. I'd never said it to any woman before apart from Lily and our families, and the feelings that gave me were hard to get past. However, despite all the warnings I kept giving myself about Mya I knew I was teetering on the edge of falling in love with her. If I had another week with her like that, I'd be sold on her.

Strangely, my feelings angered me, maybe because it felt like an unfair world. Every time I thought I had it figured out, another curve ball was tossed in my direction, and I felt that time it was especially difficult because with an ocean between us, I had no control over any of it. If we did survive together it would be a miracle. Distance and time can fade relationships.

Mya began to push me back and I thought I was hurting her but she pushed me down onto the bed and took the reins for a bit. I went down easily. As far as I was concerned she could do nothing wrong and I wanted to see what she wanted to do. I was turned on by her confidence to take over and try to please me.

Straddling me, she lowered herself onto my length and began to undulate her hips like she was in the twerking Olympics. I'd never known any female to ride me that fast and for that long before. When I voiced that out loud, Mya lost her rhythm and started chuckling but tweaked my nipples for being cheeky. Of course, I responded in kind and tweaked hers back and she cried out smacking my chest. I caught her hand and once again changed our position to lay her on her side. Lifting her leg over my hip then I began to ride her from a spooning position.

"Fuck, Mya, my dick is so deep inside you."

Mya kept trying to turn to look at me, so I held her

gently by her throat and continued to direct her by talking into her ear and telling her how I felt about being inside her. When I stuck my tongue in there she cringed and scrunched her neck up, her skin, which was glistening with sweat, was suddenly crimped in goose bumps again. When I eventually allowed her to move her head, she was so close to me we were sharing the same air with her breathing into my mouth. During that time I was watching her intently for signs of her impending orgasm.

Mya came again then rolled away from me and got onto her knees, whipping the condom off of me. She tried to take me in her mouth but pulled a face at the taste of latex. Moving quickly she grabbed a glass from the table and took a sip of wine, she then placed me back in her mouth. I was mesmerised by the fact that she hadn't given up after the first time.

Mya liked sucking dick, I could tell by the way she was handling me, sucking my balls and stroking me with her other hand at the same time. It felt amazing. Every time she tried to deep throat me she gagged and spluttered then grinned as her eyes watered and yet she did it again and again.

She made me come, and I'd have liked to say she swallowed but she pulled me out just as I began to tremble and stroked me off between her breasts. It was still one of the best experiences of my life maybe because it was her who was paying attention to me.

After I came I was feeling restless. Probably because I didn't want daylight to come. It was early morning by the time we settled down. Mya was facing me with her legs and arms entwined in mine, sleeping peacefully with deep even breaths that wafted gently on my chin. I lay there looking down at her and every time I thought about how I was going to say goodbye my arms squeezed and I pulled her a little closer to me.

At some point I must have fallen asleep because I

woke to a knock on my hotel door. Mya was still deep in slumber so I eased my way out from our entangled limbs and headed over to see who it was. Phil was standing ready to leave and asked if I wanted to share a ride with him to the airport. I'd overslept and should have been ready to head out.

Glancing back to the bed I asked him for ten more minutes to pull myself together and softly closed the door resting my head on it with a heavy heart. The time had come for me to leave her behind. Cobham Street and their crew were flying out to California at five in the afternoon, but my flight was leaving at eight fifteen. My first thought was to stay and catch a later flight, but that would only be delaying the inevitable, so I wandered over to the bed and sat down with my leg underneath me, bending down to kiss Mya softly on the lips.

Slowly, Mya stretched out with a smile on her face, her eyes fluttering open and I must have looked grim because her expression changed to one of alarm.

"It's time for you to leave isn't it?" Mya's voice sounded like I felt, heartbroken.

Nodding slowly, I took in a deep breath and sighed.

"Phil has been here already, I have less than ten minutes to get downstairs."

Mya sat up and wrapped her arms around me.

"Go. We can do this. I can do this. I'll call you later before the plane leaves and we'll make plans for when we'll next see each other."

I chewed at the side of my mouth and wondered where she found the strength to send me off without shedding any tears because damn, I felt close to them myself. My throat was closing and the sadness I felt inside me was almost overwhelming. I moved swiftly to the bathroom and had a two-minute shower.

Afterwards, I shrugged into my clothes as quickly as I could while Mya stuffed everything that was left lying around into the one bag I'd left open. She was naked and looked beautiful and my heart squeezed again at not having more time to be with her. Zipping up my bag, she lifted it to me and bravely told me to go. I kissed her, which was in no way long enough, and ran out the door. As I reached the lift Phil called to tell me the transport was waiting. I had no more time to dwell on our separation—I had a plane to catch.

Phil and I drowned our sorrows at the airport, we were sad our trip had come to an end. We'd had a brilliant time and the both of us thought we had experienced a once in a lifetime event. He was a good guy and we'd actually worked well as a team to get the articles done for the magazine, so I was in no doubt that I'd be seeing him again.

By the time we got on the plane from Frankfurt to London it was twenty five past seven and we were both pretty inebriated. After an aeroplane foil dish of what tasted like powdered omelette we both fell asleep.

Arriving back at my apartment after seven weeks felt worse than arriving back after six months because that time my emotional state was a hell of a lot less resilient than it had been in August. I'd come back full of hope and aspirations then, left to go on tour at the end of September with my heart in tatters. Now I came back to the bleak winter in London again with a saddened heart.

Being back and away from Mya made me think and although Rosie barely made an appearance in my mind those days, I had a new burden to contend with. I had a beautiful new woman in my life that meant more to me than anyone else ever had, but I was unable to see when I wanted to. The odds were stacked against us but I was determined to make it work. The only plus I could see on my return was at least the heating still worked so the place was warm but that was my only source of comfort.

I saw the light flashing on my answer-phone and

could see it was full with messages.

Dave. "Whoo! Hoo! Call me."

I sniggered and made a mental note to call him when I'd had a bath and sobered up properly because I was still a little drunk from the plane.

Sam : "Are you still in Germany? Call me and let me know."

I shook my head at Sam he hadn't developed in the smarts department since I'd been gone.

Emily: "Jack...I feel someone should tell you anyway, I mean...I know you aren't with Rosie anymore but she had her baby...a girl. She called her Ava-Jacqueline and she's happy. I just thought you'd want to know that because I know you felt bad about breaking up with her."

I guessed no one had told Emily that Rosie had her baby a couple of months ago, because her baby was born before I'd gone on tour. Maybe no one wanted to talk about it around me and that left Emily out of the loop.

Elle: "Hey loverboy! I'm coming to town on the twentieth. I have tickets for the ballet and I know how you love to look up those tu-tu skirts they wear. You are invited to come with me if you want. I'm not taking Sam because last time he talked all the way through Swan Lake asking why ballerinas didn't have breasts. I've missed your sexy arse, call me! We have planning to do and if the ballet is a no-go we're all going dancing anyway. Drew isn't coming with me so I'll be let loose for the night."

A wide grin spread over my face. Elle was, and is as independent as ever, her partner Drew was the lead guitarist in Alfie's band, and the guy just didn't have the will to tame her. She left him weak with her boundless energy. Elle and I were strictly friends since before we were teenagers and she was important to me.

Mum: "Oh, Gosh, Jack. I'm excited you are going to be home again. We've missed you terribly. Call me when you get home and don't be a stranger, we can't wait to see you."

I bit my lip knowing how hard it had been for my mother to let go and allow me to live my life my way. Several times a week she'd tell me how precious I was to her and my father, and I guessed I'm not on their level emotionally yet because my 'missing' people and theirs was on a completely different scale.

There were two messages from financial institutions offering to advise me on wealth management products and new exciting investments and the last one or the first one to be left as my answer-phone, was from Lily.

Lily: "Please don't delete this, Jack. Remember how mad I was when I found out that you and Alfie had been talking behind my back and I felt you were taking his side over mine? Did I walk away from you? Did I stop speaking to you for months? No. Man the fuck up, Jack and call me. The longer this goes on the more I wonder if I ever meant that much to you after all."

In the background I could hear Alfie laughing at her then I heard his voice closer to the phone. **"Way to go Lily, that's really going to have him rushing to pick up the phone. Don't get any ideas about joining the British Diplomatic Service if your music career goes tits up.**

265

You'd start a war with that mouth, lady."

Maybe it was because I was slightly drunk or because of Alfie's smart mouth but I started laughing. After I stopped I realised that inside, my heart was crushed when I'd heard her voice and how angry I'd made her by not talking to her. She seemed to react to men this way. She was either full on or she blew you off.

My first instinct was to call her back, but I decided to wait until my head was clear so that I had no excuse for how I treated her if I did. I knew the incident she was talking about but this was way different. I could have been a father that's in a whole different league to talking to her ex-boyfriend behind her back.

Chapter 33

Fabulous job

How many weeks would it be before I had some leave again? As I walked into my bathroom Mya was on my mind. She wasn't even on her flight yet and I was already trying to figure out how quickly we could be together again. I knew that I'd get a hefty bonus from work and whilst I'd been away I had been on Cobham Street's payroll as well.

Staring in the mirror I wondered how my editor would feel about me having time off again. I'd barely been back at work for a month before I left for the tour, but I knew that if I didn't ask I wouldn't get, so I pulled out my phone and rang Joe at the magazine and was thinking that I was glad to have had a few to drink. I'd deal with the other messages after; at that moment being with Mya was my priority.

"Jack Cunningham. Am I happy to hear from you? You home? You did a fabulous job with Cobham Street, the competition will be freaking out when we start to roll those articles out on Monday."

"Hey Joe. Glad you liked them. It was a blast but I'm

desperately fatigued my man. How am I looking for time off?"

"Are you fucking kidding me? Do you even work here? I'm beginning to wonder who works for whom? You've not been in this office for more than seven weeks in the whole of this year. No, Jack. No way. Whatever you want to do or whoever you want to tap, it or they are going to have to wait. I have another job for you, you're flying off next Wednesday but you can have Christmas week off how does that sound?" Sounds like it may as well have been a lifetime it was only mid-November.

Miserable. That's what it sounded like.

"Nothing until Christmas week? Come on, Joe, I've been on the road for seven weeks."

Joe interrupted me, "Yeah and you were sitting on your arse doing nothing for six months before that. Think about it, Jack. You're lucky I kept you on. Do you know how many applications I had for your sabbatical? Seven hundred and sixty two, so if you want to keep that privileged post you carved for yourself you'd better suck it up and look perky Monday morning, capish?"

Of course, message received and understood. No more play time for Jack. Maybe it wasn't such a bad thing because it would help me put my feelings for Mya into perspective instead of ocean hopping on a whim. I wanted to spend more time with her and my urge for more of our last night's bedroom antics was giving me a semi hard-on every time I thought back on it. As much as I hated the thought of not seeing her that long, maybe those weeks away from her would let me consider things a little more objectively.

Walking into my bathroom, I started to run a bath, stripped off my clothes and slipped into the tub still thinking on what he said.

"Fuck, are you in the bath talking to me, Jack?"

"Yeah, you are one lucky guy to be having a naked

conversation with Jack Cunningham. Women would pay to be doing this with me, Joe."

"If you were a woman they'd be calling you a slut, Jack."

"Nah, that's what jealous dried up old farts like you call me. Women call me 'Oh, Jack' or 'Oh, God', or sometimes 'Oh, God, yes, Jack', or variations of the 'God' theme."

Joe chuckled heartily, "If I didn't love your smart mouth so much, I'd fire your arse you know that?"

"There you go again with that burning desire with my arse. You're obsessed, Joe, but I'm sorry to say I'm not that way inclined. You'll have to focus on some other poor guy's rear end to light your fire under."

Joe knew he wouldn't win when I was in that mode so he fired his warning shot again about me being at work bright and early on Monday and concluded the call. I swiped my phone closed and leaned over to place it on the sink countertop before relaxing back in the tub. No matter what occurred between us, I was going to have to be patient with my emotions and wait it out until Christmas to see Mya again.

I must have dozed off because when I woke the water was freezing. I pushed myself up to a stand, grabbed a towel from the heated towel rail and went through to my bedroom.

Late afternoon in London in early winter felt like the middle of the night sometimes, especially when I was feeling weary. With no one to answer to, I peeled back the duvet and slipped under it, instantly feeling the comforts of home.

Last night was catching up with me. I hadn't wanted to waste any time sleeping when I was with Mya and then couldn't sleep because my mind wouldn't shut down. Even as I thought about it a sleepy feeling washed over me so I turned the light off and snuggled under the cover and finally fell asleep.

A distant buzzing broke into my dream and when I opened my eyes. I was confused about where I was. It was pitch dark and I lay back for a second trying to remember where I was. Once I realised I was home I turned and felt for the light before swinging my legs off the side of the bed and sitting up. The buzzing had stopped but I was wide awake and my throat felt dry so I padded through to the kitchen to get myself something to drink.

My house phone began to ring and I realised that was the source of the buzzing. Lifting the receiver to my ear I managed to croak out, "Yeah?"

"Jack? Is that you?"

The female voice was familiar but it wouldn't come immediately to my mind as to who it belonged to.

"Did you ring, Jack?" The voice was familiar and I was concerned it was one of my previous dates and I was going to say he wasn't home if it was. Then it came to me. It was a friend I hadn't heard from in ages. *Shit it's Maddie!*

"I know it's you, smart arse."

Maddie had been one of our friends but had dropped off the radar when she'd had a baby. She wasn't interested in hanging out in bars and clubs with us and if I'm really honest I hadn't kept up the friendship because…well, because I was too selfish to make time for her.

"Hey, Maddie. What a pleasant surprise. I just got home this afternoon. I've been away for…" I realised I was doing it, talking about myself and I hadn't even asked how she was or how she'd been doing.

"Sorry, sweetheart, I am a little lagged. How are you? Where have you been? How's Ethan? What is he now? A year?"

"Nathan, his name is Nathan, Jack and he'll be two in January."

Damn. What a shitty friend I had turned out to be. I

wasn't always like that, only since I'd met Rosie. Before that I saw Maddie, Emma, Emily, Dave and Sam at least once a week when I was home, so the least I could do was be honest if nothing else.

"Maddie, please forgive me, I've been a terrible friend to you. Completely up my own arse this last year trying to make things work with Rosie, trying to network for my job, trying to… be an arsehole. Falling out with everyone and generally being a self-centred prick."

Maddie cut into my self-depreciation.

"Jeez, all right already, Jack. We know you're a prick and some of those other things. I only called to ask you if you wanted to come over for something to eat because I'm at a loose end. My guy is overseas and everyone else is busy so if it makes you feel better, I'm desperate and you were last on my list. On account of you being an absent arsehole of course."

I was tired but how could I say no to her? We'd been friends for years and I hadn't even recognised her voice on the phone.

"What time is it?" I asked noting it was dark, but it was dark early in November.

"Six thirty. Are you coming or do I have to eat alone?"

I'd slept all afternoon and once she'd mentioned it I was hungry. Apart from that I really wanted to see her.

"Maddie, this prick would be delighted to have dinner with you. Give me half an hour. Do you want me to bring anything?"

"Um, dinner?" Maddie started laughing and quickly added, "I can cook if you'd prefer but we'll have more time to chat if I don't. Have you any idea what putting a toddler to bed is like? I'd rather be out patrolling the worst areas of London with a dish-sponge as my only form of protection than tell him it's bedtime."

"Okay your sympathy card worked. Indian?" At least

271

I remembered what she liked.

"You're a saint, Jack, see you soon."

The line clicked off and she was gone, so with no time to waste I dialled the local Indian and put my order in, got dressed and went to collect it on my way to Maddie's. She was only a five minute walk from mine, which made it all the more disgusting that I hadn't been round there. The last time I saw her was just after her boy was born almost two years ago.

Mya rang while I was on my way to Maddie's and it wasn't a long drawn out call. She was about to board the plane. Rick had kept her busy all day so she couldn't call me earlier. During the conversation she told me again that she loved me and I was able to reply honestly that I missed her already.

"You don't have to love me back, Jack. I can love you anyway, right?"

I swallowed hard at her comment. When she said that my heart ached for her and how she must be feeling, but she put on a brave face about it. It took a lot of maturity and guts to say something that honest. I was able to tell her that I may be over to see her around Christmas time and she sounded ecstatic about that. Rick then called her name and she told me she had to go and that she'd call tomorrow when she got home before hanging up.

Dave rang just as Maddie was opening the door and invited himself over as well. I was kind of relieved about that because it meant that some of the heat was off me.

Fifteen minutes later there was no strained relations between us, Maddie was very gracious and commented several times about how hot I looked. It was kind of embarrassing being in her home, with her husband gone and her baby in the next room, but I weathered her comments and we quickly moved on to talk about all of our friends. When the subject of Rosie came up, Dave rang the doorbell and I swear I could almost have kissed him.

Rosie was quickly forgotten but they quizzed me about the tour, Rick, and the other guys in the band. Dave even managed to hold back on asking how many women I'd had during the tour until Maddie went to the bathroom.

"One." I smirked knowingly and Dave coughed awkwardly like I'd told him I had pubic lice.

"One? Seven weeks of groupie-fest and you scored once? Man you *have* lost your Midas touch with women." Dave's eyes were almost popping out of his head with disbelief.

"Oh no, I scored quite a few times but with one girl."

Dave's interest was piqued just as Maddie came back and heard my last comment.

"You have a new girlfriend, Jack? How lovely. What's her name? What does she do for a living? Where did you meet."

"Whoa. What's with the twenty questions? It's early days and I really like her but I'm not sure where we're going with it all yet."

Maddie placed the takeaway cartons in the brown paper bag on the counter after dishing up the food and stopped to stare at me with one eyebrow raised.

"Why not? What's wrong with her? Can't she see how hot you are?"

So I explained my situation while Dave sat perched on the end of the sofa and Maddie sat on the other, crossed legged bobbing her head along as I shared some of my experience on tour with Mya. When I was done Dave slid back and leaned into the seat exhaling heavily.

"Fuck, Jack. Can't you fall for someone normal like the rest of us? Oh, no, Rick Fars niece? Do you have a death wish? Well you know you won't be getting any if you pursue her. Your dick will shrivel up and drop off if you're not getting it regularly, Jack. I know how cranky you get if…" I was making wide eyes at him and signalling frantically with them in Maddie's direction but as usual, Dave wasn't being subtle about airing his thoughts.

"Rick isn't the problem, Dave. He kind of encouraged it in his own enigmatic way."

Dave almost choked on the breath he was taking, "Fuck me, he did?"

"No, he didn't fuck you, Dave. That would be in your dreams, knowing how infatuated you are with the guy. But yeah he did, the stumbling block is my issues around Mya. She's twenty and just about to start college."

Judging by their response, I'd say my disclosure about my new girlfriend went rather well because neither of them said another word, so I left the subject at that and moved quickly on to ask Maddie how her husband, David's, new job was going. It got a little confusing because she went out with Dave before as well. Maybe she had a thing for guys called David.

Three hours later, Dave and I got up to leave and Maddie moved in to hug me.

"Jack I've loved having you tonight, please don't make me wait another two years before you come again."

"Fuck, Jack. You had Maddie tonight as well?" Dave smirked wickedly at his own joke before adding, "And, Maddie, Jack can barely wait two weeks to come, so you don't need to worry on that score."

Maddie and I both shook our heads, not wanting to dignify that with a response. Dave then invited himself to stay at my place because he was too tired to make it back to his own. At least some things hadn't changed.

Chapter 34

Sarcastic

Dave turned out to be the friend I always knew he was during the following six weeks away from Mya. Apart from a two day assignment right after touring with Cobham Street, all of my work was done from the office or local interviewing. I had fallen back into my routine and fallen more in love with Mya.

I'd heard the saying, 'absence makes the heart grow fonder', I don't know about fonder but mine beat at a much faster pace every time I spoke with her. We skyped every morning her time, which was afternoon for me, then I'd go and meet Dave or one of the others a few times a week to have dinner to help me get to bedtime. Nights were the worst. I never knew how lonely I was until I couldn't lie next to Mya at the end of the day. It had been weeks since the tour and I missed her even more every single day.

One night, Dave had arranged for us to go dancing and although I wasn't going to hook up with anyone like the old days, I still believed I could enjoy myself. And I was, until Gini suddenly appeared and slipped her hands around my hips from behind and grabbed my dick while I was carrying a few drinks back to our table. Narrowly avoiding dropping the glasses, I tried to evade her hands by moving my body to the side. When I made eye contact with her she smirked devilishly at me and licked her lips.

"Hello, Jack. Long-time-no-see. How's my favourite Tube-ride stranger?"

Knowing her situation I felt slightly nauseated that she was out cruising for guys while her husband stayed home and dealt with her latest conquests on her phone, but I still felt I had to tread carefully around her. Luckily Emily and Emma were with Dave and me so I passed Emily off as my girlfriend by way of an introduction. Dave looked pissed off that I'd done that, but it was all pretend, I just needed Gini to go away.

As soon as I winked at Emily she played the part to perfection, draping her arm around me and whining for me to go and dance with her. We had to make it count. Gini was watching intently from the side of the dance floor so Emily was a little over exuberant in her role, grabbing my arse and grinding against me. After that I think Gini felt she'd seen enough because she moved on to pastures new; with a guy that looked pretty similar to me in fact. Dave had seen enough as well judging by how his jaw muscles were tensing when we got back to our table.

Dave took the opportunity to separate me from the girls by asking everyone what they wanted to drink and as we approached the bar he spoke to me in a harsh tone.

"Nice one, Jack. Emily? Why did you pick her and not Emma?"

"Dave, I love Emma to bits but she couldn't act like my girlfriend if her life depended on it. She's nearly as sarcastic as I am. My cover would have been blown in a heartbeat."

Dave's face brightened then he smirked because knowing Emma well he nodded in agreement. Then he tried to smooth over his jealousy, but he was great at dishing out discomfort so I pressed the point.

"Dave, why don't you just man up and ask the girl out if you're still harbouring feelings for her after all this time?"

"Who? You have a crush on someone, Dave?"

Dave stared pointedly at me and almost freaked out when Emily overheard and interjected. What he'd probably missed was the slight inflection in her voice, which sounded like she was alarmed by the news, to me. I saw how she was staring intensely at Dave but turned her head to look away quickly when she knew I was watching her. I wasn't normally a betting man but would have put money on it that Emily was hot for Dave as well.

"You, Emily."

Dave's legs almost buckled and he was about to make a joke about it until I put my hands up.

"Listen guys, we're not in school now. You're both consenting adults stop pussy-footing around each other just get the fuck on with it."

Emily's jaw gaped and I leaned over closing it with my index finger.

"Talk. Enough of this angst-arguing bullshit you both do around each other. If my new girl taught me anything it's that time is short. Just make your minds up."

I didn't hang around for the outcome of my outburst and grabbed Emma by the hand dragging her giggling behind me onto the dance floor. I was feeling pretty pleased with myself, and some of that spilled over when I pretended to dance suggestively to Emma. She was half-mortified half-delighted because there were a group of girls on a night out who were all standing checking me out while she danced close to me.

After dancing to a few more tunes from my favourite bands the music changed to a slower set so we made our way back to the table where Dave and Emily had obviously broken the ice with each other. When I saw their faces I wondered who had been the first to wear the lipstick that was smudged all over both of their mouths.

Not sure how, but I survived the six weeks and on the nineteenth of December, Dave drove me to Heathrow for my flight to Los Angeles. I was excited and full of anticipation at the prospect of holding Mya in my arms again. That was only tempered by the thought that she may feel differently about me once she saw me in the flesh.

Even though I had flown to Florida to see Lily many times, the journey to California felt infinitely longer. By the time I'd arrived I was still trying to wrap my head around the time difference because even though I had been in the air for eleven hours by the time we landed it was only a few hours after we had taken off in England.

As soon as I cleared customs and collected my bag, I took the escalators two steps at a time to get to the arrivals hall and Mya. When I got there, my eyes searched frantically around, scanning the sea of faces all waiting for loved ones or business transfers. Suddenly there was this almighty high pitched shriek and Mya was running towards me. She was dressed in a small white shorts playsuit which stood out against her tanned skin, her hair was pulled back into her trademark messy bun and she looked incredible.

Dipping my legs, I dropped my bag and threw my arms out waiting to catch her. Within a few seconds all four of her limbs were wrapped tightly around my body, her chest was pressed hard against mine and she was clinging to me like her life depended on it. My heart swelled instantly in response to seeing her and finally being able to physically feel her in my arms.

Mya's stunning features barely registered with me before her lips sought mine in the most breath-taking kiss I'd ever encountered. All of my senses were in meltdown, her smell, taste, feel, sight, and finally the sound of a soft moan that escaped during our kiss made me feel wild with desire. I knew without a shadow of a doubt that I'd never loved anyone the way I loved her.

"Oh, Jack. I missed you so much. I can't believe you are finally here."

I pulled my head back to look at her and took a moment just to take in her beautiful face. My chest felt tight at how deeply my feelings went for her. The impact she had on me was an overpowering and uncontrollable feeling and I'd never felt anything on that level with anyone else.

Once we'd recovered from our very public display of affection, Mya led me to her car and I remembered her telling me about her Volkswagen Beetle, but what she hadn't told me was that it was bright purple with a black badass strip down the bonnet or hood as she called it. It made me laugh and she frowned trying to look hurt before she smirked which eventually morphed into a grin.

"Meet the number one guy in my life."

"Who me? Or were you talking to him?" I said, gesturing to the car by inclining my head.

"Jeez as if you even have to ask that. Stanley meet Jack. Jack...Stanley." I still wasn't sure if it was me or the car.

In keeping with her playful mood I fist-bumped the windshield.

"Hey, Stanley glad to finally meet you."

She giggled and unlocked the car, opened the door and then she slid behind the wheel. I opened the passenger door and climbed in before turning to look at her again.

Mya was adjusting herself to get comfortable before she started the engine.

"I never thought I'd be jealous of a car like I am right now."

Her brow bunched and she bit her lip, which made me want to jump her right there in the parking area.

"Why? He's a car, Jack."

"Yeah, well I hope you put as much effort into wiggling on me later like you just did on his seat just now." I winked then waggled my eyebrows playfully at her. She started laughing and threw her arms around me.

"Oh, God, I've missed you."

"See, there you go again adding more males into the mix. I won't tolerate it, Mya, you hear? I don't share and you're mine, understand me?"

She swatted my arm and turned the key in the ignition. Stanley roared to life and we headed to her place.

Mya's apartment was on the twenty-ninth floor and whilst I wasn't that keen on living at that altitude, her view over Los Angeles was outstanding. I could see the benefit of choosing to live high above street level. The city looked spectacular from where I stood and the sky seemed so much bigger from up there.

I was standing with my hands shoved deep into my jeans looking out the window when Mya came out of her bedroom with some clean towels.

"I thought you might want a shower after your long journey. The bathroom is through there."

"Is that your polite way of saying, 'You stink, Jack, get your ass in there and clean yourself up?'"

She grinned and shook her head.

"No, it's my way of saying, 'go make yourself smell of something other than you or I'll rip your clothes off right now'."

"Oh, Mya, I'm a very defiant boy haven't you learned that yet? No shower." I winked and she wandered over to me, snaking her arms around my neck.

"All right, compromise. Maybe I could have a shower with you too," Mya grinned.

"You're going to make a terrific mother with those negotiating skills, Mya. Obviously not that you'd offer to shower with your children, just that you have powers of persuasion to make people do what you want I mean, right?" I said, grinning and smacking her arse as she turned and led me into the bathroom.

We had been in her apartment for less than ten minutes by the time I had Mya pushed against the tiled wall of her steamed up shower cubicle. She was biting gently on the skin between my shoulder and my neck while I was holding her perfect little arse in my hands before I thrusted my dick slowly forward until I was buried balls deep inside her.

Feeling Mya wrapped around me again after so long felt fabulous. Tasting her delicious sweet body on my lips together with the stimulation of her sensual touch had me breaking a sweat in a heartbeat. The way she looked when her head rolled slowly to the side extending her long neck as the hot water ran in rivulets down her skin was enthralling. When she finally made eye contact with me the scandalous look she bore had me fucking her like my life depended on it.

Mya's pussy began to retract, clenching tightly around my dick and her body began to tremble and vibrate in my arms as she came undone in my hands. Her hands left my hair where she'd been pulling it and she dragged her nails down my back. Pleasure and pain tore through me and my own climax began to build. I had no condom so I pulled out of her and began to stroke my dick vigorously as Mya knelt before me and began sucking my balls. As soon as she did, I was done. Strands of hot cum began to pump from my body and I sprayed across her face and hair. I hadn't meant to, but Mya didn't move away, she just closed her eyes briefly until I had finished.

She cupped her hands and caught some water from the shower then washed her face so she could open her eyes. Then she smiled. For almost seven weeks I had dreamed of being with her again and during our time apart I'd never even looked at another woman. Making love to

Mya after all that time was the best feeling ever.

Having sex with her sapped the last of my energy and sleep caught up with my travel weary body. After getting out of the shower, I passed out on her bed spooning her in my arms. My last conscious thought being that, finally everything in my world was becoming right.

Chapter 35

The power of the Internet

Being kissed awake was definitely my new favourite way to start the day. Cracking an eye open I'd focused on Mya's heated glance. She began to smile slowly at me and when I took her appearance in, I noted that her bed hair made her look ultra-sexy first thing in the morning. I lay quietly watching her, both of us enjoying the still, quiet moment, just being content to be in the same room as each other.

She looked so stunning that she took my breath away, but it wasn't just how she looked. It was how she felt to me—how she made me feel. Whole. I knew it sounded ridiculous because we'd only known each other for a few months and there was still so much to learn about each other, but as soon as I'd held her in the airport I knew I never wanted to leave Mya again.

Crazy thoughts about marrying her and taking her home with me entered my head, something my conscience fought against because she was only twenty years old and she had plans, big plans, and I was...just Jack.

Just Jack with a job; granted it was a great one, but I

had no huge aspirations to be more. That thought depressed me and I had to shake it off quickly and focus on enjoying our time together.

Tricky negotiations between Rick and Joe gave me two weeks in California instead of the one that Joe had granted. Rick had requested I cover some end-of-year charity event Cobham Street was due to play at, so Joe couldn't really say no.

That morning we did what any young couple would do who hadn't seen each other in a while; we stayed in bed and made up for all the frustrations we'd felt at being apart. I still hadn't told Mya I was in love with her and I didn't want to do it while we were in the heat of the moment. When I said it I didn't want any ambiguity or doubt about it.

It was near impossible to arrange anything without her knowledge because Mya seemed to be in the room with me all of the time, but I managed to find a little restaurant on a nearby beach. From the pictures on the internet, it looked perfect for us. One of the photos looked incredible with a small dock and a few yachts moored. It had been taken at sunset, giving the photo a romantic feel to it. Another picture showed the restaurant at night which looked the kind of place Mya might like with candles and string lighting. Soft floodlighting from the beach shone towards the building, bathing the restaurant in a soft amber glow. It was exactly the right place to tell a beautiful woman she was loved. Once I had planned it, I knew I wanted to do more but I was worried that I'd scare her off if I expressed just how deeply my feelings for her went.

Later in the day as I was in the shower I heard her phone ring and from the sounds of it, I knew it was Rick calling her. It felt very weird that I was 'shacking-up' with his niece but I guessed nothing was very normal in Rick's world. I knew I'd be overly protective if I had a young female relative with someone like me sniffing around her, especially given what he'd seen of me in the past. However, since I'd been with Mya I hadn't even thought about any other woman in that way.

I grabbed a towel and headed back to the bedroom to Mya who looked deep in thought. Whatever he'd said had affected her deeply, but she smiled when she saw me and patted the bed where she was sitting for me. I walked over and sat next to her, and I instinctively wrapped my arm around her shoulders.

"Uncle Rick wants us to go over to his place tomorrow morning, is that okay with you?"

It wasn't really. I didn't want to spend time with anyone else, I just wanted my beautiful girl all to myself but Rick *had* bought me an extra week with Mya so how could I argue?

"Sure whatever you want, Mya."

She smirked and rolled her eyes at me then sighed.

"I know what you're thinking, Jack. And I just want you to be inside me all the time as well, but it's only for a couple of hours I think."

Her comment made me chuckle because she sounded like such a guy sometimes, but I guessed that was the result of being around rock band roadies.

Around six that evening I told her I was taking her out and she was surprised I'd managed to arrange something. So was I. I had ordered a black hummer with a driver because I thought it was a bit cooler than the clichéd limousine.

Mya walked into her sitting room dressed up to the nines and for the love of God, she was wearing an exquisite figure hugging, olive green dress with six inch heels that were a slightly darker green than the dress. She wore her dark hair scooped to one side so it sat heavily over her shoulder and cascaded down her front. Taking in her beauty I had to concede she was absolutely flawless.

Watching her silently, I digested how stunning she

looked again and committed the moment to memory because that was the day I would tell her that I loved her. My own efforts to dress appropriately for the occasion were met with a soft hum of approval.

"Mmm. Oh, my, Jack. You look incredibly sexy in that shirt. I love a man who wears pants for me instead of jeans. And I love the man inside these particular pants," Mya said, rubbing her hands around my hips to stroke them over my arse.

"All right Mya, don't let your mind or your hands wander to the inside of my pants or we won't be going anywhere. Come on we have to eat sometime otherwise I'll have no energy left to let you explore the quality lining of these fine threads later."

Mya grinned, kissed me passionately then stepped abruptly away. She was breathless from her own lack of restraint and heaved a wistful sigh at me with wide eyes.

"Fine, let's go now because dinner is looking less and less favourable right now."

The ride to the restaurant was comical because we both had a sly fondle as we teased each other whilst the driver talked non-stop about a trip he'd taken to London twenty years ago. He was completely oblivious to what we were doing and if you'd asked me what he'd said at any point during the journey I'd have failed that test. My attention was firmly focused on my gorgeous brunette beside me.

Mya was delighted with my choice of restaurant, she'd never been there before and I could see she was impressed with the effort I had made to reserve a table in the corner. There was a window on either side which gave us a panoramic and uninterrupted view of the sunset. Actually, I had impressed myself because I'd never given a thought to doing something like this before.

A few moments after we sat down the sun began to set on the horizon and I knew that just watching it with her sitting next to me wasn't good enough for her. So I stood up and held my hand out to her. She looked puzzled but slowly joined me. Bending slightly I scooped her into my arms and sat on her chair with her on my lap. She chuckled, slightly embarrassed, but went with the moment and laid her head on my shoulder. I had no words for the feelings that were bubbling inside me but our reverent silence as we watched the sun go down marked the significance of a perfect moment together.

When dusk fell Mya retook her seat and we ordered our food. She stared affectionately at me during dinner and I loved watching her eat because she was so refined in her eating habits and her mouth looked so tantalising and luscious I couldn't stop doing it. She looked so cute when she chewed with those perfect lips and she pouted when she had to catch some sauce from dripping from her mouth. I just found the experience of Mya eating fascinating.

For a girl who grew up with an uncle like Rick, Mya was everything he wasn't. Don't get me wrong, Rick was a great guy, but years of mixing with the edgy rock star types meant that he was very far removed from the guy I imagine he once was at her age.

During our conversation I teased her about all the guys who would hound her when she got to college and that she'd soon forget about me. I suppose it was my insecurity with her age that made me say it, but her response stopped me dead.

"Yeah, you think so? I'll remind you of this conversation when we're old and grey, Jack Cunningham. I'm marrying you whether you like it or not."

My eyes darted to hers and she stared straight at me with a smile on her face and for a minute I could see the certainty in her expression of what she'd just said, then she apologised.

"Sorry. That was very presumptuous of me to say that

when you don't feel the same."

I could see her confidence sliding from her expression and I had to call a halt to my shoddy behaviour and tell her exactly what was on my mind.

"I do."

I didn't know how to say it because anything I said may have been taken as me trying to just make her feel better. The next thing I said had to be the truth and it had to be right for Mya.

"Mya, I love you. When I held you in my arms at the airport I knew, you are the girl for me. My plus one. The *only* one. Mine. I should have told you yesterday when I saw you, but then we got carried away in your apartment and I didn't want you to think…"

"It was in the moment?" Mya nodded and looked thankful. "Thank you, Jack. Thank you for waiting. Now what?"

"Now it's a bit messy, love. You're twenty years old, you're about to go to school…"

"I can go to school in London. I'll transfer. Uncle Rick will fix it for me."

"You see, Mya? This is the problem I have. I should be able to do everything for you and I can't. I don't have a magic wand to make you older and I don't have a wand to wave you past college. What if you do this with me and wake up one morning and think that *you've* made a huge mistake?"

"Jack. You're over thinking this. Love doesn't have ages or college degrees and twenty doesn't make me emotionally immature. Can't I be one of those people in life that just know what they want from theirs and how to get it?"

I stared into her eyes as they searched my face. Her argument stood up and I knew one of those people she was talking about. Lily.

"But…"

"But, what? What if we don't last? What if we have ten babies and I get fat and you hate me for not being the slick rock chick you met X amount of years ago? What if you lose your six-pack and your hair and become a cranky old couch potato or have an affair? Jack, life is about chances and luck, and life partners are about choices and making things work, about working at it and carrying on working at it. Being with someone is about sharing life's ups and down and the humps in the road, Jack. Not fucking rainbows, sunsets, candles, and women staying size zero after their ten kids and the all other romantic shit that the media wants us to believe."

She reached out and took my hand away from the wine stem I was holding. She laced her fingers in mine then she took a deep breath and held it as she stared me square in the eye. I didn't know if she was expecting me to say something, but when I didn't she exhaled heavily and spoke again.

"Look, Jack, I can't make myself be anything except what I am. I'm twenty years old but being around my daddy and Uncle Rick with all their high profile contacts and shit has made me pretty savvy. I don't need anyone to tell me how to live my life. I don't need to be compared to a twenty-five or thirty year old woman because they may have had small lives. I've lived a huge one, trust me. I am the last person that would hook up with a guy half way around the world on some romantic notion. Sometimes you just know, right? When something is the real deal, yes?"

"So if I said marry me and come to England?"

"Is that a proposal?"

"Just answer the question, Mya."

"I will when you decide you want to ask that question for real, Jack. If you ever do that is."

My eyes dropped to stare at her fingers woven between mine and I knew she was the one for me.

Everything about our connection felt right. When my eyes flicked back to hers, I saw that they were full of determination and I could see she had no doubts in her mind. I realised that the only thing I could do was put my faith in her to know that was what she wanted. I had already made my own mind up that this was definitely what I wanted.

"So, Mya Fars. This isn't exactly how I would have planned to ask you such a life changing question, but my imagination is just about tapped out today. And for your information as soon as I saw you yesterday I knew I wanted to marry you."

I stared lovingly into her eyes and my heart beat like a thousand drums in my chest with the anticipation for the answer to the question I had on the tip of my tongue.

"So... would you do me the honour of being my wife? Because for me, I am absolutely one hundred percent certain you are the only girl I have ever loved, will ever be in love with."

"Jack, we could date for years and still be in the same place as we are right now, so yes, I'd be delighted to marry you."

"Holy shit. This should have been done so differently, you deserve..."

"You? Jack, if you'd wrote a post-it note and left it on the flusher of the toilet, I'd have said yes. I've been around pomp and ceremony all my life, being invited to prestigious events and award ceremonies. Believe me, I'm ecstatic I'm going to spend the rest of my life with you."

I still felt bad I hadn't even asked her father but I'd never even thought about marriage so I had no clue how to do it or what kind of place would be right, but when I saw the smile on her face, I knew none of that really mattered to her, it was the commitment that was key.

"Jesus, does that mean we're engaged? Tomorrow I think we need to shop for your ring before we hit Rick's place otherwise I think everyone will try to talk us out of this."

"So what? Do we care what anyone else thinks? Jack, I pity anyone who can't see what we have. We just have to prove to everyone that love doesn't come with a timestamp."

I cupped her chin, leaned over the table and kissed her softly on the mouth. Most girls would have been disappointed to have been asked for their hand in marriage like that. Mya was much smarter than me and on an emotional level I knew I'd have to think damned hard before I'd find a person with more maturity than what she'd just shown me. So I accepted that she knew what she was doing and until I had asked Mya the question and she'd replied, I hadn't realised how relieved I would feel if she said yes.

Chapter 36

Mixed feelings

Sunsets and candles didn't matter. Mya was right, and if that is a once in a lifetime feeling then why does it matter what anyone else has to say about it? In my heart I felt it, when I touched her I felt it, when I heard her voice my heart raced, when I saw her my heart had pretty much the same reaction.

My body reacted to Mya in a way it never had with any other woman before her and my dick was almost permanently hard. She had agreed to be mine forever and always and suddenly I was filled with a sense of peace I realised had been missing in my life.

Even though I was jetlagged from the flight we didn't waste the rest of the night. It was filled by my new favourite pastime—sensual and passionate love making. We experienced an earth shattering connection that was both slow and deliberate, with a mixture of soft delicious kisses, and long piercing glances, then hungry passionate kisses which ended in an almost punishing union. By the end of it she was screaming almost continually and we were both soaked with sweat. When we were finally sated, we flopped onto our backs panting and chuckling with laughter.

Curling up with her after sex was an incredible feeling but waking up next to her, was even better. She felt exactly right in my arms and according to her I was the right man for her.

As promised, I took her to find a ring and found that her taste in jewellery was very modest. She chose a simple round two-carat solitaire diamond in a thin platinum setting. Her eyes shone brightly as she watched me slip it on her finger right before I kissed her.

"I love you so much, Mya." I murmured when we broke the kiss.

Mya grabbed my shirt and pulled me back towards her, twisting the cotton in her fist and kissed me again. I was vaguely aware of the assistant sighing before we pulled away from each other. Once the ring was on her finger, it was official. She was going to be Mrs. Cunningham and I didn't really have a plan for that yet.

After we left the jewellers we headed to Rick's place. I'd never been there before but in my mind it was opulent, extravagant, and would have a swimming pool full of women. The reality was huge metal gates at the end of a quiet country lane which I realised later also belonged to him as did the last mile of road we'd driven along.

I had noted that there were some girls sitting at the side of the road wearing Cobham Street t-shirts. They were camped out and there was a guy talking to them. I found out afterwards that that's where the boundary to Rick's private land was and it was constantly patrolled to weed out fans and other fanatics that were trying to get to him.

Mya reached into the glove compartment and pulled out a fob that she aimed at the gates which opened with an alarm sounding at the same time. A menacing guy with a huge German Sheppard came out of a small cottage immediately inside the gate and nodded at Mya then turned and headed back inside and I realised just how hard Rick had to work for his security.

As she drove up the long driveway my heart began to beat faster when I noticed Alfie's vintage Aston Martin car sitting outside. I felt betrayed because my initial reaction was that Rick had arranged a reunion for me and Lily.

I still hadn't spoken to Lily and I had already planned in my head to do that after Christmas. I knew I kept putting it off but the time had to be on my own terms. My jaw ticked and I realised I was clenching my teeth as my temper rose. I hated people interfering in my life and I hated being forced to do things I wasn't ready for even more.

Mya's eyes met mine and she instantly understood what the presence of Alfie's car meant without me even saying anything.

"Look, Jack. This is a new beginning for us. You have to talk to Lily sometime so let's just get it over with. You miss her. I can hear it every time you talk about her. Let it go."

Mya was right. It had been nearly six months and I guess I'd made my point. Rosie had a new life and so did I. Nodding I pulled the door handle and pushed my weight against the door.

Rick opened his front door before we reached it.

"Sorry, Jack, come in. Alfie and Lily are here." Rick wasn't his normal sarcastic self and the feeling I had was that there was something amiss.

Rick and Mya hugged then Rick caught Mya's left hand as she was stepping back. Glancing at the ring, he instantly ran his hand through his hair with a distressed look on his face.

"Shit. No. Please, no." He was shaking his head vigorously.

Not exactly the response we wanted but I kind of figured that Mya's family wouldn't be best pleased if I scuppered any plans she had for college.

Alfie appeared in the doorway then stepped forwards with his hand out. I stared at it for a few seconds then met his palm with mine.

"Hey, Jack." Alfie put his arm around me and began to steer me into the sitting room where Lily was sitting. I had expected a punch from him rather than a handshake. Lily looked like she'd been crying and all my anger just dissipated as I strode towards her to comfort her.

"Hi, sweetheart. Are you okay?"

Lily stared at me and was so emotional that she couldn't speak and to think I had something to do with that tore me up. Glancing round for Mya I noticed that she and Rick hadn't followed us into the sitting room and wondered if Rick was giving Mya a hard time about our engagement.

Lily looked up and took a deep breath then swallowed audibly and took another breath before bursting into tears. *Something's wrong.*

Alfie pulled me to sit beside him and took a note out of Lily's bag.

"Jack, sorry buddy, you need to read this."

By then my heart was thumping so quickly that I had pins and needles in my fingers and a metallic taste in my mouth. I knew instinctively it was bad news.

Glancing down at the envelope I recognised Rosie's hand writing and turned it over thinking, the baby *is* mine. But I wasn't prepared for what the note said.

Dear Lily,
If you are reading this Stewart and I are no longer alive, so I've written this letter to be delivered to you in the event of my death. Ava-Jacqueline is Jack's baby. Anyone who looks at her can see that she's all him and very little of me. She is a beautiful, sunny little girl with a

cheeky personality— just like her daddy.

My eyes filled with tears and I couldn't read on. Rosie was dead and Ava-Jacqueline was my baby. *Jacqueline. Jack. Fuck! How did I miss that? Rosie's dead?*

No! No! I'm here to share our news of our engagement and now…I'm a father…I can't expect…No wonder Rick had reacted the way he did.

"Hold on. Where is she? Where's my baby? Why would Rosie deny me the right to see my own child? I've missed nearly four months of her life. And she never told me? I believed her when she said the baby wasn't mine. That twisted bitch! Why would she do that to me…to her child? Rosie's dead? How did she die? What the fuck is going on?"

My mind was flitting from one question to the next and I couldn't think rationally. I'd just had the biggest shock of my life and my day had gone from jubilation to disaster in a heartbeat. I was a father, my ex-girlfriend was dead and I had a beautiful young fiancé. Add to that Mya lived overseas and was about to go to college and I suddenly felt my head was going to explode.

The impact of everything I had just learned began to take effect and I felt my legs give way from under me. Luckily Alfie was there beside me in an instant and caught me before I hit the ground.

I didn't pass out but I don't know how long it was before I was coherent after the news. When I had absorbed some of the shock, Lily told me that the rest of the letter said that Rosie had not wanted me to know about the baby. Stewart's name was on Ava-Jacqueline's birth certificate and Rosie had left Lily as Ava-Jacqueline legal guardian in the event of Rosie's death.

Apparently they were on holiday and they slept in a room with a faulty heater and had carbon monoxide poisoning. My baby had been in a different room, thank God. Lily had only got the hand delivered letter that morning and had rung Rick because he'd mentioned that I was over to see Mya. So Rick actually had nothing to do with Alfie and Lily being there. He just landed himself the role of facilitator.

When I heard that Rosie didn't want me to have anything to do with our baby it felt like a knife was twisting in my gut. Was I that bad of a person to her? Just because I couldn't be with her didn't make me a bad father. I just didn't love Rosie enough when it mattered to us. I wasn't ready and now that I'd met Mya I knew I would never have been truly ready with Rosie.

I was... just Jack, a normal guy who maybe joked a little. I was as flawed as the next man and maybe a little immature, but I was a good man and I knew I could be an amazing father when I had kids. My dad was a great teacher. Rosie's judgement about my ability to parent was horribly off and that left a scar in my heart that would be there forever.

My thoughts became words and I was firing off my own questions to Alfie and Lily.

"Where is my baby now? Who has her? Where do I go to get her? Do you have a phone number? Jeez, what do I need to take care of her? Who's going to tell me what to do?"

"Whoa, Jack." Lily stood with her hands on my chest looking concerned.

"Jack, Rosie wants *me* to be her guardian."

"Well, fuck what Rosie wants...or you." I was seething that I'd had a child on this planet for over four months and it had been kept from me. Shaking my head vigorously I pointed and I stared at Lily, who had sat back down again,

"You're not having her, Lily. Ava-Jacqueline is *my* baby. What kind of a mouthful is that for a kid anyway?

I'm calling her Ava. How do I get her, Lily? Where can I collect my baby from?"

Alfie stood between me and Lily, and placed his hands on my chest which made me see red.

"Hey, it's not her fault. She told you it could be yours. Lily prompted you to go and see her, she did what she could."

"Don't fucking defend her, Alfie. She kept it from me for six months."

"Just like she could have kept this from you, Jack. Lily got that letter this morning." Alfie threw his arms out to the sides then banged his chest with one palm. "Don't shoot the fucking messenger, dude. We're here for you, aren't we?" Pointing at himself then Lily, "Look at her. I've had to watch her tear herself up every day for that one mistake. One fucking mistake, Jack. How many have you made? You could have demanded a DNA test when Lily first told you. Why didn't you do that? Because you believed Rosie, we all believed her. Don't rake over the things you can't fucking change, Jack, focus your energy on what's next."

Alfie was harsh but I needed to hear it. He was right. I'd just accepted Rosie's word. Maybe I had preferred to accept that than face my responsibilities. It hadn't felt like that at the time though, I genuinely thought I was out of the frame.

"Now, do you want our help or do we just go claim Ava-Jacqueline and bring her up as our own?"

"Ava. We're calling her Ava. I'm not having her go through life with a double-barrelled name in London. Kids can be horrible with names. It's different in the USA, in London they shorten everything or elongate it or some shit. And no she's mine. I'll get her."

I don't know why I had such a hang up about her name; maybe it was because I had nothing to do with naming her.

Lily tried again to explain the process of claiming Ava and the more she said the more livid with Rosie I became. At that point I am ashamed to say I was glad she was dead for doing this to Ava and me.

"Jack, because I have been made legal guardian, we have to fly to London to collect her, however, there are checks to be done on myself and Alfie because we are not blood relatives and paperwork to be sorted out before we can leave the country with her. She'll stay with me until you can prove you're her dad."

"She'll what? The letter says I'm the father."

Lily explained, "Jack, they aren't just going to let either of us take her because of a letter. She's in foster care. I spoke to the local authorities this morning. We're going to have to demonstrate our suitability to care for her."

"We? She's mine. You mean I'm going to be tested on whether I can be a father to my own child? By a stranger?"

Lily nodded sadly and stared seriously at me before she drew in a deep shaky breath and exhaled.

"Once you have a positive DNA test there is a thing called a core assessment. That will start to look at your suitability to take care of Ava-Jac…Ava."

What if I see my little girl and fall in love with her and they decide, like Rosie, I'm not good enough to be in her life?

Suddenly the room felt like it was closing in on me. Glancing around, Alfie, Lily, Rick and finally sweet beautiful Mya came into view. Everything that had happened in the past twenty four hours had rocked my world completely in different ways and I felt like I was suffocating. *How could I ask Mya to be a mother to another woman's child? How could I prove my suitability as a dad? How did I do any of that when I have no plan for any of it?*

"Sorry guys I need to get out of here. I need a minute to think."

Chapter 37

Proof

Absorbing everything I had learned wasn't easy. I was an absent father through no fault of my own. Rosie must have really hated me. I was trying to figure out how someone can go from loving to despising someone so much that they would hide something so incredibly important, even from the child themselves. My heart froze for a moment at the fact that Rosie was no longer walking this earth but then my anger took over again.

I was in Rick's driveway pacing back and forth, my mind so closely connected to my feelings that every time a fleeting thought came into it, it felt like it hit me square in the chest. *How am I going to get my baby back? How could I work and take care of her?* The last question was easy, thank God. I'd use the money my father gave me when I turned of age to keep us both and would write freelance articles from home. Using the money didn't make me feel proud, but I wasn't going to make life more difficult for myself or my daughter if I had the means at hand. *What about Mya? It wouldn't be fair on he;, I couldn't expect her to bring up another woman's child.*

What kind of test would they give me to decide if I was a suitable father to take care of my child?

Lily wouldn't fight me for custody but she was right, Rosie had made her the legal guardian. *Why am I still standing here? I need to get back to the UK my baby is living with strangers.* Kind ones I hoped, but strangers nevertheless.

Walking at speed back into the house, I ran into Alfie who stopped me dead in my tracks by placing his hands on my shoulders. I struggled to free myself from his grip.

"Stop, Jack, breathe. You need a clear, calm head if you are going to deal with this. They're not going to hand a child over to someone who seems hot headed and volatile." I turned and stared at Alfie incredulously because this is the guy who flies off the handle about anything to do with Lily.

"All right, Alfie, and you'd be doing what if you were in my shoes right now?"

Alfie stopped moving. He stared back at me and when I saw his jaw tick the way it did when he was pissed off, I knew he'd be reacting the same as me but didn't want to admit it.

"Go. Do what you have to do, but do it calmly. Being passionate is one thing, sounding aggressive is something else."

I went searching for Mya.

"I need to go to the airport." Mya bit her lip and looked at Rick who put his hand on her wrist.

"You're not going anywhere. I'll get Jed to drive Jack to the airport. Do you even know when the next plane leaves, Jack?" I shook my head. Rick ran his hand through his hair and looked briefly at Mya before looking back at me.

"Take the jet. I'll have it ready to leave as soon as they can get a flight path agreed." With a stern look on his face, Rick grabbed Mya by the forearm with his other hand. "But you're staying here, Mya."

Mya pulled roughly against Rick's hands to free her wrist and arm from his grasp.

"Like fuck I am. I'm going with Jack. We love each other and he's going to need all the help he can get and this affects me too. Jack and I are engaged Uncle Rick. Like it or not I'm going with him."

My eyes flicked to Lily's first and I noted how sad she looked. She understood that if I felt ready to make a commitment like that with Mya, I must love her deeply. Alfie slid his fingers into his jeans pockets and looked about as helpless as I felt. Rick's face was twisted in an angry sneer as he stalked around Mya. She had determination I'd give her that, but Rick was right. At twenty she should be at college having the time of her life. I wasn't going to tie her to someone else's child even if she was half mine. I took a deep breath and held Mya's hands.

"Rick's right, love. You can't come with me. This is something I need to take responsibility for alone. I love you, Mya, but I have a defenceless little girl who's going to need her daddy's full attention. I'm sorry we can't do this. I won't do this to you."

Mya slapped me so hard across my face making my ear ring.

"Jack Cunningham, I never had you down as someone who wallowed in their own misery. What? You suddenly don't love and want to be with me because someone wrote a letter to someone else telling them you have a child? Man the fuck up. You need me just as much as I need you. So what? We'll have a kid to care for. Why does everyone think I'm not capable because of my age all of a sudden? Get the fuck over it."

Rick stepped in front of Mya and blocked her path to me.

"No. Jack's dealing with this by himself. I understand

what he's doing. There's no room for anyone else in his life right now, Mya."

Mya burst into tears then pushed past Rick grabbing me by my shirt and clinging to it tightly.

"Jack Cunningham. You walk away from me now, don't you dare come back. You either trust me or you don't. You better think carefully about that because there are no second chances with me."

She dropped her hand and turned to walk away but came back and stepped in close to my face. "So what, Jack, life has thrown you a curve ball? Deal with the damn thing. Or are you going to suddenly turn into Saint Jack who throws everyone out for his little princess? Let me tell you she won't thank you for that when she's older and she could've had a mom. Ava-Jacqueline needs a mother as well as a father. So am I in or not? Decide. Right now, Jack. Am I going all the way with you like you said yesterday or am I being kicked to the kerb at the first bump in the road?"

Without any hesitancy at all I replied.

"Right, I gave you an out and you didn't take it, remember that Mya, because my daughter isn't going to have someone throw in the towel when it gets a little rough at times."

Inside I felt relieved that Mya fought for her position in all of this because to walk away from her would have broken me. I knew I'd never be able to let her go in my heart, but I had to be sure she wasn't going along with this just to make me happy. I'd never have asked her to take care of Ava, it had to be something she did willingly.

Rick's jaw dropped and he drew in a really deep breath as if he was about to say something, but before he could speak I silenced him. "Rick, remember, you encouraged this relationship so keep your thoughts to yourself. Mya and I know what we're doing." I had never sounded so sure of anything in my life, pity I didn't feel the same.

Before I knew what was happening, Alfie was on the phone arranging for his and Lily's passports and clothing to be taken to Rick's plane and then we were all in Alfie's car heading to Mya's apartment to collect some things before heading for the airport. We left Rick sulking in his kitchen and I guessed he'd stay that way until Mya and I proved we could do this.

The flight to the UK was much shorter than the one going out to California. Having Rick's Lear Jet made the flight much more comfortable than the premium economy seat I'd flown out on.

Lily was beat when we arrived in the UK but I had no time to lose. When she called social services we were disappointed to find that they were going to meet with her first and would have nothing at all to do with me unless I could produce evidence that proved I was Ava's father.

Luckily Alfie had already arranged for a DNA test to be carried out at a private laboratory but we needed the consent of social services to have something of Ava's. I was surprised that the standard paternity test could be done in as little as twelve hours.

I was so angry with the standoffish attitude the social workers had with me. All of us provided them with pictures of Rosie and me and there were still texts on my phone of her telling me that she loved me and still they were treating me like an absent father. Seeing those gave me a momentary lump in my throat as I remembered that she was gone forever, but I didn't feel what I had for her when I came back from the retreat, I just felt sad.

The social worker on the case was more interested in Alfie and Lily and what their bands were doing instead of taking care of what actually mattered—seeing my baby. It frustrated me because I just wanted someone to see sense and let me take her home. Finally, after a lot of discussion, the younger of the two social workers saw that sense and gave permission for the test to go ahead. A swab from my baby's mouth and a lock of hair was given and the same from me. Then the giant sized cotton-bud-like swabs were stuffed into a plastic envelope and couriered to the lab Alfie had found.

Even if the results came back and I was her father, I still wouldn't be allowed to see Ava until the professionals had assessed my suitability to take care of her. I hadn't told my parents anything about Rosie or what happened between us because I wanted to be sure Ava was mine before my mother went hysterical and invited her luncheon friends to flock around us.

After that we returned to my apartment and Mya and I were so exhausted that we fell asleep as soon as we hit the bed. We were woken up not long after by a call from Alfie to tell me the result was on its way back. Instantly I was a bundle of nerves and I just wanted to be put out of my misery. Alfie said that they would only deliver the results to me on production of photographic ID.

Lily and Alfie arrived at my place ahead of the motorcyclist who brought the result and when I showed my driver's licence he slipped the white A5 size envelope into my hand. When I'd signed his docket he didn't move, obviously waiting for the fallout like the rest of us.

My nerves caused my whole body to vibrate in anticipation of what was inside—one single piece of cheap white paper was going to change my life. Before opening the envelope I paused. *What do I want it to say?* I really wanted her to be mine even though I hadn't entertained the thought of having kids yet. Once I admitted it to myself, the pressure was really on. *What if she isn't mine?* If she wasn't, then the last forty eight hours of anguish would have been for nothing and I'd be mourning the loss of a baby that wasn't even mine.

Mya moved by my side and gripped my arm, whispering softly that she was with me no matter what it said and telling me she'd love Ava as if she was her own. I kissed her softly and shared one last hug with her, potentially our last as a couple because when I opened the result we could be a family.

With shaking fingers I tore the flap off the envelope and pulled out the folded piece of paper. I flipped it open and hurriedly read through the contents. It was a table of results and I noticed all the numbers were very high percentages. I skipped to the conclusion at the bottom and amongst other stuff was Jack Cunningham the number 99.9% accuracy and the statement—*is* the father of Ava-Jacqueline Lister. *I'm her dad.*

Mya stood in front of me waiting patiently but I couldn't speak past the huge lump in my throat. I was completely overwhelmed by the significance of finding out I had been her father all this time and my feelings of anger mingled with sadness because I was robbed of those first few months with her. I passed Mya the note and sat down whilst she read it, feeling stunned by the enormity of the letter and what it meant.

Lily sat beside me, her eyes searching mine and I could see fear in them.

"She's mine, Lily. Ava *is* my baby."

I don't know where the tears came from but suddenly they were rolling down my face and I realised it was with relief. Mya sat on the other side of me and pulled me in for a hug.

"Let it all out, Jack. That was a terrible thing Rosie did to you. No one deserves that, but at least we can move forwards now. You're a father and Ava has parents to care for her. What a wicked woman Rosie was."

Mya tried to sound measured in her statement but I could hear undertones of disgust there nevertheless. Rosie's spiteful decision had caused me so much pain and took those precious first months away from Ava and me that I'd never get back.

Turning to Lily, I saw that she actually looked relieved and wondered if the relief was that she was off the hook to provide guardianship or if it was because she'd been justified in eventually telling me about the baby. All of that slid from my mind because it wasn't important any more. I had work to do to prove myself fit to care for my daughter and show that I could provide for her. Social services had also received a copy of the results because Alfie had arranged for copies to be sent to me and them as soon as they were available. When a social worker called to tell me that work would begin to assess my suitability for parental responsibility she made an appointment for the following day. Lily and Alfie left shortly after that and I was thankful for their friendship and grateful for the way they had handled everything for me so far. The rest was up to me... and Mya.

Turned out Mya was a lists person. As soon as the others had gone, she began making a list of things she felt we needed to know and prove as to be suitable parents.

"Are we going to stay here? Is this where you want to live once we have a baby to care for?"

"Yes, we're staying here for now".

A baby is a baby, they're little and we've got a spare room. My apartment was spacious and it was close to all the local amenities and the park. Over time it might become unsuitable for a family but I wasn't going to jump in head first and start changing everything all at once.

Memories of cramming for an exam came to mind as we sat up for most of the night learning about attachment theories and what a four month baby's milestones were as well as how to bring a child up with confidence and resilience. We were actually lucky because Ava was so young it was, despite the sadness of the situation, the best time for her to have a big change as she wouldn't remember the separation and loss of Rosie and Stewart.

I wanted my daughter surrounded with love and even

though I hadn't met her yet, I already loved her and couldn't wait to have her home with us. We were in for some tough times though, I had no idea how to take care of a baby. One thing we had to sort out was Mya's status. She wasn't a UK citizen and had entered the UK on the waiver scheme that is set aside for countries that have a special relationship with Britain. But that only gave her a few months.

So first thing the next morning I rang the authorities to find out what we needed to do to obtaining a visa for her. We were informed that even if we were married, Mya may have to go back to the USA and wait for her immigration status to be confirmed. The news freaked Mya out and she rang a few universities, made some applications and found out what she had to do to gain a student visa. I marvelled at her resourcefulness and the three years she would study in the UK would give us the breathing space to work out all the legalities of her status.

By the time the social worker was due we had a pretty good idea of our position and what was expected of us.

Chapter 38

Baring my soul

I wasn't too sure what I thought a social worker would be like, but the one sitting in front of us was actually about my age and wasn't hostile or judgemental like I assumed she would be. She informed me that since I had parental qualification, whatever that meant, she could now begin her assessment of my suitability. There were tons of forms to fill in which asked about the ins and outs of my life, my emotional state, lifestyle, which people were in my support network and how I would provide for Ava.

It felt weird disclosing my most personal information to a stranger when I hadn't even told my parents that they were grandparents yet. I had to make sure that everything was a certainty before I could share that with them because I knew my mother would be buying a hat for a wedding, a wardrobe full of baby clothes and signing us all up for generational family portraits, bless her. Like me, it would break her heart to know she had a child in the family that she couldn't have a relationship with.

After we'd dispensed with the basic paperwork,

Brenda, the social worker, asked me a lot of questions about my childhood and friendships, and how I interacted with people. Was I popular? And other stuff that seemed pretty irrelevant to parenting a child but I answered honestly and she seemed impressed that I had friends I'd had since childhood in Lily, Elle and Dave. I was thankful that I had reconnected with Maddie because she then asked if I had any friends with children, so I was able to talk about Nathan and my relationship with Maddie.

Since Mya was going to be caring for Ava as well, she was also interviewed. I was nervous about that but it seemed to go okay because Mya and Brenda were smiling when I came back into the room.

The most painful part of the process was talking about Rosie and what had gone wrong with our relationship and on top of that, I had to have that discussion in front of Mya. It must have been uncomfortable for her, but she was supportive and held my hand tightly throughout. When I finished what I had to say, Mya leaned in and gave me a hug. I noticed Brenda noting this on her sheet and smiling.

When I told the rest of my friends what was going on, they were so supportive. Dave, Emily, Emma and Sam were all there for us. They took Mya to their hearts and Dave warmed mine when he punched me in the arm and told me enough was enough and I should make an honest woman of Mya because I'd never find a better match.

After a few days and many more discussions we were told that Brenda thought we were more than adequate to meet Ava's needs as parents, but that we'd initially have their support during the settling in period. So we started preparing for Ava's homecoming and a couple of days later, I was finally being introduced to my daughter. I was nervous and excited.

As with anything that is life-changing, I had periods of self-doubt during the whole process but I hid it well.

Mya was amazing and constantly built up my confidence, telling me that I was going to be an incredible father and that we'd work it all out together. Something she said made a lot of sense to me and helped me greatly. We were becoming parents together. It wasn't as if Ava was in my life before and Mya was coming in, it was almost like when a child is born. I liked the thought of that.

It was just about dawn and I was wide awake. Instead of getting up, I lay in bed with my head on my elbow watching Mya sleep peacefully beside me and thought about how lucky I was that she was mine. She was an incredible girl with wisdom way beyond her years. She grounded me and even though there were many miles of uncertainty ahead of us, she made me feel like Superman. Not like I was just Jack. It felt like there was nothing we couldn't do if we were doing it together.

Fourteen weeks from the first time I laid eyes on her was all it took for us to know we wanted a lifetime together. It felt as if I'd been waiting for her all of my life and I didn't know how I'd gotten that far without her. Lily was my best friend, but I understood Lily's position. Although she was still important to me, my love for Mya had placed my feelings for Lily where they needed to be, still in my heart but not in the centre anymore and when my heart became swollen with love it was in reaction to Mya.

As I was unable to sleep I got up and quietly sat in the chair facing the bed just taking stock of everything before the emotional day ahead of me. Daylight crept slowly into the room and Mya suddenly rolled over, her hand reached out, she waved it around before opening her eyes with a start. Catching sight of me on the chair, she pushed up to sit in the centre of the bed and took her weight on one hand. The sheet fell from her body and pooled around her waist. She looked perfect in the grey light of the room, with her sexily tousled bed hair and her amazing body innocently on show as her eyes adjusted sleepily.

"Aw, Jack. Couldn't you sleep? Come here. You should have woken me." Mya looked concerned.

"I'm okay, just taking some quiet time to reflect on everything. Today is the start of the rest of my life. Our lives. You, Ava and me. You didn't have to do any of this, but here you are. I love you so much, Mya. No matter what happens from this day on, I need you to know that." I continued to stare silently at her and prayed that everything worked out.

When I didn't move, Mya crawled along the bed, stepped off and positioned herself astride me, her warm behind settled in my lap. Feeling her skin rub against mine infused sexual feelings inside me. My hands immediately made contact with her legs just above her knees and I stroked up and down over her firm little arse cheeks. Mya slipped her arms around my neck and placed her lips next to my ear.

"You do realise that you're going to look even sexier when you're holding a baby don't you? So that's another problem you're going to have to face. Thank God we're living in London and I can justifiably carry a golf umbrella with the weather here. It'll come in handy for beating off all those young mothers in the park when we take our baby out for a stroll."

"A baby, huh? To attract women? I better get online and order myself one of those chest carrier things in that case. I think I'm going to need both hands free. And what about you? Am I going to have to join a baseball team so that I can legally carry a bat? You are going to be this hot rock chick from California with the famous uncle, truckloads of guys are going to be walking into walls at the sight of you when you start college. Just think, all those horny, hard dicks in one room for you, actually, no don't."

"Jack, we all have our crosses to bear. I may need you to pick me up with our baby to warn them off."

"Fuck, Mya, I'm not letting my daughter anywhere near college boys. I've heard and seen enough of those wild parties where girls are all fucking in the same room and sometimes with the same guy. Our daughter is going to grow up thinking men only grow dicks after they're married."

Mya laughed then slid her hand sexily down my abs and trailed down to my dick. Grinning wickedly she wrapped her fingers tightly around my length.

"See this, Jack. This is the only dick that gets attention from this girl. This is the only penis invited to party with me. I know I'll never let you down that way. I love you so much."

Smirking knowingly, Mya shifted to change her position on my lap to face away from me and positioned my dick at her entrance. Without another word she sunk slowly down onto me, burying my dick deep inside her. Fuck she felt amazing and I struggled for words to tell her how she felt around me. My arms instantly wrapped around her and I kneaded her breasts in my palms, rolling her nipples between my fingertips as she lay back against my chest and rocked gently.

Moving her hair from around her neck, I bent to kiss the sensitive spot at the side of her neck. She shivered and gasped before moaning erotically and wriggling herself a little more. I tightened my grip around her and slid down the chair a little to move more freely then began to take control. It wasn't a fast and furious session but it was one where I could feel how deeply connected we were. Mya was deliciously wet and when I thought that was how I affected her, it was all the confirmation I needed to know that I could take her how I wanted to.

Afterwards I'd walked us over to the bed and laid her down then held her tightly. I wondered if, after that day, we'd still have the same connection we had, with Ava to care for.

Two hours later we looked around our apartment, everything was neat and tidy, and we seemed more organised than I'd felt. We were going to finally be introduced to Ava and I felt sick. I'd never been so scared and so elated at the same time. I couldn't imagine how a child would feel if they were in Ava's position. I thanked God again that Ava was too young to remember any of this.

The contact centre was a place where people whose kids were in care could go to meet up with them and the meetings were all scheduled by the social workers, just like Brenda had done with my visits with Ava. She had decided not to introduce Lily to Ava because I had come forward and Lily was in agreement that if my baby was to be handed over to anyone, it should be to me. We arrived in the reception area and sat holding each other's hands. My heartbeat fluctuated between its resting rate and wildly accelerated beats. Each time the door opened my eyes automatically trained themselves to search for Ava.

Brenda arrived and greeted Mya then went to speak with the contact supervisor who was going to be observing our visit and no doubt reporting back on how we'd done. When Brenda came back she smiled warmly at us both.

"All set? Ava's already here. Please follow me."

I stood up, my heart thumping in my chest and tugged on Mya's hand to pull her with me. She didn't move but squeezed my hand quickly before letting go. I turned my head to look down at her and she had a serious expression on her face.

"Jack, we're in this together, all the way, but I think before I meet Ava you should spend some time with her alone. This is the first memory you will have of her and I want you to savour it because this will be the last time you are just Jack. You will be Jack and Ava and when she finally comes home with us we'll be Jack, Mya and Ava."

I was choked by her thoughtfulness. Where most

girlfriends would be feeling insecure and even jealous that they may have to compete for attention, she was happy to give me the time I needed to experience my first moments with my daughter alone. Her understanding was incredible and I was lucky to have found someone so rich in emotional wealth. I bent to kiss Mya softly.

"Thank you, Mya, I love you so much," I whispered against her mouth before stepping back to look at Brenda.

"So, Jack, are you ready to meet your beautiful daughter now?"

I was, but my heart leapt to my throat at her question. I'd refused to accept any pictures of her by way of rejecting the fact that she was kept apart from me. I had already made up my mind that the first time I saw Ava it would be in the flesh, just like most new fathers when they saw and held their baby in their arms for the first time.

Brenda led me along a corridor with various rooms, each with a couple of chairs and bright educational toys which obviously were meeting rooms for families or assessment rooms where children were offered some therapeutic support. My heart was racing like a train leaving a station and was gathering speed with every step I took. I wasn't ashamed to say that I was as nervous as hell.

At the end of the corridor Brenda pushed the door open and I saw a woman sitting on a chair with her back to me. My heart almost stopped when I saw a pair of little pink booties and some short dark brown wavy hair. Just like my hair. My pace quickened as did my heartbeat again until I was standing next to them. The small blond haired woman holding my baby turned around in her chair and my heart stopped momentarily as I saw my little angel for the first time. Happiness flooded my body as I took her in—she was gorgeous, with my eyes, Rosie's nose, and my lips. Beautiful, perfect and mine.

I was worried about bonding with her because of the time and circumstances but my heart had swelled to such an extent I could hardly breathe. It was love at first sight. I swallowed past the lump in my throat as I struggled to get control of my emotions. There was no way I wanted my baby to see me cry the first time we met.

Brenda placed her hand on my shoulder.

"Are you okay, Jack?" I nodded and blinked back tears afraid to speak.

"Would you like to hold your daughter?"

I could only nod for a second before I cleared my throat and a gruff sounding, "Absolutely" came out.

Reaching down I tentatively slid my hands under my daughter's arms and lifted her gently from her carer's arms. I held her close to my chest with one hand under her legs and the other splayed protectively across her back. Deciding it wasn't close enough I repositioned her onto my shoulder, hugging her tighter. Ava's little hand immediately grabbed a chunk of my hair at the back of my head and clung on tightly. Suddenly, strong emotions and feelings washed over me and I struggled to prevent them overwhelming me. Anger, sadness and betrayal came first then as quick as they arrived they left and were replaced by a wave of love and the strongest urge to protect my daughter from anyone and anything I could have thought of.

Brenda steered me towards a chair and I sat down with Ava, placing her on my knee so I could look at her properly. I was smiling widely with an instant feeling of fulfilment. When I'd stared down at her perfect little features, her eyes stared warily back at me for a few seconds before she suddenly gave me this huge gummy smile and I was a goner. I was completely smitten with her. I held out my index finger and she reached out to grasp it and held it tightly in her little fist. My world as I'd known it disappeared because I had a whole new one sitting on my knee.

I'd thought for a moment whether I was doing the

right thing, introducing Mya and my daughter to each other. Mya and I as a couple were amazing together, but I still took a moment to consider if I believed that she would stay in Ava's life as her mother figure. As the thought processed I knew my answer to that without a shadow of a doubt.

"Can you bring Mya in please? Now that Ava has met her dad I think it's time she meets her mum."

Brenda nodded and headed to the door. When I'd turned towards the door I noticed that Mya was already standing just outside and had probably been watching me meet Ava. I was really glad about that for some reason.

Mya didn't attempt to take Ava from my knee but crouched down beside us to look at her.

"Oh, Jack, she's gorgeous, what an incredible gift she is, to the both of us."

Smiling widely, I felt relief because Mya had almost the same reaction as me, her eyes brimming with tears and I was confident we could do this.

Chapter 39

Homecoming

We spent an hour with Ava and during that time I had literally hundreds of questions for her carer about her routines and how to care for Ava properly. Mya had almost as many question as me and hers were things I hadn't even entered my head. I was actually in awe of how she had such an understanding of what she may need to do in the future.

Our contact with Ava was increased daily until we were caring for her all day and had our first overnight visit. She didn't sleep for most of the night but we loved having her at home with us.

Finally the day came where we were able to close the door and take control of our child without anyone else telling us how they thought we were doing or suggesting that we do something differently. That feeling was both the best, and the scariest feeling in the world. Mya and I could now get on with living our lives and were free to make our own decisions without the pressure of having to conform to the thoughts of others.

When we went to tell my parents about Ava, my mum

cried and my dad almost fell out of his chair. But after the news sank in, they were incredibly supportive and couldn't wait to meet her. They also offered to help with anything we might need in the future. It was times like that when I remembered how amazing my parents were.

Their first meeting with Ava was precious and something I'll never forget. Watching the instant love for the latest member of the family was touching, and it made me feel proud that I had fought for my daughter. It also dawned on me when Mum and Dad saw her for the first time that they had been deprived of Ava's first five months by that time, as well. I'd never speak ill of the dead but Rosie did Ava a terrible disservice by keeping her from all of us.

Three weeks after Ava came home I was feeding her when there was a knock on our front door. Mya answered and when she came back to the sitting room she was followed by two people. I immediately knew who they were. The man looked like a slightly older version of Rick Fars and the woman an older version of Mya and neither of them looked happy.

During the previous few weeks Mya had had several heated conversations with them over the phone and I felt terrible for them. Now that I was a dad, I could understand how they would feel at their daughter suddenly leaving the country and taking care of someone else's child, but love is love. You don't choose who you fall in love with, it just happens and it happened to us. We were really happy and so was our little girl but we still had to prove to her parents we could be young, have fun and bring up a child responsibly. You would think that no one had ever had a child in their twenties. I mean Maddie had Nathan at twenty three, her husband worked away most of the time and she had done an amazing job.

Initially Joel and Sarah Fars were pretty standoffish where I was concerned, but they watched us with Ava and

I could see their frosty attitude begin to thaw. Ava was the cutest, sweetest baby ever and she could melt the coldest of hearts. Eventually we all sat discussing the practicalities of our relationship and how Mya and I had gotten engaged before we knew about Ava. I'd felt bad that I hadn't asked for his permission first, but the fact I had asked her to marry me beforehand helped dispel any suspicions they may have had that I only wanted Mya to be a mum to my daughter.

Once we'd cleared the air, they were a little warmer about Mya and I being together but her dad still had some natural concerns. He asked me how I was going to support my family and provide for their future. I had always been embarrassed by the fact that I had been given money by my father, but I was so glad that I hadn't been frivolous with it. My father gave me the apartment and I had only invested in a classic car. In truth, I was actually very well off. I had just chosen to do things on my own and when I'd told him about that, Joel's attitude towards me changed.

I had already paid for Mya's college course even though it wasn't due to start until the September. Mainly because I wanted her to achieve her own aspirations and dreams like I had mine. After watching Lily's struggle between being with Alfie and trying to keep her own dreams alive, I knew that I didn't want Mya to resent me in the future if she didn't do it.

During Mya's parents visit, Maddie, her husband and Nathan popped in to meet Ava as well as did Dave and Emily who incidentally, were now kind of living together. As usual, Dave's filter was missing but did me a huge favour when he told Mya's parents that whatever I did, I always did it properly. I never cut corners and once committed to something they could be assured that I'd do everything in my power to see it through. I made a silent note to thank Dave for the reference for the job of being Mya's husband.

After a couple of hours her parent's left to check in at a local hotel and the others all went to Maddie's place while I called my parents to ask if we could bring Mya's parents to dinner. We were already due to spend the evening there and we felt that it would be a good opportunity to put their minds at rest about our decision to be together and for our parents to know each other. My parents were delighted at the idea and were excited to finally meet them.

We were already there when Joel and Sarah arrived and initially, relations were strained. I was thankful for my parents' ability to make people feel at home. They were very hospitable people and before long they were chatting about mutual interests, rather than talking about us. Mya and I were really grateful for this and I felt that inviting Joel and Sarah was probably the best move we could have made. Sarah and my mother had a lot in common. Joel was a wealth manager and well... my father was a very wealthy man, so they had a lot to talk about as well.

When their small talk ran dry, the topic of conversation turned to us and the way my parents spoke about Mya and how wonderful she was had her parents bristling in their seats. Mya's dad listened with a furrowed brow then sounded jealous when he spoke about Mya in an extremely possessive way. My dad was intuitive enough to pick up on that and did his best to make them realise that they were gaining a son in their family, just like mine were gaining a daughter.

To be perfectly honest we could just have said, "Fuck all of you, we're consenting adults and we can do what we want," but we respected our parents and wanted to do things properly, after all, what would we be teaching our daughter about relationships in the future if we did that.

My parents had taken to Mya as if she was their own, and Mya fell in love with them almost as easily as she did with me. I think both of her parents noticed the warmth in the relationships between them that wasn't there in theirs with me. My thoughts were that they didn't know me yet, and to some extent I was the man that stole their daughter's affections away from them.

From their perspective I was a guy with a job and a baby living half way around the world and Mya was smitten. I could accept their concerns for her. I'd probably be the same if Ava presented the same circumstances to me. However, during the evening there were glimmers of hope in their conversations and I was confident they'd eventually warm to the idea of us as time went on.

The contrast between my parents and Mya's reactions were clear, but nothing more than I'd expected given Mya's circumstances. My mother, after she got over her initial shock, was ecstatic about having a grandchild and even more so that she was a girl. Mya was just accepted as Ava's new mum and as I had suspected, my mum had booked us all in for those family portraits saying it was about time the one of my grandparents, my parents and me from when I was a baby was updated.

It wasn't long before my mum brought up the subject of me and Mya getting married. Mum was desperate to throw us an elaborate affair despite Mya and I telling her that we had no time for anything as luxurious as a wedding because we were too busy with our new role as parents. The look of relief on Sarah's face at us not getting married immediately didn't escape my notice.

By the time Mya's parents left, they had a different idea to the one they had been forming in their minds about me. I had told them that I was more than happy to support and encourage Mya to live her dream and Mya told them that a part of that dream was to live as a family with Ava and me. As he was leaving, Joel asked me if Rick knew how potentially wealthy I was. I responded by saying I doubted Rick knew anything about me other than my work.

Joel smirked and nodded.

"That sounds like my brother. Unless it directly affects him he's not that interested in other people's business, and he regarded Mya as his business. I think had he known what a wise head you have and a good man you are, he'd have formed a different opinion. His assessment is that you'd play with Mya until you were bored and would use her to help you with your child. Rick said he loves you like a brother, Jack. He's a good guy and if he likes someone they are treated with care, but when it comes to Mya, his only niece, I think his judgement can get distorted."

Joel patted me on the back and added, "My daughter loves you very much and I think you'll take very good care of her. I have to go with my gut on that. The most important thing is that Mya has assessed you as someone she wants to spend her life with and she's not easily fooled, so that's good enough for me."

The relief I felt at his simple statement meant everything. I was expecting a more difficult time from Mya's parents. I believed Ava's presence helped as well because before dinner all of our parents were fawning over her and I could see that she was already staking her claim on their hearts. I'm sure when they saw how we all were together it must have been a little reassuring at least.

However Ava had been born and to whom and how she came into our lives didn't matter anymore, she was here forever and we all had a stake in her upbringing. Anyone that wanted out knew where the door was as far as Mya and I were concerned. However having everyone's blessing made it a much smoother path even if it was tentative at the start.

So after Mya's parents visited life settled down and our home life fell into a comfortable routine. I only took on local assignments for work. Joe, my editor was incredible and gave me some great pieces before giving me my own column. Most of it I could do at home between feeds, nappy changes and cooing at Ava.

Caring for Ava was a pleasure, but when she went through a phase where she became clingy I became concerned, but my mum reassured me it was normal at her stage of development. Everyone always made comments about how strongly we had bonded and that gave me hope there would be no lasting effects from being introduced to her several months after her birth.

Our daughter's cuteness factor was off the charts, she'd started to follow me around, mirroring my expressions and copying my mannerisms and when she said, "Dada," for the first time...I can't describe how that felt. The speed of Ava's progress was rapid. She went from being an immobile child that lay gurgling and cooing whilst being flat on her back into a confident toddler who thought chairs and tables were some kind of fun obstacle courses. And she tried to eat anything within her grasp. Learning the dangers to a baby around our apartment was a steep learning curve.

Every day she amazed me with something new and every day I fell in love with her just a little bit more. Above all, she was a funny, sunny baby who had an infectious giggle which sent us all into hysterics. I've yet to meet an adult that Ava couldn't wrap around her little finger.

Our work-home balance was just about right and Mya picked up the rest, but I insisted she study until her school year started; she had to keep her student visa running. Within a couple of weeks of a music appreciation course she was attending, Mya had got bored at summer school and pulled together a couple of guys and then dragged me into the mix. Somehow from that we started playing as a band for fun. Ava had special noise reduction headphones and was usually so impressed by the sound of us that she fell asleep. I really enjoyed taking part and Mya gave me the confidence to perform. Because of that I realised how much I had missed playing.

I still hadn't shared what I really did when I went on sabbatical with anyone except Mya, the guys in the band never knew my past, and she had been great at respecting that. She just knew what I needed from her. Mya was everything I'd waited my whole life for, even if I hadn't known I was waiting at the time. She was also proving to be the excellent mum I knew she would be. She was patient, kind, firm, protective and practical and Ava doted on her. My amazing girl's life was full on with all she was doing yet Mya still always seemed to find time for me.

My sexy, confident girl coped with everything from Ava's first viral infection which scared the shit out of both of us, to all the milestones of weaning, crawling and walking and she took every challenge in her stride. She made me feel like the proudest guy alive and I was in awe that she was mine.

All of our friends said we were obviously meant to be by the way we only had eyes for each other. In fact we had to push ourselves to socialise because we were so happy in our own little world. I kind of expected my friends to ease off after Ava came on the scene, but I found the opposite to be true.

Dave and Emily became constant visitors to our home and finally Emily 'officially' moved in to Dave's place, while Maddie and I met up for walks in the park with the kids when the weather permitted. Sam I didn't see as much of, but he and Cat loved partying. I guess our social scenes had changed since Ava came along but the more interactive she became the more smitten they all became with her, so I was sure they'd come back on the scene more as she grew.

We felt truly blessed. We'd survived the new couple and our sudden parent status and my friends had completely taken to Mya. They were loyal and supportive and they'd all been so encouraging during some pretty intense moments, like when Ava was sick or we were both exhausted and looked like we'd forgotten where the bedroom was.

Emily and Dave had actually turned up one evening and refused to leave unless we went out to dinner for a few hours. After using his powers of persuasion we armed them with a million instructions and reluctantly set off for the Chinese restaurant at the end of the street. I knew it took less than two minutes to get back to our place if we needed to hurry back.

It was quite funny actually because we managed to drink a bottle of wine due to us being nervous before our entrée even arrived. We were so busy discussing how they were getting on that neither one of us noticed we were downing the drink as fast as we were pouring it. We couldn't really relax during our time away and were fretting about leaving Ava at least every five minutes.

No matter how hard we tried to relax we worried about how they were coping. In the end it was the quickest dinner we'd ever eaten and we were home in just over an hour. Ava never even knew we were gone and had slept right through our dinner date. It was an amazing gesture from Dave and Emily, but I think they got the message that while she was still tiny, we preferred to socialise at home.

The first months seemed to fly by as we got to grips with parenthood and before we knew it, Ava's first birthday was coming up as was Mya's twenty-first, and it was only two weeks until Mya's music school started. It was an amazing coincidence that we could celebrate two milestones in the same weekend with Ava's birthday on the Friday and Mya's on the Monday.

When I thought about Mya's background I knew I would struggle for something special for her birthday, especially something that would involve the three of us. I could have kissed my mum when she rang to ask if she could arrange a marque and a local band to play for her birthday. She thought a hog roast and barbeque would go down well with our friends and would be more relaxing than trying to attend anything formal with Ava. I was relieved to have the whole thing taken out of my hands. I just had to find something special for both of their birthdays.

During the time we were getting to grips with Ava, Lily and I had got our friendship back on more of a firm footing. I had to forgive her because there was too much between us for me not to do so. Besides, I knew I'd never forgive myself, god forbid, if anything ever happened to her and I didn't settle our differences like I hadn't been able to with Rosie.

Lily's parents had told her what was being planned for Mya and called saying she was going to be over for the week leading up to the barbeque. Both Lily's and Alfie's bands were playing at a festival and she was excited to be able to come and see us. She sounded determined to spend time with me, and asked about our availability which I was glad about because I needed to see her making the effort. We still had some fences to mend. We'd spoken a few times on Skype and she'd watched Ava grow through photos I sent in emails, but we still had a way to go to get our relationship back to where it was.

I had accepted that we'd never be the same. Lives change and so do people, but Lily still held a special place in my heart. She had always been there, apart from the past year or so but ultimately she was still there when it mattered. So I had learned to let everything go. People are flawed, I just never figured Lily as people.

Lily arrived on the Wednesday before Ava's birthday, and she and my mum begged me to let Ava stay overnight at my parents. It was Mya who eventually talked me into it but I only agreed if they promised to call me if there was anything wrong.

Dropping off Ava and driving away was difficult for the both of us, but the sense of freedom I felt when I saw all the guys from XrAid and Crakt Soundzz in the club helped me relax and I felt like I was coming home. They were all brilliant guys. I had kept in touch loosely with Lennon and Cody from Lily's band just before Lily and I had our spat, so seeing them again was great.

For one night Mya and I had a rare night out as a couple instead of a family and we were making the most of it. Mya and Lily were like kindred spirits and were constantly laughing and joking with each other. It made my heart swell because unlike Rosie, Mya didn't feel threatened by Lily's presence and it was amazing that my three favourite women get along.

Chapter 40

Group night

During the evening Mya started doing tequila shots while I had limited myself to two gin and tonics. Like I said, we had one night—I didn't want to be too drunk to perform when I got her home. It was difficult making time for intimacy with a baby at times.

"Mya, you know how it's your birthday this weekend?" Mya smirked like she knew what was coming and leaned in to place her hands on my chest. She stared up at me and her eyes were filled with humour.

"Don't tell me, Jack, you have a present in your pocket for me. Am I right? Or are you just playing with yourself because you're so used to holding Ava and she's not here so you don't know what to do with your hands?"

Mya's questions were funny and I started chuckling but Alfie roared with laughter. "Damn, Jack. Mya's got a smarter mouth than you have."

I grinned widely, "Well I was going to say, why don't we spend a night in a hotel, but if you are dissing the not-so-little-guy in my pants he may not want to play with you at all, love."

Mya swept her hand down over the material at the front of my pants and ground her palm into my now semi-hard dick smirking wickedly. She had no issue in claiming me no matter who was looking.

"Oh he wants to play all right, Jack. Don't pretend you can take it or leave it. You're almost ready to come in your pants at the thought of having me alone in a hotel bed."

"No, Mya, I'm almost ready to come in my *pants* because you're grinding your hand over my semi. Keep your hands to yourself, love, or I'll have to cut the night short and teach you a lesson."

"Jack, if I keep my hand here you'll come and it'll cut the night short anyway, so less of the threats."

Alfie and Cody shook their heads trying to muffle their laughter then Alfie grinned widely at me.

"Damn, you two are a match made in heaven my friend."

I smiled slowly and nodded at his comment because everyone said the same and that was exactly how I felt.

Our night out was great fun and everyone had turned up to share it with us, even Maddie and David had gotten themselves a night off from Nathan to come and party with us.

We were at Konnect nightclub again, but that time was very different because being with two hot rock bands had its advantages. We had a private party room so everyone could relax without having lots of screaming and jostling when fans tried to get a piece of one of the guys as I had seen happen previously.

Cody and Lennon disappeared at one point and came back with half a dozen girls who must have been well warned because none of them interacted with Drew or Alfie at all. They looked like they were all enjoying themselves though.

Mya chatted with Lily, Emily, and the rest of our

female friends and was excited because they were all coming to the barbeque my mother was arranging. When I'd heard her talking I realised it had actually escalated from a marque and a barbeque to caterers and a sit down dinner of Italian cuisine, but that was typical of my parents. They believed in taking the stress out of parties by employing people to make things go smoothly and simple plans became more elaborate the longer they had to plan.

The rest of the night we danced and caught up with the latest from everyone and it was a great feeling to dance with Mya in my arms to one of her favourite songs 'Lost Stars' by Maroon 5. She felt perfect, snuggled up beside me.

When Mya danced with Alfie I felt more than a little jealous, she was smiling up at him and it gave me a sense of what he was feeling when Lily and I danced together all those times with him watching us, but that was all in the past now. We were good mates now.

Mya started yawning and five hours after arriving at the dance club, I could see she was dead on her feet. We said our goodbyes and I took my girl back to our apartment to show her just how much she meant to me. She was more than a little bit tipsy when we finally arrived home and she headed straight to the bathroom.

I had planned ahead and had wanted to give her a night that was a little different from all the rest, so I had hired a massage table, bought some extra luxurious massage oil and some mandarin and Jasmin infused candles.

As soon as the bathroom door closed I ran to the sitting room, lit the log burner and candles then opened the massage table. The linen cupboard where our towels had hot water pipes running through it kept our linen warm, so I pulled out four white fluffy bath sheets and draped two over the table just as I'd heard Mya padding along the wooden floor in the hallway.

Throwing the other towels in front of the log burner to keep them warm I quickly stripped off all my clothes and waited at the side of the table. When Mya opened the door she was hesitant.

"What the…"

"Well, you said you didn't want to play with anything in my pants so… ta-da, no pants. Problem solved."

Watching Mya's face light up as her lips curved up into a sexy smile was great. Raising her eyebrow she wandered around the table her fingers trailing over it until she reached my side and I didn't know who was turned on the most by my little gesture.

"What do you suggest I do now, Jack? All of a sudden I'm feeling a tad overdressed for this party."

Smirking wickedly I reached out and slowly flicked her hair over her shoulders. My hands swept around her upper arms and my fingers found her button down top. I began to unbutton the little blue silky blouse and when I'd reached the last button I glanced up at her to see her standing watching me, mesmerised. She smiled adoringly when her eyes eventually met mine and I mirrored the emotion and winked.

Slipping the blouse over her shoulders it fell down her arms until it pooled at her feet on the floor. My hands skated around her skin from her ribs to her upper spine reaching for her bra strap. Expert fingers unhooked the fasters and I peeled it away from her as well. As I dropped the offending clothing on the floor, I saw her nipples react to the cool room and bent to kiss each one of them before stepping back to the table.

"Come here." My voice was gruff with emotion as I tried to contain my own needs and focus on giving pleasure to my beautiful girl.

Mya stepped towards me and my fingers trailed from her hips to the zipper of her tight blue leather leggings. They were extremely sexy with zips up the ankles and when she had come out of the bedroom with them on and some six inch stiletto shoes I had wanted to tear them right off of her before we got out the door. Her arse looked incredible in them.

Unzipping her leggings was like un-wrapping a precious gift, I ticked each tooth on the zipper down as slowly as I could. I was tormenting myself so it had to be teasing her a little as well. Turning her around to pull her back against my chest, I slipped my hands from around the sides of her ribcage down in front of her belly and into her trousers until I found the tiny triangle of lace that did nothing to stop me from finding her clitoris through it. Mya didn't usually wear underwear so it was a special treat to find another layer to unwrap.

Exhaling heavily, Mya sighed and sagged further against me as I slipped my middle finger further down to her entrance. A loud gasp followed by a moan escaped her lips and she turned her head to look up at me. I leaned forward to meet her mouth and kissed her softly before spinning her around as quickly as I could and bending her across the table.

"Ohh, God." She muttered when I caught her off guard.

Her body trembled slightly under my touch. Her response made me smile and I pulled her trousers down to her knees and quickly pressed my mouth between her thighs as my tongue sought to taste her through her thong. She groaned and shivered, and I stood back abruptly smacking her arse a little hard, fighting to stay in control and not just take her right then. I rubbed the red handprint, gently squeezed her arse cheek and ordered her to finish getting undressed and lie face down on the table.

Without a word, Mya complied with my demand as I wandered around the table observing her form lying before me. Every time I'd looked at her I thanked God for sending her to me. She was an incredible person, beautiful inside and out. Her California tan had completely faded and her skin was an even olive tone all over. She was amazingly relaxed in my presence, even in the knowledge that I must be looking at her closely. I saw the welt my hand had left on her right buttock and bent to kiss it again. Mya moaned and her legs instinctively parted.

I'd resisted diving in and devouring her when my animalist side was provoked after smelling her scent and tasting her, and I tried to remember my plan for the night. Lifting one of the towels to cover her up from the base of her spine to her ankles I took the oils I'd left to warm up on top of the log burner. Smoothing her hair out of the way, I trailed my hand down her spine then opened the oil bottle.

When I poured it on my hands it was extremely thick and I was turned on almost as much as Mya when I began to massage it over her shoulders and down her arms before bringing it back over her back and down to her hips. The erotic noises she made at the sensation of the oil and my hands on her skin made my dick rock solid. The bottom half of her body wriggled each time she moaned.

I'd taken my time, making sure I covered every inch of her back, arms and neck with my hands working in unhurried sensual strokes to worship her beautiful body. Eventually I tugged the towel away from her and began to pay attention to her lower limbs and buttocks.

Mya's legs parted slowly as I'd rubbed her inner thighs from her knee to her groin. Each time Mya's arse arched towards my hand it signalled that she wanted more than what I was doing. I nudged her side indicating that I wanted her to turn over and once she had, my eyes fell on her gorgeous breasts. Her nipples were pebble hard as they met the cool air. Mya looked up and when her eyes met mine I could see the lust radiating from them towards me.

I poured more oil onto my hands, trying to make the massage last longer but I was desperate to be inside her. I massaged over her breasts and down towards her belly, before running my hands down her legs as I tried to keep away from her perfectly shaven pussy. My dick was distracting me by twitching every time my eyes raked over her until I eventually began massaging her clitoris with my fingers. Mya moaned loudly and raised her arse off the table in an effort to get more contact. It was actually quite fun teasing her. And when I saw that little crease of frustration appear in her brow I knew she'd be begging to have me in no time.

I dropped to my knees and dragged her width ways on the table with her head hanging off the other side and took her pussy in my mouth. She tasted incredible as always and I groaned into her core.

"Please Jack..."

And there it was. Just as I knew she would, Mya was begging me to take her and she didn't have to ask twice. Since she'd started taking the contraceptive pill I wondered how I'd ever managed to get the condom on in time before. I placed the crown of my dick at her entrance and leaned over her on the table to support her head in my hand.

When my forehead touched hers the look of love she gave me almost blew me away. I slid inside her painstakingly slowly and saw her eyes change from love to lust at the same time as her hand reached out and stroked down my abs because she needed to touch me a little more.

The feel of her clenching around me tightly always made me feel like a king and when I thrust into her and pulled out so just my tip was inside her, she lifted her left leg and pressed her heel into me to draw my arse nearer and to keep me from leaving her completely.

What started out as slow and sensual became hard and passionate and almost competitive as the both of us let loose our inner animals which turned our love-making into a wild ride. Mya moaned and screamed her way through three orgasms and I managed two of my own. When we were done we landed on the floor next to the log burner draped in the bath towels. Mya lay with her head in my lap, her silky locks of hair strewn all around her and I bent my neck to kiss her again.

We had been through so much as a couple. More than many would in a life time in terms of the barriers we'd overcome so far, and the way she just seemed to know what I'd needed was amazing. Everything she did seemed so easy, her love for Ava and me was effortless. I was a very lucky man.

After a while I lifted Mya in my arms, held her close and carried her to our bed. She slid between the sheets and I crawled in next to her, scooping her in my arms so I could spoon her. I used to like spooning with Lily but with Mya it was so much more intimate. No clothing and my dick nestled safely at the crease of her arse with her pulled tight to me and one hand securely cupping one of her breasts—it felt just perfect. What Lily and I did was nothing like that.

"I love you so much, Mya." I told her as I kissed the top of her head affectionately. I made it a point to tell her several times a day how much I loved her and how beautiful she was.

Mya snuggled into the curve of my body and I was vaguely aware of her telling me she loved me more right before I fell asleep.

Chapter 41

Exhibitionist

By the time Saturday came Mya was really into the swing of socialising and she thought it would be a real coup if we surprised everyone by playing together during the party. Apart from Mya no one knew I was now a proficient guitar player in a band she'd put together for fun and I really liked the idea, if I could get over my nerves, so I told her I'd think about it.

At that point she came clean that we were the local band my mother had referred to. That's when the panic really started to set in. A couple of the best bands in the world were going to be there and they were going to have to say that they enjoyed our little amateurish stint out of loyalty. I felt sick.

"No fucking way, Mya. No. A song maybe but a whole gig…"

Mya chuckled at me and nodded interrupting me.

"Jack Cunningham, you're doing it. Don't do it for them, do it for me. I think you're incredible, you'd give them all a run for their money and I enjoy playing with you. Please, for me? Don't say no to me, it's my twenty-first birthday."

How could I refuse after that plea? So I nodded and felt like shitting my pants because I had just agreed to make a fool of myself in front of everyone.

Mya laid some clothes out for me to wear and what she had chosen was exactly what I'd have worn for the day as well, a blue and white striped shirt from my favourite tailor and some dark jeans, but with my Italian leather shoes.

While I had been working for the magazine Mya had a hand in organising her birthday bash at my parents with Ava and I could see her little touches everywhere as I looked. The old wooden pagoda with the lead roof had been transformed with flowers and string lighting and had been set up as the band stand with a drum kit some guitars and a microphone for us. The sound system and amps were stacked discretely at the back.

Glancing up I saw that the foliage of all the trees had strings of tinsel hanging from them as well, giving a glittery effect from the rope lighting Mya had strung around the balustrade that ran the length of the back of the house as well. I was a little jealous to have missed my mother's reaction to Mya's takeover of her normally immaculately and well pruned garden.

Inside the marque that stood in the middle of the garden there were tables with small flower jars and floating candles, balloons and bunting.

Somewhere around five people began to arrive. There was a couple of hours before Ava went down for the night and everyone wanted to share in her first birthday celebration. She was thoroughly spoiled by everyone and when I saw all the wrapped presents for her, the enormity of having a growing child hit me. Our apartment was only going to be good for another year at the most. I made a mental note to speak to my father about that at some point the following week.

Lily, Emily and Elle fawned over Ava and I even saw Alfie have a sneaky cuddle when he thought I wasn't looking, but I wandered over and put my finger in front of Ava while he was holding her. She immediately grabbed it and squeezed it smiling widely at me with adoration. Alfie gave her his lopsided smile and I could see that he was taken with her. Ava began to cry for me and stretched out her little arms in my direction. I lifted her out of Alfie's arms into mine to comfort her and he looked a little awkward.

"Oh, Alfie, look at that. Another stunning looking girl with good taste, I see. How does it feel to have stiff competition? First Lily, now Ava." Giving Ava my complete attention I cooed, "Aw sweetheart you are a great judge of character, don't worry, daddy's the only rock star in your life."

Mya came up behind me and kissed my shoulder. "Ah, Jack did I hear you sharing your secret talent at last?"

"Jack's always wanted to be a rock star, I've seen him perform a few times, Mya, but those performances would normally get him arrested for public indecency, although I don't doubt in certain circles people would pay to see it." Alfie sniggered.

It was my turn to look awkwardly at Alfie, wondering if he really just tried to put my previous antics with women out there in front of Mya.

Again I was surprised when Mya pushed his jibe back at him.

"Alfie, I was telling my Jack here he could probably give you, Lily and even my uncle Rick a run for your money. He's an awesome guitar player and when he sings to me it just melts my panties right off."

Alfie sniggered and winked at Mya.

"Damn, Jack, you got yourself a fan for life there. I might just have to have the Jack experience for myself. Mya makes you sound so appealing."

Shaking her head, Mya patted Alfie's arm.

"Don't worry, Alfie, as soon as Jack's put Ava to bed, he'll be up on that stage shocking the hell out of you all."

Alfie's eyes widened and Lily walked up slipping her arm around Alfie.

"What's that, Mya? Jack's performing? I hope whatever it is, it's decent. All of our parents are going to be here later."

If looks could kill, Lily would have been flat on her back. Mya's dark side instantly showed, her mouth twisting at Lily's comment which obviously left a sour taste there.

"You may think you know Jack, Lily but I *know* I do. Be prepared to be blown away later. Y'all are going to wonder how the hell you have jobs when you hear my Jack play."

No pressure then, Mya. Right then I wanted to kiss Mya and smack her arse at the same time for talking me up like that in front of those two. If I had been feeling queasy about performing before, I was going to need to check my pants after that build up.

I knew I was stalling but Ava had her first late night where I kept her up twenty minutes past her bedtime. That was more about me delaying my performance than anyone having more time with her. Once she was tucked up in her cot sleeping peacefully, I went back to the garden to find Mya, but I bumped into Hugh, the drummer we'd been playing with.

"All set?" I wasn't I was crapping my pants but I couldn't allow Hugh to see how nervous I was because he wasn't the most confident guy I'd ever met either.

"Sure, we've got this, Hugh. No pressure." Hugh hesitated and then swallowed hard.

"If you say so, Jack."

It was a muggy night once the sun had gone and the light was kind of grey when we took up our positions on in the pagoda. I was thinking all kinds of random stuff to try and make myself comfortable in front of the mic. *God only knows how those guys do this for a living day after day. Karaoke was way different.*

Lily grinned and shook her head at me like she thought I was joking and I stepped forward with the microphone in my hand. I was shaking, the only mic I had held before outside of rehearsals was on Karaoke nights.

"I just want to say thank you to my parents for having us all over to celebrate my beautiful girls' birthdays and I want to thank all of you, my friends for your love and support during the hardest but the most rewarding year of my life so far. Before I blow you all away with my talent I have just one note of sadness to bring to the party."

"Most of you knew Rosie, Ava's birth mother. Rosie was a sweet person and I guess she felt I didn't treat her with respect for the way she kept Ava a secret from me. Now I don't want her memory sullied with opinions of what she did to us. In my heart I have forgiven her for not telling me about Ava until after she'd passed." I held a glass up and saluted her.

"Rosie, honey, if you're looking down on us, no hard feelings. Thank you for my beautiful daughter. I will do everything in my power to see that she has the best life possible." I took my glass and raised it.

"Rosie." Everyone raised their glasses and Mya did as well then we all saluted her together.

"To Rosie."

With that I turned to Mya staring deeply into her eyes but still speaking to everyone.

"I know now that I was a mess when I split from Rosie and some of you may have felt for her. I did too, believe me, however in my heart I knew she wasn't the person I could spend the rest of my life with. When I realised that, I did the decent thing and set her free. As you know I took the choice to opt out of life for a while and during that time I thought I had acted in haste. But then I met Mya and we fell in love so effortlessly. I can't imagine life without this wonderful girl by my side. She is the stars and the moon to me, heaven and earth and I don't know how I survived without her."

Mya leaned in and kissed me on the lips and murmured, "Ditto."

I broke my eye contact with her and turned back to all of my friends. "No one really knew what I did during that time away, apart from Mya, because I've never really spoken about it. Now you are all about to find out, or I'm about to make the biggest arse of myself in front of two worldwide bands."

Lily smirked and looked at Alfie and he folded his arms in an arrogant pose and smirked back at her as if to say, 'This is going to be funny'.

I nodded my head at the band and started to play the song that Mya thought suited me best, 'Smart Dressed Man' by ZZ Top. When I started singing Lily's jaw dropped and she and Alfie glanced at each other with a surprised look on their faces.

Mya's performance was exceptional as always and we played the song together like we'd been doing it for years. Lennon and Cody started playing air guitar and that made me smile. When I took on the awesome guitar solo it was like a freeze-frame as everyone stared in wonder at me. As we finished my parents cheered the loudest of everyone. They had been desperately trying to get me to play an instrument throughout my childhood years.

We went on to play five more songs and then it turned into a bit of an impromptu Karaoke where everyone else got up and sang a cover of their own favourite songs. As soon as we stepped off the pagoda I was almost overrun with everyone commenting how impressed they were. Alfie pushed his way through the crowd and slapped me on the back.

"Jesus, Jack, where the hell did you learn to play guitar like that? That was absolutely incredible, I'd buy your album in a heartbeat, buddy."

Lily stood to the side staring at me with a stunned look on her face just waiting for everyone else to finish what they wanted to say. When she finally walked slowly towards me she had a kind of sad look on her face.

"Hey." Her voice sounded small and she pointed to the pagoda where Lennon and Cody were singing a rendition of 'Pinball Wizard' by The Who.

"I don't know what to say. I mean you and the guitar, Jack?" Lily shook her head and glanced up at me again with tears brimming in her eyes. "Wow, Jack. Just...wow."

I put my arms out and Lily stepped into them. Closing them around her I kissed the top of her head and she began to cry. I pushed her away from me a little to look down at her and she sniffed laughing, a little embarrassed by her emotions.

"Sorry, that was just awesome. You are awesome. My big hero. I've always known you could do anything you put your mind to Jack, you just proved me right."

Lily felt good in my arms. I had missed her hugely but that year taught me I could live without her, except I didn't want to any more.

"God, I've missed you, Lily. I'm sorry if I took all my anger out on you, sweetheart."

Lily's brow furrowed and she shook her head vigorously.

"No, Jack, you were right. I should never have kept something so incredibly important from you."

I kissed her forehead and pulled her tight to my chest.

"Let's not get ourselves twisted any more about something we can't change. I have Ava and Mya in my life now and I couldn't be happier."

Lily smiled up at me with affection. "If I'm honest, it

makes me a little jealous to know that there are a couple of girls on this planet that are more important to you than I am now."

"Lily I still love you, sweetheart, it's just a different kind of love to that of Mya and Ava." Lily nodded and Alfie came over and pulled Lily away from me.

"Fuck off, Jack, just because you can hold a tune and play the guitar like the best of us doesn't mean you can pull my woman and make her cry."

For the first time I conceded to Alfie completely.

"She's all yours, buddy. I'm very happy with my own girl so no need to get jealous man, I love Lily, but I'm completely *in* love with Mya."

Alfie nodded and squeezed Lily to him, "And that's a fucking incredible feeling, right?"

Nodding slowly I smirked and tilted my head to the side glancing past him to Mya then back at him.

"Right, Alfie." It definitely was.

Chapter 42

Sneaky

Mya had a fantastic night and was surprised by her parents who arrived later. Her father didn't want to miss her big day and she spent some time with them talking in the marque while mayhem was happening on my mother's lawn between the XrAid and Crakt Soundzz guys. They were all behaving really childishly doing cartwheels and leap frog and my father smirked and raised his eyebrow at me.

"Thank goodness you don't do anything like that at parties to embarrass yourself, Jack."

Alfie was behind me and coughed loudly, drawing my father's attention to him. He held his hand up and pretended to be choking for a second then wandered off. I bit back a grin and nodded innocently at my dad like I'd never do anything to draw attention to myself like that.

Mya and I were staying at my parents' place that night and after one in the morning I just wanted to get into bed and snuggle up with her. I still had no gift for her because I wanted it to be the right thing and not just 'something'. When we got into bed I apologised and then asked her straight what she wanted.

"You really want to know?" Mya shifted up onto her elbow to look at me.

"Sure, it would make my life so much easier than trying to find something special. You have been spoiled by Rick, Mya. I could buy you many things, but I don't want it to be materialistic."

Mya brushed my hair away from my eyes and kissed me softly on the lips before leaning back again to speak.

"Cunningham. That's what I want for my birthday."

I was already in the process of changing Ava's name from Lister to Cunningham, and Mya had followed the paper process with me as she was adopting Ava as well. Mya was such a part of me that I never thought she may be feeling left out by not having the same name as the Ava and I. By changing her name, I was laying my final claim on Ava. I still had to do that for Mya.

"Sure. You know I'll be ecstatic when you become my wife, we just have to find the time to get married, and with school starting soon you won't have any holiday time until Christmas. Do you want to do it then? Just give me a date and I'll tell my mother. She'll plan most of it if you tell her what you want."

Mya shook her head slowly and stared seriously into my eyes.

"No, Jack. I just want it to be us. No fanfare. No rock stars. No negotiation about which side of the Atlantic the ceremony is on. We can have a wedding for them afterwards but I want a secret one now."

Glancing at her through sleepy eyes I considered what she'd been through for me and throughout our time together she had never made any demands, but part of me also thought about how that would feel to my parents knowing that their only child had gone and got married without inviting them. Then again, if there was a public wedding afterwards would they ever know we'd already done it?

"All right Mya, I'll look into it tomorrow." I wasn't sure what the outcome was going to be but at least she knew I wasn't dismissing the idea. Mulling over that thought meant it was an age before I fell asleep.

Amber rays of sunlight bathed the room when I'd woken to the sound of Ava babbling through the baby monitor. I remembered we were at my parent's house and decided I should let Mya sleep in a little. She stirred but didn't wake up when the mattress dipped as I stood up and began to walk to Ava's room. Lifting her into my arms I sat on the oversized chair that had been my mother's feeding chair when I was a baby. She was bright eyed but just sat quietly in my lap stroking my skin on my arm so I spent a few quiet minutes explaining what had been going on for all of us during the past year.

I talked about Rosie and described her as a beautiful girl with a serious outlook on life, kind of the opposite to me at the time. I was able to tell Ava honestly that I loved her mum, but that sometimes just loving someone wasn't enough.

Previously I had vowed to concentrate on the good parts of Rosie when Ava was old enough to ask me about her and I'd never hide the fact that although she had a wonderful mum in Mya, she wasn't the one who had helped to make her. Rosie may not have done the best by me, but that didn't mean she hadn't loved our daughter, and I was the better person for filling Ava's mind with good thoughts about her birth mum.

Creaking floor boards took my attention away from Ava and I saw Mya standing at the door. I wasn't sure how long she'd been standing there, but from her face I knew she'd heard enough to be affected by what I'd said. She looked emotional and at first I thought she was upset by me telling Ava about her birth mother, but instead she came and sat by my feet.

"I've never heard anything more touching, Jack. You and Ava make an incredible sight sitting in here quietly. I was happy to share my life with the both of you, but I want to belong now and I'm starting to need that."

Mya never asked me for anything. She was a born giver. The conversation she'd started before bed was still on her mind and it was my responsibility to do something about it.

"Heard loud and clear, love, we want that too, don't we, Ava?" Ava cooed and reached out to Mya as if on cue and we both chuckled.

"I never paid her to do that, Mya. Honest." I winked at Ava playfully as if we were in collaboration and Mya grinned, reaching up to hug me.

"Thank you, Jack. Normally, I wouldn't be pushing this, it's just that I feel ready for that next step with you, you know?"

I did. I was more than ready, but we'd just been so busy getting through the days and I suppose I'd been a little neglectful of Mya's feelings at times.

"Forgive me, love. I know I haven't been the best fiancé. No birthday gift and with everything else that's been going on I haven't done what I should have in respect of your status. I'm on it today."

Mya went off to her music session, the last of her summer school, and I set about figuring out how I could marry Mya. I called the British Embassy for advice and then the American one. I explained our situation and that Mya was about to go to university and was currently on a student visa.

Donald, the guy at the UK Embassy was extremely helpful and said that in our present circumstances, and with knowledge of the fact that Mya was going to be adopting Ava, we were able to circumvent a lot of the paperwork because she was already in the system. The American Embassy case officer's name, Steven Hardy, was given to Donald and he called later that day to say that they could at least grant a special license for us to marry.

Given that Mya had been in Ava's life since the same day as I had, there was more than ample evidence to say that Mya and I weren't having a 'marriage of convenience', and social services were able to supply a wealth of information to support Mya's application. All we had to wait for was her certificate of approval to marry because she was a non-European Union citizen and she had entered the UK on a visa which wasn't for marriage purposes.

Smiling excitedly, Mya couldn't wait for us to be a proper family when I'd told her and she surprised me further by opting for a civil service with a church blessing once we'd told our parents.

So Mya and I discreetly set the date for a week later, but before we married I wanted to go and see where Rosie was laid to rest. I was informed she'd been cremated and her ashes were interned in a small church yard where she grew up. I wanted to make my peace with her before Mya and I cemented our relationship forever.

Mya understood that it was something I wanted to do alone and didn't seem hurt by my need to do this. I wasn't sure what I'd wanted to get from it, but I went to see the little brass plaque with 'Rosie Lister 1987-2014' inscribed on it. She lived for twenty six years for what? A life cut short or was her real purpose in this life to have Ava?

I sat quietly and told Rosie about Ava and apologised again for hurting her then stood silently and shed a tear in respect of her memory. As I walked away I closed the door on that chapter of my life forever. There was no more to say about it.

Thursday morning the following week, without any build-up to our day, we were standing outside Chelsea Registry Office with Ava waiting for Dave and Emily to meet us.

As soon as he saw me he was gushing excitedly. We'd only called him an hour earlier asking for him and Emily to meet us there and approximately thirteen minutes after meeting them, Mya and I were Mr. and Mrs. Jack Cunningham and she was signing the register.

Watching the look of joy on Mya's face when the registrar said, "I now pronounce you man and wife," I knew I'd done the right thing. Mya unceremoniously leapt onto me squealing in delight. Her arms clinging around my neck as her lips crushed mine before I could even draw breath.

Ava was clapping and whooping along with Dave and Emily unaware of what it all meant and we all burst out laughing,

"Thank you, Jack. Everything until now has always been about other people and their circumstances impacting on us as a couple. Rosie, Uncle Rick, Cobham Street, Lily, our parents... I just wanted one day where it was just us and without anyone knowing about it. Dave and Emily permitted of course."

My wife was incredible. Most girls wanted rainbows and tiaras, designer wedding attire and a huge white wedding day, and all mine wanted was to belong to me.

Our wedding luncheon was at a local pub with Dave, Emily and our daughter, who sat in an old wooden high chair eating spaghetti bolognaise with both hands. And I couldn't have been happier.

Since we'd decided to do that I had been thinking a lot about how inadequate I'd been in taking care of Mya's needs. I'd written nine songs about Rosie and not one about how Mya made me feel, so I had tried to put that right and decided to write a song to sing to her on our wedding night. We only had one day together and I could have booked us into a plush hotel and given her the works, but that was clichéd and I wanted something a little more personal than that. Mya may have had the privacy she wanted but there was one more person I had to confide in to make the day a memorable one.

Dave and Emily had earned my trust with Ava and I'd gone as far as naming them on my will as the people I'd like to take care of Ava, God forbid anything happening to Mya and I, so I was as confident as I could be about leaving Ava in their care on our wedding night. At five thirty, we walked away from Dave's place with Mya believing we were just going home.

Mya grinned up at me looking absolutely stunning in her simple ivory linen dress and stilettos.

"A whole night with no responsibilities, what are we going to do with that, Jack?"

"Actually, Mya, I think it's too early to go home. I've neglected to show you the city you have chosen to live in. We have one night free, so if you'll indulge me I'd like to show you my home town." Mya grinned as I put my arm up to flag a taxi for us.

"Victoria Station, please."

Mya's brow was bunched and I could see that she was thinking about the shoes she was wearing.

"Don't worry, there is very little walking with what I have in mind." She sat back in the taxi and allowed me to control the evening.

Mya started laughing when I dragged her towards the classic red open-topped tour bus. She grinned widely as she boarded and allowed me to be her personal tour guide while the red London bus drove down Victoria Street, past New Scotland Yard and then on to Westminster Abbey, where Kings and Queens had walked for more years than her country had been discovered.

Next, we drove past the Houses of Parliament where the government allegedly made sound decisions and past the icon that was Big Ben. The bus ride took a left along the embankment of the River Thames passing the London Eye and The Royal Festival Hall on our right then onward again passing Tower Bridge stretching over The Thames and the Tower of London on our left. Mya was particularly impressed with those as the evening light had faded and they were beginning to be lit up.

Staring out in wonder, she was fully engaged with what I was telling her, listening intently and asking questions to gain a greater knowledge of her new city. On the way back we passed through Oxford Street to Trafalgar Square and eventually got off the bus at Marble Arch.

London's history had Mya enthralled and she didn't see me text to arrange the next part of the evening. Hailing another cab, we set off for Battersea and I could see her wonder what else was in store for her.

Charlie, Lily's dad was waiting at the helipad in Battersea for us. He was a helicopter pilot in London and the one person I'd told to arrange this for her. Mya's eyes were wide, glittering in the sunset and I could see how ecstatic she was at her surprise.

Seeing London from the ground was one thing, seeing it from the air at dusk was something else. A magical city full of wonderful architecture and even more amazing having Mya share it with me. Charlie had brought some champagne for us and we drunk the whole bottle as he weaved his way down the river sharing his knowledge of the city with us. Mya was obviously enjoying her trip judging by the amount of expressive gasps and hand squeezes she gave me.

After an hour, Charlie touched down at a City of London helipad. The City is only one square mile. The rest of London is a town which confuses people a lot. It's the financial and legal heart of London. Mya and I thanked Charlie and wandered down to the river for another glimpse of The Tower of London and Tower Bridge being flooded by light in the dark.

Smiling lovingly at me, Mya told me she thought the whole experience was incredible. It wasn't that much from my perspective because I'd wanted to give her the whole world in a box, but with the limited time and my even more limited imagination, this was the best I could think of. She had her first British fish and chips in a newspaper before we headed home to finish our night, and I have to say she still looked amazing despite our long day.

It felt strange entering the apartment without Ava but that night belonged to Mya. She had my undivided attention and it was long overdue. She left me to go to the bathroom and I hurriedly prepared my wedding gift for her. Pulling my guitar out of its hard case and slipping my slacks, socks and shirt off. I sat cross legged on the bed wearing just my boxer briefs.

When Mya opened the door she was wearing lingerie similar to the set she had the first time I made love to her except this one was white and I had to fight with my dick for control to stick with the plan and not drag her to bed and devour her.

I began to play the song I'd written for her and she climbed slowly onto the bed beside me, crossing her legs and watching me play.

I'm crazy in love with a girl who's surrendered,
But I'm complex or simple that's me,
And while most things in life can't be forced,
Others are just meant to be...

Mya had tears in her eyes as I sang of my everlasting love for her and what she meant to me. My gift to her wasn't rubies or diamonds or anything materialistic, what I'd wanted to give her was a memory of the day that I committed to giving her my heart; my life. When I'd finished the song I leaned over my guitar and held her chin.

"You once told me that I didn't have to love you back

and that was the greatest gift anyone has ever given to me. You taught me what unconditional love is, and I want you to know that."

I kissed her softly and her tongue poked into my mouth right before I broke the kiss. Mya pouted and I sniggered but carried on where I'd left off.

"And because I didn't have to love you back, that was probably the best pick-up line ever because you made me do just that."

Smirking wickedly, Mya wiggled her eyebrows and her smirk morphed into a grin.

"Ah-ha, busted, but it worked."

I grabbed her wrist and pulled her over onto her side. I slipped the guitar strap over my head and onto the floor before twisting back and nestled on top of her with my arms cocooning her head. I brushed a stray strand of hair away from her eyes, placed my forehead on hers and hardly believed my luck as I looked into her eyes.

"So Mrs. Cunningham… to my knowledge I've never slept with a married woman before, are their vaginas the same as single girls'?"

Mya chuckled, "Hmm, good question I think you should definitely investigate that or is investigative journalism beyond your scope of capability?"

I chuckled at her playfulness.

"You should know better than to challenge me, Wife. I think I need to teach you just how thorough my investigative skills can be."

Mya's laugh died on her lips as a moan escaped her when my mouth went to investigate the sweet spot on her neck.

Chapter 43

Alternative medicine

"So, Mrs. Cunningham, I hope this isn't the once or twice a month thing I've heard that happens to couples when they get married."

Mya grinned at me but was trying to keep her face straight.

"Well we have to factor in headaches and tiredness, Jack. That's a married woman's right you know, to have headaches I mean."

I smirked wickedly and pulled my boxer briefs down freeing my thick, hard erection and gestured down at it with my head.

"You've heard of alternative medicines, right?"

She howled with laughter and I began to tickle her until she was breathless and tried to continue with my explanation by holding my solid aching length in my hand. Mya glanced down at it and reached out, dragging her thumb across the head of it and I drew in a sharp breath and grinned.

"Now, I know you may think you are well acquainted with this, but there is a lot I have yet to teach you about it." I tried for a serious look but I could feel my lips curve into a smile.

"Research has shown that this is the world's biggest secret cure for headaches, Mya. It can be taken orally or via other orifices. *And*, if it is applied as per those instructions, it's guaranteed to cure even the worst migraine. It has even been known to have self-lubricating qualities for easy application in tight or hard to reach places," I said playfully.

Mya chuckled enjoying the banter and shook her head staring first at my dick then at me.

"You said all of that with real conviction there." I raised my brow as if surprised by her comment.

"Indeed. And, did you know its healing properties have all the effects of a full body massage if applied in the right way," I replied, biting back a grin as I stared down at her face, the smile she gave me would have melted the hardest of men's hearts.

She giggled, watched my face for a few seconds without speaking then rolled her eyes up in thought.

"Oh you know what, Jack? I think I feel my first headache coming on. What do you say? Should we see whether that dangly thing really is an alternative medicine. For research purposes of course?"

Mya's beaming smile momentarily took my breath away. Seeing her eyes glitter with amusement, I reached down and stroked her wet entrance with my fingertips. As soon as I did her smile became more salacious, the glitter faded from her eyes and was replaced with lust.

I should have taken my time with her but I just couldn't wait any longer to be inside her. We were consummating what we'd verbalised, and when Mya opened herself to me and wrapped her legs around my waist, I could tell she was in no mood to wait either.

Hugging me tightly inside her I began to slowly thrust deeper, sinking to the hilt then drawing back until her nails raked painfully down my back and her hips began to undulate frantically under me, as she chased to the edge of that heady pleasure. It didn't take much for her to orgasm and when she did she clung to me tightly as her head rolled back into the mattress. I had never seen anything more erotic than her in that moment and to think that she was all mine made me come hard.

When I'd finished pulsing inside her, I wrapped my arms tightly around her as we lay in silence and in no time Mya's laboured breathing became slow and steady as she fell asleep. I stayed inside her for as long as possible but eventually we separated and it was a while before I dropped off because my mind refused to shut down.

It was our day of commitment, where Mya and I became everything to each other, emotionally, legally and physically. There was a time when I thought I'd never get married and that my life was going to be work, women and play. I haven't been wrong about that. My work is important to me and I have the good fortune to be able to do most of it from home. That allows me to spend time with my women, Ava and Mya. As for the play, Mya and I have our two B's: the band and the bedroom. Both are purely for our personal pleasure.

Meeting Mya had been the most tremendous thing that had ever happened to me. When I go out alone women still approach me, but there's no room for anyone else. I might only be an ordinary man, but I have a good life. I just happen to have extraordinary friends. It doesn't impress me that Lily is a rock star. I kind of expected that, or something similar, because I always knew she was destined for great things. I am proud of her and a little in awe, impressed at the changes in her confidence. Alfie, Ellie, Dave and the rest, they are all extraordinary people either through fame or on a more personal level to me, but they are all just people behind closed doors.

Me, I am just Jack Cunningham, a guy who had some

aspirations to be a journalist and the thought that if I could combine it with my love of music all the better. I achieved that, so in a sense I am successful in my own non-earth shattering way.

I wouldn't swap what I have with Mya and Ava for the life that Rick, Lily or Alfie have, because I am my own man and I'm anonymous. I can walk down the street without being accosted and pawed, or made to feel like I'm constantly on show. I can spend time with my family when I want instead of when other people tell me I can. Those guys lost all of their privacy and in turn their freedom in order to share their craft. I suppose I understand their drive in a way, because I gave up mine as well when I chose to find out if Ava belonged with me, but that was a no brainer.

Ava's presence and Mya's love makes me feel complete and the way Mya and I took to parenthood was worth all our efforts of pursuing responsibility for Ava. We're a few years ahead of ourselves in terms of our whirlwind romance and marriage, but since I'd decided to share my life with Mya, she in turn came into Ava's life and I've never felt a moment's fear.

It was only one year ago that I thought Rosie was the love of my life and I had lost her. Broken hearted, I left on assignment to follow a band and write some articles about how they got by day-to-day while on tour. Never in a million years did I think I'd meet and fall in love with the real love of my life on that tour and that I would do it as quickly as I had with Mya. And if I'm being honest, given her age, it scared the hell out of me how much I wanted her.

A linchpin is the pin that's vital for holding everything together and my life is as it is now because of Mya and the love she has shown me. She is my linchpin, the glue that holds us all together, my new best friend and my teacher. Mya has taught me that it's okay to make mistakes, it's how you move forward that matters the most.

Thinking of the commitment we made caused an internal struggle, I could understand Mya's want for something private and just for ourselves, but a part of me wants to do the right thing and tell our parents. Sneaking around didn't sit well with me and I knew I wasn't going to be able to keep it a secret for long. I wondered what the fall out was going to be from it until I finally fell asleep.

I woke with a start about three hours later and wondered why I hadn't heard Ava over the baby monitor; then I remembered, she was at Dave's and I relaxed back on the bed. Mya turned over, stretched and peered up at me.

"All right, what's going on in there? What's the long sigh about?"

Inhaling deeply I released the air from my lungs slowly and sighed again.

"Being married and Ava being at Dave's place."

Mya smirked knowingly, "Well you are too late about the first point. I'm legally entitled to some of your cash now, so no use trying to shake me off, Jack."

I grinned at her and pulled her up the bed with me until we were both sitting. I leaned against the headboard and tucked her close to me, resting her head on my chest.

"You know what I mean."

"Your parents? You don't want to keep secrets, right?"

Swallowing back the small lump in my throat that we'd excluded them, I nodded.

"Yeah, kinda doesn't feel right, love." I gruffly murmured.

"Okay, get up. We're going to tell your and my parents that they can have their day now that we've had ours. Then we're going to pick our daughter up, I've missed her like crazy this past..." Mya glanced at her wristwatch, "Eighteen hours and thirty five minutes."

Once again, Mya was completely in tune with my feelings and showed me one of the many reasons I loved her so much. She was just so drama free and laid back about most things, but make no mistake, she was no pushover.

Driving up the private road to my parents' house I wondered what kind of reaction we were going to receive. *Is my mother going to wail and throw herself at my feet in distress at missing our wedding or was she going to go off at myself and Mya for being selfish?*

I didn't have to wait long before I found out. Weather-wise, it was a very grey, windy morning and we were barely through the door when Mya ran her fingers through her hair trying to comb it back into order. That's when my mother caught sight of her wedding ring with her engagement ring.

"You're married? You eloped and never told us?"

Hugging my mother before she became hysterical, I turned and walked her over to the sofa to sit with her and explain what and why we had done it. She choked back tears while my father stood in front of the inglenook fireplace with his hands shoved deep into trouser pockets and rocked back and forth on his heels as he digested it all.

Their reaction was muted and the opposite to the chaotic mess I was expecting, but my mother hugged Mya and said that, although she was disappointed, she understood Mya's wishes and every girl should have the wedding they wanted. She even said she was glad Mya hadn't just gone along with what everyone expected because it could've been turned into a circus. I was blown away by my mum's understanding. My father left the room for a moment and as he walked back into the room he dug deeply into his pocket pulling out a set of keys and waggling them at me.

"Jack, it's time you took this over now. It's been

empty for the past six months. I took the liberty of sending in some workmen to give it a neutral coat of paint, but you'll no doubt want to decorate it to you and Mya's tastes."

My initial reaction was to protest, but this was something I knew my father had been waiting all of my life for so I couldn't refuse his wedding gift of Meadland Hall. It was the home in rural Hertfordshire the Cunningham family had owned for six generations. The house wasn't a massive place, but it was set in twenty five acres of land and it had been a terrific, safe place for me to play freely when I was younger.

"I know you have always been your own man, Jack, but as you know the house has been in trust for you since my father passed away. You've always known it was yours and Ava is next in line for it now. I know you have many happy memories of the place when you were growing up. Ava and Mya should spend time there now that you are a family."

Mya's eyebrow raised and I nodded slowly at my father, clasping my fingers closed around the keys as I stood and hugged him. Then I turned to Mya.

"Sorry, Mya, it never occurred to me that when I married I was supposed to take this place on, but I did make a mental note when Ava got all of those gifts the other week that we were starting to outgrow the apartment. Maybe we can do weekdays in London and weekends there? Ava should start to play more independently soon and she'll need friends in both places."

Mya sat stunned at the knowledge that we had a house. We'd never really discussed my own wealth except in terms of being able to provide for Ava, and it occurred to me that I hadn't shared all of my assets with social services, just my apartment, investments and monetary wealth. Mum broke my train of thought by hugging Mya and congratulating us and I knew my parents were more than happy with my choice of wife. Too bad if they weren't, I was definitely keeping her.

Chapter 44

Hero

Dave was at the window with Ava in his arms when we pulled up and Mya was out of the car before I'd put on the handbrake. She took the steps up to his front door two at a time and I chuckled as I thought how alike we were. Mya had strong maternal instincts considering Ava was born to someone else. It's a true saying 'anyone can give birth but not everyone is a born mother', and Mya was definitely a born mother.

Emily looked sleep deprived and frazzled, and Dave... Well he just looked like shit. Turns out Ava had been up half the night and I smirked when I saw how much she had tested them in just one day. Dave passed her to Mya as soon as she walked through the door and threw himself heavily into an armchair.

"Jack, man I love Ava to pieces but you have to take her home right now before I have no fingernails left. She's driven me crazy all night, babbling, talking gibberish and then she crapped all the way up her Babygro! To her neck! How can someone so tiny and angelically beautiful make shit stretch that far?"

Mya burst out laughing and Ava cooed on her lap. When I glanced at Emily, I couldn't read her mind but I could bet she was making a note to call the family planning centre as soon as we left. To us, Ava was this amazing little human being; to them she was a constant reminder to use birth control. Dave made a great babysitter, but being a dad would be years in the making for him yet and I considered revising my will.

We drove straight to Hertfordshire after collecting Ava because I wanted to show Mya where we could potentially spend our weekends. When she saw the house she immediately fell in love with it. I had to admit that I was quite in awe myself because it had been a couple of years since I'd been there and I had taken for granted how special it was and how it must look to someone who hadn't seen it before. It looked pretty spectacular. Or maybe that is because it was no longer just a house and was going to become a home again.

Mya gasped when we reached the start of the long stretch of private road that lead to the house. The path was outlined by willows and wild flowers; it looked like something you would find in a magazine. After five minutes of driving down the private road, the house suddenly came into view. Despite practically living here when I was a child, I was in awe of the long thatched cottage that stood before me. Its Tudor white washed walls and criss-crossing black beams were beautiful but it was the thatched roof that made the house's appearance special. It was pretty spectacular as it almost reached the windows on the ground floor on one side and the two floors on the other. Heavy oak doors with black wrought iron hinges and latches gave the house an extra feeling of grandeur.

A small stream ran close to the house, completing the picture perfect idyllic setting in front of us. Positioned on the edge of a vantage point leading down to rolling green meadows, it was picture postcard pretty and people commented on that point all the time. We were fortunate to have it. It was love at first sight for Mya and she drew in a sudden sharp breath when she saw it. After getting over her initial shock, we got out of the car and she turned to me smirking.

"Nothing special for my birthday and nothing special as a wedding gift, Jack? And we had all of this..." Mya threw her hand out in gesture at the place, her eyes flitting excitedly around the scenery again while she jiggled Ava to reposition her in her arms. "I'm glad I never knew about any of this, Jack. At least you know I married you for you and for no other reason."

Grinning widely because I knew she really meant it, I winked and pulled her back to my front.

"Mya, when you have me you don't need another reason. I mean come on look at me... What's not to love? I'm a stunning, hot bodied love machine, right?"

Shaking her head she elbowed me in the ribs.

"Jack Cunningham, I have no idea what we're going to do if we have a boy next time. I'm not sure I could cope with a junior version of you if he's going to be as beguiling and smart mouthed as you are."

I chuckled and smiled affectionately at Mya and then tried to imagine the time when that could happen.

"Any son of mine will have you smitten in a heartbeat, just like you were with me."

Resting her head on my chest she sighed and I squeezed her tightly, "Seriously love, I'm not that special. I'm just Jack, the nice guy you met one day when you were lonely in a city far from home."

Mya turned her head to look at me and Ava reached out and put her little fingers in my mouth.

"Good girl, Ava. See, even our daughter's silencing you. To us you have never been just Jack. You are Jack Cunningham, our fearless hero, the brave guy who gets spiders out of the bath. You're my superhero who gets up in the night with Ava so that I can sleep because I have school the next day. This is the same guy who sends me off to school with a healthy packed lunch and a love note in my bag. And you are the gorgeous guy who smiles sexily at me and waves me off holding our baby in your arms that I can't wait to get back to."

Staring up at me with pure adoration in her bright loving eyes, Mya continued. "You're our guy who sings a mean loud tune in the bath and shower and you're definitely our rock star. Also, while I'm on a roll let me tell you something else. Your sense of humour is extremely sexy, and you have an armoury of skills in the bedroom at your fingertips that makes me want you all the time."

She smirked knowingly and slipped her free hand between us to rub it across my dick through my trousers, "And let's face it, you are an awesome headache cure, Jack Cunningham." Suddenly she stopped joking, stared intensely at me then reached up and placed her hand onto my face. I leaned into it and felt instantly comforted.

"You are so special to me because of everything you do, everything you say and everything you are. You always know exactly what to do to lift me when I'm feeling down and you're an amazingly supportive and loyal person. I'm so honoured to be your wife."

I was touched by her adulation of me. Most of my friends would say I am a very confident man. That's my public persona and I used to think I was as well. But that part of me changed when I finished with Rosie, or perhaps that's when I grew from being Jack the frivolous playboy into Jack the man. By facing up to what was wrong in my life with Rosie, I had inadvertently thrown myself the biggest curve ball life could possibly throw me. However, the twist in my journey tested me and I rose to the challenge it delivered to me in a blink of an eye.

Had I known Rosie was pregnant before we split, would I have stayed? That question mulls over in my mind every now and again and I'm glad I never had to answer it. What happened to Rosie and Stewart was a terrible tragedy and my heart aches a little that Ava will never know her biological mother. But, I've never been completely grief-stricken about it because Ava came to me because of it when I might never have known that she was mine.

Something led me to my decisions and steered me in the direction I took and it led me to Mya. One year is all it took.

When I'd first met her, I remember feeling ashamed of my experience with other women, but when I reflect on that I was thankful to have met all of them, it gave me the presence of mind to know a good thing when I saw it. And in Mya and Ava's case well… A good thing doesn't even cut it.

Turning Mya in my arms I held her and our baby close to my chest. When I bent to nibble Mya's earlobe, she cringed and Ava grabbed my hair.

"Ow."

Mya struggled to free my hair from Ava's grasp and chuckled.

"Good girl, Ava, it's two against one now, Jack," she joked.

I leaned forward, firstly to kiss Ava on the nose and then Mya on the lips much more passionately.

From that day forward, I was a husband and father, a completely different man. I'd like to think I'm a better man. A year ago I felt lost and thought I was just Jack, but maybe I wasn't lost at all. Maybe I was just waiting. You may ask what was I waiting for: Love? Romance? The stars to align? I don't know but I definitely wasn't aware I was on the path to love when I took that assignment with Cobham Street.

When we were kids Lily used to say our destiny was

written in the stars. Maybe it is. All I know is that I struggled with my identity when people stopped referring to me as part of a duo: Lily and Jack, and I'd put Lily on a pedestal by thinking I was lost without her. Now when I look back it's much clearer to me, that title was only ever going to be temporary between us.

Sometimes we have to make room to grow and in losing Rosie I grew faster than I ever thought possible, in losing Lily for a time taught me I could live without her, living without Mya taught me I didn't want to. The difference is right there. It was my decision to be Mya and Jack and in making that choice I know in the way she looks at me, in our future I'll never be just Jack ever again.

Epilogue

Three years later

Peering over the heads of all the mothers in the school playground, I caught sight of Mya, her arms waving frantically towards me.

"Quick, Jack, she'll be out in a minute."

Squeezing past the bodies all around me, I passed one young mum who caught my eye when she raised an eyebrow at me and licked her lips; she gave me a certain smile I recognised from my single days. She was coming on to me. Right there in the playground in front of my wife. She wasn't in the least bit fazed by the month old baby I had wrapped in a sling around my front with my hand held protectively at the back of his head.

We had been caught in traffic and were late back from visiting my parents while Ava was at school on her first full day. I had dropped Mya off at the school gates and drove the short distance to park the car at home then walked back with our baby son, Freddie, swaddled against me.

Mya had given birth to our boy a week before Ava started school and that felt a little cruel having a new born baby and sending another off to the care of someone else during the day. However, Ava is a secure little girl and has the smart mouth gene from the both of us. I've never known a child with the level of psychological smarts she's been dealt and took Freddie's birth in her stride. Her only comment was to warn Mya that he looked like her daddy so she'd probably kiss him a lot.

As the youngest kid in her year at school, Ava had only turned four the week before school started. That caused us issues with sending her off into an environment where there were kids of eleven in the same building. I mean some of the kids were huge and boisterous and I was ready to do battle with anyone who hurt a hair on her head or who gave me cause for concern about her. We'd opted for state school because I was determined that Ava should learn to earn her way in the world and not live a life of privilege until she understood the value of money and how hard everyone else had to work just to get by.

The bell rang just as I reached Mya and she glanced at the woman who had been checking me out. Mya looked her over from head to toe and then smirked knowingly as she tugged gently on the sling to draw my face nearer to hers. Kissing me slowly on the lips, Mya was making a bit of a spectacle of us, but I hadn't had any action for a month and a half so I wasn't going to complain about her amorous little show of affection.

Just as she broke the kiss, Ava came bounding out of the door, hand in hand with Nathan who was in his last year of infant school. She was carrying a drawing of an elephant Nathan had given her and proudly thrust it in Mya's face.

"Look, Mummy, Nathan did this for me. Can I have one for Christmas? Can I mummy please? Can Nathan come for tea? Please Mummy, please?" Ava gave Mya a stare like she was pleading for her life and I grinned because, Lily used to have the same skill in her armoury to achieve what she wanted and I'm pretty sure it was one that Mya also had.

The emotional blackmail escalated when Nathan entered into the conversation.

"Ava asked me to come to tea. Should I tell my mum you said yes, Aunty Mya?"

I'd spoken to Maddie about how the kids should refer to us because of my own experience with Lily. I'd have hated them to feel the same way about each other as we had as teenagers. They were close and we encouraged that, but I didn't want any blurred lines for them later. It wasn't that I was a killjoy, I just wanted to save them some of the angst I felt when I had with all those mixed up feelings about Lily that prevented me from forming platonic relationships with other girls at school.

Besides, Ava was a girl and if Charlie had known about Lily and I having spooning sessions he'd have kicked my arse black and blue. If I could protect them from some of those feelings I saw that as my mission in life until they were old enough. If anything developed between Nat and Ava later, then it would be a natural progression and not through confusion.

As a family we were settled and secure. Mya and I were as close as any couple could be without smothering each other. We had great balance. She'd graduated from music school and we bought a small commercial property in Meadlands Village and one in London where she ran music schools for kids. The one in London was for music appreciation for kids from underprivileged families. Her status had long been resolved a few months after our wedding but she'd had to leave the country for two weeks during a recess in her studies while that happened. Ava and I simply went on holiday with her to her parent's place.

During our visit I came face to face with Rick again, who hugged me tightly and couldn't stop staring at Freddie

and Ava.

"So...Jack. Family man? No after parties in that gig are there?"

Smiling slowly I raised my brow.

"All the after parties involve your niece these days, Rick."

He gave me a low growl and Mya wandered over and snaked her arm around my waist.

"All our parties tend to be at home these days aren't they Jack? He hates buffets, Uncle Rick."

"Jesus, you've even primed her with that response." Rick chuckled heartily.

Mya looked puzzled and bunched her brow at him.

"What's funny? Partying at home or having buffets?"

Rick looked a little awkward and changed the subject and it was funny to see Mya put him in his place, but he couldn't deny how happy we were and finally apologised for his 'shitty behaviour'.

My parents and friends took time out from work as well and came to California with us because Mya and I took the opportunity to have our wedding blessing in front of our parents, friends and families in the church she attended as a child. Mya was insistent that it not be a grand affair so the atmosphere was relaxed and romantic and it turned out to be a really fun day for everyone. Both of our mum's bawled their eyes out and I noticed my dad touch the sides of his eyes with his thumbs more than once. It was emotional but in a good way.

I finally met all of Mya's friends and realised just how much she'd given up to be with me. Two friends in particular were of interest to me: Jacob and Alison. Jacob reminded me of myself and Alison of Elle. When I asked Mya about them she told me that her and Jacob were close friends as kids but that they dated for a while when she was eighteen. It didn't go well and she called a halt to it and since then they weren't as close as they used to be. It

explained how easily Mya accepted my friendship with Lily. Mya had been there already but had taken the plunge. It also made me think about how she'd been brave enough to take that risk with me.

After the wedding dinner Sam had obviously had more than a few and approached me wanting to tell me about him and Lily because it had been playing on his mind for a while. Slapping his back I took him over to the edge of the room, I thanked him for trying to be honest about it but it really wasn't my business and from what Lily said, he'd done us a favour. Dave and Emily had gone from strength to strength and Dave confided that he was ready to ask Emily to marry him. When I joked he'd be having kids next, I chuckled as I noted how pale he became.

As we stand, Mya and I are more than happy with our lives and feel blessed by our beautiful children. I still have a column in Muzikvibe and Mya's music schools are doing well. Our test for the coming years is to keep our kids grounded around their extended rock star family. Lily, Alfie and Rick have all become stakeholders in the upbringing of our children and Ava is already exhibiting some of her mother's musical talent.

I can also see some of the same traits in her as I saw in Lily when she was that age so if my powers of observation are correct I have a feeling she's never going to be just Ava.

The End

About K.L. Shandwick

K. L. Shandwick lives on the outskirts of London. She started writing after a challenge by a friend when she commented on a book she read. The result of this was "The Everything Trilogy." Her background has been mainly in the health and social care sector in the U.K. She is still currently a freelance or self- employed professional in this field. Her books tend to focus on the relationships of the main characters. Writing is a form of escapism for her and she is just as excited to find out where her characters take her as she is when she reads another author's work.

Social Media links
Facebook
https://www.facebook.com/KLShandwickAuthor

Twitter
https://twitter.com/KLShandwick

Website
http://www.klshandwick.com/

Made in the USA
Charleston, SC
06 March 2017